THE HOUSE ON HARRIGAN'S HILL

To Vera,

May you enjoy!

Claire

Noonan

THE HOUSE ON HARRIGAN'S HILL

C. J. NOONAN

Santa Barbara

Published by

Sea Hill Press, Inc.

P. O. Box 60301

Santa Barbara, California 93160

www.seahillpress.com

Design and Layout: Walter Sharp

Author Photography by Anja Ulfeldt

ISBN: 978-0-9708050-6-5

Printed in the United States of America

HISTORICAL NOTE

The House on Harrigan's Hill, while fictitious, follows major events in the real life of the Edwards family. I have remained true to some of the facts and lore surrounding the life of Mary Edwards and her family. Though names of real people have been used in this book, the personalities and dialogue of the characters are products of my imagination. Truckee, California, is a real place in the Sierra Nevada, though not all of the sites described in this novel were ever found there. The historical circumstances and my portrayal of the events in this story are extrapolated from oral histories and historical documentation. Most revealing, the novel depicts actions surrounding the October 10, 1911, special election to pass the Woman Suffrage Amendment. At that time, California women gained the right to vote.

1

October 1985, Friday Evening
Colfax

THE BLACK OAK tree clung to the slope that plunged to a narrow creek behind Alta's little house near Colfax. Dusty leaves dropped to the ground. I leaned on the porch railing and looked up, studying the Sierra foothills, scraggly Digger pine interspersed among oaks, then higher, Ponderosa pine and Douglas fir. I raised my gaze to take in the first range of mountains, the forest so thick with Jeffrey pine and white fir I couldn't see the road climbing toward Donner Summit and over to Truckee, no matter how well I knew the way. Merely a narrow cut split the green-black spiky silhouette of the top ridge in the twilight.

Squinting through my glasses, I watched stars glint on one by one. Quiet. Not a chipmunk ruffling the leaves, not a jay squabbling with its competitor.

My granddaughter, Polly, moved her chair, and next to me, Lane, my twelve-year-old great-grandson, crumbled leaves and asked the names of mountain peaks. He wore jeans and a sweatshirt, never overalls or a jacket like his great-uncle Raleigh wore on the night long ago that came to my mind. Maybe the autumn scent of pines reminded me of the old days.

"I wish Raleigh hadn't been fooling around with those wild boys when the hotel caught on fire. Easy to say now, but he wouldn't have fallen on his wrist and twisted it so bad."

I turned and leaned back, my elbows resting on the verandah railing. I pulled the heavy sweater tighter over my shoulders and took another sip of sloe gin, never whiskey, not after the heartache it caused in my family. And no cocktails anymore. I was too old for them.

Head down, Tiny stirred with a swizzle stick.

She sipped her gimlet and said, "I don't know, Mary. So long ago."

I thought she must've been tired from cleaning up. Quite a job, closing a house. She was my sister, but she wasn't strong like me, though she held her own when she was a ten-year-old tomboy. Two-years apart, I was eighty-seven, and Tiny was eighty-five. Besides, she was still upset about Alta up and dying, after we'd taken care of her most of our lives.

But my mind wandered. I was thinking about my brother, Raleigh.

"It's like the weather on that October afternoon at the train station."

I thought for a moment.

"Seventy-six years ago."

My great-grandson looked up.

"Mr. Hoy, who looked like the devil, would never have noticed us at the train station except for Raleigh tripping and falling on his wrist again, still swollen from the accident at the bonfire."

I couldn't help it. Like Mama, I made a *tsk* with my tongue against my teeth.

"He screamed so loud," I said. "Poor Raleigh."

Tiny sighed and said, "Don't you think, Mary, Mr. Hoy knew we'd been up there on the hill when he saw our faces? Scared out of our wits when he came to the house."

"I know he couldn't have heard us when we ran back down the mountain. The air was full of that man sobbing. It seems crazy we had the idea to go up there."

Tiny smoothed one hand with the other and twisted her diamond ring.

Finally, I said, "The last bad thing for Mama."

"All because we wanted to see those Indian pictures scratched in the rock. I thought it would be fun," said Tiny.

"Can I see the pictures? I want to go," said my great-grandson.

Her diamond clinking against the tumbler, Tiny said, "I don't know why not, Lane. Lots to see in Truckee, if you knew about it. Plenty to entertain us, anyway."

We sipped our drinks. I didn't need my glasses to point out the Big Dipper in the black sky, same as nights long ago in the mountains, and the old town on the other side of the summit floated before my eyes. Polly had been to Truckee, so she kept reading her magazine. Lane listened, but it felt like I was talking to myself.

"Just twelve then, I was happy to see the steep gable of our weathered clapboard house the time we waited on the Truckee train station platform after we came back from the first trip to Sacramento.

"I was happy to see Mr. Faye's saloon, the grocery, the stationery store on Front Street, then the school and the Methodist church clustered down by our street. Already Truckee looked like an old town filled with ordinary people who lived as if it was still pioneer days. Mama often said she might as well have been back home in Montrose, Missouri, where I was born in 1898. Except it was 1910 when we inhabited that remote part of the mountains, each person with his own small business, no great companies like in Sacramento or San Francisco.

"Barren hills surrounded the town, pines long since logged. Not a romantic place like the villages in my books. Weeds all along the railroad tracks, paint peeling from buildings, even the houses for the rich people weren't beautiful Victorian dwellings like we'd seen in Sacramento. Hardly a flower or fancy bush. Still I remember hoping the next day we'd traipse down to the Truckee River and through the far meadows into the woods.

"Too young, I didn't know about the state's financial crisis after the 1906 earthquake in San Francisco. I only remember the petrified families coming through by train on the way east through California. If I'd been an adult, I would have seen how the price of land around Truckee had collapsed when the bankers and railroad owners in San Francisco lost money.

"What a raucous place. I thought men with those injuries inhabited all mountain towns—an arm chomped off by a bear, bowed legs from endless mule trips up and down the summits, a jagged facial scar from a slashing argument about a gold claim, or cheeks damaged by small pox. That fat constable, Mr. O'Brien, with his bushy red mustache, huffed and puffed after gunfighters and robbers from one end of town to the other. We heard a lot of those stories after we went to live on Harrigan's Hill and became his neighbor.

"Alta was a beauty and a devil for me in those years." Polly grinned at my older sister's name. "It was just like Alta to laugh and drag me to look at those thieves who stole from Mrs. Tucker, the Whitney Hotel owner. Everyone went by the jail to look at those losers.

"No doubt, Mrs. Tucker was some woman, always outspoken about her rights. She led the suffrage campaign of 1911—a big issue in a small town. "So listen to this," I told Lane. "She used her new telephone and called all the hotels and stores in Reno and told them to watch for her liquor, telegraphing an exact list of what was stolen. That's how she got most of it back."

"I think I've had enough," said Tiny, tapping me on the arm, calling me back from my evening ramble.

Polly announced that supper was ready to come out of the oven and they might just as well wash up and set the table.

Tiny placed her hands on the arm rests, and with Lane's help, she lifted herself up and took a step, testing her legs, while Polly gathered the tumblers and napkins. As always, Tiny let the door slam when they went in for supper.

My mind roamed from Sacramento to Colfax and far into the mountains. Who else? Let's see, when we lived in Truckee there were a few rich people. At least we four kids thought they were rich. Respectable, church-going, they made money from every drifter who stepped off the train. Wasn't it why we lived there, Papa being a train brakeman? Mama was the boardinghouse manager, not a lowly kitchen maid.

Yet we knew we were the poor people who slogged through snowy, muddy roads and dusty summer days cooking for boarders, burning garbage, building the winter toboggan run and the Ice Palace for the tourists, rebuilding when fires roared through entire rows of shops.

Still we young ones had our little advantages—fooling around at the edge of the icy cold Truckee River and twirling in the grassy meadows to make the shining granite mountain peaks spin around us. We'd hide out in the dark woods and poke our noses in and out of the back streets where the Japanese laundry man collected the sheets from the inn, while the red-cheeked ladies stared out windows on the alley and the honey man cleaned the outhouses.

The only people we didn't know were the Paiute and Washo, except for Minna who was Mama's friend and a nurse, lucky for us. The other Indian families kept to themselves on the other side of the river or farther away on the Reno side of the mountains.

"Tiny, remember when you found out in school the word Truckee is Paiute for 'all right'?" I called. "Even if it was hard for Mama in that town, it was all right for us, wasn't it? You, me, Raleigh, Alta. Of course, we didn't know better, did we, until everything began to go to pieces after we became horse owners."

My great-grandson pricked up his ears.

"A horse? You had a horse? Tell me about it."

Molly. One of the few happy surprises in those two years when, surely, we grew up.

The cold evening breeze was rising. Slipping my arms into my sweater sleeves, I stepped forward to the kitchen door.

"It's a long story," I said. "But we have all weekend."

I jiggled the old, glass knob, then let go and listened to my thoughts. A story about another family, it seemed, though I'd witnessed most of it, and by now I hope I understood the why and wherefore.

My hand shook, but I tightened my grip, turned the knob, and pulled the door open.

2

Summer 1909
Church Street, Truckee

No DAY TO wander around, raggle-taggle, getting into mischief, as often happened after finishing their chores at home. Mama had seen a car at Mr. Faye's Last Chance Saloon, so the four Edwards children marched themselves to Front Street on that August Saturday to scrutinize his Model T Ford, the first automobile purchased by a Truckee businessman.

"I saw a rich man's car in the spring," said Raleigh, rubbing his stubby eight-year-old hand over the arc light lanterns hanging at the front. "How'd they get here to go fishing with the roads so bad? Their car had room for six and windows on the sides and the cover folded back like this one."

Raleigh turned to his sister, just one year older, who dressed like him in well-worn overalls and Papa's old flannel shirt. She had curly auburn hair, while his was still reddish-blond.

" 'member, Tiny?"

She nodded and climbed onto the running board to peer inside, feel the stained wood steering wheel, touch the black leather seat covers, and inspect her cute tomboy self in the mirror.

Alta, twelve, the oldest and prettiest, with thick, black hair and violet-blue eyes, strolled around the car with her arms folded, examining the wheels. She slid her hands over the shiny gray paint on the fenders and pulled on the door handle to the back seat, as if she were deciding whether to purchase it herself.

Mary, eleven, the plain middle sister, stood in front of the car, observing her brother and sisters while they put their hands all over the car's fixtures and argued about how to drive it. Though she had never been this close to a car in her life, Mary didn't want to touch someone else's property.

Irresistibly tempted, Mary moved closer and peeked inside at the levers and pedals. Mrs. Faye charged down the last step of the stairs to the offices above the saloon. Handsomely dressed in a pleated brown skirt and snow-white blouse with puffed sleeves, she took two steps across the porch, grabbed Tiny, pulled her off the running board, and dropped her in front of Alta.

Mrs. Faye pointed a finger and said, "Stay off my car."

"Hey! Leave her alone!" hollered Alta, balling up her fist.

Alta lowered her hand when Mrs. Faye looked up. Tears ran down the woman's face. She looked blotchy and puffy with strands of hair flying about.

Mrs. Faye shook her own fists and yelled over the children's heads, "I can drive this car! I will drive it! You can't stop me! There's no law against me driving it!"

The children whirled about. Mr. Faye stood on the last step of the staircase, a flush rising from his chin up over his nose. At that moment, shirtsleeves rolled up, one suspender unattached, he didn't look like the suave fellow from the Eastern saloon-keeping family he assumed in front of townspeople. Though he was well established in the saloon business, it was known he wasn't a drinking man, so liquor didn't explain the quarrel.

The two adults and their audience of four posed like statues by the car. Then Mr. Faye's hands rose, palms up, as if appealing to his wife's good judgment.

He opened his mouth to plead, "Grace, please don't be angry. I'll take you anywhere, or the boy can drive you. It doesn't look right."

The siblings turned back to watch Mrs. Faye's lip tremble.

Related to the wealthy railroad Harrimans of San Francisco, she had a reputation for calm, correct manners. The children were surprised to hear her cry out, "I don't want a chauffeur. And I don't care what those old ladies think, sneering at us about everything, especially when we pass out suffrage flyers. I won't let them decide what I can do—and you can't either."

Mr. Faye put his arm carefully around her shoulder. He whispered in her ear, but she pulled back, and the children heard him say, "Maybe we can go out along the road to Colfax, and I'll let you try then. Please, Grace."

Mr. Faye looked up, his face flushing again, and he realized the four children had witnessed the entire spectacle. He knew it, and he knew them too. Their mother had been the midwife for his children. He winked and smiled.

"Well, married people don't always agree about everything, do they, Mary?" he said.

She shook her head slowly.

Frowning again for a moment, he said, "Listen, since you all're too young to have a car, how'd you Edwards children like to have a horse? I don't need old Molly anymore, and she's not worth enough for me to sell. She's out there in the field below McGlashan's house. If your mother says yes, and if you can catch

Molly, you can keep her."

Mary looked at the other three. Of all the children, Mary loved animals the most. She cuddled every dog and cat wandering near the boardinghouse Mama and Papa managed. A horse was more than she'd ever imagined. Even Alta, eyes round and lips curved, seemed astonished by their luck.

Tiny raised her eyebrows, and Raleigh, slapping his knee, yelled, "Let's go!"

They raced to get the bridle from the saloon shed and took off up Front Street toward Church Street and their house.

The late summer sun was shining straight down. Dust from the road kicked up and settled on the hairs on their arms. Sweat glistened at each child's hairline. Raleigh, robust but small, lagged behind, and the three girls stopped to let him catch up. All had opinions about their good fortune, and because Mama had always insisted each child be allowed to put in his or her two cents, Alta began.

Flicking away a fly that had settled onto the sweat inside her elbow, she said, "Mr. Faye's letting us have that horse so we won't tell everyone about the fight he was having."

Raleigh straggled up. He bent over, putting his hands on his knees to catch his breath. Dust turned to muddy lines and streaked his sweaty neck.

"And Raleigh, don't think you're going to be first to ride all the time. I'm the oldest, and I'll decide," added Alta.

"I hope Mama lets us keep Molly," said Tiny. "I don't care if Mr. Faye's getting us not to tell. When I get bigger, no one's going to boss me around either."

Mary said, "When I grow up, I'm going to buy my own car. Then no one can tell me what to do with it."

Straightening himself up, Raleigh said, "Go on. That's fine."

Mary added, "And how about we tell Mama she can ride Molly when she goes out to a farm to help with a baby."

Mary lifted her arms, placed her hands under the long, blond hair framing her plain face, and flipped it away from her neck to cool off.

They scuffed along the street, more and more delighted they had shown up at the right moment. Mary thought about feeding bits of apple to the horse and whispering to it. She, who was the most wary of all new things, especially something Mama would say "showed up out of the blue," did what she had been warned against time and time again. She threw caution to the wind, feeling certain Mama could be persuaded.

They reached the white clapboard two-story building where Mama kept ten boarders in addition to the family. The children climbed the porch steps, but Mama didn't appear. They flung the door open, clattered through the long, dark hall past the parlor and sitting room used as bedrooms, peeped into the dining room, and finally barged into the large kitchen. Mama was looking out the back screen door across the field toward the woods. She turned as they jostled through the door and stood in a clump. She rubbed her stomach, starting to protrude from another pregnancy.

"There you are. I was beginning to wonder," said Mama, looking them over. "What's in your hand, Tiny?"

"This?" Tiny asked, holding up the bridle.

"Where'd you get that?"

Alta stepped forward and said, "Now, Mama, Mr. Faye said we could have old Molly. You know that Model T Ford he bought? We walked by to look, and he said we could go get Molly if you said yes."

"We can have fun, and it only eats the grass, Mama," added Raleigh.

Mama looked again at each child, and they all returned a look of innocence as far as Mary could tell. She was certainly trying to appear earnest when Mama turned to her.

"Mama, Mr. Faye said he didn't need Molly anymore, and you can ride the horse to go help when someone's having a baby," said Mary.

Ready to peel a potato, Mama picked up a paring knife.

Pointing the knife as if it was her forefinger, she said, "I suppose I can go talk to Mr. Faye tomorrow. So no harm in trying to catch Molly."

She swerved the knife, aiming straight at Mary and said, "But don't get too attached because you might have to take her back."

Mama's words didn't refer to little pets like chipmunks or mice or lizards, but to the kind requiring a lot of food. The last time Mary wanted to keep a large mutt, Mama had said to stop the crocodile tears and contrary desires. It was enough trouble taking care of four, soon five, children and ten boarders without adding dogs. Let alone adding horses, Mary thought.

While the children ate bologna and bread, Mama continued making dinner preparations for the boarders. In her plain brown dress and an apron used as a towel, she moved back and forth from the large table in the kitchen's center, a table mainly used for food preparation, to the metal sink with a pump handle that raised water from the well. The stove, fed with wood, had four burners and a spacious oven, so it was easy to cook large pots of soup or stew and bake cakes at the same time.

Mama put the potatoes on to boil. She pulled out the pickle jar from the large pantry by the small room not rented at the moment and gave each child a pickle. She remarked that Molly reminded her of a "when I was little" story. Mary pulled her stool up closer and set her elbows on the table and her hands on her cheeks. Besides animals, Mary loved stories, and Mama was a great storyteller.

"I lived on a farm, you know, although my father was a veterinarian rather than a farmer. We had three or four horses, as I recall, and at that time all four of us older children had to take care of them and the cows and chickens and pigs. Sometimes on a summer afternoon we would ride the old horses bareback around the yard. I was very small, like you, Tiny, and I remember my older brothers, your Uncle Lauf and Uncle Frank, hoisting me up onto the horse's back. I would hold his mane while the horse walked around."

"That's what we're going to do," said Mary.

Mama took a bite of the pickle.

"One morning Lauf and Frank were harnessing a team of horses for spring planting, and one horse bolted, catching Lauf's right hand in the hitch. Frank got Lauf's hand out, cutting the straps with his knife, but when they rushed into the house, blood dripping all over, my father saw Lauf's right thumb and two fingers were crushed. My father had to cut off the first joint of Lauf's thumb, and the first bones of his forefinger and middle finger with the veterinarian's surgical tools. Then he stitched everything up. Lauf was always our favorite brother, and Margaret and I cried as loud as Lauf. Even little Ola cried when she saw the blood."

"Oh, Mama," said Mary.

"It seemed a long time before we rode the horses again. So you must be careful around Molly."

"I would've cried too," said Raleigh, and then, "How come Uncle Lauf's never been here? I wonder how he holds things."

Mama said, "He was here once, before any of you were born—soon after your father and I moved to Truckee."

"When's Papa coming home?" asked Alta.

Papa had been gone for a long time.

"Another week maybe. A lot of men've been sick this summer—ague, typhoid, consumption—and so the healthy ones have to stay on."

"Hmm," said Mary. "There're a lot of trains in California. Can't they hire some more workers?"

"It's been a bad time for railroads and money people since the San Francisco earthquake. You'd have to ask Mrs. Faye's cousin. He's still a big railroad man," said Mama.

CATCHING MOLLY WAS no trick at all, thought Mary. Tiny went first, and they took turns riding on her back with no blanket or saddle all afternoon in Mr. McGlashan's field. Molly was really a wagon horse for the shay the Faye family used, but she didn't seem to mind when Mary climbed onto her broad, brown back and clutched Molly's sides with her knees. Mary leaned forward and held onto Molly's dark mane and the rope attached to the bridle. Molly walked around the fenced-in field time after time. While Mary gave her a piece of apple, Molly would look at her, an all-knowing kind of peace in her eyes. At least, that's how she remembered the horse, and she was the one who thought she loved Molly best of all.

At last the angle of shade from the fence posts told them it was late, and they walked Molly halfway across town to live behind their boardinghouse on Church Street, grazing in the small, narrow field that separated their home from the second growth woods.

When the weather changed and was too cold, Molly stayed in the shed, wandering in and out to the field as she pleased. Hiding behind the school building, Raleigh traded treasures with friends who had no horse, leading them, when the bell rang, to the field for a ride on Molly. Days slid by, and the Edwards girls found other diversions when their brother was busy providing rides. They hurried through their boardinghouse duties, and when no other attraction appeared, favored sitting cross-legged among the weeds under the Truckee River bridge singing and listening to the echoes. By the time the winter snow began to melt, Mary had not bothered to find out whether Mama really went to see Mr. Faye. No longer encumbered with coats, hats, and wool stockings, the siblings could venture on their horse to any corner of the Truckee valley.

3

April 1910
Church Street, Truckee

BEHIND THE BOARDINGHOUSE on a Saturday late in April, Alta and Mary tinkered with the wheels of the neighbor's wicker baby buggy. The new baby sister, Florence, had been presented with it.

"Oh, bother," muttered Mary, as Tiny and Raleigh raced up the back path from Mr. Titus's grocery, hollering over each other that snow from the highest part of the mountains had finally begun to melt. The river had almost reached the top of its banks.

Alta put down the pliers.

"Let's get Molly and the four of us go up the river past the mill where we can watch stuff coming down."

Alta gazed at the three imperiously to see who would dare object to this proposal for the day. Far up the river, near the reservoir, people used a hidden weir as a dump. Every spring a bizarre mixture of trash swept down with the rushing water.

Suspecting Alta had more in her head than merely watching the river, Mary frowned, opened her mouth, and then held her tongue. Alta always needed an accomplice when she wanted to do something forbidden. Like last winter when Alta bullied her into sneaking off to the toboggan run early in the morning. Mary admitted to herself she'd wanted to be first, and she pushed off so fast the toboggan slid out from under. She flew down on her bottom, scraping her hands and legs. Alta had laughed and held tightly onto the front piece curled up to protect the rider. Mary limped home hurt and furious, but never told Mama since she knew they would both get a whipping. Instead, Mary kept herself covered up for several days and out of Mama's sight.

Still Mary couldn't imagine Alta had cooked up a scheme so quickly. She slid into the kitchen to put some bread and bologna in a bag while Alta walked out toward the field, pulling up grass—the usual way to coax Molly close enough, so Raleigh and Tiny could slip the bridle over her neck. By the time Mary walked outside again, Alta was sitting regally on the horse with Tiny and Raleigh at each side.

"You look like Lady Rowena with her pages in *Ivanhoe*," said Mary. "I guess I'm the lady-in-waiting."

She took her place behind Alta, and the royal party traipsed down the street toward the Truckee River bridge. Instead of crossing the river to play on the rock outcroppings in the far meadow, they turned west up the path parallel to the water. Here the banks were wetter and grassier, but the sagebrush and manzanita near the bank were still scrubby, only a few new leaves budding.

The river was running fast, and small waves formed as water rushed over the rocks. Broken tree limbs, fallen into the water from heavy snow, were caught between the boulders and raised more waves. Alta slid down, and Raleigh and Tiny scrambled up to ride tandem on Molly, as they continued out of town toward the mill.

A half mile farther, the path became gravelly. They stopped for a rest at a patch where no bushes covered the bank, which sloped down to the water. Alta picked up some pebbles, and standing close to the water so the dead, mashed-down grass squished under her shoes, she skipped stones across the surface. Tiny and Raleigh joined Alta and yelled, "Watch this!" or "Lookit!" and howled, *"Aw-w-w!"* at pebbles that sank straight away.

With no gift for skipping pebbles, Mary climbed the slope and gathered wildflowers. She scuffled around the bunchgrass on the other side of the path and bent over a rock to slowly, cautiously, drop her hand onto a small golden grasshopper. Sure she had captured it, but the insect crawled out between her ring and baby finger and leaped away, startling her. She yelped, scooped up the flowers, and stood when Tiny called.

Mary clambered up on Molly's back for her turn as Lady Rowena, and they wandered along the road. Poking the bushes with a stick, Raleigh startled a fat quail hiding in a brush thicket. It rushed across the path, black plume bobbing, whistling to a string of chicks skittering behind.

The air was still and warm, the sun shining overhead, when they reached Franklin's Mill. Every person in Truckee knew it used to be one of the biggest businesses besides the saloons. Even after the lumberjacks had left only stumps on the hillsides around town, wagons brought logs from nearby hills, and more logs came down the river to the mill. An area of flat, smooth dirt spread out in front of the huge mill building. It was quiet this Saturday, and even on a weekday it wasn't busy anymore, since mines were closing and the railroad was finished.

Raleigh had never been to the mill before. "Hey, this is a swell place to play," he said. "We should get my pal Joe and his cousins to come with us next time."

Mary and Alta had been to the sawmill with Papa. They pointed the way over to the river side of the building to watch the water wheel. Raleigh and his sisters stood frozen, as if caught in a trance by the turning wheel.

Molly snorted and Mary said, "See the round thing? Water turns the wheel that turns that thing that moves the saw inside the mill. The saw cuts a log into lumber like all those boards we see on the flatbeds of the train."

Mary slid off Molly and led her over to the big mill door, but Alta had beaten her to it and yanked on the lock, which didn't give, so they couldn't peek inside.

"It just makes you sneeze in there. It's full of sawdust," said Alta.

The children had to turn away from the river, cross the mill yard, and cut around the building to see the upper part of the river. The mill had been built at a spot before the river widened, so water flowed deeply and more rapidly above the mill in the narrow channel, giving more power to the mill wheel.

When Tiny and Raleigh reached the bank on the upriver side of the mill, they howled in excitement. If the water had seemed turbulent below the mill as it roared to the town power station, it rushed so fast and strong here it plucked small bushes off the bank and dragged them into the current. The water churned around the few large boulders still revealing their granite tops.

Running along the bank away from the mill, they found a good spot to watch all the junk race down from the dumping spot below the reservoir—splintered logs, some broken boards, one with a table leg attached. Still far away, they watched a wooden rocking chair on its side sliding downstream.

Alta said, "Let's pull it out, Mary."

"What d'you mean? I can't swim so well, and we can't reach it."

"Yes, we can," Alta said. "Hold onto the branch of that aspen and lean out to pull it. The branch'll bend. I'll catch hold when you've pulled it over a little."

Astonished at her sister, Mary grimaced and turned to find a bush to tie Molly's reins, so the horse could graze.

"Okay, Raleigh, you do it," said Alta. "Crawl out on the branch and push the chair toward the bank with your foot. Then I'll grab it."

Mary whirled back and hollered, "No, it's too dangerous."

Being the little brother, Raleigh said, "It's all right. I can do this."

Grinning at all three, he sat down on the bank, rolled up his pants, and pulled off his boots. Alta smirked at her sisters and put her hands together to make a stirrup. He put his foot in it and held onto the aspen trunk while Alta slowly lifted him up. Finally, Raleigh grabbed the branch, swung himself up, and straddled it. It bent with his weight as he edged his way along, out over the river. He waited until the chair was right underneath. When he hooked his foot under the top rung of the chair, it yanked him into the rushing river. As he fell, an aspen limb with a sharp tip scraped against his leg, leaving a wide bloody cut along the side of his calf, and he screeched.

Alta's face went white.

Tiny jumped up and down and screamed, "He's bleeding, and he can't swim good enough! It's freezing in there! He'll crash into the mill wheel!"

Raleigh rushed along, holding onto the chair to stay above water, and Mary yelled, "Raleigh, kick your feet and aim toward the bank, or we'll never catch you!"

Then Mary ran along the bank to get below Raleigh, stripped off her skirt, and stepped into the icy water. She held her breath and waded out into the current.

As Raleigh slipped by, she yelled again, "Hold your arm out and push off the chair with your foot!"

When he did, he gulped and sank, his head disappearing. She grabbed his hand, still above the water, and pulled him up and over. Her feet began to slide through the mud, deeper into the river. She held onto Raleigh, and her head went under. She pushed with her feet, and when she came back up, she slid her hands under Raleigh's armpits.

Tiny yelled, "Kick, Raleigh, kick!"

Mary felt Raleigh rocking as he kicked hard. She curled her toes into the mud and then dragged one foot behind the other, moving back toward the bank. Raleigh choked and gagged. Mary lost her balance when she stepped on a rock that dug into the arch of her foot. She and Raleigh slipped under again. When Mary bumped her bottom on the mud, she realized she wasn't that far from the bank. With one more heave, she stepped onto the slope, where it was much less mucky.

Alta grasped Mary's blouse and pulled. Tiny caught Raleigh under the armpits and dragged him, while he used his feet to push himself up out of the water. Coughing and spitting, Mary and Raleigh spread out on the grass at the top of the slope in the sun. Alta and Tiny helped pull off cold garments, until both the rescuer and saved lay in their underclothes, Raleigh snorting and moaning about the long bleeding cut on his leg and Mary breathing heavily through her mouth. They rubbed Raleigh and Mary's red toes and shaky legs.

Finally, Alta leaned over Raleigh and said, "You were supposed to push, you dope. You better not tell Mama."

Tiny said, "What did you want that old chair for anyway?"

Alta answered, "You better not tell either, Tiny."

Lying there with her hand over her heart, feeling it slow down little by little, Mary said, "It was your fault, Alta. The only reason we won't tell is because Mama will whip us all."

"What about Raleigh's bleeding leg? Can't you see all the blood dripping onto the ground?" said Tiny.

"Let's put a spider web on it. That'll make it stop," said Alta.

She searched around the tree and out in the field until she found two webs and wrapped them around Raleigh's leg.

They were quiet again. Tiny retrieved the bag of bread and bologna, and the children lay there munching, drying out in the sun.

At last Mary said, "I know. You were going to bribe Mama for something by giving her the chair."

Then a new thought entered her head, "Or you were going to sell it to Mrs. Bridges on Back Street, weren't you?"

She stopped, seeing Alta's eyes squint and a frown form.

Mary said, "Oh, forget it. I don't care. Let's go home. We'll be dry by the time we get back. And Raleigh, remember. Don't tell! We'll all get in trouble. Your leg'll be all right."

"Yeah," said Raleigh. "I don't think I'm going to come up here with Joe or anyone else. He can't swim very well either."

The children started back, allowing Raleigh to ride Molly all the way. By the time they reached the spot where the gravel turned to dirt, he'd recovered enough to relive the adventure with Tiny. Danger past, thought Mary. Raleigh's like the Black Knight from *Ivanhoe*, celebrating victory.

Turning onto Church Street, they were a bedraggled lot. Raleigh's pants were still damp, but rolled down over the wound. Mama was standing on the porch with baby Florence in her arms, watching as they straggled along.

She called out, "Mary! Alta! I've been waiting. Get in the house to set the table. Raleigh and Tiny, take this money. Now. I need some sugar."

Raleigh slid down Molly's side and yelled, "Mama, guess ... "

Alta grabbed his arm and pinched hard.

"O-w-w-w!" he yowled.

Mama stopped giving directions, shifted the baby onto her hip, and said, "All right, Raleigh. What happened?"

Raleigh limped up, and Mama made him lift his pants while blood, drop by drop, pooled on the instep of his boot. Just then, Mr. Thomas, a longtime boarder, walked up the path with a new boarder. Too late now—the story came out, Mama's face turning pale, eyes darkening, teeth clenching.

When the near drowning had been described, Tiny telling about her fears and Mary's bravery, Mr. Thomas whistled, and the new fellow shook his head and said, "Well, I'll be damned. Excuse me, Mrs. Edwards. I mean darned."

Mama said, "Go get Papa's shaving strap, Tiny. Alta, you're first."

Arms folded and legs spread, the boarders stood at each side of the porch and nodded approval.

Mama cradled the new baby in the little basket she used to cart her around. She took the strap, made Alta turn around, and whacked her across the behind. Alta never cried or yelled when she was punished, but when Mama finished, Alta walked down the street, around the corner, and didn't come back until Mary was already in bed. Next Mary, then Tiny, and then Raleigh were whipped, as they knew would happen, Mama wincing as the strap cracked.

"My God, that was a near disaster," said Mr. Thomas. "Now maybe they'll listen."

The new fellow agreed and said he wouldn't have been able to sit for days if he'd done what the four children did. No one asked to see the wound. It was like all other cuts, even if long and raggedy. Anyway, everyone knew spider webs were the certain cure.

"I ... HATE ... her," mumbled Mary under her breath, as she slapped each piece of silverware down on the long table where the boarders ate.

Her lips quivered in fury.

"She gets us in trouble, and then I have to do all the work too because Mama won't go find her."

Tiny wandered into the dining room and said, "I'm not going anywhere with Alta for a long time. Raleigh isn't either. She's always getting us into trouble. I hate her."

Mary kept slapping the knives and forks onto the table. By the time she finished folding napkins, Mary started to argue with herself. "I should've stopped Raleigh. I should've pulled Raleigh away. Why do I ever do what Alta tells me? To see what will happen?"

Raleigh was the happy survivor. He lay around the house for a few days, as the cut developed a long black and blue bruise and continued to hurt when he walked. He had a long scraggly scar down his calf for the rest of his life.

Sitting on a rock out behind the school building, Raleigh entertained his pals with the adventure, rolling up his pants and stretching out his leg so every boy could examine the lumpy red skin where the limb tore into his calf. It got better every time he told the story, and he'd remind everyone it wasn't the only time Alta meant trouble.

He'd say "Am I not right, Mary?" and she nodded.

"YOUR MOTHER HEARD that story and saw the scar," said Mary.

"I saw the scar too," said Lane. "When I was little."

4

May 1919
Sacramento

LIFE, OF COURSE, is a long trail of memories. Especially those that make us choose what to do next. I was thinking of my twenty-first birthday, nine years since those children we were ran along the mountain trails unaware of danger.

I walked up the dirt road in the far south part of Sacramento, admiring my new shoes, the ones I'd fancied at the classy Braddock and De Land store. I stepped carefully to keep from tripping on stones and sticks strewn in the path. A string of ants scrambled along the weedy edge and skirted a pebble, oblivious to my shoe next to their trail, and they entered the opening into a dirt mound.

Behind the row of olive trees, my eye caught a view of the rented house and Mama waving from the rocker on the rickety porch. The two regular visitors, kids who lived next door, played on the steps. I pulled at a strand of hair, thinking how Mama collected kids to keep herself from being lonely once we moved to Sacramento. Raleigh, Tiny, and I found jobs and other places to live.

The neighborhood kids didn't know Mama's house was an old, beat-up place like the one we'd moved into for a year and a half in Truckee. How would they know Mama only cared that it was clean? Those kids liked to play in her yard, with no one hollering at them and Mama telling them stories and poems, funny sometimes and hair-raising other times.

I tucked my hair back up under my hat. It'd been a long trolley ride, traveling way out here farther and farther from the Capitol. The sun, heating the field grass and the country trees, soaked the air with fragrance. After dabbing my forehead with the hankie Tiny had sent me as a birthday gift, I pulled on the branch of the olive tree out in front of the house to see if any fruit had set. Not yet. Pinching off a cream-colored flower and putting it up to my nose to smell the sweet perfume, I climbed the wood steps to the shade of the porch.

Mama said, "Happy birthday, Mary."

"Happy birthday," said the kids, grinning, front teeth missing.

"I made a cake for you, Mary. Raleigh will be here soon to have some, too, for his birthday," said Mama. "Too bad Tiny moved to San Francisco. She could've had some cake for her birthday."

I laughed, spread my arms to take in the warm air, and hugged Mama. My brand new Brotherhood of Bookbinders union receipt card stuck out from my purse. Mr. Wiseman hired me as a clerk four years ago when I quit high school. I was the business's only female bookbinder, someone who was quick at fine finger work. Mama, being a steady supporter of woman's rights, showed the card to the little audience, tickled I was on the side of the union build-up after the Great War. She declared Alta and I both could vote in the next president's election, now that I was twenty-one.

The curly headed little girl piped up, "Mr. Faye came by. Alta said he had a swanky new car. He brought us Coca-Cola and a box of candy for Dolly. Told about things in Truckee."

Mama rocked, fanned herself, and smiled, saying Mr. Faye and his wife were visiting in Sacramento, but Mrs. Faye didn't come by.

The door squealed open and Alta leaned against the frame, slightly inside and out of the sunlight, waiting for our idle talk to cease. The unlit interior lent a ghostly ashen color to her figure. She looked skinnier than in the winter, when we were so hungry. Her beautiful black hair was greasy and snarled and full of lint. Her eyes were half shut against the daylight, so I couldn't see the violet irises that made everyone look twice.

"We all had a piece of candy," said Alta, "but Mr. Faye left after a few minutes. I guess he realized Mama'd never be alone in this place."

Lips cracked and dry, Alta smirked at me and at Mama, who looked away and flicked her fan.

"Oh, don't look so surprised," she said in the querulous voice she always used to defend herself. "And how come that man didn't bring you on his motorcycle?"

Mama told her to leave me alone, but the way Alta looked, I'm not sure she remembered what I'd already told her.

"All right," Alta said. "All right."

I'd already told them Abel's mother didn't approve of me. Not from the right family, I wasn't good enough for her son, the brave soldier in the Great War, with mustard gas burns to prove it. I'd tried to be friendly and helpful, but she was unkind, as Mama would have told me if she'd been there. I'd been unhappy and tearful, but now I was over it. Tiny had said Abel was a mama's boy. All the same, it was mean of Alta to bring the man up. Why did she act so on my birthday?

Still standing in the dark in the doorway, Alta said, "I don't suppose Mama told you I'm going to San Francisco."

Mama held up a letter.

Alta said, "It's from Tiny. She wrote her roommate is leaving."

Waving the envelope, Mama said Tiny and her roommate argued. Tiny was worried she wouldn't have enough money at that secretary's job to pay for her apartment. It was expensive there, and she ate out most of the time.

Alta stepped outside, sat down on the porch steps, and lit a cigarette. She blocked the sunlight with her hand and interrupted.

"So, I said I'd go. Mama gave me train money."

Standing up, Mama asked me to go with her into the kitchen to get the cake and plates. Alta sat on the step, leaning over and whispering to the kids, making them laugh when she blew smoke rings. How could she be so sweet to those little kids when I suspected she had a plan up her sleeve that would make us all unhappy?

"Don't talk about me for too long," Alta called.

In the kitchen I said, "What are you thinking? Tiny can't cope with Alta. She'll take Tiny's things. She'll take Tiny's money. She won't spend her time at the library! She'll go down to … to … wherever people go in San Francisco to drink and smoke and gamble. Have you looked at her?"

Mama tightened her lips and said she didn't want Alta to live with her anymore. She found out Alta was hanging around with a crowd of gamblers and drunkards in the saloons near the Sacramento River. All those places were closing down because of the temperance laws, but Alta knew where they were still open.

Picking up the plates and forks, I remembered Mama's face after Raleigh fell into the river and she'd whipped us. I'd thought Mama'd been upset because she couldn't protect us. Now, she'd chosen to let Alta go.

"Do you think it'll be better in San Francisco?" I wailed. "I can't have her live with me though. Never. I think she needs to see a doctor. I've heard about doctors."

I knew Mama'd never find a doctor. She barely had enough money for herself. Alta had a job playing the piano in the barroom still open on Fifth Street, and she sang, still with a lovely voice. Alta made a lot of money in tips, which she spent on liquor and cigarettes, but she never gave Mama rent money. This is how it always was, and why, tired of being poor, I'd dropped out of high school when we moved here—to give Mama money. Alta couldn't keep a job even when she did manage to get one, and now she was going to give up the job on Fifth Street.

Mama said Alta always wanted to live in San Francisco, so it was an

25

opportunity. The lady down the street let Mama use her telephone to call Tiny at her secretary's office. She talked Tiny into it. I never could imagine how.

We walked out to the porch with the cake—vanilla with chocolate frosting. Mama must have saved pennies to buy the ingredients for such a treat.

I went back for the iced tea and glasses. Alta followed me, holding onto the chair back and the edge of the table, as she slipped into her tiny room. When I came out of the kitchen, she'd washed her face and combed her hair, but her dress was wrinkled with a button missing. She was struggling with her coat, a faint pungent smoky odor floating in the air.

I asked if she was meeting up with her latest, Bill Hutchinson.

She snapped, "Mind your own business, will you?"

I pleaded with her to at least stay for the cake, since Raleigh was coming over. She was licking her lips, turning from side to side.

She picked up her purse, looked into it, and said, "I need a dollar to take the trolley."

"The trolley doesn't cost a dollar," I said.

"Are you going to give it to me or not?"

I didn't want to argue with her in Mama's house. She looked so bad, squinting and holding her stomach like she was nauseated. I gave her the dollar, even though I was hoarding every nickel because I had to pay for my room and food all alone. I'd even skip the trolley and take short cuts to work down Sacramento's back streets. I knew the scent of opium. She was doing something besides drinking.

She hurried out the door and down the steps, calling, "I'll be back, Mama."

I brought out the tray and sat down on the steps. Mama had cut the cake and given a piece to each child. They played with bits of rock and pieces of wood and took bites of cake almost too big for their little mouths. I cut a slice for myself. Raleigh walked up the path. I hadn't seen him for a couple of months, and my brother had become a good-looking young man—not tall, but nicely built with the same cheerful smile he'd always had.

Mama, smiling and winking, gave him some cake.

"Happy birthday, son."

The kids said, "Happy birthday, Raleigh."

He rubbed the tops of their heads and they laughed.

"Want to see my scar?" Raleigh asked. "Scary story."

The boy shook his head. "We've seen it."

"That reminds me. I ran into Alta at the corner," Raleigh said. "She got me to give her two dollars. Doesn't she ever have any money? She was lucky today. I made a few dollars playing cards with my pals."

"That's it. Alta's gotten money from us all," I marveled.

We sat on the porch eating cake. A breeze ruffled the billowing branches of the olive tree, and behind the tree on the far side, a barbed wire fence separated the dirt road from the fields. Wild flowers and tall grass spread color over the meadow. A few jays called out. Otherwise, it was quiet and peaceful in the countryside of Sacramento.

I calmed down until Mama said, "Raleigh, did I tell you Alta's going to stay with Tiny in San Francisco?"

He snorted and said, "You're going to let Tiny have a go with her? I'd like to see that one."

"It doesn't matter if Alta's getting money or getting away. No matter where she is, she'll be unhappy," I said.

"Sometimes she takes us to the park. We go on the trolley. She tells us funny stories," said the curly headed girl.

There was the problem. Sometimes she was kind, and most of the time she was tormented, even now we were grown up. She took after Papa who could be jolly like the day we left for Sacramento and went over the Donner Summit, but then he'd lose himself.

Mama sighed, "I think Alta wants to meet Bill Hutchinson in San Francisco. He's joined the Merchant Marine. He's a nice man, so maybe things'll settle down for her there. Though I didn't tell all that to Tiny."

Mama pushed the rocker back and forth and stared at the olive tree, a sure sign she wanted to stop talking about her oldest daughter, the one she dearly loved, but couldn't handle.

So I said, "I've met another man. A girl from work and her boyfriend introduced us at Alta's bar. He's a bit older. Named Henry. He travels up the valley buying vegetables and fruit to be sold at the wholesale market near the river, like Mr. Archer did when we lived with his family. I've been so lonely since Tiny went to San Francisco. He's fun to go out with."

Mama rocked and hummed Alta's new favorite song, "Till We Meet Again," while we ate cake and gazed through the olive leaves across the dirt road into the field where oak trees swayed.

The first time we came to the city, Alta and I did have three weeks of truce where we helped each other. I was thinking about when we arrived in Sacramento and had to live with Mr. and Mrs. Archer. We were lonely then, and we only had each other.

5

End of April 1910
Donner Summit Road

PAPA MUST HAVE stopped at the Last Chance Saloon when he got off the train from Sacramento. He stomped his foot on the front porch step, and he had to steady himself before dragging the other foot up.

The evening had been peaceful enough. Alta had cleared, Mary washed, and Tiny dried the dishes. Raleigh had carried the food scraps out to the garbage pile behind the shed and carried the other trash to the brick pit for burning. The four children had taken off to play Run, Sheep, Run in the field behind the houses with Joe and his cousins who kept showing up, some of them speaking only Italian.

Hot and thirsty, Mary had run into the kitchen for water. Leaning against the counter, patting Florence on the back in the evening silence, Mama heard the noise and mouthed "Papa."

He opened the front door and called out "Dolly?" as Tiny, the last child in, banged the kitchen door closed.

"Liquored up," Mama whispered, the children following in a line to the front hallway.

"You're home," she greeted her husband.

Usually he loomed in front of his children, long-legged, with black hair brushed back from his thin face, a sharp nose, and deep blue-black irises. The photograph in Mama's bedroom depicted a handsome man, but now his eyes were bloodshot, his skin blotchy. He swayed side to side, keeping one hand on the doorknob to steady himself.

"Say hello to your Papa," Mama commanded. Pale and stiff, her face betrayed how much she hated Papa's drinking.

Alta's and Mary's wary voices chimed in with Tiny's and Raleigh's obedient,

"Hello, Papa."

A crooked grimace appeared on his lips—the smile before any number of unpredictable acts. Would he dig candy from his pocket? Would he kiss Mama even when she turned her head to the side? Maybe he'd harrangue Mama and any child nearby? Instead, he simply stood rocking.

Mama said, "You'd better go upstairs."

Papa grunted, let go of the doorknob, and stumbled to the steps. He ascended to the second floor, holding the banister with one hand and pressing the other palm against the wall to balance.

THE NEXT MORNING, hands in his pockets, face amiable, Papa came down to the kitchen. Sitting at the kitchen table, eating and talking over each other, all four children suddenly closed their mouths. Only Florence cooed and kicked in the basket on the counter, and Papa picked her up, giving her a finger to grab, as she waved her tiny hands.

"A darling, isn't she?" he said.

He continued to gaze at the baby and smile.

After a while, Papa asked, "How's the horse, Raleigh?"

"First-rate, Papa."

"I was thinking of making a wagon for Molly to pull," Papa said.

"That'd be swell," answered Raleigh.

The three girls put their heads together and whispered, wondering why Papa had suddenly thought up that idea. Later, staring after Papa who headed off to the Last Chance on Front Street, they didn't stop offering opinions.

Tiny said, "He won't get around to the wagon for a week or so."

"How d'you know?" asked Raleigh.

"Because," said Alta, "he's on a binge. And it'll last about four days. How much you want to bet?"

She looked around for takers, but everyone knew she was right. Yes, yes, Mary said to herself. If we badgered him while he was drinking, he got angry.

Sure enough, on the fourth night he reached the top step of the front porch, sat down, and threw up. Mama put him to bed, fed him broth, and put cold rags on his head. Trying a new tack, Mama didn't snap at the children and didn't shout at Papa either, although Mary did overhear her sigh in the kitchen, *"Life's but a walking shadow, a poor player … ."*

Three days later, Papa pulled himself out of bed and began to construct the wagon. He sang while he worked, and he told stories about his trips up and down the valley. He bought four wheels at the livery stable, and the children, with Molly's help, dragged discarded lumber from the sawmill. Soon they had a buckboard, plain with no trimmings. Alta was disgusted and said so, but Raleigh and Tiny took it out to show off. Mary thought Molly was beautiful, and Molly made the wagon look fine.

THE DAY AFTER the wagon was finished, Papa slid into the house through the back way, and Mary was party to one of her parents' last calm talks. She was rocking Florence, and Mama sat at the table, counting out rent from the boarders. Papa sat down quietly and gazed at Mama with eyes as radiant as when he coddled the baby.

Mama glanced up, wariness in her eye.

"Well, Tom?" she asked, placing a stack of pennies on the table.

He took her hand and smoothed his palm softly along the back of it.

"Dolly, they want me to pick up trips from Sacramento for a while longer," answered Papa.

Mama pulled her hand away and picked up a pile of pennies. She spread them on the table and began to build another stack of fifty.

"What do they mean by 'a while'?" she asked.

Fiddling with the dollar bills, Papa said, "Too many men up here and not enough down in Sacramento, Dolly. They didn't say how long. Just 'go'."

"We're barely getting by, Tom," said Mama, voice quavering. "We need the money from this boardinghouse, but I don't want to be here alone with five children."

Mama's voice rose, "Lord help me, you know Raleigh almost drowned."

Papa sagged into the chair, his gaze darting from the baby to the pot of simmering potatoes to Mama's serious face.

"It's not like before when there were only two of us, coming and going as we pleased. Or when the children were little and followed around like ducklings in a line," said Mama, a wistful turn to her lips.

Papa breathed deeply, smoothed the bills, looked straight at Mama, and said, "I guess we'll all go."

"What do you mean?" asked Mama. "How long before you have to be there?"

"A week," Papa sighed, taking Mama's hands again and leaning close to her. He smoothed her palms, fresh from soap, and lifted them to breathe in the scent. Smiling, the radiant look appeared in his eyes once more, as if by willing happiness, all would be well.

He said, "Dolly, it'll be better than the time we lived in Bakersfield. Better houses in Sacramento and lots of stores and big schools."

"Perhaps, but Tiny was a newborn in Bakersfield and the girls were too young for school," Mama said. "Now I have a newborn and four children in school.

What we'll need is money, Tom. It won't do if we're as poor as we were in Bakersfield."

She pulled her hands back and placed her palms on the tabletop.

"Not only are there stores," she said, "there're saloons in Sacramento. I thank you for the wagon, but I can't thank you for the money you drink with."

Papa frowned and turned his gaze to his baby, picked Florence up, and smoothed her cheek.

"Oh, Dolly, I want us to be together again," he said. "You'll like it in Sacramento. You'll see. The park around the Capitol is beautiful. The rivers are much different than the Truckee. We can window shop at all the fancy stores.

"I can take our things down in the wagon with Molly. You can take the train with the children."

Quietly watching Papa's smile, smoothing her hands along her skirt, Mama said, "How're we going to have money, Tom? Do you hear me? I can live on very little, but we've five children, Tom."

Papa stood before he answered. "Do you hear me? I won't have a job at all if I stay up here. I must go to Sacramento."

He smiled at the baby.

"You can come with me or stay here."

Mama frowned and turned to look at Mary and the baby.

Voice welling up in frustration, she said, "The river incident was the last straw for me, Tom. We must find a place where I can watch the children better. Maybe food will be cheaper. Maybe you won't drink so much. Maybe … "

She paused, trying to control her voice.

"Tomorrow I'll tell Mr. Englehardt I won't be managing the boardinghouse anymore."

She circled the table and lifted Florence from Papa's arms, patting the baby and shushing her.

"I'm telling you, Tom, I'll have to find work, and I'll need your help. Or we won't make it."

For a while longer, smiling and nodding, Papa gazed at Mama. Then he tickled the baby, patted Mary's head, and walked to the kitchen door.

"Please Tom, take only one bill," said Mama.

As it turned out, Mr. Englehardt found someone to manage his boardinghouse, a boarder's wife from Nevada, and they only had one child. Mr. Englehardt was happy, as more rooms became available to rent without Mama's big family taking up three bedrooms.

Though Mary was the one who doubted the move to a large, intimidating city, she had already wrapped her two prized possessions, the bedraggled *Ivanhoe* and *The Marvelous Wizard of Oz*.

Tiny carefully packed her jewelry and elocution book, all of which she had found by lounging around the train station. After finding the elocution book, she had decided to be an actress. For weeks, adorned with necklaces, she'd walked around the kitchen, reading poems out loud to Mary, Florence, Mama, whoever was available.

> *Blow, bugle, blow; set the wild echoes flying,*
> *Blow, bugle; answer, echoes, dying, dying, dying.*

Tiny tried to imitate the echo with a high falsetto, and Mama applauded, hugged Tiny, and explained the difficult words in the rest of Tennyson's poem.

Raleigh packed his yoyo and the little knife he had traded for with Joe. Alta wouldn't let anyone see what she had accumulated in a purse she said she found, but her siblings assumed she had swiped the purse from her best friend Sally Faye.

ON MOVING DAY, Alta and Tiny departed by train for Sacramento with Mama and the baby. Everyone wanted to go by wagon down to Colfax and then to Sacramento. Mama refused to let Alta go off with Papa, expecting she would discover trouble wherever they spent the night. Tiny agreed to go on the train after Mama curled Tiny's hair and let her wear hair ribbons, a real change from overalls and a flannel shirt.

With boxes on board and Molly hitched up, Papa, Mary, and Raleigh set off early. Not far out of town, they saw the steep, granite cliffs that led to the pass beyond icy blue Donner Lake. Snow still filled deep, permanently shaded crevices. The horse clopped along the narrow wagon road on the shore of Donner Lake. In the distance, Papa glimpsed the ruined hovels from the Donner Party's 1846 winter of starvation and pointed them out to Mary. All Truckee school children knew about the mothers, fathers, and children who were trapped in deep high mountain snow only four miles from Front Street, and Mary was glad a warm breeze brushed her face, assuring her snow wouldn't blow over them that day.

Molly began the steep climb to the summit. About half way up, Mary and Raleigh jumped down, jogging along, throwing rocks off the ledges, and poking sticks at the budding monkey flowers until Papa told them to stop beating them. He pointed to a young jay, its black crest shining in the sun, flying up from the brush, squawking *chey-chey-chey*. A crew of shaggy ravens swooped onto a long branch, ignoring the jay. They turned their heads to watch the wagon and croaked loudly out of reach in the white pine.

At the summit, out of breath, Mary and Raleigh climbed back into the buckboard.

Papa said, "Watch what happens as we go down toward the foothills."

Truckee had squeezed itself into a high mountain valley near the tree line, with stumps from logging all around the town. For a short way, the mountainsides were still granite outcroppings with trees perched in the crevices. Papa pointed to the railroad tunnel that his trains used to go to and from Reno and points east and Sacramento.

Papa said, "See the thick, dark trees. They remind me of the forests where we used to play back in Tennessee. I loved those woods."

Pines and fir reached to the sky on both sides of the road.

"Did I tell you I was the youngest boy for a long time until my baby brother was born?" Papa asked, out of the blue.

"I was my grandmother's favorite, and of course, she let me do whatever I wanted. I raced a pony through the forest to her place most every day, even when I was only five. She liked the outdoors, and I'd help her in the garden and feed the pigs and chickens, not that she had many. We were poor at that time, you know, being that the War Between the States had just ceased. Some of my father's people still hadn't returned from prison at that time. But not too many of her relatives fought."

Papa stopped speaking and clucked at the horse. He flipped the reins to encourage Molly, as the road became narrower and broken up where loose dirt on the mountainside had slid down during the winter.

Raleigh asked why not, and Papa said, "She was Cherokee, at least mostly, though many had already been driven off to Oklahoma by then. Her people tried to stay out of the way of all that killing in the war."

Papa watched the horses and the road for a minute before he said, "I was so young, so it's hard to remember what she looked like. Anyway she let me play with toys she had from her people. Let's see … my sister, Martha Jane, and I played with the hoops and my favorite toy was the singing spinner. If you twirled the leather string until it was twisted tight and then pulled, the button spun, making a singing tune. You can make one. It's easy."

Papa's conversation trailed off. He steered the horse around a huge hole in the road so the wheel wouldn't get caught. Noise from the wheels made a few mule deer peep out from the edge of the woods. Sharp-eyed Raleigh pointed out a black-tailed deer deep among the trees that bounded off when Raleigh called out.

Going up a rise, the wagon slowed. Mary caught sight of tiny gold blooms pushing up among the rocks. The more Mary gaped, the more wildflowers she saw sprouting. Suddenly remorseful about whacking the monkey flowers, she promised herself someday she'd learn all of their names.

"Your Cherokee grandmother knew a lot about plants and flowers, Mary," said Papa. "She'd make a paste of some plant to put on my mosquito bites and other muddy-looking stuff for my cuts. I bet she would have fixed up your gash lickety-split, Raleigh. She saved a soldier who had gotten lost in the battle at Stones River. He became feverish from a wound, but she cut out the bullet and used one of her concoctions on him. He wandered off after two days or so, and she never did know which side he was on."

Papa laughed, a puzzled snort.

"By then soldiers were wearing each other's clothes. Stuff they'd pulled off dead men," he confided. "But, you know, every family had stories like that to tell."

After the Cherokee great-grandmother tale, bumping along in the wagon became tedious until Papa let each take turns at the reins. He sang out his favorite railroad song,

> Oh, in eighteen hundred and forty-one
> My corduroy britches I put on,
> My corduroy britches I put on
> To work upon the railway.

Two horsemen rode by, raising their hats. At a curve in the trail, a shay appeared, going up the grade. Both parties called out directions as the wagons squeezed by each other, without a wheel sliding over the edge of the cliff. On and off, the two jumped down and walked to stretch their legs and spare Molly. Even Papa was tired by twilight, but he knew where he wanted to stay.

EVENTUALLY, PAPA TURNED the wagon off to a large way station, short of the Colfax turn-off. Papa unhitched Molly, but Mary and Raleigh led her to the barn. They rubbed her down, found her stall, and got her a big pail of oats, all the while talking to her, calling her "good horse" and "our pal, Molly."

Neither had ever been to a way station, all was new from the enormous barn to the vegetable garden, full of soup and stew vegetables already growing at this lower elevation. They played tag in the barnyard, hollering and sprinting and leaping over the woodpile. Finally reaching the entrance, they halted in a large room, dark and smoky. A few long wood tables filled the space on one side where families might sit, although no chair was taken.

At the bar on the opposite side, Papa appeared and disappeared in the smoke. To reach him, they had to pass a table with four hulking men hunched over bowls of stew, chewing steadily and sipping from whiskey glasses after each swallow. At the next table, one slim man in a tight gray suit dealt cards to three others in miner's get-up—Levi's, threadbare flannel shirts, and ratty jackets. The pale gray-suited man poured a round of whiskey. The miners dared each other to bet, puffed on cigars, and guffawed at a joke delivered by the one with a mustache.

Embarrassed, Mary gritted her teeth, held Raleigh's hand tightly, and forced herself to walk into the saloon with her head up. He swaggered, trying to act grown-up.

Raleigh poked Papa on the arm and said, "We're hungry," in his high, clear voice.

Snorts of laughter erupted from the tables. Mary cringed. Papa squinted down at the children, recognition appearing in his eyes, a revelation that he had forgotten about them. Mary's heart pounded. She put her hands against her temples to stop the thumping and squeezing, afraid she would spend the trip making sure she and Raleigh got food and a sleeping place.

Then Papa called to the woman at the far end of the bar, "Miranda, my boy and girl are with me. Can you get them something?"

Miranda disappeared, but in a few minutes she came back and ushered Mary and Raleigh to the family side. She laid out soup, bread, and milk. As Miranda leaned over to see if everything was all right, Mary smelled the whiskey on her breath. Miranda was a large, friendly woman, plump, with red hair, like the women on Back Street. She didn't appear drunk, so, like Papa, Miranda must have been able to drink a lot before she began to sway and slur.

Hands on her hips, watching them eat, Miranda asked, "Where're you from?"

"Truckee," said Mary, "but we're going to Sacramento because Papa works on the railroad."

"That's how I got here," said Miranda. My Da helped build this railroad track all the way past Reno before he got the typhoid and died. My Mam and us three kids were happy until that trouble, but we survived. I've worked here since my own man died in a rock slide while repairing the track up by Donner Lake."

"Maybe I won't work on the railroad after all," said Raleigh.

Miranda laughed, "You might if that was the only way to make a living."

A boisterous voice called, and Miranda disappeared into the haze at the bar side of the saloon. Mary, soothed by the food, and Raleigh, sleepy after the excitement, put their heads down on the table until Papa came over and shook them.

With a voice thick from the whiskey, he said, "There're no rooms upstairs, Mary.

Miranda says you can sleep in her room. Raleigh'll sleep with me in the barn."

Mary recognized the fib, Papa'd spent the money, but she rolled herself into the blanket on the cot in the corner of a room off the kitchen.

She dreamed. It was a hot, hot morning. She dawdled along Front Street, watching farmers dressed like Munchkins from *The Marvelous Wizard of Oz* stand by their wagons, bellowing to customers, hawking their vegetables and fruits—enormous and more colorful than any Mary had ever seen. Miranda, plump and pretty, flounced down the middle of the road, herding sheep and singing. She was showing off a huge ram.

Mary jerked awake, hearing Miranda singing, stumbling, and then falling onto her own bed. Mary listened for a few seconds, and it came to her, "The Derby Ram," the song from school, the funny rhyme about the biggest sheep in England. Mary listened some more. She blinked, blinked again, and sucked in a breath. Those weren't the words. Miranda sang the raucous, bawdy verses over and over, more loudly each time like the saloon ladies in Truckee.

The room reeked of whiskey from Miranda's breath and smoke from her clothes. Mary turned over and covered her ears and nose with the blanket, but it was no use. Finally, she threw off the cover, tiptoed over to Miranda, who didn't seem to be asleep, and stuck her hand out to shake the woman's arm.

Miranda bawled out,

They brought the beast to Derby-town,
Drove him with a stick
And all the girls in Derby-town
Paid a quarter to see his ….

Hands clapped over her ears, Mary shoved her feet into her shoes and retreated to the kitchen. She roamed around in the dark, coat over her head, while Miranda reeled off the chorus,

Maybe you don't believe me,
Maybe you think it's a lie,
But if you'd been down to Derby-town
You'd see the same as I.

From the back door, a half-moon high in the clear, black sky, the ground glowing, Mary easily crossed the yard and pushed open the large barn doors. Horses were awake, munching oats or shuffling in their stalls. Molly, peeking over her gate, whinnied softly. She slipped over to the stall and rubbed Molly's nose while she looked around and finally saw the mountain of hay in the far corner. With her eyes half-closed, she staggered to the pile and threw herself down close to Raleigh.

In the morning Papa, didn't ask why Mary was in the barn. He brought biscuits from the saloon, and she and Raleigh ate, lying under the blankets while he rearranged boxes and bags in the wagon. The next night they stopped near Auburn. The third evening they arrived in Sacramento.

Mary always supposed that Papa had seen the resentment in her face because he cheered them with more stories about Tennessee and their Cherokee grandmother for the next two days. At the way station near Auburn, he didn't go near the bar. He sat and ate supper with them. In the barn Mary pushed hay away from her face, thinking it was funny she didn't want to go anywhere, but ended up on this journey.

In Sacramento, Mary recounted Papa's stories about their Cherokee grandmother, but Alta and Tiny much preferred the mad night of the Derby ram and laughed as raucously as Miranda sang.

<hr>

"I THINK YOUR great-uncle was almost nine, Lane, younger than you, when we begged to take that wagon ride," said Mary.

6

Three Weeks in May 1910
Sacramento

MARY SAT ON the left, with Raleigh, Tiny, and Alta next to her on the top porch step. They straddled carpetbags between their legs and threw prickly balls they found under the sycamores. The children aimed for the far side of a much wider street than any in their mountain town. The boardinghouse, where the four train passengers had stayed, fronted a long street shaded by the broad-branched trees in the old part of Sacramento, near the American River.

Alta listed the places they had seen, informing Raleigh and Mary that Sacramento certainly wasn't Truckee. The day before, they'd wandered along K Street, loitering at swanky shop windows, scrutinizing the fancy restaurants.

"I wanted to give bread to the squirrels at the Capitol Park," said Tiny, "but a lady warned us not to touch."

Mary threw her last bristly ball and sat thinking about the big city, waiting to set off for new lodgings.

THE EVENING BEFORE, Alta and Tiny sat cross-legged on the rug in the parlor, hovering over Florence, who gurgled and grasped at their fingers. Tight-lipped, Mama sat on the edge of the sofa. When Papa, Raleigh, and Mary came in, Mama patted the cushion. Papa placed his arm on the sofa back, in easy reach of Mama's shoulder.

"Tom, I have work for the time being, nursing for a woman with a new baby," she said, "but I can't find any rooms or a house that we can afford near her home."

"Dolly, don't ... ," Papa began, stifling a yawn and smiling.

She interrupted, "Florence and I can live in her servant's room, and you can stay in the room with me when you're in town."

"Don't worry. I can ask the fellows at the railroad office," said Papa, leaning over to catch Florence's little fingers. "They'll find something."

Mama rubbed her eyes. "Tom, I've seen every building. I'm ready to give up. I've talked to Tiny and Alta. They'll explain to Raleigh and Mary. I don't want to, but Raleigh and Tiny are young enough for the orphanage in a house donated by a rich lady. They can go to school. They'll be taken care of."

Raleigh and Tiny hid their quivering lips and the tears in their eyes. They only knew about the orphanage in *Oliver Twist*. Expecting the worst, a knot of sorrow closed Mary's throat.

Wiping his forehead, Papa looked at his children's grim frowns before he grinned and wiggled his eyebrows, anything to make them smile. Then he took Mama's hands and held them on his knees, the wide smile still on his face.

"They'll be all right. They'll be all right. I asked around for Alta and Mary too," Mama said.

"I've found a lady with small children who'll let Alta and Mary live in her maid's room. The girls can take care of the little ones to pay for board and room and they can walk to school."

Mary shook her head hard and fast.

Papa said, "Dolly, I thought we'd all be together. It's hard to imagine what's happened."

Mama let out a breath and said, "Perhaps by the end of the month we'll find a house. But, Tom, you know that's all the time we have. Mr. Englehardt's giving that woman a month. If she's good, it's too bad for us. If she doesn't work out, we can go back. If we don't go back, he'll get someone else. Lots of people need work up there."

Edging off of the sofa, Papa said, "We'll find a place. My railroad friends are smart fellows. Who would've thought it was hard to find a house in a big town like this?"

Mama covered her face. Raleigh brushed away tears with his fist. Sitting around Florence, the three girls looked down, unable to smile at their baby sister. It was obvious to Mary that Papa wasn't going to be any help. Papa made Mary laugh, except when he drank. The railroad company said he was a brakeman to be trusted, but Mary knew he wasn't going to find a house. Papa barely held himself together when he, Mary, and Raleigh came down the mountain.

Papa lifted Mama's head and gazed into her eyes. He took hold of her hands and held them against his cheeks.

"Dolly, it'll be all right."

He hugged her and headed for the door, but Mama cautioned him, "I'm praying for patience, Tom. *'The end is not yet,'* Matthew 24:6."

MARY AND ALTA boarded on J Street and 17th, not far from lavish shops and downtown restaurants. Robert, tidy in short pants and jacket, and Jane, charming in a fluffy pinafore, kept their hands behind their back and their gaze on their mother, Mrs. Archer. Tall and plump like Miranda at the Colfax way station, but imposing rather than friendly, Mrs. Archer showed Mama and the girls around. All looked fine until they saw a tiny room with a bed so narrow they'd have to sleep head to foot.

Feeling an eleven-year-old's sense of doom, Mary grabbed hold of Alta's hand.

"Two weeks," Mama announced. "I'll come visit on my day off."

"What if we need you?" asked Alta.

"Mrs. Archer will send for me," Mama answered, kissing and hugging them. "Don't worry. I only wish you to do what Mrs. Archer asks. *'Whatsoever thy hand findeth to do, do it with thy might,'* Ecclesiastes."

As she walked out the door, Mary wondered if the last two days of Bible verses were meant to reassure the girls or Mama herself.

The girls came home as soon as school was over. Every afternoon, Mrs. Archer stood at the door holding a watch, her lips pressed together, reproving them, and then she left without a word about where she was going. The girls took care of the children until she returned. Each afternoon, they gave snacks to the children and ate some too. With only oatmeal for breakfast and a small sandwich for lunch, they were hungry most of the time.

"Should we tell Mama?" wondered Mary, already making a list of the miserly things Mrs. Archer did.

"Sure," said Alta. "That lady must think we're dumb country folk."

On the weekend Mr. Archer came home from buying and selling vegetables up and down the Sacramento valley. The family took off to a new park for a picnic in Mr. Archer's vegetable business wagon, much more finely built than the one Papa had made. Alta sneered about Mrs. Archer, so high and mighty, but who didn't have a car.

The girls hadn't been invited to the picnic and were told to stay in the house, but after the wagon rounded the corner, they strolled along J Street inspecting all the shops near the big, white Capitol building. They walked into the large stationery and candy store to see what it contained. It looked so different from the tiny shop at home in Truckee.

Mary asked to look at the greeting cards in the glass case. The girls pored over the elaborate designs. Since they had no money, they thanked the clerk and walked out. A few steps down the street, Alta pulled two horehound sticks out of her sleeve and gave one to Mary. Hungry for sweets, she popped it into her mouth and took a long suck before misgivings took over and she held it out wet and sticky.

Alta crunched on her candy, and Mary thought of no way to justify herself and sucked again on her sweet stick. Letting the flavor slip down their throats, they watched the Saturday shoppers. They had no desire to go back to the house they disliked.

Alta fumed, "Why didn't Mrs. Archer take us to the park?"

"Maybe she didn't want to spend the money on food," offered Mary.

"They're cheap and mean," Alta said.

Nodding, Mary said, "Except Robert and Jane. They're sweet. How did that mother raise two nice children?"

Back at the house, Mary finished her homework and watched the porcelain clock, ticking slowly. Alta wandered around, picking up every knickknack that Mrs. Archer wouldn't let anyone touch. Finally, Alta perched on the piano bench. Before Raleigh and Tiny needed clothes and books for school, Alta had taken a few piano lessons from a lady who lived on McGlashan's Hill.

"Such a beautiful voice," Mama had said. She had talked Papa into paying for lessons.

Alta played and sang "Sweet Adeline" while Mary waltzed around. The girls leaned over the piano, their heads close together, and bickered about which song to sing next, "The Glow Worm" or "Meet Me in St. Louis." Their heads bounced up when Mrs. Archer, her lips pinched dourly, rapped on the piano lid.

"Why are you touching my piano?" she snarled.

Mary looked from Mrs. Archer to Mr. Archer, who didn't seem disgusted. Mr. Archer acted surprised, whether at their disobedience or at his wife's anger, Mary wasn't sure. Mrs. Archer struck the cabinet with her fist. Mary jumped back and sheets of music slid to the floor.

"We didn't know … ," Mary's voice squeaked.

Alta interrupted, "We're not hurting anything."

Then she leaned forward and blurted out, "Why'd you make us stay behind if you didn't want us to touch anything?"

Mrs. Archer's face flared, eyes glaring at one girl and then the other. Alta sat back, a flash of fear crossing her face. Mary sucked in her breath when Mrs. Archer abruptly raised her hand, but Mr. Archer reached for his wife's arm.

Mrs. Archer croaked, "Go to your room, both of you."

Gathering the music, Mary laid it on the top of the upright. Alta closed the cover. Mary clasped her palms together at her waist, while Alta let one hand slide along the buffet table and over the top of the arm chair, as they silently walked out of the sitting room all the way to the maid's room and lay down on their bed. Alta closed her eyes.

Footsteps clumped into the kitchen, cabinets opened.

Mr. Archer said, "Alicia, you're being too hard. Their mother agreed to a good arrangement."

A cupboard door slammed and Mrs. Archer hissed, "Those mountain girls look at me funny. Too snooty for their own good."

"You're seeing things, Alicia. Robert and Jane talked about them all day. How much fun they are," he said.

"Their mother acts educated too, and she's no more than a mountain woman. And those girls are always reading," said Mrs. Archer.

Alta turned, eyes as wide open as Mary's.

Mr. Archer whispered, "If you don't like them, then we don't need help. We can do fine."

"How else will we save enough to buy a car?" retorted Mrs. Archer. "Can you tell me that?"

"Saving for a car?" asked her husband. "Then what're all the new things I see around here?"

Steps retreated to another room.

Alta mouthed "crazy." Never in Mary's life had anyone ever called her family snooty.

The last straw fell when Mrs. Archer entered the house from her afternoon outing and told Mary and Alta they must do the ironing. Mary stared at her, thinking they'd kept things as neat as a pin. Why should they iron too?

Mrs. Archer said, "After all, your mother said you know how."

She pointed to the pile of laundry left by the washer woman, and the girls set the irons on the stove to heat, while the wicked witch, as they called her, walked out of the room in search of her children.

ON SATURDAY, MARY and Alta told Mama everything Mrs. Archer did, even before they squabbled over who would hold Florence.

Mama frowned, patted Florence's back, and quickened her steps. Mary and Alta charged after Mama to catch the trolley for the orphanage. The director brought Tiny and Raleigh out to the foyer, one child at each hand.

Standing in the foyer, regarding her brother and sister, who looked healthy, neatly dressed, and contented, Mary felt hungry and tired and untidy. She guessed Alta did too. Then Mama smiled, and Mary repeated to herself, please, please, please don't forget about mean Mrs. Archer.

Raleigh and Tiny let go of the director's hands and threw their arms around Mama, trying to see Florence and get the first word in about everything that had happened. After another trolley ride, they followed along the path to the park, yakking about the trolleys and the indoor toilets at the orphanage, which wasn't like *Oliver Twist* at all.

Crossing to the entrance with Southside Park embossed on an elaborate metal sign, Mary laughed because it was the same park that Mr. and Mrs. Archer had visited the previous weekend.

Then Mama stopped and the trail of children jostled up against her. Five women with yellow sashes and posters walked back and forth, passing out flyers. One woman asked a passerby to sign a letter to the legislature about woman's right to suffrage, like Mrs. Tucker and her women friends in Truckee.

Mama signed the letter, took a flyer and said, "I'm with you. Keep it up."

Mama set out the picnic while humming "Oh Dear, What Can the Matter Be," the old song with new words the ladies had been singing. She nursed the baby and read the flyer, saying, "Who would have guessed we'd see suffrage ladies at the park."

All four children played in the park together. Alta shouted and Mary ran around for the first time in two weeks. The children came when called, and they gobbled ham sandwiches provided by Mama's employer.

Then Mama said, "Close your eyes. I have something special."

When she said to open their eyes, they saw a plate with four little cakes on it.

"Happy birthday, Mary and Tiny and Raleigh! Surprise!"

Passing out the cakes, she said, "I'm sorry we weren't together these past two weeks to celebrate."

Mary took a big bite. For a few minutes the delicacy filled her mouth, and she enjoyed the buttery stickiness of the icing and the soft, crumbly feel of the cake. It seemed a distraction from all worry.

Mama said, "Mrs. Dodge let me make these in her kitchen. She's been very kind while I've worked for her."

"Did you find a house yet?" asked Mary.

Mama shook her head and the smile slowly disappeared.

"I wish we could be together," said Tiny. "I wish Papa was here."

"Yeah," Raleigh said. "They're nice to us, but it's lonesome at the orphanage."

Alta said, "Mrs. Archer is not nice at all, and I want to go home."

The ducks swam and quacked in the pond.

"I don't know what to do. I'm obligated right now to the lady I'm working for," said Mama. "Money. It's worse than Truckee. I'm going in circles like those ducks."

Mary took Mama's hand and said, "Can you please talk to Mrs. Archer? We don't have anywhere to go when she's mean to us."

Mama cleared her throat.

"Mrs. Archer seemed nice enough. We're in a bind, aren't we?"

She rubbed her forehead and hummed the tune to "America" that had new suffrage words, and they gathered the picnic things.

After a long talk, Mrs. Archer nodded and patted Mama on the arm. Their mother said good-bye to Mrs. Archer, although Mama didn't look reassured. Mary and Alta were left to cope.

THE GIRLS DRAGGED around until early the next Saturday morning. Mama knocked, opened the door, and strode into the kitchen. She leaned over the table to look at the meager bread and milk breakfast, and she told Alta and Mary to pack their things. She waved off Mrs. Archer's excuses, and Mr. Archer sat in silence at the entry of this tiny, unprepossessing woman with the stern look. When they saw the girls waiting with their carpet bags, Robert and Jane began to cry, but Mrs. Archer continued to excuse herself as they walked out.

"You're unkind, Mrs. Archer. Unkind," said Mama, reproof enough to stop Mrs. Archer from slamming the door.

Mama handed Florence to Mary and marched them to the corner, talking the entire way.

"She didn't have to be so grasping. You saw how those children cried. That's because you were kind to them. I don't know how she acts to her husband and children, but I asked around, and she's arrogant and tight-fisted. If only I'd checked more carefully."

She juggled her bags and said, "Please don't ask about your father. I left him a message at the train station."

Holding Florence, who was smiling and oblivious to all the drama, Mary waited as the trolley trundled around the corner.

She whispered, "We've been saved."

Alta murmured back, "From that wicked witch."

On the trolley, seated and packages arranged, Mama calmed down and said, "We're going to pick up Raleigh and Tiny and take the train back to Truckee. I received a telegram. Here."

Neither of the girls had ever held one, and they squished together to examine the message.

Mrs. Navarre sick and fights with husband. Going to Reno. Can you come?
Englehardt.

Mary looked at Alta, who looked at Mama, and they laughed.

Finally, Mama wiped her eyes and said, "Thank the Lord, Mrs. Dodge and her baby have found a nanny. We've tried our best. I still hope Papa can change the trips he works soon, so he'll be home more often."

Huffing and puffing when they reached the train, Raleigh and Tiny spread out on the seats, guarding the bags. Each child bit into a sandwich made by Mrs. Dodge, another example of kindness as Mama pointed out. Watching her brother and sisters fall asleep, wondering what it would be like as a mountain girl once more, Mary's eyes shut, then opened, then shut, to the rhythm on the rails.

⟶•◦•⟵

"IN TRUCKEE WE rarely thought about Mrs. Archer, and it seemed a long time there, Lane, until we grew up," said Mary.

7

March 1921
Sacramento

I WAS NEARLY twenty-three, no longer the young Mary who was confused about the adults in her life, even her mother. Confined to bed, I had plenty of time to think.

My insides were sore and my bones hurt. Mama had never warned me how hard it was to deliver a baby, no matter that she knew a lot about birth. The doctor said I was too narrow, and my daughter struggled all the way down. I saw the tiny mark from the forceps used to pull her out. Thank God, Mama stayed with me during labor. What would I have done all by myself? Henry was at a speakeasy.

When I was sent home, Mama came every single day, washing clothes, making supper, and hugging and kissing Betsy, my beautiful girl with dark red hair and long, delicate fingers like her father. When she opened her blue eyes it seemed as if she recognized me. She would be smart. That I knew.

I lay there in the bed in the small house Henry had rented a long while before we were married. I wished I could get up, but I hadn't been so tired since I had the typhoid when I was thirteen. One night, drifting in and out of my little world while rocking Betsy to sleep, I looked at her and thought it was baby Florence, so sweet, so quiet, so happy. Startled, I blinked and put my hand on my baby, uncertain what was real and what was memory.

It was a cold, drippy March. Whenever I managed to stir from my bed and slump in the armchair to stare out the window, people suddenly appeared near my house, out of the tule fog drifting along the street, so low it was like the person walked out of a cloud. One afternoon when waiting for Mama, a ghostly man emerged and my heart jumped. I felt sure Henry had come home early.

Calm had finally fallen over me when I became Henry's lover, as I'd been more lonely than I ever remembered when Tiny went to San Francisco and Alta followed. Once in a while I saw Raleigh, and often I went to see Mama, but she was always busy with those little neighborhood kids who were drawn to her house, playing among the trees and helping in the garden, as if it was the most entertaining part of their day. It wasn't their job to be my friends. Anyway, what was I thinking? I had friends, but they weren't around all the time like my family had always been.

Henry had wandered into the bar, still open before Prohibition, my friends called to him, and he sat across from me, smiling like Papa the charmer. He made me laugh, told good stories. At that time we got along, even though he was much older than me. He'd been divorced and had a son, but I only met the boy once. A sweet kid. Why didn't I find out about his divorce? Because I was happy that a man of the world liked me, or so I thought.

Holding his arm, I stood at the door of this house. I'd hardly ever kissed anyone before. Only Abel, with the motorcycle, and the sailor who gave me the belt made with sailor's knots, which I still kept in my drawer, designed just for me, he said. Still, the sailor's family was Greek, and I was afraid of them. I hardly knew where Greece was in the world. He was too different. Henry was suave, and I was drunk and lonely. Anyone can guess what happened. Before I knew it, we were together.

Henry had taken me to Frank Fat's the July night I told him I was going to have a baby. I loved Chinese food, though looking at the chow mein that evening made me feel sick in the stomach. He gripped the edge of the table, and his red Welsh cheeks turned pale. What did he think was going to happen? I'd never talked about those things with Mama or my sisters. I didn't know how to prevent a baby. I thought he did. He took me back to my tiny room at the hotel. I didn't say anything, and neither did he.

Mama was surprised too. She found out the day I went to visit and threw up. I was the good girl, and she never thought I would be caught in this situation. Those were her words, though I'd certainly learned in Truckee about loneliness and desire and chance. She had me lie down on her sofa, brought me tea, and talked about babies, but not about how hard they were to deliver. She said I could come live with her. That's the kind of person she was.

Instead, I did what Aunt Ola did when she hid her past. Mr. Wiseman from the bookbindery needed someone to work at his shop in Reno, so I said I'd go. I lived with the only person I knew, Aunt Margaret, and I hardly knew her. Odd, no one asked me about the father, though I had a story. I supposed in Reno, as rowdy as Truckee, it didn't matter. Everyone had a story.

At first, I was afraid of the changes to my body. Then I felt happier and happier, and when the baby began to kick, I realized everything was all right. One day I walked down the street in Reno and beheld myself in a window, stomach full and round, face smooth and calm. I smiled.

As my stomach ballooned, loneliness came back. Constantly called away by her family, Aunt Margaret let me be. Letters from Tiny and Mama weren't enough, so when I went to Sacramento for Christmas, I was happy Henry showed up at the train station and finally asked me to marry him. I thought I could do everything myself, but even at twenty-two I was too young.

I sat forward in the chair and looked out the window again. The door didn't open, so it wasn't Henry who had loomed out of the fog. Where was Mama? Caring for her sick neighbor? It might seem like Mama was crazy while we were growing up, especially the first time we came here to Sacramento. One minute she wanted us all to be near Papa, so he could live with us. Next minute she'd left Tiny and Raleigh at the orphanage and Alta and me with those horrible Archers.

It was true Mama did have a hard time in that hard place in the mountains, so many children to care for, but she didn't give up on us. I hoped I'd have as much gumption as she had. I shifted in the chair and pulled the quilt up over my shoulders. The memory of Mama with four little kids clambering onto the train rose in my mind. Alta was seven, I was six, Tiny was four, and Raleigh was still a toddler when we took the train trip all the way across the country from Truckee to Murfreesboro, Tennessee, stopping in Montrose, Missouri, to see her family. A far distance.

I hardly remembered our trip to the big world, except it took a long time, and we crossed wide rivers and mountains higher than the Sierra Nevada. How did Mama ever feed all four of us? Or keep us entertained on those long rides? I did remember Alta ran off, to explore she said, and Mama had to find a conductor to haul a squirming, protesting girl back to our train car.

I thought I heard a step and lifted my head in time to see a squirrel ruffle the dead leaves still clinging to the elm as it ran along a branch into the mist. Settling back in the chair, my pretty, spunky sister Tiny stood before me. Funny how little squirrels and chipmunks made her come to mind. Poor Tiny. Pale. Smile gone. Shoulders slumped forward. Not the flirty girl who made me so mad sometimes and made me laugh most of the time.

She'd never become an actress, though she'd recently finished her own short dramatic performance. She married a piano player, Patrick, last year. He was her San Francisco catch, Tiny's best line in the drama. She dragged him here to Sacramento to meet Mama, and then Patrick's mother made him annul the marriage. Something about Tiny lying to him. That was crazy. If anything, he lied to her. Mama put on her good coat and hat and took the train to San

Francisco to stand up for Tiny, of course, and brought her home when the show closed. I shook my head, and she vanished from view. In truth, she'd already returned to San Francisco, to try again as she claimed.

I heard Betsy's muffled burp and scuffle against the sheets. I hoped Mama would come soon. Before Betsy cried, Mama would gather her up. Mama would tell me funny stories. How I longed for them, as much as I'd missed them in those days when Papa was so bad, and Mama was hurting in her heart, but not letting on.

I was trying to lift myself out of the chair, when a knock sounded and the front door opened. Mama came in, shivering, and sat by the fire to warm her hands and feet. She whispered the nursery rhyme,

> *Little Polly Flinders*
> *Sits by the cinders*
> *Warming her pretty toes ...,*

and I laughed.

"You'll never guess what's happening now," said Mama.

I shook my head. Whatever the story, I was grateful for the news, fatigued by the voices in my head. Mama picked up Betsy, holding her tiny head, and gave her to me. She placed her fists on her hips.

"That girl Raleigh's married," said Mama, "is going to have a baby. And she's so sick the doctor says she'll have to stay in bed, or she won't keep it."

I shifted in the chair.

"I told Raleigh to bring Maggie over to our house. They're going to stay with me."

"In your little place?" I asked.

"What else to do? Raleigh's wild about that girl. I don't want anything to happen to the baby," said Mama, "but she'll probably lose it."

Raleigh, the youngest, the most protected ... it never occurred to Mama to do anything other than take care of us.

Like my feelings about Betsy. I patted the baby's back, knowing it was only the comfort against my body making her lips open, making her smile already. I smiled back. Betsy in my arms, nothing could make me unhappy. Though I should have known life wasn't like that.

8

May-June 1910
Church Street, Truckee

ON THE WEEKEND, Papa pulled up in the wagon in time for supper, not a whiff of whiskey about him. Mama smiled, accepted a hug, and set another plate and fork on the table.

"You made it. All those twists and turns on the western side of the summit," she said.

Papa put his hands on her shoulders, grinned, and winked at his children.

Sitting down to eat, Raleigh and Tiny chattered about how smart they were because they'd been to a big city school. Though Papa had to go by morning train back to Sacramento, Mama's face was calm, the family together, the disastrous trip behind them, everything peaceful.

All week, Mama had been her old self, full of energy, reciting her favorite poems while her children yelled out the chorus. Not once had she punished anyone, even when Alta talked back. One afternoon Mama stopped making biscuits and helped Mary fix a cap for Florence.

Brushing dough off her hands, Mama held the cap on Florence while Mary measured ribbon and cut it.

She went back to plopping dough on the tray, then leaned over the table and said, "You're a lucky girl, good with your hands and good with books too."

Smiling, Mary took care to make precise stitches while a memory poked its way into her head.

"What's a mountain girl, Mama? And are we snooty like Mrs. Archer said?"

"She doesn't like other women to show they're smart," said Mama. "That's what she means by snooty. She wants the upper hand. I say she was too smart for her own good. Lots of people assume mountain girls and women are stupid and can be made to do anything."

"We didn't try to act smart," said Mary.

"I meant educated smart," said Mama, "not talking-back smart. We're lucky to be educated and enjoy books. Not all people in the mountains are so fortunate."

A month later, Mary wandered up Harrigan's Hill to show off Florence to their new neighbors. Thinking about that happy week, Mary wondered what might have happened if Mama had been smart enough to see Papa had exhausted himself far from home on another round of trips up and down the Central Valley.

ATTENTION WAS LAVISHED on Molly after she returned to Truckee with Papa, even though to keep them from trouble, the children weren't allowed in the far meadow across the river. Alta disappeared anyway, but the field where Molly grazed became the playground for Mary, who brushed Molly and brought her treats, and for Raleigh, Tiny, and all their friends, who took turns riding bareback.

Old pal Molly was forgotten once more when Mama displayed another telegram. On the appointed day, Raleigh, Tiny, and Mary, out in the field, ran around and stopped at the bottom of the front porch steps to gaze at the young lady who looked like Mama looked in the fancy photo when she was a teacher. Exact smile, but this woman's hair was long and full and blonde instead of dark brown. This woman had clear, shiny skin, almost glowing. Mama's skin had pulled tight over her face bones.

Mama stood with her arm linked with her sister's. Her sister held Florence and smiled at her beatific baby face. Mama said, "Here's Aunt Ola from Missouri. Remember when I worried because she was sick with consumption? Now she's better. The doctor advised a warmer, dry place."

"How'd you find us?" asked Tiny. "We've been living in Sacramento, a big place."

"Your Aunt Margaret told me you were there," said Ola. "I stayed with her in Reno. When we heard you'd come back to Truckee, I came on."

She turned to Mary.

"I remember when you were born at the farm in Montrose. Alta was just beginning to walk. Where is she?"

Mama unlinked her elbow from Ola's and stared at Mary. She and Alta had stuck together in Sacramento, but she wasn't going to cover for her now.

"Alta went to play at Sally Faye's house," she admitted.

"Go get her," said Mama.

Mary took off, determined to get that girl and bring her home where she belonged. Reaching the wood fence at the end of Church Street, Mary found a stick and dragged it against the pickets as she sped along the walk. *Plock! Plock! Plock!* On Front Street she dallied around the Last Chance Saloon, sneaking a quick look to see what was going on.

She turned up McGlashan's Hill toward Sally's house, tall trees still intact on the property, one of the few yards with a flower garden. Alta told her that each child had a bicycle. The best, though, was the real swing attached to a pine branch at the perfect height and angle. With nobody around, Mary took a few swings, leaning back until her hair scraped the ground.

Satisfied, she knocked, and when Mrs. Faye opened the door, Mary was led into the dining room to see Alta and Sally, each holding a forkful of cake.

Mary's eyes opened wide, but she only said, "Mama wants you to come home. Aunt Ola's here."

Alta, polite and charming when it suited her, stood to face Mrs. Faye and said, "Thank you very much for having me over. The cake is delicious."

As they walked out the gate, Alta waved to Sally and called in her sweetest voice, "I'll see you soon."

How pretty Alta was, how she got away with anything when she lifted her eyebrows and smiled. Still, Mary bet herself Alta wasn't really invited over. She had hung around, being friendly to Sally until she could invite herself in.

By the saloon, Alta said, "Remember Mr. Faye's new car? I found out what happened."

Mary didn't answer, both cake and Aunt Ola on her mind.

Shaking Mary's arm, Alta said, "Mrs. Faye couldn't talk Mr. Faye into letting her drive for the longest time. Then it was too snowy. In April, she tried to start the car with the crank when Mr. Faye was at the saloon, and while we were gone Mr. Faye took her out on the road to Colfax like he said."

Mary thought of the wagon trail to Colfax, crooked and full of holes. What would it have been like in a real car?

"He still won't let her drive through town, though," concluded Alta.

"She will," laughed Mary. "I wonder how long before?"

IN THE HOUSE, Aunt Ola called out, "Alta, I'm glad to see you again."

Sitting next to her aunt, using her gracious voice, Alta asked about all their relatives, an attempt, Mary surmised, to distract Mama.

Not a day later, Aunt Ola took over Florence's care. She gathered the pile of mending, Mama bragging that Ola was an excellent seamstress. When asked, Aunt Ola repaired clothes for the boarders, whether or not they could pay the fee. She chatted with the neighbors, as she walked around town, and soon ladies asked her to make dresses. She taught fancy embroidery stitches to Mary.

"Did you know that your mother taught me how to sew?" she asked.

Mary shook her head and said, "Usually, Mama doesn't have much time for us, but I know she can make pretty things when we have money. We've a photograph of Alta, Tiny, and me in Easter dresses, but that was a while ago when Raleigh was a baby."

"A happier time, wasn't it? But, everybody loves the youngest, protects that one," Aunt Ola allowed.

Ola played cards when she wasn't busy sewing or caring for Florence, and one evening said, "Let's play Commit. No one here is against putting counters into a pool, are you?"

Ola insisted Mama join the play. The kitchen clock chimed nine o'clock while they threw pennies into the pot and called for one more round.

Mary decided her aunt had a sweet nature. One day, Mary and Alta showed Ola the way to Sally Faye's house, summoned there to make dresses to wear at a wedding in Sacramento. Mrs. Faye waited with silk and batiste in her lap.

Ola fingered the silk and admired the color. Mary handed over the drawings of dresses for which Ola had patterns. Mrs. Faye and Ola huddled over the chosen illustrations, deciding how to change the sleeves and other fussy details. Then Mary wrote down the numbers while Alta helped Aunt Ola take measurements. In the meantime, Mrs. Faye chattered on about how busy she was with the saloon and her work with the Woman Suffrage Campaign. She made Sally fetch the new woman's right to vote flyers.

When they prepared to leave, Mrs. Faye, with her hand placed to her forehead, said she'd been so worried about the dresses. She exclaimed that Aunt Ola seemed so calm. Aunt Ola smiled as if she knew the secret of happiness.

The next day, a drowsy afternoon, Mary was rocking Florence when Aunt Ola slipped into the kitchen and picked her up.

The baby on her lap, she laughed, "Mother surely loved babies, didn't she, Dolly?"

Mama smiled as she sliced some potatoes and added, "I remember how she'd hold both you and Cyrus on her lap at the same time and sing a hymn until you fell asleep."

"This baby reminds me of ... of ... Frank's sweet baby," Ola said.

Mama looked up, as Ola waved her hand in front of her face, softened and rosy, a tiny tremble in her chin. She handed the baby back to Mary, who, rocking the cradle once more, asked herself, "What did this mean?" Odd that Ola looked sad all of a sudden, she who thought the youngest and protected were always the happiest.

HOME AGAIN IN June, Papa passed out oranges. Eyes lit up, Mama hugged him, and he greeted Aunt Ola with a joke about long train rides. He didn't disappear to the Last Chance and Mary wondered what had gotten into him.

While Mary shuffled the deck of cards, Tiny and Alta pulled up chairs for a game. Papa said, "I'm home for three weeks, Dolly."

Cards in hand, Mama said, "That'll be fine, Tom. I'm hoping you can do some repairs around the house and Mr. Englehardt will reduce the charge for our rooms. It's easy carpentry."

He rocked Florence, grinning and tickling her. He looked up and nodded to Mama.

Mid-morning the next day, Papa sat around drinking coffee and talking with Aunt Ola while she sewed. Tidying up the kitchen counters, waiting to catch Aunt Ola, hoping to learn another fancy stitch, Mary noticed Papa looked flushed and squinty-eyed. Otherwise, he was his talkative self.

"How's that brother of yours Lauf? What's he been doing since he went back to Missouri?"

"He's off in Chicago and St. Louis. You know he doesn't get along with Father or Cyrus. Do you know my brother Cyrus?"

Papa shook his head.

"Actually, Cyrus won't speak to Lauf," said Ola. "He and Cyrus got into it about religion. Funny, my brothers and sisters always called Lauf the bad boy before the Lord took him over."

Papa laughed. "Lauf's a strange one all right."

"Cyrus won't speak to me either," she said in a whisper.

"I can't imagine that," said Papa, leaning forward and patting Ola's knee, so that a blush flared on her cheeks.

She blurted out, "Religion. Cyrus is a good Methodist, but Lauf wanted everyone to pray all the time, and soon enough the two of them began shouting, Cyrus saying to leave him alone and Lauf exhorting Cyrus to let the Lord guide him. Cyrus stomped out of the house and wouldn't come back until late at night, after everyone was asleep."

"Oh, that happens all the time between brothers," said Papa, "but why won't Cyrus speak to you?"

"He didn't like the man who courted me, which is funny because Cyrus introduced us. Cyrus said he was no good and never would be. You know, I loved that man and miss him so."

Ola dropped the sewing into her lap.

"That's why I had another spell of the consumption, what with Cyrus angry all the time and Mother not being able to get Lauf to stop evangelizing every time he walked in the door. And Father on Cyrus's side. It was an unhappy time," Ola said, cheeks flushing again.

Taking Ola's hands, smoothing them with his rough ones, Papa said, "You're here now. You got over the spell. We'll take care of you."

Aunt Ola sat back in the chair, blinking to hold off her tears.

She picked up the next shirt in the pile of mending and whispered, "I don't know what to do. Everyone's kind to me, especially Dolly, but sometimes I'm very lonely."

Papa set about to jolly Ola up by recounting one of the many fights with his next older brother in which they stalked each other in the woods until they fell down dead tired, declared a truce, and walked five miles to get home for something to eat. Mary had heard this story and wandered out, seeing that she wasn't going to get Ola's attention that morning. In the late afternoon, Papa started off for the saloon.

WHILE HER BROTHER and sisters vanished each day after finishing chores, Mary hung around the house, absorbed in learning embroidery. Mama wandered around the kitchen, cooking and muttering to herself. Her eyes burned when she looked at Papa, departing for the saloon each night, getting up later each morning.

On the fourth day, before noon dinner, when Mama almost chopped her finger, Aunt Ola stopped her and said, "What's wrong? Why isn't Tom doing the repairs?"

Mama flared, "Because he's drinking right here in this house, not only out at the saloon every single night. He yelled when I asked why. He never used to drink in the boardinghouse with the children here."

She sat down at the table, massaging her fingers, and said, "It was an illusion he was better."

Mama picked up the knife, but Ola took it from her.

"He's angry because I asked him to do some work! But he would've been insulted if Mr. Englehardt had suggested the deal. He said he was exhausted, and I should let him be when he comes home on a break from the trains."

"That's why?" asked Ola. "He was kind to me the other day."

Mama burst out, "You'd best beware, Ola. You shouldn't sit and talk with him. Or laugh at his stories. He likes you. I see the look in his eyes. He'll sit all day and carry on, jabbering about his escapades to impress you, getting you on his side. You'll see. You'll see."

It's not as if Papa was oblivious to Mama's feelings. He tried to mollify her, playing with the baby and jollying up his children. Raleigh and Tiny laughed when he put his head in the kitchen doorway and winked while scanning the room for Mama.

On his way, the afternoon of Mama's outburst, he looked over Mary's shoulder, whiskey on his breath, saying she was almost as good as his sister Martha Jane who did beautiful needlework. Folding the linen and thread into her lap, Mary listened to Papa's words in her head. He only said that to get on her side. He talked to Raleigh about fishing and Tiny about acting too. Alta was smart enough to stay away, saying Mama'd never get him to pick up a hammer until he felt like it.

ON FRIDAY, MARY was alone at the kitchen sink peeling potatoes for noon dinner. Papa's feet stomped down the hallway. When Mary turned, Papa was braced in the doorway, each hand holding a side of the frame. The look on his face wasn't kind.

He said, "Who made up the beds today?"

She answered, "Me, Papa."

"Where's the bottle?"

"I don't know. I didn't see any bottle," she answered.

In a second, he grabbed the wrist of the hand holding the peeling knife and twisted it until Mary bent to the side. With his other hand, he pinched her cheeks between his thumb and forefinger.

"Where's the bottle? Tell me what she did with it," Papa hissed in Mary's ear, as he squeezed her cheeks and twisted her arm.

"Stop, Papa. You're hurting me," she sobbed, hardly able to say the words.

Her fist opened and the knife slid out and clattered on the floor. Papa looked at the knife and saw Mama standing at his side. He let go of Mary so quickly that she fell on the floor.

"Who do you think took the bottle?" Mama said, her lip twitching. "Mary doesn't look under the bed. She's not married to a drunk."

Papa's hands shook. He blinked slowly and sucked in a deep, whistling breath.

Words poured out. "I emptied that bottle and the one I found in the cellar, too. I'm tired of you and I don't want to nurse you after you've made yourself sick for four days before you'll do any work."

Mama bent over Mary, still on the floor. Papa grabbed Mama's hair and pulled her head back. She took a step back and slipped on the knife, falling on her tailbone while she grasped hold of her head.

Mama screamed, "Let go! I despise you! Let me go!"

He put his head down by her ear and shouted, "I'm the one who'll decide what goes on here. I'll drink when I want to. You do what I say."

Pulling her by the hair across the floor, he lifted and shoved her onto a chair, and slammed the back door. Mama held her head in her hands and cried.

Mary picked herself and the knife up from the floor. She put the knife on the counter and then turned to Mama who sat slumped over, rubbing the back of her head with one hand, drying her eyes with a towel in the other. Mary crept to her side and hugged her, placing her mouth next to Mama's ear and crooning, "It's all right, it's all right," as if Mama was a baby. She clutched Mary, reaching up to smooth her blonde hair before leaning forward, head down, murmuring *"the end is not yet."*

Perhaps those words comforted Mama, but Mary was not soothed. She collected the peeled potatoes that had rolled off the table and dumped them in the sink, where she washed them off and set them in the pot to boil. Then pulling a pickle out of the barrel in the pantry, she went to sit in the outhouse where she could do her worrying in the dark and quiet, even if it did smell of caustic lime.

It hurt where her cheeks had been mashed against her teeth. Her twisted shoulder hurt. But most of all her heart hurt. She loved her mother and knew Mama was right. She rubbed her shoulder, wondering what had happened to Papa. She bit into the pickle and chewed slowly as if food was going to bring an answer. Then she cried.

SITTING ON THE back steps after a sad noon meal, Mary pulled up some grass for Molly, who ambled over to nuzzle. Mary fed it to the horse, sighing, "You're a good old pal, Molly."

Aunt Ola, frowning in dismay, carrying several dresses, came out the door and said, "I'm sorry, Mary. I'm so sorry."

At supper Mama announced, "I received a note yesterday to stay with the family that lives near the reservoir while the woman has her baby. I've accepted because Ola, you've been around long enough to take care of the boarders. Everyone knows their jobs. I'm taking Florence with me, of course."

Face puffy and pale from crying, Mama did not heed entreaties, not from Ola nor from any child, her little boy, the youngest girl, the middle sister, the worrisome oldest.

"No, no, no," she said. "We can use the money. Your father'll go to bed any day now, and he'll see what it's like to take care of himself. Your aunt can take care of you. You know where to send for me. It'll be better if I'm away for a while."

Their mother had nursed women before and Mary resigned herself, and so did her brother and sisters. They were used to it. On guard, Mary was going to stay as far away from Papa as she could. The next morning, as Mary had foreseen last summer, Mama harnessed Molly to the wagon and left.

As they waved good-bye, Alta declared, "There may be a baby to take care of, but we know why she's left. She's as mad as a hornet after what Papa did. He's off his nut, y'know. But she'll be sorry."

Suspicious, Mary said, "How d'you know?"

"You're so busy being a good girl, you don't know anything," responded Alta, flouncing off up Church Street. Mary squinted after Alta, wondering what she saw and heard along the back streets of Truckee that made her so sure of herself.

AUNT OLA MANAGED to get food on the table in time for the boarders and Papa didn't go to bed as Mama had predicted. Mary had even sneaked a look under Papa's bed and hadn't found a bottle. On the second afternoon, watching a small rabbit leap and stop to nibble a wildflower, Mary heard Papa's affable talk in the kitchen. She wondered if he had pulled himself together, though still not helping much around the house. Ola seemed content to chatter with him. Mary kicked a stone, scaring the rabbit into the woods, reminding herself that she didn't care and was staying far away from her father.

A chair moved, a muffled scraping noise on the kitchen floor.

Papa whispered, "Ola, I thank you for helping with the children. We all love you for that."

A soft breathiness came through the window.

"You needn't say all that, Tom," said Ola.

Then again that evening, Mary overheard crying and looked in to see Ola by herself in the kitchen, singing a mournful, lonely tune,

Down in the valley, the valley so low,
Hang your head over, hear the wind blow.

Later Papa appeared and sat with his elbow on the table and finger on his chin. Ready to entertain Ola, he fixed his eyes on her blushing face. She smiled. Even to Mary, who felt far less mature than Alta, it looked like flirting. After supper he left, heavy steps stumbling up stairs, waking Mary late at night.

On the third day after Mama left, while Mary set the boarder's table, Papa wandered toward the kitchen and called out, "Ola?"

In a voice as cheerful as the one she used when she first arrived and enchanted them all, she answered, "I'm here, Tom."

"How're you doing for money?" asked Papa.

"We're fine, Tom," she said. "Dolly left things in good order."

Papa lowered his voice, and without snooping, Mary only heard his gallant tone and Ola's soft laugh. Then no sound at all. Then a shuffle of footsteps. Then the rustle of clothing came to Mary's ears, enough so she held her hand in place instead of smoothing the napkin on the dining table.

At dinner, Aunt Ola said, "It's a good thing after all to have your father around, for your sake."

LATE THE NEXT afternoon, Mary settled on the front porch steps. Her gaze followed a red-tailed hawk that soared slowly over the mountain ridge behind the big houses. Mary thought Alta had better come home soon to help with supper.

Veering at the angle in the road beyond the picket fence, Alta appeared on a bicycle. She put a foot down to stop at the front porch, lifted her leg gracefully over the frame, and grinned.

"Look what I found in the river," crowed Alta.

Mary said, "What d'you mean 'in the river'?"

"Down past the train station, under some bushes in the river. Want to try it?"

It wasn't rusty or scratched up much. Still, it was dirty with rotting leaves caught in the chain, so Alta might have been telling the truth. Mary had only ridden a bicycle twice, but sat down on the seat and rode unsteadily down the path.

"Where're you going to keep it? You'd better show Papa," said Mary when she returned to the porch.

"In Molly's shed. And don't open your tattletale mouth to Papa," said Alta.

"I'm not speaking to Papa ever," said Mary. "Don't worry."

After hiding the bicycle, they entered the kitchen to see Papa tilting the chair back with one foot, the other crossed and resting on his knee, hand waving as he told Aunt Ola a joke. He gazed at her with a satisfied smile on his face and soup ladle in hand, and she laughed. Mary walked through to the dining room and laid out the tablecloth. Alta took silverware out of the buffet drawer.

"It's a good thing Mama isn't here right now," whispered Alta, slapping down the forks and knives. "Papa's acting like a boyfriend, and Ola's not singing those misery songs anymore. I saw her humming and waltzing at the sink."

Pulling napkins out of the drawer, Mary thought Mama would be angry because Papa still hadn't done any of the repairs, not simply because he was flirting with Aunt Ola.

IN THE MORNING, Alta disappeared on the bicycle without letting Raleigh and Tiny have even one quick ride each. Late afternoon, Mary sat idly on the front steps again, watching the red-tailed hawk dive and rise, mouse legs wiggling from its beak. Then Mary spied Mr. Faye striding up the road with Sally, Alta, and the bicycle. Leaning inside the front door, Mary called to Papa. Mr. Faye waited, the prosperous Truckee businessman, one hand holding his bowler and the other in his sack jacket pocket. Alta squinted, as if she was thinking of a good lie.

As soon as Papa walked into the front hall, Mr. Faye said, "Your daughter stole my Sally's bicycle. She was caught riding it in town."

Papa turned to Alta, but she said, "I found it in the river. Ask Mary. She knows."

Mary told the truth.

"Alta came home with the bicycle yesterday. She told me she found it in the river."

He looked over the bicycle and grabbed Alta's arm, who, caught and wriggling, yelled, "I didn't, I didn't."

Papa shook his head and told Mr. Faye to take it. Sally climbed on, arranged her dress, gave Alta a look of triumph, and pedaled down the path while her father, bowler back on his head, followed.

"Mr. Edwards, you'd better do something about your daughter. Stealing a friend's bicycle. In this day and age," Mr. Faye called.

Papa dragged Alta, protesting all the way, through the house to the back porch where he kept the strap to sharpen his razor.

Holding onto his arm, Aunt Ola begged, "Tom, please. Somebody else might've taken it, and she found it."

Mama always carried out punishments, and Papa didn't know what to do. He took deep breaths. He looked from Alta to Ola to Mary. How strange, she thought, four days ago he had hurt her badly when he was drunk and enraged, but now his hands shook at the thought of whipping his child.

Then Papa pulled his arm away from Ola and said, "Leave me alone. She's always lying and getting in trouble. I'm teaching her a lesson. Get out if you can't watch."

Hands over her face, Ola ran to her room. Mary crept out the back door where Raleigh and Tiny peeked from the edge of the porch, too scared to go in.

They heard the crack as the strap hit Alta across the back of her legs. They didn't hear her cry out though. A few minutes later, walking stiff-legged, Alta came out the back door and went into Molly's cool, dark shed.

Papa stormed out, stopped at the shed door, and yelled, "Stay in there until you learn to tell the truth."

He stalked down the path behind the houses on Church Street, the back way to town.

When Mary, Raleigh, and Tiny entered the kitchen Aunt Ola was crying while mixing batter for biscuits.

"How can your father be so hard?" she said. "I don't think he was drinking. She's just a girl. My father was strict, but he didn't do that to me. How could your father?"

Her hands shook as she tried to measure more milk. Mary took the cup and made the biscuits while Ola sat down, distress in her weepy eyes, her down-turned mouth, her hand wringing. Finally she managed to finish cooking, but it was Raleigh and Tiny who set the table, Mary who helped serve the boarders, and all three who cleaned up as best they could.

In bed exhausted, Mary lay wide-eyed, but pretended sleep when Alta, groaning as she lifted her legs, slid into bed.

⇒•⇐

"How was the man Papa related to me?" asked Lane.

"Your great-great-grandfather. And now you know, he was a mixed-up man," said Mary.

9

June 1926
Sacramento and Roseville

HOW UNSETTLING IS my memory of the day I drove Mama all the way to Roseville to visit Papa. I'd finished with my father, and I didn't know what Mama still saw in him. She talked up how Betsy should spend time with her grandfather, how enjoyable it would be to motor in such beautiful weather, how Henry would be happy to have the house to himself. Really, she didn't want to take the train all alone.

Getting no response, she said, "Please, Mary. You like to drive."

She waited for me to agree, knowing I was proud of myself. After all, at twenty-six I'd done what I said I would do when we saw the Model T in Truckee. Henry did give me money, but mostly I'd saved the three hundred dollars to buy my own automobile. Mama knew I'd debated with myself about quitting school. I'd wanted to be a teacher. Instead, I worked and opened my account at the bank. Unlike our days in Truckee, I felt rich.

There I was, wearing my jaunty car suit, with Mama in the front and Betsy in the back, dressed in the plaid dress with the white collar, paid for by her father. As her custom, Mama wore the travel dress I'd seen on her since we lived in Truckee, completely oblivious to dressing for a special day.

My touring car was black, not gray, and the levers and pedals didn't seem as unwieldy as the ones for that first Model T we'd pored over, thank goodness. Henry kept using his horse and wagon to go up the valley for fruits and vegetables, but I said soon his boss would see automobiles were the better choice. Since they'd been paved, a lot of trucks maneuvered around the old streets of Sacramento near his business.

Out of Sacramento, a good part of the road ran alongside the railroad track. The flat, dirt road stretched ahead, a pebble here and there flying up and pinging against my beautiful painted hood. Nothing like my journey over the Donner Summit.

I think the warm air and the clear blue sky kept Mama chattering as if she'd never been up there. To keep the grazing cattle in the grassy fields, a barbed wire and post fence separated the fields from each side of the road. She pointed to the scraggly morning glory climbing up the posts and the buttercups clustered around the rough wood where it had been sunk into the ground. Between the fence and the road squatted oak trees with their branches spread and full of leaves, still shiny green, not yet dulled by dust. In some spaces with no oaks, tall iron bark eucalyptus had been brought in and planted to provide a wind buffer I supposed. Between the trees, on the ground among the fallen leaves, a few stray Sweet William popped up and the last glorious golden poppies.

The wheat fields, still green, sent out a warm, earthy smell. We inhaled deeply to catch the scent as we drove along. Leaning over the side of the back door, Betsy stretched out her hand to feel the wind and watched a gregarious swarm of red-winged blackbirds swooping down for seeds, calling *konk-a-ree*. She leaned forward and called, "Mom! A hawk," and pointed out a red-tail soaring and searching. Mama said to keep an eye on the wheat wavering like blown by a breeze. The bit of movement signaled where the rabbits were running to their holes under the grain.

Then Mama saw the old fox's nose peek out from the row of wheat. As she yelped "Mary, watch out," the fox, gray whiskers standing out against his ginger fur, scampered across the road, not even looking at the car, completely uninterested in us. I started to brake, but we hardly needed to slow down. The fox had disappeared across the cattle field to the woods long before we would have hit him.

As we approached the town of Roseville and the sanatorium where Papa lived, Mama stopped talking. She watched the side of the road, dandelions and other weeds poking out of the broken up stones along the way. She smiled at the dark-eyed juncos picking at bugs on the ground and flying up to the branches of the eucalyptus, but she remained quiet. Betsy dozed on the back seat.

"What're we going to do when we get there?" I whispered.

Mama shook her head and waved her hand as she always did when she wanted to dismiss what was in her head. I drove along, watched the road, and waited.

Finally, she said, "He lives in a little wood shack away from the main building. If it was painted a long time ago, no one would guess. It has a bed, a table, a chair, and two windows. He has some books. I don't know what he does out there. He doesn't seem to drink, but who knows where he hides a bottle. Or where he gets one. No one says anything to me. Maybe they don't care. Perhaps

Raleigh brings a bottle when he visits, but he's only come all the way up here three or four times, as far as I know. Every time I visit, your father's skinnier and skinnier."

Mama came every couple of months, and I hadn't expected her to carry on so much about Papa's life in Roseville. Her voice sounded rueful and resigned at the same time.

"Once they wanted to release him, saying the consumption was in remission. That's what they call it when he's not coughing and feverish and he can eat, but I told them he couldn't live with me. Alta was at the house at the time. I didn't want to put up with both of them. Maybe that's why he's out in a cabin, not with the regular patients. He's old and will never leave, and he keeps an eye on the big place. He tells me long stories about all the patients."

We'd seen a few farms in the distance at the back edge of the fields, but all of a sudden, we drove onto the main street of the little town of Roseville with shops and a restaurant. After we passed the last house, we turned off to the right and drove down a long tree-lined path to buildings close together on each side of a large hospital-like building.

After sitting and dozing so long, Betsy hopped out of the car and ran across the grass to get some exercise. I wondered if Mama walked all the way from the train station in town, out and up this driveway to get here. What was in Mama's mind that she would do that for Papa, an old man who had treated her and us children badly?

Mama walked into the large building to let the supervisors know she had arrived. By now I was tired. We'd been up since seven in the morning, and it was near noon. The sun beat down on the car. It was warm, even with the covers for the side openings rolled up. I found a shady spot under one of the oaks and Betsy flopped down next to me, fluffing her dress to cool off.

I thought about how good it was for Betsy to visit her grandfather, but I couldn't bring myself to forgive him. In fact, forgiveness was more difficult this long after we had grown up. All I remembered was the evening he stared at Raleigh and me and didn't recognize us, he was so drunk, and the day he twisted my arm and pulled Mama by the hair, not to mention the money he spent on liquor and his other bad habits.

That's not all. Henry appeared in my mind, tall and portly, with thick eyebrows. He was doing the same as Papa did all those years ago, sneaking out or coming home late. Refusing to do the few jobs I asked him to do. Playing with his adored little girl, but ignoring me. How did I make such a mistake?

Henry rarely took me out for the evening anymore, not like the times after the Great War when we went to hear Alta play the piano in the barroom on

Fifth Street and sing "Till We Meet Again" with her lovely voice. We'd dance all evening, enjoying the night like everyone else. The war was over and the horrible Spanish flu epidemic passed.

Mama returned and pulled the picnic basket out of the car. I didn't have any more time to think about Henry. Mama and I walked, and Betsy ran along the path to Papa's cabin, her long skinny five-year-old legs churning. She pounded on his door, and he came out wearing a jacket I must have seen a million times and his old brown felt hat that had looked snazzy when it was new, but now looked like he'd found it in a garbage pile.

He carried a hammer, switched it back and forth from hand to hand, and dropped it at last onto the porch railing. I studied that man I remembered who had a smile and clever word on his tongue, and who was dashing and neatly dressed even though we didn't have money. Mama was right. Now, he stooped a bit. His chest was caved in from the consumption. His clothes hung loosely.

He took Mama's arms and looked at her standing in front of him, plainly dressed, pale faced, gray-streaked dark brown hair pulled back in a bun. Papa had a gleam in his eyes and a smile on his face like this was the first time he'd ever seen such a fancy woman. Then he hugged her tightly.

She finally pulled back and said, "That's enough now, Tom. Your daughter's here and your granddaughter."

I was astonished at the look of love in his eyes. Maybe I'd been too young to see it or too upset by the hard words they spoke to each other when we lived in Truckee. No one, certainly not Henry, had stared at me with such a glow.

Then he sat down on the stoop in front of his house and asked Betsy to sit at his side.

"Aren't you good-looking in your smart dress," he said.

With straight dark red hair cut in a pageboy style, Betsy arched her head, showing her beautiful wide smile, and giggled. Eating bologna sandwiches and pickles with gusto, Papa and Betsy proceeded to chat about school and play. He told her stories about his life in Tennessee, all of which I'd heard long ago. Betsy hooted at the funny parts, bright eyes lighting up her face.

Papa showed Betsy the hiding place among the trees behind his cabin. Then my gaze turned from my daughter to Papa, who carried out a chair for Mama and ushered her to the seat as if she were a queen. He cozied up to her on the stoop like a jester at her feet, distracting her with gossip about the people at the sanatorium. She laughed as she stretched out in the chair, ankles crossed and hands folded across her stomach. A long time had passed since she'd appeared so relaxed, but she jumped when Betsy ran back from the woods, yelling and whooping like Mama's neighbor kids.

As we prepared to go, Papa said to wait one minute. He had something for us. The hammer was out because he was tacking some photographs up on his wall. He gave Mama one of himself when he was young, dressed in a suit, saying he didn't think she had that photo.

Then he said, "I always liked this picture of you and Alta and Tiny in your Easter outfits, and the photographer made several copies, Mary. You can keep this one. I certainly had pretty little girls."

There he was trying to get on my side, an old man's effort to be kind. We all were cute in that picture, but he knew I was never the good-looking daughter. Was this his way of asking forgiveness? Why didn't he say he was sorry all those years ago when I was young and my anger might have eased up? Still, I thanked him for the photo.

WE STOPPED BRIEFLY in Roseville at the gasoline station and drove straight back to Sacramento. It was late when we arrived at Mama's house, which she owned now free and clear. Tiny and I had helped her get enough money to pay for the house, bought for a reasonable price because it was so far out on the edge of town and called a country place. Betsy bounced up the steps as if a handsome, sturdy dwelling graced the old property. She was too young to notice it was falling apart. She loved to run around and hide in the backyard shed near the overgrown vegetable garden and the chicken coop. I was glad she had a place to enjoy herself. Our house was small, neat, and quiet. Henry didn't like noise.

I brought in the picnic basket and took Mama's purse into her bedroom.

"Stick the purse on the bedtable shelf," she said. "That's where I keep everything."

Surprised, but by then I should have known what she was like. She remembered long verses of poetry and many, many sayings from the Bible, but she wasn't interested in organizing her belongings. I turned to the small table with a drawer and the shelf. The delicate black Chinese box with red lacquer flowers Papa had given her sat on the table top, and next to it rested Mr. Faye's gift, the beautiful tiny Washo basket. I stuffed the purse on the shelf. In the partly opened drawer, I saw a messy pile of letters, bank papers, and sumptuous, delicate cards. I picked one up and turned it over. On the back was Papa's signature.

"Mama, I've never seen these. They're beautiful. They look like some Alta and I fancied at the stationery store the first time we came to Sacramento."

Mama picked some up and smoothed them with her hand.

"That's how your father caught me," she said. "He knew how to make a woman feel like she was the only one. I was in Reno staying at Margaret's, and he came to a New Year's Day party. Margaret introduced us. He spent the afternoon telling funny stories and eyeing me. You can't imagine how that charmer's glint made a woman want to be around him."

Mama took a step toward the front room, then she stopped and picked up another card even more elegant with gold paint and swirls around the words that said, "Love."

"You know, even then he saw what he wanted to see. Many other girls had prettier hair and fetching dresses. He didn't notice. I was smart, and at that time, he smiled when I said something clever. We talked about books and poetry, and I laughed at his rogue's stories. He would go away to work on the railroad and I missed him."

She sat down on the bed and smoothed the cover with one hand while she stared at the card. She pulled some more out of the drawer and laid them out on the bed as if searching for her favorite.

"I was teaching in Reno, but I didn't like it at all. He asked me to go off with him to be married and live in Truckee. I had no idea what Truckee was like or who lived there, but the railroad wanted him stationed there. Margaret spoke against it, but I wanted to go off and be on my own."

She smoothed her hands along her skirt and a smile lit up her face.

"He was so charming and elegant when he wasn't working, and when he did work and wore his rough clothes, he swaggered down the street. I was happy such a man wanted to be with me. I wouldn't listen to Margaret, of course. I was already twenty-six and thought I knew everything."

"But Mama," I blurted out. "You could have gone up on a train to Truckee by yourself to see what it was like. To ask about Papa."

Mama gathered the beautiful collection and lay down on the bed. She held them like a hand of cards, rubbing a frilly edge, staring, blinking, staring, blinking. Meanwhile I walked back and forth along the bed, twisting the strand of hair that had fallen when I pulled off my straw hat. Mama shook her head slowly.

"No. I never thought of that. That's what happens when you're in love, Mary. You don't do what you ought to do. He seemed to be in love too. We went up to Truckee. I think I was going to have Alta even before we saw the minister. For a clever girl, I was much too innocent. Later I found out about counting the months when I learned about nursing."

Mama looked at me. Did she wish she'd told me how to prevent having a baby? Did she want to tell about Papa's recklessness? Or own up to her other brief, but consuming, love attachment? I never would have asked. I only knew what I saw.

Instead, she said, "I loved Alta, you know. All the people in town exclaimed over how pretty she was, but she was a difficult baby. She cried all the time. She didn't want to nurse. I walked around our rooms all night, rubbing her back and singing to get her to fall asleep. Your father was off working all the time to get money for us. He'd been drinking before, but I never paid attention. All men drank. Now I knew he was out carousing. I waited up for him, and I smelled it on his breath when he finally came home at night.

"Only us women didn't drink or go out. I was so tired and sad all the time. I left him, you know, to go back to my parents in Missouri. That happened a month before you came along. Alta began to walk, and then run. Thank goodness, you were a good baby, and my mother was around to help me. He sent me some of these cards when I was in Missouri."

So, that's what had happened. I didn't think she ever would have explained things if I hadn't seen the elegant greetings. She sat up and put the cards in the drawer and waved her hand in front of her face. She took a deep breath and let out a long sigh.

"That's how it was when we were in love. I came back from Missouri and followed him to Bakersfield and Colfax. Finally, I told him we'd stay in Truckee, except when we tried out Sacramento that one time. The real world had pressed in on us. You remember Minna? I'm so thankful she helped me learn to be a nurse. That's how I made all our money before the boardinghouse."

Sitting up on the side of the bed, Mama cocked her head, listening for Betsy. I stood in front of her, rocking from side to side. This time Mama couldn't walk away from me and start to sweep or slice potatoes to keep from talking. Even so, I was the one with no words.

I thought about Papa, now an old man who I wouldn't hurt, but I wouldn't forgive either, no matter what Mama said. In any case, I was worried about my husband. How was I going to ask Mama about Henry? Out drinking every night. What could I do? I wondered if Betsy and I would run away from him and come here to stay with Mama. Would we come to this unpainted, gloomy house like the one where we ended up in Truckee?

10

June 1910
Church Street, Truckee

A ROOSTER CROWED, and through the window, rays of sunlight touched Mary's eyelids. Her stomach growled, and she thought of the sugar cookies on the kitchen table.

Lifting the covers so as not to wake Alta, Mary tiptoed down the stairs, slipping into the kitchen, intent on a cookie. Voices came from Ola's room off the pantry, and she stopped, holding her breath.

Ola whispered, "You shouldn't've whipped her."

"She tells stories. She steals. She needed a whipping," murmured Papa.

Ola sighed, "I didn't think you'd do anything like that."

"Dolly should've been here. I shouldn't have to do the punishment. I don't want to talk about it."

"Are you sure she's not coming back?"

"I don't think so. Not this time. She … she's left me once too often."

The bed creaked and Ola sighed.

"I've been so lonely, Tom. Ever since Cyrus sent him away."

"It's all right. It's all right. M-m-m," murmured Papa, and the bed rocked.

Leaning on the kitchen table, Mary stretched her neck to peek into the room, its door opened slightly. Each eye opened as round as a dish. Even though she was twelve and knew very well what was happening, her fingers pressed against her lips to keep from yelling, "What're you doing?" Papa was lying in the bed naked on top of Aunt Ola—under the covers, but naked all the same.

Mary ran to the outhouse and sat down in the dark, her hands and legs shaking.

Oh, Lord, what's he doing? And Aunt Ola? What'll Mama think now? What am I going to do? This all flashed through her mind as she covered her face.

MARY'S EYES POPPED open and her head jerked back, her skull knocking against the outhouse wall. Her eyes blurred. Then leaning forward and raising her hand to rub the back of her head, she focused on the door latch, snapping up and down.

Alta whispered, "Mary, you in there? Open up!"

Mary mumbled, "I fell asleep for a minute."

"I don't know how you can sleep in there. It smells!" muttered Alta.

Mary lifted the hook, and the door swung out violently. While pulling the door at the same time, Alta groaned. Her legs buckled from the pain of the whipping.

"Damn," Alta snarled. "Get out."

She grabbed Mary's forearm.

Mary held onto the door frame and whispered, "I want to tell you something about Papa."

Alta tilted her head and turned her lips up at each corner.

Stepping inside, she placed the hook in the loop. Folding her arms, she asked, "What?"

"It was horrible. Papa was in Aunt Ola's room this morning … and … and they were talking about you. But Papa wasn't only in the room. He was on top of Aunt Ola!"

A rude laugh came from Alta.

"Mary, you really are the stupidest girl. Aunt Ola isn't the only one Papa's been on top of. What do you think happens when he's off down the valley on the train all month? Why do you think Mama's always mad at him? I already told you it's not simply because he doesn't do anything to help around here!"

Alta glared at Mary still on the outhouse seat.

"You know why you don't know anything?" she said. "Because you stay around this house all the time. If you'd come out with me, you'd hear things … you'd know something!"

Mary rubbed her temples and said, "Why'd Aunt Ola let him do that?"

Indignation making her face red, Alta replied, "You're the stupidest girl, and Aunt Ola is the stupidest woman I know. She probably let Papa sweet-talk her into feeling sorry for him. He does that to Mama too—you've heard him. How do you think baby Florence was born?"

Alta paused, then added, "Maybe Papa made up stories about Mama to get Aunt Ola to feel more sorry for him."

"Even so, Aunt Ola's her sister!" said Mary. "But, y'know, she had a fellow back in Missouri, and she was lonely."

Alta said, "So that doesn't mean she and Papa can do it!"

"You've got to tell Mama. She listens to you," said Mary. "Remember you talked her out of leaving Papa the time before we got in trouble about the river. Of course, I don't know what we want her to do."

"How'm I going to tell Mama when she isn't even here?" snapped Alta. "Besides, Papa'll say I'm making things up because he whipped me."

"I'll write and tell her to come home because we miss her. Then you tell her, and when you do, I'll say you're telling the truth. I saw it."

"Fine," said Alta, "but I'm not staying around waiting for her to show up. Anyway, get out of here. I have to use the privy."

AT THE BACK door Mary listened to Tiny and Raleigh argue about who should clear the bowls off the table. Aunt Ola asked if they knew where Mary and Alta were, but she didn't hear her father, so she went in.

Aunt Ola turned when she heard the door slam and said, as if all was fine, "Oh, there you are. Can you help Raleigh and Tiny in the dining room?"

Mary mumbled, "Yes," hating the thought of talking to her aunt. She ran upstairs to change.

Dress and apron pulled on, she slipped into the dining room to see what the boarders needed. Just then, Alta walked in with a plate of eggs, and Mary's mouth dropped open. What was she doing? She never helped.

Alta hissed, "Shut your mouth. Papa was coming into the kitchen. D'you think I wanted him to find me?"

Mary stood way back and leaned forward to quickly drop the biscuit basket on the table. Alta extended the plate of eggs before her, sidestepping to avoid Mr. Thomas's arm sliding around her waist. The cup in his left hand shook and coffee slopped out.

Alta murmured, "My mother's coming home, and I'll tell if you do that again."

Mary grimaced and wished Mama was there. Those boarders were more cautious then. Tiny and Raleigh were already in the kitchen laughing about the spilled coffee.

Once Papa was gone, Alta said, "We really hate it when those old men touch us, Aunt Ola. Always when Mama's not here. Now you better tell Papa. Let's see if he'll do something about Mr. Thomas. And … and there's a lot of things going on Mama wouldn't like."

Aunt Ola said, "Now, Alta, your papa punished you because you stole something."

Alta answered, "That's not all that's going on."

Aunt Ola stopped washing plates. Tiny and Raleigh stopped laughing. In an instant, Mary knew she'd better stop Alta from saying anything else. She grabbed Alta who pulled away and lowered her head, brows pinched together, eyes glowering.

Turning to Tiny and Raleigh, Mary said, "Show us where you set the chipmunk traps."

She shoved Alta ahead of her, Raleigh and Tiny following out the door.

"That Ola. I don't think she got it," said Alta, shaking her head, pushing bushes aside at the edge of the woods.

STRAGGLING BACK HOME at noon to find some lunch, Alta turned up the path that led to Front Street, saying she was going to her friend Violet's house. Alta asked Mary to come. Mary wondered about a hidden motive for the invitation, but Alta looked innocent enough. Even so, Mary shook her head.

"OK, but I told you. You'll never know anything staying around this place."

Raleigh piped up, "I'll go with you."

"I don't want you hanging around in the way. Go make some more traps. Maybe we can sell the chipmunks as pets and get some money," scoffed Alta.

She walked off, kicking each dandelion that leaned into the path. Tiny sidled up to the kitchen door, listened for a minute, and beckoned them to come. They washed down salami and bread with lukewarm tea.

Mary said, "I'm writing to Mama and telling her to come home."

"Tell her we miss her and Molly," said Tiny, wistful and teary.

"Tell her we're making money, so she doesn't have to go off being a nurse anymore," called Raleigh, as they wandered back to the woods to see if they had caught anything with apple pieces in the chipmunk traps.

Down the dark corridor in the front hall, Mary climbed the stairs, double stepping the ones that creaked. She tiptoed into her parents' bedroom in search of pen and paper. Thin cotton curtains had been closed to keep the room cool. Clothes were folded on the cedar chest, and a quilt was smoothed over the bed. Only a dish of Mama's hairpins sat on the dresser. Mary gingerly opened the drawer and extracted a sheet of writing paper, pen, and ink. She stood, holding the paper. Still air and tidy things made the room feel as if no one had entered since Mama had left. Uneasy, Mary hurried down to the dining room to compose.

She twisted the pen, thinking how to start, never having written to her mother before. Finally, she began,

Dear Mama,
We miss you. Tiny cries.

Raleigh's request came next. Then Mary asked Mama to please come home, as Papa said she'd be gone a long time. She folded the letter and opened the tiny drawer of Mama's black Chinese box with red lacquer flowers, a wedding present from Papa. Mama kept coins in the box, and Mary lifted a nickel out of the box, more than enough for an envelope and a stamp. Mary made her way along Church Street to the post office.

Going home, taking her time, Mary reached the juncture of Front and Church Streets where a dirt path led up to Minna's house. She was Mama's friend, but Mary was fond of Minna too. Minna started down the path carrying a beautiful Washo woven basket full of tamales. Mary waved.

Daughter of a Washo mother and a white father, Minna had straight black hair pulled back in a low ponytail, a short heavy body, and a round face with smooth brown skin. She had showed Mama how to nurse mothers and newborns. Mary didn't know why she lived in this town since she was trained as a real nurse. Minna could live in Sacramento and make a lot of money.

Minna's daughters played by the scraggly bushes of the front yard. Eight-year-old Hazel, Tiny's playmate, was a white man's daughter, and she had much lighter hair fixed in long braids. Delilah's father was Washo, and only three years old. She was chubby and black-haired.

Mary often confided in Minna, who seemed to know everything and always had a kind word whether she had just heard a good or bad story. Mary waited, but Minna turned off on Back Street with her tamales.

Walking along, thinking about Minna, Mary watched a tiny woman lugging a huge basket of groceries. A man on the train platform, top hat and satchel in hand, pulled out a watch. The young Japanese fellow in the wagon full of bags crossed the bridge to the laundry where the Chinese herb shop used to be. Mary found it hard to tell which of those people saw the world like Minna.

Little Florence was always content. At first, Aunt Ola seemed happy enough, but not now. Raleigh and Tiny? Good sometimes, sometimes not. She, herself? She couldn't tell. Be kind, be content. This felt hard to do after all the anger and deceit of the past two weeks.

Alta was going to have a devil of a time. Mary looked up at the back side of the school and there was Alta. She was not with Violet at all, but with Georgie Vaughn, son of the newspaper publisher. Standing in the shade, Alta pulled on a cigarette offered by Georgie. Then she turned and punched the boy in the stomach. He bent over, and she pushed him to the ground, hollering.

Stabbing the cigarette toward the boy, she said, "Who d'you think you are? Talking about my family. What business is it of yours if my mother has gone away for a while?"

Mary watched them quarrel. Maybe Alta was beating him up, so he wouldn't talk about Papa and Ola, if it got out. Alta finished the cigarette before she let him up to limp home. She brushed off her hands and tossed her black hair before sauntering up Church Street as if nothing had happened.

THE THIRD WEEK in June, Tiny was first to see Alta promenade along Front Street wearing a wide-brimmed hat, primping before the store windows. Mary, Raleigh, and Tiny were sitting on the pile of granite rocks jutting out of the weeds between River Street and the railroad tracks. Each grasping a pile of pebbles, they waited for the afternoon train to come through, ready to throw them at the words and pictures on the sides of the freight cars.

Spying on everyone along Front Street, past the tracks and up the rise, they watched Mrs. Goode open the stationery store, the butcher shake a customer's hand, and the constable walk out from behind Mr. Faye's saloon. A man came out at the same end of the street where he had entered. They laughed because he had, most likely, turned into the alley that went to Back Street.

"Oh-oh," said Tiny, pointing. "Where'd Alta get that hat? Nobody gave her money to buy a hat."

"Maybe she stole it from Sally," offered Raleigh.

"No, no, no," said Mary. "D'you think she wants to get into trouble with Mr. Faye and Papa again?"

Tiny practiced throwing pebbles.

"What could Alta trade for that hat?" she asked. In a flash, Tiny began to climb down the rocks, her toes feeling for footholds. "She took that necklace I found at the train station. I know it. I'm going home to look."

Mary shifted her eyes between Alta, who walked down the street looking in the windows, and Tiny, who slid down the rocks. Just then, a wagon turned onto the street.

She shouted, "It's Mama! There's Molly and Mama ... and Florence! Look, Tiny!"

Tiny stopped for a second, then yelled, "I'm still going to look for my necklace. I'll see Mama at the house," and raced up River Street.

It seemed too soon for Mama to have received the letter. Could someone have told her?

Raleigh punched Mary's arm and pointed. Alta stepped into the alley between the saloon and the dry goods store. They realized Alta must have seen Mama too. Raleigh made a bet she'd sneak down the back way and come home without the hat. Mama stopped the wagon at the butcher, and in a few minutes, she came out and went into Titus's Grocery.

"Meat and potatoes," Raleigh said. "I wish she'd get candy."

Mary said, "I don't want to wait for the train. Let's hurry."

They slid down the side of the rock and ran to beat Mama home. Sweaty and panting, they came up Church Street to see Aunt Ola bending over the fence.

"Hey, Aunt Ola. We saw Mama in the wagon. She's coming home," called Raleigh.

"I know. I'm watching for them."

She pulled the gate open and waited while Raleigh and Mary, placing their hands on their knees, caught their breath.

"Tiny already told me when she got here to find her necklace. Your father's in the kitchen."

"Going to get it now, I hope," Mary said.

Ola said, "That's not kind, Mary. I'm surprised at you."

"You know how Papa hasn't fixed anything. Mama will be m-a-d!" Mary said. She was surprised at herself and suddenly angry with Ola instead of feeling bad that Papa seemed to be tricking her. On the other hand, Mama was coming home, and everyone should feel sorry for her.

It seemed like a long time passed. Ola and Mary and Raleigh leaned on the fence and watched a jay dive at a crow skulking across the scrap pile behind the church. The front door slammed. Tiny stomped down the front steps. Just then, horse hooves clopped along the curve near the church.

Mary watched solemnly as Mama waved to everyone, while she pulled up the reins. Ola opened the gate.

At that moment, Alta, without the hat, walked around from the back of the house and yelled, "Hi, Mama!"

Then they all yelled and ran to hug her. Each took Florence and gave her a kiss, but Mary held her and began to straighten her little jacket.

After giving Ola a reserved hug and handing out a horehound candy stick to each child, Mama said, "Where's your papa. I need to speak to him right now."

Alta said, "I saw him in the kitchen."

She glanced at Mary and said, "Before you go in there, Mama, I have to tell you something."

She pulled her mother by the sleeve up the hallway stairs. Tiny and Raleigh took the reins and led Molly around behind the house. Ola bit her lip and patted her hands on her apron before disappearing down the hall into the kitchen. Mary followed with Florence and sat part way up the staircase to hear the hushed voices.

Mama was taking off her jacket and hat while Alta whispered, "Now, Mama,

I don't want you to get mad about the bicycle … if you heard about the bicycle. Papa whipped me already. But I want to tell you, Papa has been wicked. He …. "

"I know what's been going on."

Mama walked stiffly down the stairs without a word to Mary, sitting there with her hands clasping Florence so tight the baby squirmed. Patting the baby's back, she sneaked out the front door with Alta. They scuttled around the house to listen under the kitchen window. Mary laid Florence down on her blanket on the grass.

They missed the beginning.

Voice calm, Mama said, " … going to close the boardinghouse, Tom. I spoke to Mr. Englehardt today. You're going back to work in a few days, and that's when the children and I will move up to the empty house on Harrigan's Hill. I'm not going to live here anymore. I can rent that old house real cheap from the lumber company. You'll have to find a room."

They peeked in and saw Ola twisting a napkin, her hands trembling.

"Dolly, where'll I go? I have enough money to send for Amanda. I thought we'd be staying with you," she said.

Mama answered, "You can't now. Mr. Englehardt said I can't keep the boardinghouse without a man's name on the manager's contract. Maybe you can move with Amanda to Margaret's in Reno."

Alta and Mary sat down, surprised.

"Who's Amanda?" mouthed Alta.

Ola's tears flowed, and Mama sighed, "Ola, you're so foolish."

She tapped her foot. Her voice rose and trembled, a telltale sign that she was trying to keep her temper.

"I said it before, and now this is the last time. I'm not putting up with you anymore, Tom. You might as well leave us alone except to bring me money to help your children."

At first, a grunt came from Papa's throat. A chair scraped the floor. They peeked again. Papa grabbed Mama's elbow, whispered in her ear. She yanked her arm away.

Papa yelled, "Who'd want to live with you anyway? All you think about is money. I've tried, haven't I? My children love me. I should take them."

A chair fell back and whacked the floor. Heavy steps clomped across the kitchen floor and back.

"You don't mean it. You never do. Anyway, she'll come with me," burst out Papa.

He hit the table.

Ola said, "Tom. Please don't yell. And don't throw things. But, Dolly, he's been worried. He has."

"I don't believe you, Ola. Not after what happened," whispered Mama. "I can't bring myself to put up with you, Tom."

Mary peeked again just as Mama pointed she was going upstairs. Papa gripped her shoulder and lifted his hand. Mama grabbed her hair. Ola clutched his arm.

"Don't," Ola cried. "My father roared, but he never hit Mother."

"I'm not drinking," Papa whispered, voice shaking. "I didn't want her to leave."

He banged the door. Florence was still lying on the grass, kicking her legs, squeaking, trying to roll over, but Papa didn't notice. He stalked off along the back path to Front Street.

MARY AND ALTA knew about the lumber-company house on Harrigan's Hill. Sometimes they played in the big barn, full of lumber waiting to be loaded onto a train. A foreman had lived in it when the mill was busy. At one time, Mary had peeped into a broken window to see a front parlor and a bedroom. There was a kitchen attached like a shed. Raleigh had climbed an old ladder up to the roof and peeked into an attic room above the parlor.

"Yikes! You should see the chipmunk nests in here!" he'd yelled.

The clapboard siding must have been painted when it was built, but to Mary it had always been faded. She had pushed the door open and peered through the gloom at the walls, whitewashed at some long ago time, but now cracked and yellowed and smoky from the fireplace and wood cooking stove. It didn't have a pump in the kitchen for water like the boardinghouse did. It certainly didn't have electric lights or a telephone.

"How could Mama do this? We're going to live in that horrid old house?" Alta asked, squatting next to the baby, pulling weeds from her mouth. "I'd rather stay here. Let Papa and Ola do it. Mama hates him anyway."

"It's not right what Papa did. I'd rather move," said Mary, straightening Florence's blanket.

Thirteen and always talking about her friends' pretty things, Alta answered, "Now we're going to be really poor. No money from the boarders. You don't think Papa will have money to give to Mama, d'you?"

At that moment, Tiny pranced around the corner with Alta's hat sitting on her red curls, Raleigh marching next to her, their elbows linked, pretending to be rich people with their noses up in the air.

Tiny stopped in front of Alta and said, "Look what I found in the shed. Isn't it pretty?"

Standing to grab the hat, Alta snarled, "Give me that. It's mine."

Tiny jumped back and yelled, "Hold her, Raleigh!"

He seized Alta's arms and pulled her down onto her back.

Tiny threw the hat on the grass and yelled, "Mary, get her leg."

Mary laughed and grabbed Alta's leg.

Holding the other leg, leaning over Alta's face, Tiny shouted, "Where's my necklace?"

"I don't have your ugly necklace," grunted Alta.

"I know that. But it isn't behind the dresser either, is it? Where I hid it. What'd you do with it?" yelled Tiny. "Who did you give it to? Sally?"

"Yes! Yes!" Alta shouted back. "And I got the better deal too. It was a cheap necklace."

At that, Tiny made a fist and punched Alta in the stomach.

"I hate you, Alta. Always taking our stuff. Now I've got the hat, and I'm not giving it back!"

She punched Alta again.

"I'll get it back anytime I want," retorted Alta, tears swelling out of her eyes.

Mary looked at her, surprised they had made tears appear. Florence snuffled and rolled onto her side to grasp a dainty silk leaf from the hat. The petals of a pink rose lay on the grass. Tiny screamed, scaring the baby, so she let go of the leaf and put her fist in her mouth, tears dripping down her cheeks.

Tiny snatched up the hat and ran across the meadow into the woods. Jumping up, Raleigh ran off in the direction of the river. Mary took her weight off Alta's leg and prepared to dodge if Alta tried to hit her. Mary wondered why Mama or Aunt Ola hadn't come out after all the shouting.

Instead, Alta lay there, spread out on her back, pulling at the grass with her fingers.

"I'll get her later. And Raleigh. I'll get you too," she said finally. "Really, I'm mad about moving to that old shack. Just think. Not one piece of furniture. We owe everything to Mr. Englehardt at this place, except Mama's bed and dresser. What're we going to do? I wonder how much money I need to get away from here."

Mary shook her head. She didn't know and didn't care about the money. Somehow Mama found ways to get them food or a dress when they needed it. Mary didn't care about the old house either. She wanted to get away from Papa. In her heart she wondered how Mama would ever be content like Minna seemed to be.

To distract herself, Mary found the wicker buggy, stuffed Florence into it, and wheeled over to the neighbor lady to show the baby off.

<hr/>

"Did great-uncle Raleigh know what happened?" asked Lane.

"He was only nine and always off playing. But, you know, you are the same age I was when that happened," said Mary.

11

July 1910
Harrigan's Hill, Truckee

TINY YANKED OPEN the kitchen shed door, her hand on the chest pocket of her overalls. She stood grinning.

"What's in your pocket?" said Mary.

"I'll show you! Come on out, Billy."

Up popped a chipmunk. It sniffed and jumped onto the table.

"Probably it's a girl, but I'm not sure, so I named it Billy."

Mama flipped it over, felt its stomach, confirmed it was female.

"I taught Billy a trick. Watch."

Tiny tapped her finger on the table, and Billy crawled up her arm to sit on her shoulder. She gave Billy an acorn.

"Me and Raleigh will take Billy to the train station to do tricks, and people will give us money."

Mama laughed outright and said, "Don't catch any skunks."

"Oh, Mama! The trap's too small," Tiny said, backing out of the kitchen.

Mary's curiosity about the traps piqued now that her sister had actually caught something. She called, "I'm coming too," and followed Tiny up the hill.

Mary regarded the flimsy apparatus and blurted, "I think Billy wanted to be caught."

Indignant, Tiny said, "Mr. Titus gave us crates, and we used bits of wire to hold pieces together. The food goes in the back and the wood door slips down between slats. We found a lot of string at the dump by the river."

Tiny set it up. "Pull the stick away with the string after the chipmunk grabs the food, *shshshp*, the door slides down, and another one's trapped."

Tiny smiled with satisfaction and put berries inside the trap. They waited behind a tree, ready to pull the string. Nothing happened.

"Maybe they're not hungry right now," sighed Tiny.

On Saturday, standing in the center of the station platform, the chipmunk ran up and down Tiny's arm.

Someone, usually a lady, said, "How darling," and Tiny asked, "Do you want to see another trick?"

Afterward, Raleigh, blue eyes opened wide, tapped the person's sleeve, pointed off in the crowd, and said, "That man gave us a nickel for that trick."

Almost everyone dug out some change.

Tiny and Raleigh handed over most of their chipmunk nickels to Mama. She was digging a cooler for vegetables and singing,

Blow, boys, blow for Californio
There's plenty of gold so I've been told
On the banks of the Sacramento.

Glad for the nickels, as if they were gold, she said they were bound to make them rich.

But soon Mama's face settled into determination. The three girls and Raleigh complained to no avail when all except Florence dug up the dirt for a vegetable garden. Yelling out the verses to "Comin' Round the Mountain," they dug enough to plant lettuce and turnips.

Watering the garden was the worst. Someone had to go to the pump down by the barn to get water for everything.

"Stop fussing," said Mama. "We don't have gold, for sure, but we'll have vegetables in our stomachs. Better off than those poor miners dragging themselves into town."

Still, as pennies disappeared, they spent most of the day scrounging food. Raleigh and Tiny scouted the woods for wild berries. Mary helped Mama search for wild onions and pulled out watercress at the creek. Minna told her about pigweed the Washo cooked like spinach, and Mama wandered down the road and cut some once in awhile.

One morning Mama called Raleigh. They returned a couple of hours later, Raleigh holding a rope attached to a Jersey cow's neck.

He yelled, "We went to the dairy and bought this old milk cow. What'll we name her?"

Always called Jersey, the cow and Molly roamed the hillside eating grass all summer. The Edwards family was living in a raggedy house, searching bushes for food, counting pennies, but keeping two big animals as pets, which baffled Mary. Mama, though, was smiling again for a while.

THE KITCHEN CALENDAR highlighted July fourth, Independence Day. Stores displayed flyers singing the praises of the parade, the races, the ice cream cones.

Watching Tiny and Raleigh hurry down to Front Street to show off Billy, Mary imitated Alta's saucy saunter, swishing the skirt of her good chambray dress. Each had won the lottery to represent her grade on the school float, a wagon decorated with paper and tissue flowers. As she waited, Mary kept her eye on the ground, scouting for dropped coins.

At last they climbed onto the wagon, while volunteer firemen marched off. Then the railroad men's band played "Yankee Doodle" and "When Johnny Comes Marching Home" all the way down Front Street. Horses pulled the school float, and Mary waved at school friends. At the end of Front Street, she and Alta jumped down to watch the last of the parade.

Ladies with wide yellow sashes marched by, carrying a Campaign for Woman Suffrage sign, loudly singing the "Oh Dear" song. Mr. Vaughn, publisher of the *Truckee Star News,* drove his 1909 Model T, which everyone knew he purchased after he saw the enthusiasm with which people admired Mr. Faye's car.

"What a show-off," Mary overheard the fellow next to her mumble. "A touring car with white tires and Brewster Green paint. Who polishes those brass lamps?"

"He's an arrogant man, hard to work for," said his friend.

The fellow snorted, "Vaughn's rich enough to buy a Pierce Arrow or Cadillac, you know. Look at him in the duster with hat and gloves. I heard the dealer in Reno told him to make do with the Model T as the wretched mountain roads would ruin a fancy Eastern car."

Mr. Vaughn's son, Georgie, in matching duster and hat, shouted to his pals. Alta ignored him but pointed to Mrs. Faye driving their car with the top down and decorated with red, white, and blue ribbons. Sally and her brother, Zack, knelt on the back seat, waving to everybody.

"Mmph," said Alta. "It took awhile, but Mrs. Faye finally got to drive around town, didn't she?

From the front passenger seat Mr. Faye, parade organizer for the year, threw dimes into the air. Mary and Alta stepped on dimes to hold them while they bent down to pick up others. Alta counted six, and Mary calculated she had enough to buy material for a new school dress and ice cream in a cone, a first for the July Fourth celebration in Truckee.

Alta disappeared while Mary picked up a penny by the saloon near Church Street. When she looked up, Raleigh and Tiny were yelling at her from the bench in front of Mr. Titus's grocery.

"Look who's here," shouted Raleigh, holding a bottle of Coca-Cola and pulling up his pant leg to show his ugly scar to a little girl.

He pointed at Aunt Ola, gripping the hand of the child wearing a dainty white cotton dress with puffed sleeves and tucks all across the front of the bodice. She looked about two years old with hair crimped in sausage curls, blond like Aunt Ola's.

"Amanda, this is your cousin, Mary. Say hello."

The little girl stared and then looked at the ground. Mary smiled because she liked the dress and little kids, but then, recalling she was still disgusted with Aunt Ola for what she did with Papa, stopped grinning.

To Raleigh she said, "Did you use your dime to buy Coca-Cola?"

Raleigh said, "No, Aunt Ola bought it. Tiny has one too."

"Would you like one, Mary?" asked Aunt Ola. "You can get a bottle right in the store here. I have a dime for you."

Mary shook her head.

"No, thank you. I'm not thirsty."

"Suit yourself," said Aunt Ola. "Now I've found all of you except Alta and Florence. The baby's with Dolly, but where's Alta?"

"I bet she's talked her way into a ride in Sally Faye's car," answered Mary before she could stop herself, disdain already gone.

"Maybe we'll see her. I must tell Dolly about Missouri and … and … about what I'm going to do," said Aunt Ola. "Can you all take me up to your new house?"

"It's not new. It's older than old," said Tiny. "There's no electricity, and we have to go down by the barn to get water from the pump."

"Different then," said Aunt Ola.

Climbing up Harrigan's Hill, she asked, "Is your father around?"

Mary couldn't believe Aunt Ola didn't know where Papa was, but Tiny answered, "Nah. He's been going down to Bakersfield as brakeman since we moved. Anyway, Mama won't let him in the house. Don't you know that?"

Aunt Ola didn't answer, so she said, "He has a room at the Whitney Hotel. Mama makes Raleigh check at the railroad office to see if he's left us money."

Mary added, "I don't know why she didn't come into town today. Mama loves parades. Maybe she thinks people will talk about her."

"I suppose she's still angry with your father," said Aunt Ola. "Maybe she thinks he'll be in town today."

That thought hadn't crossed Mary's mind.

Raleigh pointed out the features of the hill, the lumber barn, the despised pump, and the best view of the Truckee River. He assured Ola they would be safe from robbers because the constable lived on the hill, and he told about the old woman Crazy Lady Harrigan.

"She goes around her yard talking to herself and leaves out food for the rabbits. Sometimes she's got her clothes on backwards and buttoned wrong. Nobody lives with her anymore."

They rested on the flat rock in front of the pine tree, the river, meadow, and mountains pearly in the sun.

Raleigh said, "Look how you can see everything going on."

PUSHING WITH HER knee to rock Florence's cradle, humming "Hush, Little Baby," Mama didn't seem surprised to see them when they arrived at the house, and she didn't give Aunt Ola a kiss or a hug.

She said, "So here you are back again. Is this Amanda?"

"Yes. I named her after you, Dolly, such a beautiful name. Mother and Father have taken good care of her," said Ola, voice bright and earnest. "Mother said she's a doll like you were."

Placing Amanda on her lap, Ola said, "Dolly, you know Mother and Father tell the truth, but they did say to skip some words in the letter I sent. People wouldn't accept me if they knew I had a baby, but they wouldn't mind if I was getting over consumption."

Mama looked up from her sewing and said to the children, "Take Amanda outside to play in the yard. There's ice cream in the old freezer I kept from the boardinghouse. Lucky we have a cow, isn't it? For the cream. Pretty soon you check it, Mary, to see if it's frozen enough."

With looks of relief, Tiny and Raleigh took Amanda in hand and trooped outside. Mama, leaning toward her sister with an offended scowl on her face, and Ola, shrinking back in her chair, were right in the middle of the confession, so Mary guarded the freezer and listened.

"Amanda's father was a sweet man, but he didn't have any money, and Father hates that, you know," said Ola.

"Money helps. Look where I am, giving up the boarders because of the good-for-nothing I married. Even his parents called him the black sheep," said Mama. "I'm sorry I laughed when he first told me that story."

Awake, swinging her fists until she whacked herself in the eye, Florence burst into tears. Mama patted her back vehemently until Florence squealed.

Ola offered, "Tom has the railroad job."

"But he's never around. And look what happened when he was home," retorted Mama.

"Dolly, he told me you weren't coming back. That he needed me to help him take care of the family. That I was the only one."

Mama rolled her eyes.

Ola added, "It was only one time. I felt so bad I locked the door, so he couldn't come in again."

Mama shook her finger at Ola and said, "You were the baby girl of the family. Everyone protected you. You can't believe anyone would tell you a lie."

The baby whimpered, so Mama pulled her up to nurse.

"I'll bet the sweet man in Missouri said the same thing," Mama added.

Mama rocked then burst out, "Do you think I'd leave my children?"

Hands clamped tightly, fingertips pressing the skin white, Ola answered, "Dolly, Father always said you were willful. Don't you remember when he whipped you after you ran off to town with Frank and Lauf? Maybe you wouldn't have come back, but sent for the children."

Mama sucked in a breath and lifted Florence to nurse on the other side.

Ola added, "It's why I didn't tell you the truth about Amanda right away. You're so strict, Dolly. Like Father. I was sure you wouldn't let me come and start over."

"Two wrongs don't make a right," sighed Mama. "But … that you believed Tom! I've said it before and I'll say again—you truly are the most foolish girl. I don't know how you were born my sister to be so heedless."

She smoothed Florence's blanket with her free hand.

Finally, she said, "Now, I don't know. I'm so angry with Tom, I don't care."

"Dolly, I went back to get Amanda because I'm going to keep house for Mr. James and his children on McGlashan's Hill. His wife died when you went to Sacramento. He said I could bring her," said Ola.

"What story did you tell him?" Mama snapped.

"That there was no room in this house, and I had to find another place because I wanted to bring my daughter," said Ola. "He didn't ask anything else. I think he needs someone pretty badly."

"You're right, this is my home, but not Tom's," agreed Mama.

"It's very small and bare," said Ola, scrutinizing the cloths covering the windows with no panes.

"We'll fix things. I may be willful, but I can work. I'm like the ant, and Tom is the grasshopper," said Mama.

"I didn't say one thing about you or me or Tom to Mother and Father," said Ola. "Only about Mr. James."

OLA LIFTED FLORENCE to coddle, and Mary remembered the ice cream.

Mary took off the gunnysack and poked her finger into the freezer bucket. It was ready.

Mama warmed the fried chicken, made from Crazy Lady Harrigan's squawking hen. Mrs. Harrigan showed up early that morning holding the chicken by the legs. Mama'd wrung its neck, chopped the head off, drained the blood, plucked it, and floured it for frying, all before anyone left for the parade.

Raleigh and Tiny told Amanda about the doomed chicken while consuming a boardinghouse feast of fried chicken, hot biscuits, berry cobbler, and ice cream. Mary ate the last wing from the plate of chicken, feeling even better when Mama handed cobbler to Aunt Ola and smiled.

AUNT OLA BOUGHT sparklers while Tiny, Raleigh, and Amanda watched the races in town. Mary, Florence, and Mama delivered berry cobbler to Mrs. Harrigan. The lady fetched the teakettle for her company sitting in the front room. Teacups sat on a spindly table, and Mrs. Harrigan bent slightly to pour into the strainer. Light streamed in from the window, striking wrinkles radiating from the woman's mouth as she tilted up the kettle. She asked how Mama had come to live on the hill. The room faded to soft voices, the two women leaning toward each other, Mama telling Mrs. Harrigan all about Ola and Papa—why she'd been so angry and then had forgiven her sister. The old lady laughed, Mama cocked her head, a half smile on her lips.

Patting Mama's knee, Mrs. Harrigan said, "Indeed, Dolly, in this forsaken place faithfulness is a sometime thing. Every man around here, as restless as your husband, is looking for some unknown thing, perhaps a quick buck like the gambler who tricked Mrs. Tucker at the Whitney. Hardly any of them steady or prosperous. They meet up with women who come here because they have to look out for themselves. Something is bound to happen."

Mrs. Harrigan sipped tea and spooned up cobbler. "That's how I came here. My family had no money, and I thought I'd be a teacher. I ended up cleaning the hotels until I met my husband. Do you think he cared? Who cares where anyone comes from? Or how long they stay? Some husbands vanish. Some just up and die, like mine. Wives too. The young ones find someone else and usually join together for bad reasons. Money. To get away from a worse place. Loneliness. Maybe that's why you've given up being mad at your sister. She hasn't disappeared on you.

"Faithful. Absurd word. But don't worry, I won't say anything. Everyone tells me their problems. I'm the wise, old crone in fairy tales. At least they think I am," laughed Mrs. Harrigan once more.

Mama fluttered her hand in front of her face, as if the uneasy look might be fanned away. Mary poured the next round of tea, and then left to make her way to town, scarcely understanding what the old lady meant. At the kiosk selling ice cream cones, she spent a nickel to treat herself. She watched the potato sack races, licking her fingers as the ice cream dripped down the sides of the cone in the hot sun. The crunchy sugar cone gave her something sweet to think about.

WHEN ALTA SHOWED up in the evening, everyone spun flashing circles with the sparklers. By kerosene lamp light, the two oldest climbed the ladder and walked over the kitchen shed roof and opened the attic's tiny door. Pulling on nightgowns, Mary confided about Aunt Ola.

"I think she knew Aunt Ola was coming back, but I still wonder why she didn't want to come to the parade even though we were on a float."

"Ah, she's seen us on those floats before. Aunt Ola was right for once. Mama thought Papa would be there," Alta said. "That's something he would do. He likes to be around at holidays."

"Well, he didn't come. I hope he stays away," said Mary.

Then Mary passed on Crazy Lady Harrigan's advice.

"I told you to come out with me. Then you'd see what that old lady knows," said Alta. "I wonder what she was like when she was Ola's age?"

They felt their way along the rafters to hang their dusty, wrinkled dresses on the nails at the front corner of the attic. Laughing her devilish laugh, Alta changed the subject.

"I'll tell you something about cars. Sally let me ride with them for a while today, but you know what? This town is so backward and the road is so bad you can't go fast at all. Even out on the road to Colfax we can go faster on Molly. Isn't that a joke?"

They lay down on the batting on the old straw mattresses and pulled up the scruffy quilts.

Mary said, "Aunt Ola did you-know-what with Papa because she was lonely, and she'd already done it with the fellow she wanted to marry until her Father said no. That's how she ended up with her baby."

Alta snorted, "Anyway now we know who Amanda is."

She was quiet for a minute and then exclaimed, "At least, Aunt Ola's had some adventures!"

Mary fumbled for the knob to turn down the lamp wick before she lifted the glass to blow out the last spark of light.

AT THE END of the month, Tiny dragged herself into the kitchen, enormous tears running down her cheeks.

"Billy's gone!" she wailed. "I've looked everywhere."

Wiping her hands on her apron, taking Tiny in her arms, Mama said, "There, there."

Mary pursed her lips at Tiny's theatrics, but by then the howls had brought everyone into the kitchen.

Tiny sobbed, "We were playing with Florence yesterday and Raleigh tried to pick her up."

She hiccupped, "She kicked her little feet."

Raleigh folded his arms and stared at Tiny.

"It's all because her kicking made Raleigh trip, and he stomped all over Billy's little cage, so I didn't have any place to put her last night."

Raleigh shouted, "I didn't mean to."

"I tied her to the bedpost and made a little rag pillow. But she wasn't there this morning!" she wailed again. "I don't think I'll ever find a pet as good as Billy."

Mama said, "You will. Be patient."

She paused, and then said, " *'Patience and time run through the longest day.'* "

Alta rolled her eyes, Raleigh sniffed, "Oh, Mama," but Tiny nodded, her face serious, taking comfort from the saying.

"Let's get Molly. Go to the woods," proposed Mary. "Maybe we'll find a chipmunk."

Everyone scattered, while Florence rolled over, grabbing the chair leg. Mary pulled Florence up by her hands and steadied her so she was sitting. The baby let go and sat there, a satisfied smile on her pink face surrounded by dark curly hair like Alta's.

"Mama, come quick!" yelled Mary. "The baby's sitting all by herself."

"Well, I never," said Mama and gave Florence a kiss on each cheek.

"Can we take her with us? She can sit up, we can take care of her, she'll have fun," implored Mary, laughing at how Florence found an opportunity to go exploring.

MOLLY SPENT THE day as a pack horse for the caravan, led by Alta holding the bridle and escorted by Mary with Florence, Tiny, and Raleigh. Eventually they gathered more companions when Hazel and Delilah appeared at the corner of Front Street, falling in behind Tiny. Minna had said to play while she visited with her cousins. Soon Raleigh hollered to Joe, the Italian boy from Church Street. His mother had sent him out to play while she took care of her sick nephew, who had just arrived from Reno.

The meadow was blazing hot until they reached the shallow creek. Trees that grew along the riverbanks shielded the children's heads from the hot sun. Mary gave Florence water, while everyone else slurped from the creek. Joe had a metal cup he kept with other treasures in his trapper's bag. Raleigh envied the cup and had been saving pennies to buy his own. Joe passed the cup around to scoop up water when their hands began to freeze in the stream.

Kicking off their shoes, they splashed through the cold water, even dipping Florence's toes in. They picked wild blackberries to eat, ignoring the stickers, and then went back to the creek to wash the purple off their fingers and tongues. Finally retreating to the shade in the woods, Alta split up bread and bologna among seven. Florence sat up while Mary fed her applesauce. After she ate, Florence toppled onto her side and fell asleep.

Taking off into the woods, Joe and Raleigh pretended to be hunters. Tiny, Hazel, and Delilah waded in the creek and peeked under the plants at the edge, hoping to catch a frog. Delilah slipped in the muck. With her muddy bottom high in the air, she lifted herself up. Hazel guided her back into the deep shade. The warm afternoon made all the girls drowsy, but when the boys crashed through the bushes, sweaty and flushed, Mary's eyes flipped open.

"Guess who's with us?" panted Raleigh. "Captain Ben, Minna's old cousin. He was hunting up rabbits for his wife and Minna, and he showed us how to catch them."

Captain Ben, short, round-faced, straight black hair, with his flat-topped, wide-brimmed hat, appeared from the woods holding two rabbits. Their heads had been flattened with the mallet in his hand. He tipped his hat. Delilah and Hazel hugged him and hustled behind, as he strode off to their house to deliver the rabbits.

Watching the hot air ripple as Captain Ben crossed the meadow, Joe said, "Let's go home. My head hurts."

Alta and Tiny argued about pennies to buy candy. Florence rolled over and squeaked and rubbed her tiny fists all over her sweaty face. Mary dipped a rag in the water and washed the baby's face, and the baby stopped fussing. With their belongings on Molly's back, they leaped the creek and dashed over the meadow to reach the shade of the town buildings.

"I don't feel like candy now. My head still hurts. See you later," said Joe, rubbing behind his ears, turning off at Church Street.

Tiny and Alta chose peppermint sticks. Raleigh proclaimed candy was the best way to end a long day, and Mary rubbed the stick on Florence's tongue. They laughed at how Florence squinted while savoring the sweet taste.

12

August 1910
Harrigan's Hill, Truckee

AT LUNCH TWO days later, Raleigh rubbed his forehead, and Mama examined the fine, red spots behind his ears.

"Oh, my Lord Almighty," she said, ticking off the rashes she knew about to his sisters, who jumped up and bent their heads over him to see.

"It's likely scarlet fever, which came to me at age seven. Lucky me, I wasn't bad, but Mother took care of three others. Margaret was spared, and my cousin died."

Raleigh was settled in bed, cold rags on his head. The girls were ordered to the attic to throw down Raleigh's clothes and stay away from their brother.

Soon Alta stepped out onto the kitchen roof and yelled down, "Mama, it's so hot up here. Can't we please go outside under the trees?"

She waited, flapping her arms up and down, and shouted again, "Mama!"

"I can hear you," Mama called. "Keep the baby out of the sun. She got sunburned yesterday."

After Mary threw the clothes down from the roof, Mama disappeared with them into the kitchen, re-appearing to call, "Hold on. Tiny can take care of Florence. Alta, you and Mary go find Dr. Charles."

Mary was certain Alta was going to run off as soon as they found the doctor, but she had no chance.

"Good Lord!" he said. "Another one. Don't you dare leave this office. You're going to be quarantined too. Let me put the string and signs in my bag."

"Get a move on," he urged, shooing them ahead. "I put the Italian house on Church Street under quarantine late yesterday. I hope this is the only other one."

Mama was hanging Raleigh's clothes on rope between the trees. Wringing her hands, she led the doctor into the front room.

"What am I going to do, doctor? I have so little money," she said.

"You're going to keep those cold rags on his head and neck. No onion poultices or mustard rubs or the like. The rash'll move onto his chest and his armpits. It won't itch too much; good, because he won't scratch. His tongue will get bumpy and red like a strawberry. If he doesn't start to get better in a week, call for me again."

"So it is scarlet fever," said Mama.

"Yes, and I'm putting a quarantine string around this house for five or six weeks. Don't let the girls go outside the string. They'll probably come down with it soon."

Dr. Charles looked around at their house with cloth over the window frames and no proper sink. Then he walked outside and looked up the hill.

"You'd better see if your neighbor can take lists down to Mr. Titus. He'll send a grocery boy with the box of food and leave it somewhere to pick up."

Pale, hands shaking, Mama bit her lip.

Finally she said, "What about my baby?"

"Babies don't often get scarlet fever very bad. A little fever and a little rash," he assured her.

"Can you wait while I write a message to telegraph their father? He works on the railroad. He should know," pleaded Mama.

She found some coins in the Chinese box, and the doctor promised to drop it off at the telegraph office.

"One more thing," Mama said. "I'm not burning anything, only boiling the clothes. I don't have money to get more for these children."

"Yes, yes," said the doctor. "I don't know if burning or washing all their things really helps. Just stay home, so it doesn't spread. And, madam, if you please, you're going to need panes in these windows come fall. These children will be sick with colds this winter if you don't."

With sticks from the barn pounded into the dirt, Mary, Alta, and Tiny helped Dr. Charles tie string from post to post until a large square isolated the house. The doctor tied quarantine signs to each stake and strode off, swinging his little black bag. Mary had doubts the signs were going to save anybody. Alta said it was like being in jail.

Finally connecting the news between the Italian family's quarantine and Joe's headache, Mary said, "Mama, Joe was sick too. And yesterday Hazel and Delilah played with us in the woods."

"Heaven help us," she said. She stopped hanging up clothes, and in spite of the doctor's warnings, sent Mary to the constable's wife with a note for Minna.

As Dr. Charles foresaw, Alta and Tiny complained of headaches the next day. Fortunately for Alta, she progressed from headache to sore throat to body rash quickly. Tiny endured a severe headache and earache, high fever, and bright red rash.

Three lay ill in the front room. Outside, Mary cared for Florence. Mama put cold rags on everyone's forehead and boiled clothes. The following day, Alta and Raleigh were ready to wander around. They stood by the front window and entertained Mary and Florence, pressing their fingers on each other's stomach until the red rash disappeared and white spots showed up.

By the afternoon they were out of everything—bread, salami, flour, bacon fat, even kerosene for the lamps. Once more, Mary delivered a note to the constable's wife and came back with a basket of eggs Mrs. Harrigan had collected.

"Thank goodness, we have some friends up here," Mama said.

Mary waited for a Bible saying or proverb, finally guessing Mama was too tired to think of one.

"Can't we send a note to Aunt Ola for help or maybe Minna? She's a nurse," asked Mary.

"No, that's how the fever spreads," said Mama, eyes half-closed. "Can you play with the baby while I rest for a minute?"

That evening Mary's head and throat hurt. She looked in the mirror at her tongue, red and bumpy. Florence had fallen asleep while Mary read to her, even though she knew the baby didn't understand the words. Now Florence's tiny face was red and hot. She breathed with her mouth open, her tongue bright red.

Woozy, Mary wobbled to Mama, who was out hanging clothes.

"Florence is sick. And me too."

Mama's shoulders slumped. She sighed.

"Very sick?" she asked.

"No, but Florence is. She's very hot."

The basket of clothes on one hip, Mama pulled Mary along, saying, "Put Tiny in my room. You stay in the front room with Raleigh and Alta."

Mary didn't sleep well, listening to Mama change the wet rags for the two sickest girls. The next morning, Mama dragged herself out of bed to milk the Jersey. Alta soaked the last of the bread in bowls of milk, so everyone had something soft to eat.

Mary lay around all day. Raleigh and Alta played cards until he saw Alta cheat. He leaned forward to holler when she pointed out the window. The grocery boy was putting a crate next to the quarantine post. On top sat two cardboard boxes, green with red and black letters like Alta had seen at Sally's house, but Mama would never have written the name down on their grocery list.

"Cornflakes!" she yelled, then covered her mouth.

Alta rarely helped with chores, but that day she dragged the crate to the kitchen, and Raleigh helped her empty the entire box. Eating cereal from one hand, the box of cornflakes under her arm, Alta slowly carried a bowl of cereal with milk to Mary.

Alta said, "Wait a minute until it gets soft, so it won't hurt your throat. Then you'll see. It's delicious."

Hard to believe Alta was being thoughtful, but Mary took the bowl and ate it all.

"I guess Mr. Titus feels sorry for us," said Alta, marveling at their sudden luck in the middle of catastrophe. "Sally told me he'd ordered some from the cereal salesman, and they're brand new."

Black clouds built up in the sky and lightning flashed in the front room, then thunder boomed from the other side of the valley. Still they couldn't bring themselves to work up the shivers of scary excitement they usually enjoyed during a thunderstorm, so somber were their rooms.

Mama tiptoed back and forth, carrying wet rags to cool the baby. She whispered to Tiny, but it sounded like a mumbled nonsense answer. Alta, Mary, and Raleigh made themselves supper from more cornflakes and milk. The green boxes decorated the kitchen table, one bright, colorful thing in their sad house.

When evening shadows and silence after the thunderstorm enveloped the room, Mary and Raleigh climbed onto the bed and sat close together against the wall. Alta paced back and forth and then beckoned them to peep into the bedroom. Mama was asleep in the rocking chair.

Mary picked up Florence. She felt sweaty, so they pulled off her nightdress and washed her entire little body. Raleigh discovered the pile of boiled baby clothes, and they dressed her and laid her in the cradle. Tiny woke up, and Alta brought her a bowl of soft cornflakes, whispering about the cereal so she wouldn't wake Mama.

They stumbled back and laid themselves in a row on the bed. Mary woke up during the night, thinking she heard rain, but finally recognized the rocker thrumming back and forth on the floor while Mama hummed and nursed the baby.

Two days later, Raleigh and Alta straddled logs they lugged from the woodpile. They chattered to Mary, wrapped in a blanket on the chair by the window, until Raleigh yelled, "There's Papa. I know it's him."

Walking up the hill, a box of food in his arms, he stopped at the quarantine sign and then stooped under the string.

Raleigh shouted, "Papa, the doctor said no one can come in or out. Are you going to stay?"

"I don't know, son," called Papa. "Depends which way the wind blows."

Raleigh tilted his head, not quite sure what Papa meant. Papa approached the doorway and said, "Stick out your tongues."

The roughness had begun to disappear, and the bright red returned to a normal purple-pink. He commented, "Still a rash though. How're the baby and Tiny and Mary?"

Alta reported, "Mary wasn't very sick. She's right there," and pointed to the window.

Papa peered in, but Mary refused to wave.

"Tiny's better, but she still has a rash. Florence was not supposed to get sick, but she's hot and red. Mama's very upset. She spends all the time with her," said Alta.

Papa entered the house, calling, "Dolly?"

Clothes disheveled, face surrounded with strings of dark tangled hair, Mama shuffled out of the bedroom. Holding the baby tightly, she looked like she was ready to fall from fatigue.

"Oh, Tom, she's so sick," she moaned. "I don't know what to do."

Eyes blinking in the gloom, Mama held the baby out to Papa, who sat down to rock Florence in his arms.

"Dolly, sit down," said Papa. "Now, listen. The railroad loaned me some money to pay for the groceries. I've money for the doctor too, and I'll ask him to come again."

She nodded, and he continued, "You go get cleaned up. Let me sit with the baby for a while, then I'll go. I have to get back to work on the train from Reno to pay off the loan."

Eyes closing, Mama nodded again and disappeared into the bedroom. Tiny came out and climbed into the front-room bed with Mary. Alta and Raleigh plopped down on the bed.

Papa said, "We all love Florence. I wish we had one of my grandmother's root and herb remedies. She'd get better right away. We'll have to make do with the doctor."

Papa cuddled the baby. Although she was limp and barely seemed to breathe, he whispered in her ear. Finally, he gave Florence to Mary, hugged everyone, and left.

Alta said, "I've never heard Papa talk like he knew what to do."

"Maybe it's because he wasn't drunk," said Mary.

Raleigh asked, "Will Mama and Florence be all right?"

"Mama'll be all right, but Florence is awfully sick," answered Mary.

"I hope he doesn't forget the doctor," said Tiny. "You know how he forgets things."

Mary was startled when Alta, with little faith in Papa, said, "I think he'll remember this time."

ALTA AND RALEIGH waited by the quarantine sign all morning, as their excuse to get out of the dark, noiseless house. They escorted Dr. Charles into the hushed bedroom. He held Florence in his arms as if she were his own baby. Placing his finger on her tongue to see how red and rough it was, he gently opened her eyelid to see if she reacted to the light. He placed his stethoscope on her tiny chest to listen to her lungs.

All the while, Mama stood against the doorjamb, arms folded across her chest, hardly breathing herself. The four children sat on the floor, against the wall, two at each side of the door.

"She's having a hard time. I don't know why," he said. "It hasn't settled in her eyes. She seems to hear. But she's very weak. I have powders to keep children from getting rheumatic fever. I'm afraid she might get it. Measure out one-fourth of each packet and give it to her with porridge or applesauce."

"She barely nurses. How am I going to get her to eat porridge?" asked Mama as she took a deep breath and massaged her eyes with her fingers. "What's in the powder?"

The doctor frowned and said, "Aspirin mixed with salts of mercury. They say it helps with rheumatic fever. You must be careful to give her only one quarter of the packet at a time."

Mama contemplated the doctor's gentle, kind face. He knew more about sickness than she did. Fearing Florence might die, she accepted the small white packages. Alta and Raleigh walked to the string with Dr. Charles, who warned them it was foolish and dangerous to disobey the quarantine.

SCARCELY A WEEK later, the rashes on Mary, Alta, and Raleigh disappeared, and they peeled skin off each other. Tiny regained some energy, and her skin began to peel too. The baby slept most of the time and nursed fitfully. She moaned when Mama slipped porridge mixed with medicine into her mouth and massaged her throat so she would swallow.

After a supper no one wanted to eat, Mama saw tiny sores in the baby's mouth, and Florence cried when Mama touched her stomach. Mama picked Florence up from her cradle, laid the baby across her lap, and stroked her arms, legs, and tummy. She carefully brushed back the soft, dark baby hair. From the bed, Mary watched through the doorway, as Mama rocked and sang to the baby in the shadowy bedroom.

ONLY MAMA WAS allowed to leave the house and go to the town cemetery. Aunt Ola went, of course, and Minna. Her daughters hadn't even been a little sick. The following day, Minna disregarded the quarantine and came to see Mama. Minna told the children Ola had broken down, as if Florence were her own baby.

"Your mother," Minna said, "stood stiff like a soldier, staring at the coffin. Not one tear. She didn't seem to be on the earth, as if she were following the baby into the other world to make sure she was safe. That's what the Washo say happens."

According to Minna, few other townspeople came, everyone being fearful of catching the germ. Only the butcher, Mr. and Mrs. Titus, and Mr. and Mrs. Faye attended the funeral. Mama sent a telegram to Papa, but she knew he wouldn't get it in time. She burned Florence's few small clothes and blankets out beyond the vegetable garden.

THE FOUR CHILDREN watched Mama pick her way down the hill until Mr. James, Aunt Ola's boss, met her and took her arm. The children ventured as far as the pine tree to peer down the hill, looking for the cemetery where the tiny casket would go.

Red-faced and teary, Tiny said, "Florence was the prettiest of us all, wasn't she? I wish we'd bought a fancy dress to show her off on the Fourth of July."

Voice gruff, Alta said, "Ah, what good would a fancy dress do now? She's going to be down under the dirt. That doctor shouldn't've given her those powders. I think they made her die."

Raleigh believed he'd made Florence sick, even though his sisters kept reminding him they'd all been sick. He threw his arms around Mary's waist and buried his face in her stomach, hiding his tears and muffling his sobs.

Patting his back, Mary mumbled, "It's all right, it's all right," although she was crying too.

All her life she'd remember how Mama rocked back and forth in the dark, rubbing the baby's tummy, whispering

Hush, little baby, don't say a word,
Mama's going to buy you a mockingbird . . . ,

even after Florence stopped breathing.

———⋙◦⋘———

"OH, GRANDMA," SAID Lane.

"That was the first sorrow," said Mary.

13

April 1934
Sacramento

WHO WOULD HAVE guessed when the next truly personal disasters occurred? Not until I was thirty-five and Raleigh was thirty-two. And I wasn't thinking about the Depression, although we were all in trouble in Sacramento by then.

In the hot summers before that awful October 1929 day, I drove my Model T to the Sacramento River park, lawns shaded by spreading oaks, wild brush cut away from the edge of the river, and set out a picnic. The deep river rushed along, especially when, heavy with melted snow from Mount Shasta, it rose high along the shore. From the riverbank, Betsy kept her eye on tugboats pulling barges loaded with boxes of produce for towns up and down the river before highway trucks took over. Watching the steamboat churning up the river current, she waved to passengers as we waded along the shore.

One Saturday Betsy and I brought the food, laid out the lunch, and waited for Mama and Raleigh's family—Betsy sitting on a rock and kicking her feet in the water. Jays fought over crumbs on the ground, scaring away the juncos trying to snatch a morsel. I brushed the dust and twigs off my dark blue dress, straightened my stockings, and made sure my new hat fell properly over my forehead. Then Mama, Raleigh, and his family showed up, laughing and yelling. Betsy stood up on the rock to wave, slid into the turbulent muck of the river, and shrieked.

All I saw was her plaid dress, buoyed up and splayed out under her arms as the skirt whirled and pulled her into the current. Unlike the time at the Truckee River, Raleigh jumped in to yank Betsy out of the water. She stood, shivering and muddy, while I pulled off her drippy clothes and made her lay out in the sun. Lucky for her, I had some overalls and a shirt in the car, while she only blubbered about the pretty plaid dress and the birds that had silently disappeared when everyone, shouting and pointing, ran across the grass. Another in the long line of small adventures in that comfortable time.

Nearly every Sunday in those years, Mama had us out to her house for midday dinner, especially when Tiny and her husband came to town. Often there were too many people. We each brought a dish, spooned food onto our plates, and sat everywhere, the kitchen, the porch, the grass. For Raleigh's children, the ritual was to go off with Betsy to inspect the beehives at the Noguchi fruit and flower farm far down the path.

On one of those beautiful Sundays, while on a mission to buy more cheese, Tiny and I wandered across the field, pulling out dry grass caught in the open insteps of our shoes, looking ahead at the flat field broken up by oak trees and cows. Then walking along the far dirt highway, we watched for the farmer's dairy stand that sold cheese and tins of milk to those driving along the newly smoothed road. The air was full of dry grass scent, and the sky was so clear one could imagine it never rained to spoil the scene.

Now that Tiny was again a married woman in San Francisco, she walked as if through crowds on a city street, arms swinging, eyes darting from side to side, hands smoothing her dark red hair, curled in the latest style.

She was her dramatic self, disclosing tales about the people she knew in San Francisco. People like the rich Mrs. Spry, who lived in a hotel and had a chauffeur and maid. Tiny had been her secretary, although I always thought my sister was a poor speller. The woman had dinner parties, and Tiny and Fred met many of the well-known families who lived in San Francisco like the Harrimans, Crockers, and Hopkins, names we knew from our Truckee railroad days. Fred was impressed and found it easy to socialize with San Francisco's upper class.

In fact, Tiny was infatuated with that man from an old San Francisco family. Fred knew how to live and took Tiny to restaurants and speakeasies and to the racetrack and golf clubs. Tiny said he was swell, but when I met him, a thin-lipped smile peeped from under his black mustache and small eyes flitted up and down analyzing my dress, legs, and hairstyle. His puffy tie and twirling cane told me here was a city man, not a country fellow, and I kept my eyes on his hands.

Then the good days came to an end, though I can say we held on. My bank didn't crash, and Mama only kept cash. She sold her chickens and vegetables, what she didn't give away. Raleigh still had his job at the cannery for the time being. Tiny wasn't working. Alta kept singing and by 1932 made money in taverns that thrived when Prohibition was overturned. We should have been breathing relief.

BETSY, A TALL, bright girl who thought up all the fun with her friends, turned thirteen in March 1934. Even then I noticed a limp once in awhile, but one evening in April, she held onto the chairs and table, swinging her left leg so as not to bend it. I made her sit down and pull up her skirt.

Her knee was swollen and red and hot to the touch, while she assured me, "It'll go away, Mom. I bumped against the wall at school."

Oh, my Lord! I don't know how she made it up the stairs to our apartment. Just like Mama knew the scarlet fever rash behind Raleigh's ears wasn't a little thing, I knew Betsy's inflamed knee would not heal itself and leave us be. I blinked, determined not to cry, questions jostling for a place in my head.

Should I tell her father? He'd rarely come around since I'd separated from him. He'd say, "Mary, Mary, it'll be all right. Calm down." He wouldn't have money to help anyway since the grocery business closed and he'd lost his job.

What about the doctor? Thank goodness, I'd kept my savings at a bank still secure. Thank goodness, I still had a job at the state bookbindery. If necessary, I could ask Tiny. She loved Betsy, and I thought she had money.

The next day, Betsy's doctor said he'd make an appointment with the children's arthritis doctor in Woodland, about twenty miles northwest of Sacramento. I gasped at the distance. Grabbing tight hold onto a strand of hair, staring at the numbers on the telephone dial, the miles to Woodland rolled along in my mind's eye, a whole day to get there and back. I had to work to make enough for Betsy and me, and I didn't get paid for days I missed. How often would we have to drive up there?

The doctor whispered into the phone, "Miz Ashton, Miz Ashton, are you there?"

Tucking the hair behind my ear, I asked him to make the appointment.

Afraid to be alone, beside myself with worry, I called Mama's neighbor. She found Mama, who agreed to ride along. I think she remembered how it was with the scarlet fever because the only thing she said, holding my hand tightly, was, "don't be downhearted." She told stories and sang songs to Betsy all the way to Woodland. I kept my eyes on the road, so we didn't hit any holes or rocks.

Betsy, my brave girl, had to stay at the hospital in Woodland for several days. The doctor said she'd have to take aspirin three times a day and keep a cast on for six weeks or so while the rheumatoid arthritis went into remission. It was a scene getting back into the apartment with her knee in the cast.

We were lucky Raleigh came by, good soul that he was. With one arm around his shoulders, and me on the other side, she hopped all the way up the staircase to the second floor, laughing at how awkward we must look. When Betsy reached her bed and lay down, Raleigh and I stood at the end to catch our breath. It came to all three of us what a problem this would be, and, at that time, we didn't know she'd have to stay home for a year until the remission truly began.

"Golly, Mom, how'm I going to answer the door? You'll have to leave it unlocked. For Daddy. And Grandma. And my friends," said Betsy.

"I'll bring over a big stick so you can hit any stranger," joked Raleigh.

"You can leave a sandwich by the bed, but I'll have to use the crutches to get to the bathroom," said Betsy.

Raleigh walked around the small room and moved chairs out of the way and opened the curtains to let in the sunlight.

"Mom, what about books?" Betsy said. "Who'll bring me books? I have to have something to do."

Raleigh piled up all the books on the small table by the bed.

"Maybe your father can go to the library for you," he said. "Or Mama. She'll bring some of her books."

Betsy smiled, but I saw her worried glance around the room while she estimated the number of long days ahead. I came home so late, working overtime to make enough money. She enjoyed being with people, not shy like I was at her age. She had a lot of friends, but I suspected children who were thirteen would forget to come after a while.

She was unhappy to miss school like me with the typhoid, and I didn't have money for a tutor. Still, she was smart, and I brought her some schoolbooks with binding mistakes from my job. That's how she studied math.

Then Tiny sent a radio to keep in her room. Betsy learned all the popular songs and hummed "Moonglow" and sang "On the Good Ship Lollipop" over and over until I was sick of it. She listened to all the popular shows, especially the comedians, as she said it felt good to laugh. Then she wrote letters asking her friends to bring books and naming the one she wanted each to bring. They came over, too, each with a book. So she figured out how to keep her friends.

Late one evening when I came home, the radio blared so I could hear it on the stairs. Her friends were waltzing around the front room, and even Betsy was standing with her crutches, swaying and singing the words to "Blue Moon" as loud as she could. Such an ordinary afternoon of fun. I felt bad when it was time to send everyone home. I could easily see Betsy was tired, her face looked pale with circles under her eyes, but she was angry too.

For the first time she shouted, "Can't you leave me alone? I know what I'm doing." She turned with her crutches and swung into her room.

She did know how to do for herself. At the same time, I couldn't stop myself from protecting her.

Usually on Saturdays, Mama stayed over. She and Betsy listened to news programs, especially anything about Roosevelt. Mama thought FDR was wonderful, and she explained the National Recovery Act to Betsy and the banking problems that had led to such chaos. It was surprising how much Mama knew, even though she lived out in the country. Then Betsy wrote to Roosevelt and told him about the good things and the bad things in California.

Betsy was a good artist, and she sent a card with a drawing of the house across the street to Alta for her birthday in April. Alta wrote her a long, kind thank you letter—always amazing how endearing Alta could be when she wanted to be.

WHAT OF BETSY'S father? Even during the good days, he didn't like to go on outings with my family. We separated in 1929, though Betsy tried to talk me out of it. Henry'd never finished school, and once he lost his job, he didn't know what to do with himself. To save money, I didn't drive my car most of the time, so everyday on the trolley, I was afraid I'd see him among the hundreds of men in town who were hungry, and who sat on the benches in the park by the Capitol or waited in the soup lines in the old part of town.

Henry managed to keep a small room in a boardinghouse, but I don't know how he found enough money to buy liquor once Prohibition had been repealed. He had no money to help his daughter, but he dropped by once a week, bringing books and chatting with her, so she said.

One evening, Betsy had pulled herself into a sitting position on her bed and was listening to the radio when I came into her room. She flicked off the music and pulled her hair back, tears dripping from her eyes, lip quivering.

"Mother, I don't want Daddy to come anymore," she cried. "He was so drunk this afternoon, he could hardly stand. He almost fell on my leg, and then he started apologizing, asking me to forgive him."

I didn't know how to answer, but I did remember how I'd avoided my father, hiding in the woods, taking walks up to Minna's, reading at school with my friend Etta. I realized she couldn't get away if she didn't want to be around Henry.

"He was mumbling how bad he felt because we didn't live together, but I could hardly understand him," she said. "Please tell him not to come."

Which reminded me of why I'd separated from her father. Henry and I never did have much in common, except for Betsy. He'd still been working then, but he'd come home with the same whiskey smell we'd all gotten used to with Papa when we were young. Though I'd never forgotten what Papa did, and I always kept my eye on Henry, I'd always minded my own business. Betsy knew how to stay on Henry's good side. I took care of Betsy and kept her away from that unhappy man when he wandered around the house, too drunk to care, falling against the furniture and collapsing on the bed.

Then, like Mama, I became fed up and said so one evening when he stumbled into the front room. He'd never threatened me before, but that night he grabbed my neck with his hands and began to shake. He yelled never to say anything about money or liquor again. I don't know, maybe that night he knew he was going to lose his job. The next morning, I packed Betsy's things and my things, and we left.

We never stayed with Mama. I couldn't do that. We stayed in the spare room of another family I'd met in Sacramento until, fortunately, I found an apartment I could afford downtown. Like Mama, I wasn't lucky in love. When Betsy got sick, it came to me, I was the one who would save her. She was the one I loved. So I talked to her father, and he rarely came back during that long, long year and never when he'd been drinking.

I WAS BETTER off than Raleigh. Not even three weeks after he helped Betsy climb the stairs, he came over, so he said, to see if his children could visit one day. Of course, Betsy was overjoyed.

I looked at him again. He sat on the edge of the chair next to our table in the front room, leg bent and foot resting on the opposite knee, head down. Except for the hand constantly kneading his calf, he sat frozen as if by any other slight twitch he would collapse.

He pulled in a deep breath and said, "Maggie's in the hospital. She complained of pains in her stomach. On the second day, I took her over there."

She was in the surgery right while he was telling me about it.

The next moment, my brother, the young man who rarely talked about himself, let out a rush of heartsick words. How he adored Maggie. How he knew the evening they met at a dance his pals had taken him to. How Mama had told him they were Romeo and Juliet. How he was devoted to his children, but he should've known when Maggie lost the first baby. She wasn't as strong as she looked, and the children were wearing her down. How he didn't have enough money to get her some help before she got sick. And he'd put off taking her to the hospital. Finally, he confided he'd lost his job at the cannery, sobbing he didn't have money to pay for the surgery.

He put his hands over his face, while I could only think of our sister and said, "Write to Tiny. She gave me money to help with Betsy's hospital bill. She'll find a way."

Betsy called for me, and Raleigh jumped up and said, "I have to go. Maybe she's back in her bed."

The next day, Saturday, when I went to the Sacramento hospital, Raleigh was sitting outside the door to the women's ward. I looked through the small window at pearly white beds, pearly walls, light fixtures on the ceiling with translucent pearly globes, dusty windows framed with oak, so families sitting at the bedside could hardly see the woman's body. Raleigh was sobbing. He grabbed my arm.

"She's dying," he said. "She's dying."

I looked through the ward window again to see if I could find her—dark hair, round face, pointed chin. Maggie lay with her eyes closed, completely covered except her pearly face, not far from the door, no nurse near her, as if she was an "in and out."

"The doctor said it's cancer of the pancreas. He said to take her home to see her children, but she's going to die. What'm I going to do?"

Like the day we watched Mama go to the baby's funeral, he hugged me around the waist, his head on my stomach, groaning.

That evening, when Betsy had fallen asleep, I went in to turn off the radio. I sat at Betsy's bedside and held her hand. I fixed on her poor leg sticking out, stiff in a new cast, and wished I could make her well again. I wished I could find a man to love who would love us and be company for our troubles " 'til death do us part" as the words go.

Only Raleigh had found a woman he loved, and he didn't know how to go on without her.

RALEIGH WAS INCONSOLABLE. He wept, and then he drank. He used my car to take Maggie home from the hospital. Mama walked over to their house every day to wash and iron the clothes, get the three oldest children off to school, babysit the toddler, cook meals, and nurse Maggie. Raleigh, when he wasn't drinking, looked for work. Victim of the economy, like most men in the middle of the richest valley on Earth, he only got day work, for which sometimes he wasn't paid.

In a week, Maggie was gone. Tiny borrowed money from her husband to pay for the hospital and the funeral. Raleigh was thankful, of course, but we all knew it would be a long time before he could repay the loan. Tiny took a train the evening before the funeral, stayed with Betsy and me, and spent the time whispering to me about her husband. I listened, but all the while I was thinking how everything happened at once. I wished this was the end of it.

While times were good, Tiny and Fred lived in a flat on Russian Hill, not far from Chinatown, a glamorous part of the city built up after the Great War when young people swarmed into San Francisco. When Betsy and I took a train and ferry to visit, we stayed in the guest bedroom with a view out toward Angel

Island in the middle of the bay.

It turned out Fred wasn't so rich. For three years he hid from his wife how much he'd lost in the stock market collapse. Tiny wasn't sure where he got the money to help Raleigh, and she said he never spoke an unkind word, but as anyone could have guessed, he'd been drinking his anxiety away and spending time with other women. Tiny was another one who sat down, covered her face, and sobbed into her hands.

She cried, "D'you know how I found out?"

I waited.

"Alta, sweating and shaking when she knocked on the door, told me. I bet she thought he was at the apartment and wanted to ask him for money. For whatever she was taking."

Alta had fallen into a chair, rubbing her arms, grumbling about the fog. She'd claimed she ran into Fred at the saloon where she worked. He'd asked her to dinner, and she wasn't one to let a meal go by, so she went out with him a couple of times. She swore they didn't do anything. She was disgusted with his whining about money.

I asked Tiny if Fred tried to hit her, that being the important part.

"After Alta, I yelled at him and said he'd better not flirt with his brother's wife," Tiny said. "That shook him up. And no, he never hit me."

Tiny walked to my window, gazed at the new leaves on the crowns of the trees, gold in the setting sun, and said the trees at Fred's grandfather's ranch in Redding were probably budding like the ones out the window. Fred's mother had told him to quit the apartment on Russian Hill and move to the ranch he had inherited, well north of Sacramento, to save money. They were moving in a month or so.

"At least, it's far enough away, so it'll be a trek to get to other women," she said, "though he'll still drink."

Tiny snickered.

"And, luckily, I know how to use a rifle up there in the country, wild as Truckee. Remember, last summer I shot a rattlesnake."

I remembered.

Then Tiny said, "And don't worry. I'm not leaving Fred. We do have good times."

Tiny stood and fluffed her curly hair. She wandered from the bookshelf to the buffet.

Her lip trembled, as she said, "Alta's off with another sailor, not Hutchinson anymore, and she still has that rundown apartment. Funny, after she was the one who always wanted to find a nice place."

Tiny fussed with the dishes on the buffet before she admitted she'd given Alta money and told her to stay away from Fred or she'd tell Mama about the drugs.

THE NEXT MORNING we drove to the small Catholic church not far from Mama's house. Maggie's family all lived in Ireland. Along with some of Maggie's friends from her work days, only Tiny, Mama, Raleigh and the children, and I sat through the funeral mass. I never knew why she came all the way to California. Like Mama, I supposed, to find something new.

After the cemetery service, Tiny and I climbed the porch steps, one on each side of Raleigh, pulling him along while he mumbled about Maggie. Mama and his two older children, seven and eight, sat on the couch, one holding the five-year-old, and Mama holding the toddler. The boys wore neat cotton shirts tucked into little boy trousers held up with suspenders. The girls wore smocks with tucks in the bodice. Who knew where Mama found those handsome clothes?

Mama was bone-thin, wearing the brown suit she'd had forever. Except for the gray strands flecked through her dark hair, pulled back in a bun, she looked like she'd never left Harrigan's Hill.

The children smiled at their father when he reached the front room. Raleigh took the littlest one and sat her on his lap in a chair next to Mama. He was boy-like at that moment, with his red hair flopping forward and his cheeks bright from the cool April air. Only his eyes were red and puffy, from crying or drinking, we weren't sure.

Though the rest of the house was dark and bare, with a sleeping space up in the attic like the house on Harrigan's Hill, Mama had gathered more furniture for this room. It had a homey feel with a sofa and armchairs and an ancient piano. Raleigh's oldest girl, Rosalyn, sat down and played "Twinkle, Twinkle Little Star." Then her brother Frankie said to play "Sacramento," the song about gold on the Sacramento River. The tune Mama used to sing to cheer herself up, and it seemed to carry away the woe.

Tiny and I went into the kitchen, large like the one in the boardinghouse in Truckee, to bring out some food to set on the dining table. Now, of course, this kitchen had an icebox and a water faucet in the sink.

The doors were open from back to front. It was obvious children had been chasing each other, down the front porch steps, around the side of the house, and back into the kitchen, then through the front room and out the door, like we did at our house when we were little, laughing and shouting the entire time. All at once, a breeze wafted through the doors and sunlight reached into the room from the large window over the sink. Both Tiny and I lifted our heads to breathe in the earthy April smell, the air brushing against our cheeks.

I looked out the window over the sink to the huge fig tree beginning to show hard, small, green ovals. Come summer, neighborhood children would pull a plump oval off a branch, split the purple skin open, and eat the soft flesh right on the spot. I turned to see the olive tree branches out the front door and the fields beyond the road still green and shimmering in the sun.

Then Mama's voice in the front room floated above the *caw-caw* of crows inspecting the garden. Mama told Raleigh she would keep the children at her house until he found another job and a new place to live. Tiny and I looked at each other and sat down at the kitchen table. What did this mean? Mama loved small children. Maybe she wanted another family. That was Tiny's thought. I was certain Mama felt sorry for her only boy. He seemed so lost.

When we carried in the food, she spread her palms out and said, " *'To every thing there is a season, and a time to every purpose under the heaven,'* Ecclesiastes."

I remembered that verse and the others that followed, not all so hopeful. A week later, along with thousands of poor families who streamed into California, and who were talked about on the radio all the time, Raleigh left to find work on the surviving ranches north of Sacramento. He sent money, which was more than Betsy's father was able to do.

I drove home to take care of my own child who needed her supper. That's how we found a way to keep going, like we did when the sorrow was on us after baby Florence died.

14

September-December 1910
Harrigan's Hill, Truckee

RALEIGH STOOD AT the door, shoving pennies into his pocket. Alta appeared, reciting the names of books to buy for school, although Mrs. Goode knew what any student needed. Mary and Tiny had already sorted the books to pass on to the next youngest.

"I wish Mrs. Goode had something new in her store besides boring slate pencils," said Tiny, the last one out.

Looking down the hill to Front Street, where they had not set foot for six weeks, Mary said, "After buying school things, let's go find Florence."

Mrs. Goode stood silently behind the counter, and the four children didn't chatter and shove each other aside while inspecting the displays. Mary examined a lead pencil. Raleigh put down a small knife. Tiny poked among the pens and nibs. Alta accepted the books she needed and four slate pencils, while her brother spread out the coins to pay.

"You needn't pay for the pencils. I know how poorly you feel," said Mrs. Goode, pushing coins back and patting Raleigh's hand.

They hurried down the street toward the last houses in town, ducked into the cemetery, and wandered until they found the baby's grave. Tiny had picked some wildflowers, but old flowers wilted there already.

"I bet Mama comes here sometimes," said Tiny.

"Maybe Aunt Ola comes," said Mary.

"Maybe Papa," said Raleigh. "He loved Florence too."

After the funeral, Mama had worked frantically, cleaning the house, searching the fields for wild onions and parsnips, finding old jars for wild plums so they would have food during the winter. Frowning and edgy with her children, the siblings stayed out of sight.

"I know when Mama goes to the cemetery," said Alta. "After she's snapped at us."

"Oh, and then she picks flowers. I've seen her," said Tiny.

"And arranges them on the grave. She looks calmer when she gets back," said Alta.

Not only Mary, the other three also wanted school to begin, a relief from the summer sadness. Tiny wore the hat she had taken from Alta. Mary put on the new dress made with calico bought after the Fourth of July, and they had all bathed even though it was a lot of trouble bringing up the water from the pump to heat on the stove and pour into the tub. Raleigh had to be rounded up, avoiding the tub most of the summer. As Mama scrubbed, she told him school was a new beginning, so he might as well start off clean.

Just as the bell rang, Alta sauntered onto the school playground from the opposite direction of their house, waving to her friends.

"Still trying to pretend we don't live on the hill," Tiny declared.

Mary shrugged, but the more she thought, the more shaken she became. No doubt, Alta would become more trouble in spite of her sad words at the cemetery. Mama would expect Mary to keep Alta in sight and watch out for Tiny and Raleigh. Alta was giving her a headache before the first day of school even started.

OAK LEAVES WITHERED, days shortened and cooled. No one caught a cold. No one complained of skimpy food. No one squabbled, which took effort in the rooms they occupied. Near Thanksgiving, a small event buoyed them up.

Mary placed the iron kettle on the stovetop just as Raleigh walked in. He said he wanted to recite at the school program, the poem Mama wrote about pumpkin pie.

"Teacher said I have to wear a suit."

"Suits don't grow on trees, Raleigh," replied Mama, sipping her tea. "Let me think."

By the next evening, Mr. and Mrs. Faye had agreed to let her clean the guest rooms above the saloon. The butcher agreed to let her clean house and cook Sunday dinner.

"You know," she said, "he's never married and needs help. So, if we're careful, we'll have enough food, and I can make Raleigh a suit."

Mary thought Raleigh looked like the boy in *Little Lord Fauntleroy*, white shirt with a high collar spread out over the lapels of the brown jacket, knee breeches with metal buttons, high socks, and shiny brown shoes. Mama coached him to use gestures while speaking and to pause at the proper moments just like she had practiced with Tiny.

On the chairs at the school meeting room, Mary leaned forward and looked at Mama, no frown between her eyes or tightness to her lips, and at her sisters, patient in their seats, like a regular family. Raleigh stood at the front of the school stage, pink-faced, short legs stiff and spread apart, and began, " 'Thanksgiving Pumpkin Pie' by Amanda Miller Edwards."

HE JINGLED COINS in his pocket when the rhyme said the English boy was going to New York with money he'd saved. He rubbed his stomach reciting how the boy roamed New York until he was too hungry to walk further and stopped to eat. Then he reached the part of the rhyme Mary liked best no matter how many times she had heard it.

> *So he ordered a turkey and pie at once,*
> *And when they brought it, he quickly said,*
> *"Why that pie's not big enough,*
> *I want one for all the pies I've missed."*

Raleigh made a big circle with his arms and opened his eyes wide. He recited how the huge pie was made and pretended to eat, while smiles spread on the audience's faces.

> *'Til the market man heard him say,*
> *"I guess the turkey will have to wait . . . ,*

holding his stomach, he paused,

> *"for another Thanksgiving Day!"*

He bowed and grinned when his head came up, the audience clapping and calling "bravo." For days, people on the street asked him to repeat the poem and gave him a penny or sometimes a nickel.

"I'm a lucky fellow," he said, grinning when he gave Mama a penny.

"Thank you, sir," she said.

AS CHRISTMAS APPROACHED, Mama changed again, working so hard she didn't have time for Tiny, who had perfected cartwheels, or Raleigh, who brought up water without being told. She'd stop sewing and stare out the window, like she saw something hidden to her children. Mary thought Mama had withstood the grief over the baby's death. Now it seemed wretchedness had returned.

Most agitating was the day Alta stepped into the attic, hands on her hips, and said, "Mama's awfully thin."

Searching through a box of clothes, Mary flapped one of Papa's old sweaters up and down to get rid of the dust and pulled it on.

"I just went into the bedroom," Alta said, "looking for a hair ribbon to wear to Sally's Christmas party. Mama was changing, so I waited, and her bones were showing. I said we'd better go back with Papa. She put an arm in each sleeve, pulled down that brown dress, and stared, so I left."

Mary smoothed the sweater, and then they heard Aunt Ola's voice calling "Dolly, you here?" Puzzled over why Ola showed up, they hurried to the front room and flopped onto the bed.

"Dolly, you seem peaked this afternoon," said Ola, "but, it's all right, I won't stay long. I'm inviting you and the children to Mr. James' house for Christmas dinner. It was his idea to have a party, as it's been a long time since they've had a gay feast, as he called it."

Mama coughed, hard like the crow's caw.

"Dolly, let me help you. I thought you would enjoy this party since things have hardly been easy since you moved up here."

Deep, raspy breath and coughing led to footsteps shuffling in the bedroom.

Mama burst out, "Ola, don't try to persuade me about Tom. He's beyond redemption. Even if Tom did come when the children had scarlet fever, I won't live with him again."

"You're trembling, Dolly. Please, please sit down. I didn't come to persuade you."

Mama raised her voice, "I know Alta's been talking to you, hasn't she? Wanting to go back with their father."

She coughed again, a deeper, gagging sound, then shouted, "It was his fault she died. If he hadn't been drinking and carousing, we'd be together in a proper house, and I could have sent Florence to a nurse. She'd never have gotten sick!"

Mama sneezed and wept. Mary tiptoed to the bedroom door to see Ola holding her shoulders, while Mama's hands clutched her chest.

"Dolly, please, you're overcome. Lie down. Lie down," murmured Ola.

Mama's hands fluttered before her face, and Ola gave her a handkerchief to blow her nose. Alta peeked in.

"Now you know what I think," Mama said. "So don't tell me we should go back, Alta," and she fumbled in the dressing table drawer and pulled out a purple grosgrain.

"You'll find out, Alta," she called. "Here. This ribbon goes with your eyes."

Mama shook the ribbon at her, and Alta took it.

She felt behind herself for the bed and lay down to catch her breath.

Ola whispered, "I'm so sorry, Dolly."

She pulled a blanket over Mama and smoothed her hair.

"It's all right," Ola said and tiptoed from the room.

"You must remind her about Christmas dinner. She's worn herself out. We'll have to think of something."

Aunt Ola's lip trembled. Her eyes stared at one bare wall and then the other as if an answer might appear.

"Aunt Ola, it's true. I told Alta," said Mary. "Papa was trying to pay back for what he did when he came to see the baby, but it was too late. I hope he doesn't come back."

Alta stared at the ribbon in her hand and said, "Yes, well, look at us … ."

She put the ribbon in her hair, searched for her coat, and left for the party at Sally Faye's house. By the next afternoon Mama was truly sick with a cold.

TRAIPSING UP THE hill and along the ridge, Mary lugged the ax used to chop wood. The flat gray Sierra sky assured her Truckee was between storms that had raged all month. Raleigh and Tiny rushed ahead, their breath turning into little clouds of vapor. The snow had hardened, so high top shoes didn't fill with icy globs as they stomped along. Reaching the ridge top, they were hot, with red cheeks, and sweat at their hairline.

Raleigh and Tiny unbuttoned their coats and flapped the front while they scouted for a short, sturdy Douglas fir, needles sticking out neatly on branches, just enough space between each for ornaments. The tree was hidden between a row of tall firs from which snow slipped off the branches, separating into flakes as it fell and sparkling from the slit of sun shining through the overcast.

Alta laughed, snow on her hair, while she held the trunk and supervised the chopping. With Raleigh and Tiny gripping the trunk in front, and Mary and Alta holding on in the back, they hauled the fir back to the house without knocking every needle off before it reached the front room.

The fir was propped up, the six remaining glass ornaments Mama had brought from her home in Missouri perfectly displayed. Tiny draped strings of popcorn and Alta found the candle clips, so they counted their coins and bought twelve candles. Slipped into the holders on the candle clips, ready to light on Christmas Eve, they smiled in admiration at their attempt to decorate.

GAUNT AND BEDRAGGLED, Mama called Mary into her room and counted six dollar bills.

She pulled her sweater close and said, "You must take Raleigh and Tiny to get ice skates. I've been saving since last Christmas. It's their present, and I hope you'll teach them how to skate, as I'm too tired and your father isn't here."

Papa had bought skates for Alta and Mary two years before. They didn't skate at the Ice Palace near the toboggan run, built for the winter tourists. He had taken them to one of the ponds that froze quickly in the far meadow, deep enough to harvest ice, with ice cutters relegated to the far side and townspeople skating at the near end.

Alta, a natural, skated off gracefully, *scoot, scut, scoot, scut,* Papa grinning as she raced around the pond. Timid, Mary needed a lot of advice before she pushed off and glided smoothly. Papa had been patient and held on around her waist, so her ankles wouldn't hurt.

For a moment, tears were brimming, as Mary remembered how kind Papa had been then and how much she distrusted him now, but she pocketed the money since she was older and knew how to teach her brother and sister to skate.

COATS BUTTONED TIGHT, socks pulled high, Mary said, "You get ice skates because you're big enough now to skate on the pond."

Tiny said, "You know what this means, don't you, Raleigh?"

More interested in kicking snow-covered tree roots to watch the powder puff up in a spray of white, Raleigh shrugged.

"It means," she paused, "... there isn't any Santa Claus."

"How d'you know?" he said, blue eyes opened with the same look of amazement he used at the train station.

Tiny faced Raleigh, placed her fists on her hips, and said, "Why would Mama give the money to Mary and tell us to go buy ice skates? If there's a Santa Claus, ... he'd bring them, of course."

"Oh," he answered, head up as if the wind blowing from the hills whispered confirmation.

Raleigh scuffled behind until they reached Mrs. Goode's store. They didn't buy expensive, leather boot ice skates, but skates like Mary's with clamps between, with which to fit a shoe and tighten with a key. They had leather straps to buckle across the toes and over the instep. By the time Mary had paid for the skates Raleigh was full of energy again and determined to try skating immediately.

Mary, Tiny, and Raleigh set off to the ice pond, and he said, "I'm not a baby like Amanda. I know there isn't a Santa Claus."

"*Huh!*" snorted Tiny.

AFTER WADING THROUGH slushy snow, the three children brushed off a log and sat while fastening the ice skates. A sunny day, the pine trees on the far side of the pond stood out sharply against the bright blue sky, and they breathed the scented air fresh on their faces, warm enough to take off their mittens, making it easier to tighten the clamps. Putting one child at each side, Mary slowly skated off along the edge of the pond. Tiny and Raleigh, sturdy little bodies and strong legs, skates singing, *scoot, scut, scoot, scut,* pushed and glided, not falling once.

They didn't pay attention to steps slogging along the edge of the pond until Alta called out, "It's a lucky day. I saw Papa at the trainmaster's. He said I looked fine and healthy."

To Mary's eyes, she and her brother and sisters looked raggedy, always tired, doing for themselves because Mama was working and worrying so much. Why was Papa saying these things?

"He's received some money from his cousin who died. He wondered if I could talk Mama into moving back together. How about it?"

Tiny said, "Suits me. I want to move back to the big house."

"Sure we'll ask," said Raleigh.

Mary guessed Raleigh was overwhelmed by all the girls telling him what to do and would be happy to have Papa around.

"He also offered to take all of us for a ride on the toboggan run by the Ice Palace tomorrow afternoon," said Alta.

Mary's suspicions were overcome by her desire to try the toboggan again, though she knew for sure Mama wouldn't approve of spending money on such tomfoolery. Mary agreed with Raleigh and Tiny to meet their father at the Ice Palace the next day. Still, they wouldn't all live together again, not if she could help it.

CHRISTMAS EVE MORNING, Mama sent Mary to see Aunt Ola about dessert for dinner the next day. All four children were expecting wonderful food because, in their eyes, Mr. James was rich.

Opening the door, Mr. James's son, Jack, put his finger to his lips, beckoned with his hand to follow, and the two of them peeked through the crack into the front parlor to hear Aunt Ola mumble.

Then Papa remonstrated, "But Ola, I said I was sorry. I wasn't thinking then. I've been a good Methodist for five months. Hardly a drink. Not one look at another woman. I've saved as much money as I can. I even have money from my cousin that passed, and I haven't spent a penny of it. I want to go back to my children. All I'm asking is you put in a good word for me with Dolly."

"I don't think she'd listen to me even if I agreed to talk to her, Tom. She's still very angry," whispered Ola. "She blames you for the baby's death, you know. And you lied to me. You have to ask her, not me."

Papa paced back and forth.

Ola said, "Stop, Tom. It makes me dizzy watching you go in circles."

"What'm I going to do?" said Papa, his voice rising. "I hate living at the hotel. I don't have enough money for the children because of the hotel bill. But she won't believe me, I know that."

"You'll have to figure out what to say, Tom. I'm not a smart woman, but I do know it's up to you, not me," Ola said.

For confidence, Mary grasped Jack's hand and walked into the room, dragging him along. Papa was leaning against the wall, tapping his foot in agitation, looking out the window at the roofs of the buildings on Front Street.

"Hello, Aunt Ola," said Mary, hoping her face appeared innocent. "Jack just let me in. Mama wants to know what we should bring for dinner tomorrow. She said she's saved apples and can make a pie, but she'll need sugar. It's so expensive."

She turned and said, "Hello, Papa."

Papa squinted, staring without blinking. Mary, unwilling to let him know she had heard the conversation, kept up what she hoped was her innocent look, eyes wide, legs spread apart, hand clutching Jack's.

Instead of answering, Aunt Ola said, "Tom, I'm trying to be a kind and forgiving woman, and since you're part of the family, I'm inviting you to Christmas dinner tomorrow. One o'clock. Maybe you can speak with Dolly then."

To Mary she said, "Let's get sugar from the pantry. I'd love to have your mother's apple pie. Wouldn't you, Tom?"

She waited for Papa to nod. His eyebrows were raised in surprise, but he did tip his head.

"Jack, can you show Mr. Edwards the door while I take Mary to get the sugar?"

Papa said, "I'll see you this afternoon at the toboggan run, Mary. Tell Raleigh and your sisters to be on time."

"Yes, Papa," said Mary, keeping in mind she wanted a toboggan ride, no matter what she didn't want.

After wrapping the sugar in a brown paper package, Ola sat Mary on a chair and said, "You'll have to tell your mother I invited your father to dinner. You say

I felt sorry for him and thought he'd like to have dinner with his children. And that's the only reason."

"Yes, ma'am," said Mary who felt like she was being asked to memorize a psalm for Sunday school.

She walked home slowly, looking down to save herself from sliding on the ice. A voice rose in her head advising her to tell Mama right now she didn't want Papa to come back. That Papa would start to drink no matter what he said, but her shoe slipped and she flinched, thinking no, she would just repeat Aunt Ola's message. The voice persisted, saying "here's your chance."

Mary placed the package of sugar on the table and hunched her shoulders to prepare herself, waiting for Mama to put down Tiny's only dress with the torn waist seam.

Arms at her sides, feet together, Mary said, "Hello, Mama. Aunt Ola gave me plenty of sugar and asked me to give you a message."

Eyes on the sewing, Mama said, "Well?"

The message recited, Mama sat quietly. Mary stared at the walls, comparing them to the warm house full of furniture and knickknacks where Aunt Ola lived. She didn't care, she said to herself, she'd still rather be in their little old place than back in a big house, everyone arguing and accusing each other.

"Mama, Papa wants us to move back together, but I don't want to. He said he wasn't, but what if he begins to drink again?" said Mary.

Mama took another stitch and then dropped the dress to her lap.

"Yes, I know. Still we'll go to dinner tomorrow and be kind and polite. I'm grateful Mr. James is willing to invite us over."

MARY PASSED THE Ice Palace on the way to the toboggan run. As she peeked in, one of the winter tourists commented on the spectacular castle, not knowing it was chicken wire, sprayed with water that froze into icicles. Mary loved the beautiful outfits, she hummed the tunes played by fur-clad musicians, she watched the arc lamps create a shimmer on the ice track. Still she had her own ice skating pond and felt lucky, really yearning for rides on the toboggan, not fancy but definitely more exciting and scary.

The entrance to the toboggan run stood next to the Ice Palace, where Raleigh, Tiny, and Mary stomped their feet and wiggled to keep warm. Alta moved in a long oval, out of line and back to their place, craning her neck to catch sight of Papa.

He showed up from the direction of the Whitney Hotel, not the saloon, which, Mary and Alta agreed, was a good sign Papa was sober. While they waited and climbed the wooden stairs to the shed at the top of the run, Papa smiled and patted their heads, all except Mary who stood back diffident and on guard no matter how often he grinned.

Papa's pals, working at the top, helped arrange them, so they had good weight distribution on the toboggan. Squeezing her eyes shut, screaming all the way down, Mary scrambled off the toboggan at the end, convinced she would live, and ran with the others to get back in line for another turn.

Papa disappeared while they waited. On the lookout for any backsliding, Alta shook Mary's arm, as he walked away from the Last Chance, obvious he hadn't been inside long enough to do more than down a quick one.

After the second breathtaking ride, Papa again urged the four of them to talk to their mother. He said he would see them on Christmas at Aunt Ola's. Crossing the bridge, Alta began to boss them, decreeing once more they'd better persuade Mama to move back with Papa or they'd always live in that ugly house. Mary remembered her worry way back on the first day of school, but stumbling on a rock, it popped into Mary's head that her sister, in truth, had not been in one single scrape since school began. Mary refused to let Alta start now.

"I'm not going to say that. I already told Mama I don't want Papa to move back with us."

"Are you as simple as Aunt Ola?" hissed Alta, her fingers balling into fists. "Or as crazy as Mrs. Harrigan?"

Mary didn't move, though Raleigh and Tiny had backed away, giving Mary room to retreat in front of Alta's outrage.

"You know as well as I do, Aunt Ola isn't as scattered as she likes to pretend," said Mary. "Mrs. Harrigan isn't so crazy either. And we can count on Mama to stay with us and not get drunk and wander off."

Tiny spoke up, "That's not true all the time, is it Raleigh? Mama left us in Sacramento, didn't she? And she went off to nurse that lady when she got mad at Papa."

"Yes, but Papa did bad things and ... and ..." said Mary.

"You'd just better keep your two cents to yourself this evening. We're going to get Mama to change her mind," said Alta.

After a pause, everyone waiting for someone to speak, Mary added, "Mama said we need to be polite and grateful at Christmas dinner tomorrow, so I say you'd better start now and not talk to her like you're talking to me."

"Of course, Miss Good Girl," said Alta while she glared at Raleigh, staring into the sky, and at Tiny, fidgeting, to make sure they agreed with her.

That evening Mama lit the candles on the Douglas fir, and the flames delivered a flickering gleam against the antique ornaments. She gave Mary and Alta long wool stockings with wild stripes, which must have been knitted by Crazy Lady Harrigan. They had warm milk and shortbread left over from the grocer's cookie bin along with two penny candies each. Then Mary remained silent and sucked on a penny candy. Alta must have gathered enough good sense to calm down when she and Raleigh and Tiny did their best to convince Mama.

SITTING ON THE sofa and talking with Jack, Mary and Alta imitated the illustrations of demure young ladies in magazines at Mrs. Goode's store. Elizabeth sat primly while Tiny sprawled back on the smaller sofa's cushions and Raleigh swung his legs. Amanda ran between the two sofas, chattering and laughing. Jack and Raleigh received new yo-yos, and the girls received lead pencils, much to Mary's delight. All was affection and cheer, just as Mama had hoped.

Dressed in his one good suit, which his family knew he preserved carefully, Papa arrived as everyone was drifting toward the dinner table. He had a touch of whiskey on his breath, but his voice was charming and congenial. Mama let him hug her while he asked how she was feeling after her bad cold. Though thin, Mama wore her good brown suit, giving her face a warm glow. She had pinned her hair into a Gibson Girl style. No longer puffy-eyed, she looked pretty.

Mary claimed she had nothing to do with how things turned out at the very end of a satisfying afternoon, and Alta, who always wanted her way, had more to do with the trouble than anyone. Alta, in turn, blamed Mary for trying to hurry Mama out of the house. Raleigh, especially, and Tiny moped for a week afterwards.

The apple pie finished, Aunt Ola, Mama, and seven children trooped into the front parlor to play cards like they used to do when Aunt Ola first arrived in Truckee. Papa and Mr. James stayed at the dining table to have whiskey and a holiday cigar. Mary was sure everyone had counted the number of times Papa excused himself from the table, and they ignored what was happening. At any rate, the flask in his coat pocket made Papa jovial and loquacious that afternoon, not feisty or sharp-tongued. Papa must need a few shots of confidence, Mary sighed.

Aunt Ola proposed Snip, Snap, Snore 'Em, an old-time game with a chance to win the pot. Guests and hosts shouted and smacked cards onto the table, but Mary watched the clock, hoping Mr. James would keep chatting about his business.

Finally, when she thought Papa was probably incoherent, she leaned over toward Mama who, just then, stood, stretched, looked out the large parlor window at the dark clouds, and said, "It's getting late and looks like snow."

Mary answered, "I think we'd better hurry before it starts," and walked toward the front hall.

"But Mama," Alta remonstrated, "remember Papa has something to tell you. I know he does. I'm going to find him."

Aunt Ola said, "Wait, Alta. Mr. James doesn't like to be interrupted."

Lips pressed in a defiant grimace, Alta kept moving to the dining room.

She called out, "Papa, we have to go now. Don't you have something to tell Mama? You know, about your cousin's money."

Alta held onto Papa, lurching, mumbling, "Thanks for the cigar" to Mr. James, and shoved him into the study. Pulling Mama's hand, she pushed her into the room also.

From the front window, Mary watched the trees and thought about rushing through the cold air before it snowed. She already felt the temperature dropping every minute the wind blew, entire branches swaying with the gusts, and freezing air pressing against them, as they set off down McGlashan's Hill.

She hoped snowflakes wouldn't fly into their faces, making it hard to catch a breath until they came to the small bridge cutting across the river to Harrigan's Hill. The wind would blow up under their skirts and coats on the bridge, fun in a summer rain, but not when an icy spray whooshed up between their legs.

Tiny and Raleigh wandered into the hallway lit by electric lamps. Aunt Ola helped collect coats and caps, shushing them at the same time, so she could hear the voices. Mr. James frowned when the murmurs behind the closed door turned to shouts.

Papa railed, "My God, Dolly, I've tried to change. Like I told Ola, I've been a good Methodist for five entire months. This is the one and only time I've had too much."

A *clip, clip* of footsteps came toward the door.

Mama said, "That's the trouble, Tom. You can't keep yourself together. You think everyone's going to forgive you. I thank you for the money, which we can certainly use, but we're not so poor we can't get along."

Heavy shoes stomped around the room and up to the door. Everyone in the hall stepped back.

Aunt Ola reached for the doorknob, but it swung open when Papa charged through and called back, "You're hard, Dolly. You're a hard woman."

Face filled with tears and disbelief, Papa staggered as he pulled his coat off the hook and struggled to put it on. His children watched silently, Alta angry, Raleigh with his shoulders slumped, Tiny wide-eyed, and Mary torn between relief and sorrow at the unending battle. He stopped to hug each child, including Mary who had no time to withdraw, and flung himself out the door.

At that point, Mama appeared at the study doorway, hair disheveled as if she had pressed her hands against her head to muffle the shouting. Mr. James helped her, now shaking, with her coat. Mama said she was sorry Mr. James and his children had to hear the argument. No one had a word to answer, so the family left and walked quickly through the icy wind in the twilight, down one hill and up the other.

Mama went straight to bed and curled up under the blankets. The four children slept together head to toe on the bed in the front room, since the attic was too cold and snowflakes blew in through the roof.

Mary, defending herself again, whispered, "I know what Mama wants, and she's right. He won't change."

Alta shot back, "You're wrong. You'll see. Remember what Mrs. Harrigan told Mama."

"This is different," said Mary. "And I'm not afraid of him anymore. I know how to stay away."

Alta began to cry softly. As the clouds separated, a dim light from the waning moon glimmered in the room, enough so on her side, palm holding her head, Mary saw Tiny bite her lip to keep the tears back.

Raleigh whispered, "I wanted to move back with Papa. You need to stop, Mary."

"He never twisted your arm until you thought it was breaking, Raleigh," said Mary. "One day, you'll find out. Just be careful."

The next morning, Mama, lucid enough to think about her children, sent Tiny and Mary to ask Crazy Lady Harrigan if they could take eggs from the nests. Mama often said Mrs. Harrigan may have been losing her mind, but she was a generous woman.

After Mrs. Harrigan saw their sad faces and wheedled the story out of them, she didn't laugh.

Instead, she held their hands and said, "Holidays make good things better and bad things worse."

That didn't sound crazy to Mary. Mrs. Harrigan gave them a half-dozen eggs.

MARY SAID, "MRS. Harrigan just did odd things. I never forgot what she told us."

"Tell what happened next," said Lane. "I thought my great-great-grandfather would save you."

15

MAMA RECOVERED FROM her relapse while blizzard upon blizzard rolled over the mountains, burying Truckee in snow for the new year. One afternoon, between storms, unable to open the kitchen door, Raleigh lifted the bedroom window sash, pushed snow away, and all four climbed out. They floundered to the barn in time to hear a terrific crack, and from the opening at the far side saw an explosion of white snow burst off the far ridge and fly through the air, forming its own cloud until it crashed to the valley floor. Even Molly and the Jersey lifted their heads and snorted.

"Sure **enough**. An avalanche," said Raleigh, snuffling and wiping his nose with a rag.

They struggled back into the house to describe the stupendous uproar, but instead of wonder, Mama held the kerosene lamp to her son's face. For days she fed Raleigh tea with honey to soothe his throat. She shoved wood in the stove to dry the wet clothes when Alta slipped in the snow, dropped the water bucket, and rolled down the hill to the pump. After that, Alta refused to trudge down, and instead, she filled the bucket with snow by the kitchen door. When Tiny complained about freezing, Mama cleaned the crumbling fireplace to increase the heat from the burning wood. Though no longer feverish, Mama declared she felt sick at heart something awful would happen to another child in the icy, dreary weather. The dead cousin's money was soon used up, thirteen dollars and fifty-nine cents as it turned out, and Mama ended each week counting out the coins she had left and clicking her tongue against the roof of her mouth.

But not until the middle of January did the children understand exactly how poor they had become. Mama counted out five pennies and told Mary to ask for old bread at the bakery, so they could have breakfast. Raleigh begged to go with her, and they slogged down the hill during a break in the snowfall. They crossed the bridge and stopped at the top of Front Street to catch their breath.

A tall, heavy man in a beaver coat picked his way down McGlashan's Hill, poking the snow with his cane as he took a step. They saw the cowhide boots, the leather gloves, and the fur hat pulled down over the ears of none other than Mr. McGlashan himself, one of the richest men in town, who wrote books and articles for California's newspapers. Raleigh and Mary knew him, the man famous at their school for his speeches about the treacherous Sierra.

He also stopped to catch his breath in the frozen, white world.

Voice gruff, he said, "Where are you going so early?"

Raleigh piped up, "To get bread."

"That so? I'm out to take a walk after the blizzard. The stove makes the house stuffy and full of smoke. The papers say these are the worst storms in twenty years. What do you think of that? But, everyone should get out, even in this cold."

Mr. McGlashan stopped talking and looked them over.

Then he dug into the beaver coat pocket and said, "Here. Here's a quarter. Buy some doughnuts to eat for breakfast and save the bread for dinner."

Mr. McGlashan walked off down toward River Street, lifting his gloved hand as they called thank you to his back. Mary reached for Raleigh's arm to pull him along toward the bakery. He held a glove over his nose, blue from the cold. His teeth chattered and he stamped his wet boots to keep the blood moving in his feet. He wore his sister's shabby wool coat, not that he cared who owned it. Mary looked down at her own faded blue coat with sleeves too short, wiggled her freezing fingers covered by Papa's old gloves, pulled up the heavy wool stockings bunched around her ankles, and stiffened her trembling knees.

Raleigh said, "Mary, you're sucking in your cheeks and they're blue."

"Let's hurry up," she said, "or the doughnuts'll be gone."

Standing in the bakery doorway before returning home, they licked the sugar off every one, their treat for going out in the snow.

After Raleigh recounted the purchase of bread and doughnuts, Mama said, "Oh yes, *he* is like the Good Samaritan. It doesn't matter to him you don't live on his hill. But don't you forget the Lord helps those who help themselves."

ALL FOUR CHILDREN stopped worrying when Mama came home from the saloon one Saturday evening with some extra money, saying Mr. and Mrs. Faye had given her a raise. Thank goodness, thought Mary, since Mama had fallen asleep in the rocker after wrapping herself in every extra quilt to keep the chill off. Her face was scrawny, as Alta said, a word she used a lot about each of them.

Then in February, the two oldest stopped thinking Mama was skinny. All because coat wrapped tightly, collar pulled over her ears, Mary had stood in the middle of the school yard and saw Georgie, Mr. Vaughn's son, bully her brother.

Raleigh and Georgie were playing Smack Hands, one player holding out his hand and pulling it away before the other can slap it.

Raleigh put out his hand, but Georgie grabbed the wrist and then smacked it. "Surprise," he laughed, lip curled in a smirk.

Rubbing his hand, red-faced and frowning, Raleigh turned and caught Mary's eye. The principal wasn't around so Mary stalked up to Georgie, as he commanded Mr. Faye's son, Zack, to play.

Mary said, "Hey, you can't do that," and smacked Georgie hard, turning his palm bright red.

Bewildered, Zack looked from one to the other. Raleigh hooted and pointed, jeering "Georgie-Porgie, pudding and pie." Mary told Mr. Faye's son to go play with kids his own age and walked off across the yard to take cover in the group of friends around Alta. After school, Zack ran out from where he was hiding behind the building and walked with them along Front Street because, he said, he was afraid of that bully.

Raleigh and his sisters would have left the boy at the saloon door, but Mama came out and heard the story. Taking Zack's hand, she set off into the saloon, looking for his mother or father, and everyone trailed behind. That's the first time Mary recognized the glow in Mr. Faye's eyes, folding his arms on the saloon bar, leaning forward, his face close to Mama, who appeared unaware of anything but her desire to get the boy justice. Her children arranged themselves in a half circle around Mama, and after describing Zack's plight, Mr. Faye agreed to talk to Mr. Vaughn.

Smiling, Mama, with her children behind her, crossed the bridge and hiked up the hill.

At the end of the line, Alta whispered, "Did you see his eyes? Now what?"

By then with some understanding of adults, Mary pulled at the strand of hair fallen over her face, questioning why Mr. Faye was attracted to Mama. He was married, and she had four children to care for. Yes, now what, she thought, and pushed the hair into her hat.

DESPITE THEIR NEW view of Mama, Mr. Faye faded from their thoughts. In March, Alta was picked to sing in the school show, and Mary had been selected to participate in the recitation contest.

"How're we going to get money for dress material?" Alta fretted. "I don't have any, and I think Raleigh has ten cents."

"Mama still owes money for winter hay for the cow and Molly," said Mary.

Feet stomping and breathing heavy, Tiny leaped over wet places in the path and yelled, "Wait, wait!"

"Oh, bother," said Alta. "I wonder if Tiny has any money."

She paused, then added, "Like as not, even if she does, she won't give it to me. You'll have to ask."

"If you'd stop taking Tiny's things, she might give us some money," said Mary.

Still down by the tree, Tiny called out, "Guess what? I'm going to be in the show because I told the teacher I've been practicing elocution. She thinks I'm as good as Raleigh. But Mama'll need to make an outfit. Hope I have enough money."

Glaring, Alta spread her feet in the path and leaned forward toward Mary.

"Stop being such a goody-goody," she shouted. "If Mama would move back with Papa we'd have a decent place to live where we wouldn't be freezing and hungry all the time. We'd have money to buy material."

Mary shouted back, "You're always saying that. If Papa hadn't been so bad, we'd be together. But he was bad, and I'm glad we're not living with him. Why don't you save your money instead of spending it on candy or ... or ... I don't know what! Mama says we have to help ourselves!"

"But, but," said Tiny, turning her head from one to the other.

The oldest stalked off down the hill. Tiny headed uphill, saying she was going to count out the money she'd saved. Mary looked up to their run-down house and then down and across to McGlashan's Hill with all the big houses. She hurried to Mr. James' where Aunt Ola kept house.

Amanda opened the door, wearing a fine wool dress with ruffles at the bottom of the skirt and inserted at the shoulder seams, which meant Ola must have yards of material left over from some rich lady's outfit. Aunt Ola gave Mary a hug and pulled her into the kitchen for tea.

As she was summoning courage to explain about the show and the outfits, Aunt Ola said, "I'm planning to go visit your mother on Sunday, though I know she's still upset with me much of the time. I know she thinks I'm the baby and have no mind of my own, but I'm going to prove her wrong."

Satisfaction on her face, she said, "Mr. James asked me to marry him. He said I've been kind and helpful to him and the children, and he loves me for it. He said he thinks Amanda is a sweet child, and I really have grown fond of Jack and Elizabeth. I won't be a burden to anyone now, will I?"

Mary tipped her head, amazed at how Aunt Ola relayed the news in such a matter-of-fact way.

"Amanda and I'll have a comfortable home. Isn't it pretty?" she added. "Mr.

James is very generous, so I'll have money. He is older, but he's never had a bad word spoken about him."

Mary knitted her brow, wondering if Aunt Ola loved Mr. James. She hadn't said anything about that.

Aunt Ola tapped Mary's hand and asked, "Why'd you come today, dear?"

Describing the chance to perform, Ola clapped, delighted.

As for the costume predicament, Mary said, "Mama doesn't have enough money. I thought you might have leftover material from dresses you're making ... to give us ... enough for three dresses ... we're not very big. Maybe I could watch Amanda sometimes ... to pay for it?"

"Of course," said Ola. "I've some yellow silk and some blue chambray. Mrs. Faye buys yards more than she needs when she wants a dress made. I'll even make the gowns. Your mother is so busy, I'd love to help since she won't take anything from me most of the time."

CLIMBING THE HILL, Mary told herself when the time came to explain, she'd tell Mama to be content because they were doing what she said, taking care of themselves. Then Mary reached the pine tree and came to a halt, wary because Tiny and Raleigh sat on the flat rock watching her.

"Mama's upset," said Tiny, "because you didn't come home right away."

Mary sat down to think this news over.

The three of them kicked at old pinecones on the ground until Raleigh said, "Alta was smoking a cigarette out behind the school with Georgie, and the principal found them, so he took Alta to Mama at Mr. Titus's grocery. By the time they got here, Mama was crying, and Alta was yelling and then she ran off."

Mary slid off the rock, fuming to herself that Alta had made a mess of her plan to get what they wanted. She suspected the principal had told Alta she couldn't be in the show, and Mama was too weary to persuade Alta to apologize.

Taking the kitchen chair opposite her mother, Mary waited, Mama sitting, which she never did, drinking tea, and waving a handkerchief before her face.

"Now, Mama. Raleigh told me what Alta did," she said. "I don't have to go find her. She'll come home by dark. It's cold."

Mama patted her eyes with the hankie.

"Alta made a bet with Georgie she could smoke a whole cigarette and not get sick. He was going to give her a quarter. She wanted money to buy material for a dress for a show?"

"She didn't have to do that," said Mary. "Aunt Ola said she'd make dresses for all three of us. I asked after school."

Mama waved the handkerchief again.

"I thought you girls wouldn't do things like your father does, drinking and smoking. Evil comes to those who evil do."

"I try to watch out for Alta, Mama. I can't be with her all the time," said Mary.

"You're the good girl, Mary. You have to help. It seems like Alta gets in trouble, no matter what I say."

Mama sighed and dabbed her eyes. In the kitchen twilight, Mary watched the teacup, trying to calm herself, thinking she had a plan and it was all going to bits. Alta would simply have to say she was sorry. Then Mama would be happy again, and Mary would be loved.

Stirring the tea with her old filigree spoon, Mama said, "I would have found some money and been happy to make the gowns. I found the money for Raleigh's suit, didn't I?"

"We've been trying to help ourselves like you said after Mr. McGlashan gave us the quarter," Mary said. "Aunt Ola is trying to pay you back for being bad, isn't she? And even though Alta was being bad, she was trying to do something good, wasn't she?"

Dabbing her eyes again and sipping tea, Mama flicked the handkerchief and shifted her eyes. Mary waited for words to come, but her mother had none to offer.

When the sun disappeared behind the western ridge, Alta came home and hid in the attic. She balked, but by the time they went to bed, Alta agreed to apologize to the principal, knowing it was the only way she would be allowed to participate in the show. Shrugging into her coat over her nightgown and pulling up an old pair of wool stockings, she even promised to tell Mama she would never, ever smoke another cigarette, although Mary knew it was a lie. All night, Mary tossed and rolled, her mind filled with surprise she had taken charge and solved the family's trouble for the moment.

At the show, Aunt Ola and Mama agreed the yellow dress was just right for Alta, and the blue looked good with Tiny's dark red hair. She was a good actress, reciting the Tennyson poem with dramatic action and emotion like Mama had showed her. Then for the finale, not a foot shuffled nor a paper rustled, the audience delighted by Alta's enchanting soprano.

Sweet Adeline, My Adeline,
At night, dear heart, For you I pine;
In all my dreams, Your fair face beams.
You're the flower of my heart, Sweet Adeline.

In April, when Mr. James and Aunt Ola celebrated their wedding, Mama attended in her single spring and summer party frock, pale blue muslin with a fitted bodice and lace at the edge of the sleeves. Raleigh had grown, so his

Thanksgiving suit needed to be altered. Mary and her sisters showed off the dresses made by Ola.

Sitting in the Methodist Church on the corner across from their school, Mama remarked she was going to keep her eye on Mr. James to see how he treated Ola. The minister began the ceremony with the Song of Solomon, words Mary thought were perfect for a wedding.

> *Set me as a seal upon thine heart,*
> *As a seal upon thine arm:*
> *For love is strong as death.*

Mr. James held Aunt Ola's hand and listened to the minister. He turned his head to smile at Aunt Ola and turned back to the minister so many times, Mary felt as nervous as Mr. James must have been.

Finally, the minister pronounced them man and wife. Mr. James gave Aunt Ola a kiss, and Mama whispered, "Thank goodness, I was getting dizzy watching him."

Mr. James had invited a lot of well-to-do families to the reception, including Mr. and Mrs. Tucker, Mr. and Mrs. Titus, and business friends. Several ladies paid their respects to the couple and then sat and whispered to Mama about the suffrage campaign. Mama was happy because Ola had found someone and because of the woman's vote. Intrigue gleamed in her eye every time someone mentioned suffrage.

At one point, Mr. and Mrs. Faye sat down next to Mama. Mrs. Faye said she was happy the voting rights amendment was getting a lot of attention in the newspapers, even the *Truckee Star News.* Then Mrs. Faye stood and walked over to speak with another woman who had beckoned.

Mama turned to Mr. Faye, as he was often mentioned in the newspaper and never had good relations with the publisher, Mr. Vaughn. Gossip was, they rarely talked after he had spoken to the publisher about Georgie. At least that's what Mary assumed was going to be their next topic.

Mr. Faye, though, crossed his legs in his well-creased trousers time and again, pulled a cigar from his pocket until Mama made a fanning movement with her fingers, put it back, folded his hands, and placed them in his lap. All the while he smiled at Mama as she chatted about the newspaper. In fact, same as in the saloon, he didn't take his eyes off Mama's face. Mama's cheeks flushed, she pressed the skirt of her dress, tucked a stray hair into her fluffed chignon, and finally pressed Mr. Faye's arm, excusing herself to stand with her sister.

Rosy-cheeked Ola held court in the pink wedding dress she designed for herself, chatting and laughing and urging guests to eat. Puffy lace sleeves reached the elbow, fitted at her wrists, and a long embroidered silk skirt floated out in the back as she walked and turned, the curved neckline showing off Ola's pretty chest, but not so much as to be immodest. Mr. James seemed satisfied, sitting with a contented smile at the reception, receiving congratulations and best wishes, smoking a cigar, patting his new wife's hand whenever she came around to him.

Mama sat down with her children. She observed that between Mr. James's generosity to them at Christmas and his kindness, Ola would be able to count on him.

"As long as he doesn't expect Ola to use much judgment," said Mama, taking a bite of cake and eating slowly while she studied Mrs. Faye and Mrs. Tucker, holding onto the hands of all the women in the room and whispering in their ears.

Mary and Alta walked over to the table for a second helping of cake and punch and put their heads together.

Alta said, "What is Mama thinking? Aunt Ola's learned to use some judgment if you ask me. Who's got some money and a nice house?"

The truth be told, thought Mary. Did Mama see what was really there?

16

May 1911
Harrigan's Hill, Truckee

SITTING ON THE log pile by the front door, Mary contemplated the wild lilac covering the hills behind the town, turned to the buttercups blooming where it was damp around the pump, and fixed on the shooting star bowing and straightening, as a breeze blew along the edge of the river. She waited for her brother and sisters to finish their chores, and Molly waited to take her first trip out to the far meadow on this last April Saturday.

Drifting to the back garden, Mary watched Mama poke squash seeds into the ground along one row in the small plot and drip tiny carrot seeds in another. Jays swooped down onto the lowest tree branches, jostling for space to be first to peck at the seeds. Mama hummed "Oh Susanna" and then softly sang out,

> *... don't you cry for me,*
> *I'm bound for California*
> *My banjo on my knee.*

Mary hummed along, smiling at the change in lyric to California, while thoughts wandered in and out of her head. It didn't seem so long, but Papa had been living at the hotel for eleven months, and she was going to be thirteen a few days away in May. She lifted small hands over her head and stretched her skinny legs, but in her mind she felt adult-like. Why else would she and Alta have noticed Mr. Faye's attention to Mama? Turning fourteen, Alta imitated a womanly way of walking, slightly swinging her hips, trying to be worldly, as Mama said. Now eleven, Tiny was no longer childish, sometimes helping Mama without being told. Even Raleigh, ten in April, sometimes said no to Alta. Florence, their precious baby, was fading into memory without tears filling Mama's eyes.

Raleigh and Tiny, bridle in hand, found Molly up beyond the garden not far from the Jersey, grazing on sweet new grass. Swinging the bag of leftover biscuits and salami, Alta slipped out the door. Still humming, Mary fell in behind, as the party marched off to the bottom of the hill before they counted out to see who would be first to climb onto Molly's back.

ON MAY DAY, nursing shin bruises won in the tug-of-war after the Maypole Dance at school, Tiny and Mary watched a man with bulging muscles and a strong square jaw hike up the hill. The famous Uncle Lauf had arrived.

Tiny yelled to Mama, who reached up to give the fellow a hug and said, "I should know you'd show up without a word. How'd you find us?" Though they all supposed he'd asked, since almost everyone in town knew where they lived.

First thing, Raleigh said, "Uncle Lauf, show me your hand, the one with the fingers sawed off."

"I told them that story," said Mama. "As a warning."

All four children crowded around to look at the strange hand with three short fingers. He said losing his fingers was nothing and told the tale of the time his best pal, Irish Mac, and he joined a lumberjack outfit in the Colorado Rockies. He yelled "Timber!" and paused, tears filling his eyes, before he showed how Mac was squashed by a giant trunk. Tiny put her hand over her mouth when he fell, showing how Mac looked under the tree.

He'd built a sod house on the Colorado plains, but gave it up to make his way to Reno, hoping to stay with Aunt Margaret until he found his next mission. Margaret had suggested he visit Mama, which, after it was all over, Mary thought should have been a clue something was up.

Mama laughed again when her best-loved brother spread it on thick about rounding up mustangs and mining for silver in Nevada, finally calling him a vagabond storyteller from the olden days. Lauf grinned.

Mama said, "What now?"

"Ah, Dolly, 'tis a long story," said Lauf, imitating the dead Irish Mac.

Even Alta giggled as Lauf wiggled his heavy black eyebrows. Mama said it was time for bed, but not before Lauf suggested they say prayers together. Surprise spread over everyone's face, but they posed their hands and listened to Uncle Lauf pray.

THE NEXT NIGHT, at home in the big chair, his face animated, Uncle Lauf said, "Shall I tell you what happened the first time I went to Reno? Lumberjacking was my daily work, but Lady Luck was at my side, and I won money, a lot, at the gambling tables. The next year with the purchase of a cigar and tobacco shop in Reno, I had a lucrative business."

Uncle Lauf rubbed his hands together.

He said, "I made so much money I bought a dandy's wardrobe. I was young and full of myself. The night I laid eyes on the woman who would become my wife, my heart started to pound like an electric current was going through it."

Uncle Lauf patted his heart, though Mary had little experience with electricity and wondered what the current would feel like and how it fit with what she'd read about love.

To Uncle Lauf, Roxane was exquisite with dimples and ruby lips. She tossed her black hair and swished her sapphire blue dress, as she winked and sang to the rowdy crowd. He was caught.

Later Alta and Mary decided he sounded like he'd been reading lady's magazines from the stationery store.

He bought her expensive gifts and took her to the good restaurants and casino shows in Reno. She married him, and then he disclosed his greatest desire … to have a family. He sighed and shook his head.

"She was a temptress and villainess all in one. Two months later, she absconded with the cash from the store and my savings from the bank. She left town with the San Francisco cigar salesman. I was in despair."

Uncle Lauf nodded his head gravely, then looked up to see Mama who had been standing in the doorway for a while, eyeing him.

He added, "There's a lesson here. Be wary of beauty. Of clever words. Of fancy clothes. It will bring trouble. *Man is born unto trouble as the sparks fly upward,* Job 5:7."

Chuckling and pointing to himself, Lauf asked, "Well, Dolly, what d'you think? Who was the troubled fool in that story?"

Mama rubbed her shoulders, then said, "That's enough. Time for bed," but not before they put their palms together and listened to their uncle pray about man being born to trouble.

AT BREAKFAST ON the third day, Uncle Lauf offered to stay around the house to chop wood and clear weeds. Tiny, Raleigh, and Mary rushed home after school, curious to see the baritone singing "Will There Be Any Stars in My Crown?" to the Steller's Jays settled on a pine branch, cocking their black-crested heads and eyeing the large, loud man who straddled the tree stump by the kitchen door. Molly and the Jersey grazed a short way uphill, lifting their heads when Lauf bellowed a new verse, no frown between his eyes, a smile at his mouth, a spark in his blue-gray pupils.

He called out, "D'you know that song? My mother used to sing it all the time.

She was a good person, even if she did take my brother Cyrus's side when he refused to do family prayers."

"Aunt Ola said your Mother wanted you both to stop arguing," said Mary.

"That's how Ola saw it. Cyrus was the baby boy, and they protected him," he said, "like they did Ola."

"Oh. Well, we sing that song at church on Sunday," said Mary.

Looking puzzled, Tiny said, "You're not sad today. Does that song help you forget about Roxane?"

Raleigh picked up pieces of cut wood to put in the pile by the back door and asked, "Have you saved up enough money again from the cigar shop?"

At that moment, Alta slouched around the corner of the house and said, "Who's watching the store in Reno while you're here?"

Uncle Lauf furrowed his thick eyebrows and launched into a speech saying, "This is how it happened … "

They waited.

"I still think of Roxane, but I've learned about forgiveness. One day wandering in the Reno park near the Truckee River, desolation clouding my mind, out of the clear blue sky a prayer came to my lips, entreating the Lord to help me find a better way."

Right then, Mary realized he was giving them a sermon like the revival preacher invited to the church at Easter.

"The next week while strolling down the street, watching the moon and the starlit sky, I heard,

> *I am thinking today of that beautiful land*
> *I shall reach when the sun goeth down … ,*

"a verse to 'Stars in My Crown,' and I was drawn into a mission tent where an elderly gentleman was relaying the age-old message of God's love for the sinner. The power of God swept over me, and I stumbled to the front, fell to my knees, and accepted the Lord as my personal savior," Uncle Lauf said, mimicking the preacher's sing-song voice.

Raleigh and Tiny, mouths opened, stared at Uncle Lauf, falling from the stump to his knees, stretching his arms up over his head, holding out his palms, raising his face to the sky. Uncle Lauf bent his head down to them with eyes radiant, as if he was walking across clouds leading to heaven.

Watching Uncle Lauf's theatrics, Alta's angry mouth changed to an irreverent grin, and she said, "Uncle Lauf, we want to know about the cigar store and the gambling."

Flicking his palms outward and raising his eyes again, he said, "Ah, I've removed myself from gambling and worldly pleasures. I found my way, saved from a life of sin and disillusionment. My new friends helped me enter the ministry."

Mary said, "What kind? Do you have a church in Reno?"

Thick eyebrows tightened in a puzzled clump, Uncle Lauf looked from one to the other of the children. His mouth still smiling and his arms still stretching out with palms held up, he gazed off at the pines and then down again at the children. He didn't seem to be liquored-up like Papa at the way station last May, but he was drunk on some entrancing scene. Finally, recognition appeared in his eyes, and he returned to the yard where they were standing.

"I don't have a church in one place," he said. "I've been all over gathering people to meet, wherever the good Lord has led me."

"Did you save them like you were saved?" asked Mary.

"I don't count, but I've witnessed many people receiving the Lord," he said.

"But you still don't have a new wife. What're you going to do?" asked Tiny.

"I've been called to Seattle to go as a missionary to Japan."

"Japan!" said all four with nearly the same breath.

"I didn't tell you about my vision, did I?" asked Uncle Lauf, and all four shook their heads.

"It happened in Ordway, Colorado, riding my horse in the warm, country air when I sensed a presence and a voice said, 'Will you go to Japan for me?' For a moment I was stunned, but I had promised to offer my life to the Lord, and with tears in my eyes, I said, 'Yes, Lord.'

"I prayed and meditated, and two weeks later a letter came from the home mission asking me if I would go to Japan. Not only that, I sold my horses for one hundred fifty dollars. No obstacle remained. All things work together for those who love the Lord!"

Tiny jumped around, saying she wanted to see Japan.

"Do you? I'd love to have a family with me to help with the mission," said Uncle Lauf.

"What do you do there?" asked Raleigh.

"We'd live like the Japanese live. Maybe one of the women in the mission would help you with your lessons. You'd learn to speak Japanese and help the good people who become Christians learn English. Let's see, and you'd help at the meetings, taking collections and singing. You'd see all the strange buildings and places in Japan. I've heard it's beautiful," said Uncle Lauf, sounding to Mary like he had the list prepared in his head.

Timidity taking over, Mary said Mama would have to agree. They couldn't go by themselves. Then Alta said the idea was much better than trying to get Mama to go back with Papa. None of their friends had ever been to Japan. They'd be famous.

The look of enchantment came over his face again as Uncle Lauf said, "And I will have saved you children from the evils in this world. You'll be doing the work of the Lord."

A potato sack of bread and cheese over her arm, Mama opened the kitchen door. Red flared up from her neck to her cheeks.

"Hello, Dolly," said Lauf. "I've been telling the children about bringing the Lord to the poor Japanese people."

"That's exactly enough, Lauf," said Mama. "They go to services and Sunday School every week. I'm doing my job to make sure they get their religion. They don't need you to help them be received by the Lord."

"Ah, Dolly ... ," Lauf began, but Mama marched up, her forefinger almost touching his nose.

"Lauf, I love you because you used to be my clever, comic brother who went everywhere. But now, if you don't stop preaching and trying to get my children to be your family, I'll send you to Ola's tonight, even though she hasn't been over because you frighten her with your obsession."

Mama stopped and looked at her four children—Mary with an anxious frown from Mama's stern voice, Tiny with her arms folded across her stomach, Raleigh with his feet spread apart and hands behind his back, looking up at the trees, and Alta with a wide smile and daring gleam in her eyes.

"But Mama," Alta said, "we want you to come too. Of course, he'll have to sell the cigar store first, so we have some money to get there. He only has one hundred fifty dollars from selling his horses."

"All right," Mama said, voice rising. "First of all, the stories about logging in the mountains and Roxane happened a long time ago. Before you were born."

"Now tell them the real story," demanded Mama, turning back to Lauf.

Shoulders sagging as this small woman, fists on her hips, glared at him, Uncle Lauf said, "I was sick after Roxane's evil doings and I drank and gambled. I was addicted to morphine from my illness ... "

Mama interrupted, "What else, Lauf."

"Well, it's true I did relax in the opium rooms behind the local saloon after a long day," Lauf confessed.

Then stiffening his back, triumph in his voice, he said, "But remember, the Lord spoke to me and filled my heart. After a few months I sold the cigar store. It was a stumbling block. It was too easy to go to the saloon next door and waste away my life."

"You sold your store?" asked Raleigh, disbelief on his face.

"What'd you do with the money?" demanded Alta.

"I gave some of it to Margaret. I sent some of it to Missouri. The rest I gave to the mission that saved me from damnation," answered Lauf.

At this revelation, Raleigh sat down on the tree stump. The three girls watched Uncle Lauf, cheeks glowing pink, eyes glittering, hair poofing out in a brown halo. Ah, thought Mary, Uncle Lauf wasn't going to carry them off to a better place in this world. Alta turned away and Tiny's smile disappeared.

"The Lord will provide," said Uncle Lauf.

Mary blurted out, "Mama says the Lord helps those who help themselves, don't you Mama?"

Mama stood stiff, arms crossed, lips pulled together.

"The Lord shows me where a job is at hand to pay for food and necessities. Sometimes folks who want to do good give me money, but I only take what I need and give the rest to the mission. That's what we'll do to make our way to Seattle and take the ship to Japan," said Uncle Lauf.

He looked up at the jays still tipping their crests and eyeing him from the branch.

"Our poor feathered friends don't know, but it's another great awakening, Dolly. I've seen it from Chicago to California, thousands of people accepting the way. Now you have the chance to go where we can help other lost souls in this world."

"Yes, yes, yes," said Mama, unable to hold down the fury in her voice. "You may do that, but we're not out of our mind."

Stomping into the house, Mama yelled back, "We're not going."

The children wandered down toward the pump, shuffled into the lumber barn, and hunched over on the piles of boards to think.

Raleigh said, "It'd be something to go off on a ship and have an adventure in Japan, wouldn't it?"

"That's because you're a boy, and boys like to wander around," said Mary. "I think we'd be working harder than we do right here in Truckee. Uncle Lauf didn't tell the truth, did he? With no money, how'd we be able to go anywhere?"

"Why'd he trick us, I wonder?" asked Tiny. "It's too bad. I already know what I would've taken, and I have a whole twenty-seven cents to ask Mrs. Goode to buy a dictionary with Japanese words, so we'd know what to say."

Finally, Alta put in her two bits, saying, "It is too bad because I'd go anywhere to get out of here. Uncle Lauf is a little crazy like Mrs. Harrigan, don't you think?"

"Much crazier," said Mary. "Mrs. Harrigan is usually all right. I don't think Uncle Lauf sees the same world we see."

When they sat down at the little table in the kitchen to eat, Uncle Lauf didn't bring up the Lord once.

EARLY THE NEXT morning, Uncle Lauf and Mama stood outside the kitchen door to say good-bye.

He must have recouped his evangelical spirit during the night because he said, "Ah, Dolly, I ask you to take the Lord into your soul. He'll help you forgive Tom. You'll find consolation for the loss of Florence while she's waiting for you in heaven. He'll show you the way to provide for your children."

At first Mama answered, "I think, Lauf, the Lord is already in my soul, and he's telling me to find a way all by myself."

Then Lauf took her hand like a preacher does when he wants to give strength through his touch.

"The Lord is asking me to help you, Dolly," he said. "If you and the children come with me, I'll care for you as if you were my own true family. You'll be saved by helping all those poor souls in Japan. It'll bring peace to your heart like it does mine."

"Will you stop!" shouted Mama, raising her hand as if to slap him.

"I'm at the limit of my patience, Lauf. You're speaking to me like someone possessed. You think the Lord is telling you what to do, but it's the Devil himself playing you for a troublesome fool. You say there's an awakening, but you're caught up in your own wishful dreams."

Stopping to catch her breath, she then spit out, "Go to Japan! Give your money to the mission. How do you think my four children would get by, wandering around like beggars, all over the earth, asking for bread, so you could save someone in Japan?"

Uncle Lauf, eyes wide in alarm, dropped his carpetbag and tried to take her hand again.

"Lots of missionaries bring their families with them, Dolly. I was thinking of the children. Margaret wouldn't let her boys go. So I thought ... ."

Pulling back, Mama said, "So that's what happened. Leave us alone. That's why you can't find a wife. What kind of woman would straggle from place to place with children in tow so you can be a revival preacher?"

She grabbed the edge of the door frame to steady herself.

He took Mama's arm once more, but she pushed him off and burst out, "It's true. I'd love to have some steady help, but I know I'll have to raise my children myself. Any of our brothers would be more help than a wandering forty-two-year-old sermonizer. Even Ola is more help. She's the lucky one who's found a kind and steady husband."

Uncle Lauf stared at the far-off granite mountain ridges.

Clenching her jaw, Mama said, "I could have kept the boardinghouse if there wasn't a rule women couldn't manage a place without a man on the contract.

If you'd been around, I could have kept the contract. Well, what do you know? Finally, a woman's voting rights are being discussed in the legislature. There might be an election. Did you know that? Then it won't be so easy to make silly rules. I'll be caring for myself."

Uncle Lauf had a look in his eyes as if, Mary believed, he didn't understand how Mama could contradict him.

Then Raleigh handed Uncle Lauf a brown paper package, saying, "You forgot the biscuits and cheese Mama wrapped for you."

In a few seconds, Uncle Lauf's face changed from pathetic, skin almost blue, to peaceful, a smile bringing back the tan color to his cheeks.

Putting his arm around Raleigh's shoulder, he said, "Thank you, nephew. You're a thoughtful boy."

To the girls he said, "Take care of yourselves, nieces. I'll come back someday."

Uncle Lauf picked up his carpetbag and started off down the path.

When he reached the pine tree he waved and called out, "Good-bye now, Dolly. I'll be thinking about what you said. Remember *'man is born unto trouble as the sparks fly upward ...'*."

Mama grabbed hold of the door frame again and whispered, "For the love of God," shooing her children off to school with her other hand.

———⟫•⟨———

"DID YOU GO to Japan?" said Lane. "Did he save you?"

"No, he didn't. And only Tiny went to Japan when she got really rich," said Mary. "Mama was sure in trouble about then."

17

January 1949
Sacramento

SETTLED ON THE sofa, I'd fixed my gaze out the wide window. In this home a year already, I couldn't remember such a bleak January afternoon, low fog in the plum trees, my camellias' pink-tinged blooms awash in mist.

I'd picked up my portfolio of flowers, the book I'd promised myself while riding over the Donner Summit, and opened it to the exquisite drawing of violets. With plenty of time to care for flowers, it was funny that my favorite, clumps of tiny purple-blue blossoms planted along the path to the porch, had spread without any help at all.

Then I'd laid down the book and pulled up the quilt. People might say I'd decided to go back to work because I was lonely on a five-acre ranch, surrounded by brown, unkempt fields, but that wasn't my intent. Until that day I was happier than I'd been in a long time.

The minute I'd separated from Henry, dead now twelve years, I knew I'd have to look after Betsy and myself. She'd been so sick, and then she got better and her life seemed wonderful. She married a college-graduate, a navigator on Army bombers. She had two children like millions of other families after her husband returned from Europe.

Still, loneliness had hit me hard when Betsy started at San Francisco State College just before Pearl Harbor. The only compensation for World War II was with all those men gone to the army, I'd worked overtime, and was not alone in the apartment too often.

How else did I save myself from loneliness? My friends and I passed the evenings watching movies at the Empress Theatre or at clubs around the Sacramento capitol. That's where my girlfriend's husband introduced me to the man I loved the most, and I was happier than I thought possible.

Everything I'd learned disappeared into the thin air of wishful thinking. I knew I wasn't flirty or beautiful like Tiny and Alta, and Mama was no help, an old woman then, who, when Papa died about the same time as Henry, only said a long time had passed.

Although, after she threw Papa out, Mama couldn't believe when Mr. Faye showed interest, probably what enticed her. Not long ago Minna sent a telegram, which said Mr. Faye had died and had asked Minna, his nurse before he passed away, to let Mama know. She sat and held the telegram for quite awhile, but then she smiled and, again, said a long time had passed.

I didn't have that perspective on love. So when Lanford asked me out, I was caught, like Mama said about Papa and old Uncle Lauf said about Roxane.

That first evening at Bedell's, Olivia's husband called over to Lanford. He joined our table, and the four of us talked about Europe and war news for a while, and about worse news of Coral Sea and Guadalcanal, and of news about the internment of Japanese families from Sacramento, all people we knew.

Then I linked arms with Lanford when he offered to take me to the Senator Hotel bar for a nightcap. He shook hands with several men he introduced as Assemblyman So-and-So or Senator La-Di-Dah. A good story to tell Mama— how I met all those men I'd heard of, but never seen, even though I'd worked for the state as long as they had.

Lanford was a handsome dresser, who wore a sharp felt hat, three-piece suits, starched shirts. I wondered how he had money for all those expensive clothes, but he worked for the state government, not the legislature, in one of the departments high up with the bigwigs, as he said. In fact, I think he put my name in to work on the World War II secret project called "Toy Horse," which I've always said was doing my part for the war effort.

Already a supervisor at the state printing office, it was my job to organize the plans for placement of the equipment to print Japanese currency at the state fairgrounds. I took it seriously because the project supported the planned invasion of Japan, mostly all we cared about here in California—although my son-in-law languished at a prisoner of war camp in German-occupied Poland.

None of us were supposed to talk about Toy Horse at the time. Still, Coast Guard men, who stood around protecting the fairgrounds, checking papers, inspecting trucks that unloaded paper and ink, said people who lived nearby knew something was going on.

Olivia counted boxes and boxes of yen. On moving inland, the Marines and the Navy would use the counterfeit currency, knowing there were destitute Japanese willing to take any kind of money. Of course, then the A-bombs exploded, and Toy Horse destroyed the fake money.

As for Lanford, I laughed because, jealous of my Coast Guard men friends, he picked me up in his car at the fairgrounds. Yet, my favorite date was an unbearably hot Saturday when we took a ride out of town along the road by the American River past Folsom where trees provided precious shade. I often wondered how he was able to get fuel, but he said it was easy, he worked for the state. As for that bit of ethics, I was happy to have a companion I loved and unwilling to cause myself trouble.

I set out our picnic on rocks near the riverbank. Lanford didn't even know all those boulders were left over from dredging the bottom of the river for gold, though most of those tailings, thrown up on shore, were long ago home to sweet-smelling grass. We waded at the river edge, low and slow in summer. Four noisy children splashed and tussled, oblivious to the cold water or to us. Lanford leaned over me, and buoyant and content, I talked about trivial things on a dazzling green and gold day, breeze ruffling my skirt and keeping the heat at bay.

Sunday evenings, he came to my apartment for supper. I liked to cook and he was always complimentary. Why not? He ate in restaurants all the time. He made me laugh at gossip about the state government. I shared Betsy's lively letters from San Francisco where she finished college, waiting for her husband. Noisy by day, with anxious sailors waiting to ship out for the Pacific, and quiet by night, shades pulled, street lights covered on top for fear Japanese bombers were heading to San Francisco. He never spoke about his family, except he was born in Maryland. Why didn't I ask? I was foolish with love, ignoring Uncle Lauf's cautionary words about trouble.

Sometimes he stayed at my apartment, and I was glad, lonely even when I had the radio on. What did it matter? I'd already been with a man before I was married, kept my child, separated from her father, all those things one shouldn't have done. Lanford was wonderful. I never guessed I was capable of such feelings especially since the first time Henry asked me to stay I was tipsy and so lonely I cried the entire time. Now I smiled. I'd lived a long time before I felt such waves of warmth and desire to hold someone. When Lanford caressed my body and whispered in my ear, I was overwhelmed with a fever to kiss his face and feel my body against his. Afterwards, it was a pleasure to fit into the curves of his body and slowly fall asleep.

Once or twice a week we went out to a club. Lanford always took my elbow to guide me, rubbing his fingers on the inside crease as we walked, both the most comforting and most loving gesture. He did so the evening we met Olivia and her husband once again at Bedell's.

I didn't want to drink much, tired since I'd already worked a long shift, and I excused myself to find the powder room. Olivia, mouth pursed in concentration, followed. I washed my hands and dried them, found lipstick and spread it on. Olivia watched, opening her mouth and closing it again, so in the mirror I could see her jaw tighten.

I turned and said, "What do you want to tell me, Olivia?"

Maybe her daughter was pregnant. Perhaps her son-in-law was trapped in the Pacific on one of those islands overrun by Japanese.

Instead she blurted out, "Lanford Truitt's married and has been married to a woman who's been ill for the longest time. He'll never divorce her."

I sighed and fiddled with my purse. There it was, the thing I'd ignored. In love. Unreasonable.

Olivia said, "That first evening, it was a casual thing, you understand, to make a table of four."

"What am I going to do? I like him. I like him a lot," I confessed.

"I can tell him you didn't feel good and went home," said Olivia, but I shook my head.

"No, I'll ask him to take me home and think about it on the way."

I suppose I didn't look too well when we returned, wobbling at the table until I grabbed the banquette. Lanford took my elbow, drove straight to my apartment. When I stretched out on the sofa, he placed a blanket over me. He smoothed my hand.

"I have some news," he said. "Good and also troubling."

He didn't know how every piece of news that evening was troubling. Like Uncle Lauf, he'd conveniently left facts out. Still, I wanted to be with Lanford, so I didn't know if I could save myself from this muddle.

"I've been offered a job with the War Department in Washington, D.C. My work for the state has really been to handle plans for the California war effort. Now I've been asked to go to D.C. Do you think you can come with me? Why not? Your daughter is off at school, and your mother takes care of Raleigh's children. Their father is nearby. Nobody needs you here."

I stared at him.

Finally, I said, "Olivia told me about your wife this evening. What about her?" I didn't let one tear fall down my cheek, though my heart was thumping so, I wanted to look down to make sure my blouse wasn't puffing up.

His earnest, endearing expression changed to bafflement, lips and tongue forming "no," red climbing from his neck to his cheeks to his nose.

He stammered.

"I'm … I'm going to ask her for a divorce. I have money for her, and I don't have any children. She'll be fine. But you can move with me, we don't have to wait. We'll be happy."

Then I cried. I knew how long a divorce took. He grasped my wrist and pulled me to my feet. I was shaking, but he was gentle, murmuring loving words, and soon I was under his spell. That night I thought I would move to Washington, D.C. I, the timid one, who always wanted to stay in one place.

A few weeks later, we planned to meet Olivia and her husband at the Senator Hotel for a dinner party in the posh Florentine Room. I looked forward to a wonderful evening without worry about a fury-filled world.

With fabric purchased from a shop that always secured the best, I'd made a beautiful rose wool suit. I thought I looked good and was happy to go out with a handsome, jovial man who cared for me and smiled as I came toward him. Leaning against the bar, waiting for other guests to arrive, I watched another government pal of Lanford's walk up and hold out his hand.

Lanford introduced us, and the man said, "What a lucky fellow. I'm pleased to meet you, ma'am."

I smiled at the word ma'am, like he was from Texas.

Then he turned to Lanford and said, "Wasn't it a good to-do last week? How come this attractive lady wasn't with you at that affair?"

My smile began to twitch. I hadn't been invited last week, though I didn't have anything else to do. I peered through the smoky haze to see red spreading up Lanford's neck again.

"Well, well, well," stammered Lanford. "I … I … ."

The man blabbed on, "It's too bad you weren't there, ma'am. Who was that … ?"

Enough. I'd heard about women who hung around the Capitol. This Texan was flattering me, as if I was one of those ladies.

I took my elbows off the bar and said, "Nice to meet you. Excuse me, Lanford. I'll be going now. Don't follow me."

I managed to walk off, hearing the man tell Lanford he was sorry, he didn't know, too bad. Then I was weaving between tables, unable to see a thing. I bumped into a waitress with a tray of drinks, I knocked against a chair, and finally the maitre d' helped me to the door. My God, it was like the October evening a long time ago when I watched Mr. Faye, stricken by whatever Mama had said.

I worked a lot for the next couple of weeks and tossed out Lanford's letters. Olivia called to say he told her it was an old friend.

I said, "I know when men are playing around. He's excused himself before, and I let it go. Tell him to leave me alone."

The night he came over, I wouldn't let him in. I wasn't going to be lied to when it came to love. It was one thing when we first went out. Another when he wanted me to move to Washington, D.C., and live with him.

Slipping on the stair, he hollered, "You're a hard woman, Mary."

I shook at those words and almost gave in. Then I remembered that was the fate of my family, except for Raleigh and maybe Mama and Mr. Faye. To lie or be lied to.

I'D ENDURED THE last of the war years like everyone else in California, unscathed compared to the poor souls in Europe and Asia. After, I relied on my friends and visited my daughter and her family in Los Angeles. The mailman had delivered a happy letter telling me Betsy was pregnant again the very same day Raleigh told me he'd run into someone I knew.

I thought Raleigh would tell me about his latest woman friend. He'd never remarried, but he had a steady stream of girlfriends and never seemed lonely. Instead, Abel, my old boyfriend with the motorcycle, a widower with a grown son and daughter, had asked Raleigh about me. He owned this ranch where we live. Taking me to the movies, to dinner, on drives in his round-topped Dodge along the Sacramento and American rivers, Abel knew how to court a woman as well as anyone. Quiet, content with his farm, he was the opposite of voluble Lanford Truitt.

Soon Abel asked me to marry him, and it dawned on me I didn't want to continue alone. It seemed we'd be good companions, even if I didn't love him like I'd loved Lanford. Abel assured me he could take care of me for the rest of my life, and like that, I resigned from the state printing office, relieved to relax and devote myself to a bungalow surrounded by a copse of pine and a perfect garden.

Not only camellias, I planted brilliant pink peonies and dark red roses. All the quince, plum, apricot, and pear trees reminded me I'd never have to go begging from the neighbors as we did in Truckee. Abel had planted rows of blackberries right outside our door. No scrounging in the thorny bushes by the Truckee River for wild berries.

Abel painted an old bench, placed it by the path going out to the street, and next to it, he set planters of bright red fuchsias to fuss over. The stray dog we adopted sat with me to be scratched and roamed the fields with Abel. I listened to our guinea fowl calling to each other in the trees. We didn't share a passionate love, but an idyllic respite in a bucolic part of Sacramento.

STRANGE HOW WHEN feeling content, others are assailed with upheaval. Soon after we'd married, the biggest dust up in our small area of Sacramento blew in when the Japanese families returned to their farms. A few had found a sympathetic person to guard their property, but the people Abel helped didn't have that luxury. Mr. and Mrs. Noguchi, owners of the fruit and flower farm with the beehives Betsy used to visit when she was small, had stopped to greet Mama before driving on to their old farm to see what was what. It took all that time after World War II when they were let out of the internment camp way up north at Tule Lake to even get to visit their old property.

Mama, always on the side of the helpless, got Abel involved because the Noguchis had lived in Sacramento as long as she had. Calling from her neighbor's phone, she talked to Abel for a long time. I could imagine, fist on her hip, tapping her foot, holding the phone away from her ear while Abel explained why it would do no good, then coercing him to help anyway.

They spent months driving to the courts downtown, defending and swearing on the family's good citizenship, but even though Mama said *"the end is not yet"* over and over, it didn't matter. The Noguchis were defeated and had to find new land to purchase to set up another farm. Luckily, south Sacramento was wide open. Abel ended up witnessing for the family, so they could obtain loans. Honestly, the state was against those people, no matter how much money they had managed to store away.

AFTER THAT, I'D thought the world's cruelty had ended. One Sunday in October, I'd settled onto my bench, and Raleigh showed up, fit to be tied.

He started in about Margaret, his youngest daughter, the adorable little girl Mama raised from a toddler on, who drove him crazy. Mama and he were dazed by her antics, skipping school, escorted home by the police, who lectured about boys full of bravado and money to spend after war rationing and privation when they were kids. Her gang had been arrested for speeding and drinking.

Mama had remonstrated, "You're fifteen. Are you the baby like my sister Ola and think no one can lie or hurt you?"

Putting her face up to Mama, Margaret said, "And who's going to hurt me?"

But no, the worry was Alta, the original rebellious one, who showed up at Mama's front door, slurring her words, "I just got here from San Francisco. Oh, not really. I came yesterday. They're looking for me. Let me stay."

The last straw for Raleigh.

"Jeez, Mary," said Raleigh, "she nearly fell into my arms, skinnier than the winter when we were really hungry. She said to hurry because they might be following her, but I'm not sure she knew what she was saying."

She whispered she had hidden a knife in her coat pocket, so they could never hurt her. He held her arm while she dragged herself inside and collapsed on the sofa, pulling out a flask and taking a long swallow. By then, everyone was standing around her.

Margaret, hand on her hip, smirked, "Happy Halloween."

"So Raleigh, is that the baby?" Alta said, voice garbled. "I haven't seen any of you in quite awhile. You're so tall. Happy Halloween to you too."

She was sweating on her upper lip and put a hand in her pocket to pull out a handkerchief, but she kept missing, her hand shaky and uncoordinated.

Finally she wiped her face, and then Mama knelt down on the floor, rubbing Alta's arms and brushing back messed up hair, the same gesture of love she'd always used when she wanted to protect one of us.

She whispered, "I'm here, Alta."

"Mama, if I only had some money to get back on my feet," murmured Alta. "I'd be all right."

Raleigh's boys helped put Alta in her old room.

WE CUT THROUGH the fields to Mama's. I stood at Alta's bedroom door, thinking did she do this on purpose to spoil the days for her mother? Raleigh said we needed to do something before Mama gave Alta all her money, ha ha, as if she had any to give. Alta was spread all over the bed, hot to the touch, but sound asleep, mouth open, a soft whoosh as she breathed.

Mama twisted the cold cloth she had used on Alta's forehead and whispered, "She's so thin. She's starving. I don't want my first born to be left with nothing and no one."

"Oh, Mama," I said. "She's been taking care of herself. Didn't she take Tiny's money—twice—and marry Hutchinson, though it didn't last?"

"She's not starving because she has no money like the shantytown kids you gave food to before the war," said Raleigh. "She spends her money on pills and heroin."

Mama gasped, though I'm not sure why, since she knew what Alta did. Raleigh stopped talking and looked up at the ceiling like he always did when he had no more to say. He knew about hunger. He remembered when Mr. McGlashan gave us a quarter.

"She owes money. Some men in San Francisco are trying to get it from her. That's why she ran to us, Mary, to hide," said Mama.

"Listen," I said. "Tomorrow we'll take her to the hospital. We'll sign her in as A. Edwards. Even if bad men, if there are some, do look for her in Sacramento, they'll ask for 'Hutchinson.' "

Mama stopped clutching at her stomach when I said, "Maybe the hospital people'll help her or maybe she can go home with you. It'll be her hide-out."

Alta wasn't wrong. In November, wearing overcoats and fedoras like those Al Capone fellows in the movies, two fat men did drive up to Mama's house. They knocked, just as I flung open the door and swept dried mud from the neighbor kids' shoes onto the porch, my hair wrapped in a kerchief and wearing Mama's housekeeping dress. The man with the mustache stepped back, the ash from his cigarette dropping onto the pile, as he asked for Alta Hutchinson. I said that person didn't live here, and then Mama peered out and said she didn't know who that woman was. Such an old lady, hair scraggly, sweaty neighbor kids in overalls peeking out behind her loose brown frock, what did those men think?

They left, shaking their heads, and Mama laughed, saying we'd fooled those fedoras. It was years before Alta went to the city again. From time to time, Mama sent money to pay off the debt to the saloon where Alta worked. It was the closest we ever came to nasty men from San Francisco.

Then to our surprise, Alta brought Margaret around. When I arrived a week after Alta got out of the hospital, there sat Margaret on the porch step, legs crossed, cigarette dangling between her fingers, as if that made her sophisticated. Alta sat on the porch steps too, whispering and laughing, and Margaret seemed calmer. She didn't snarl at Mama, rocking and humming "Sweet Adeline." She was telling Alta about a book she'd read. A coffee can sat on the step between them where they tossed their butts.

THAT JANUARY MORNING I made my last serious decision in a decade of unimaginable rage. On the bench, bundled in an old coat, I was smiling as a squirrel leaped onto a quince tree branch to escape a frustrated jay. Abel called me into the kitchen where he did all his business.

"I'm short of money, Mary."

I grimaced, as I'd heard that one from age ten on. He smoothed papers out on the table. He pointed from one calculation to another as if the numbers might change under his finger. All the land he'd inherited from his parents and all those crops. He was a good mechanic, and I had a bit of my own money. I must have looked puzzled.

"The depression is over and the war is over," he said. "Seed and seedlings are more expensive, and the price for food crops is going down as more of the valley is planted. I have to sell a piece of land, I suppose, to help us out."

I spoke some comforting words, but back outside in my private Eden, breathing deeply to clear my mind, I watched the fog lower over the treetops. Mama's answer to crazy Uncle Lauf came to mind, the day she hollered at him, wishing for help, but knowing she'd have to help herself. That's what I'd have to do once more. After noon dinner, I called my old boss to ask if there were any openings at the printing office.

Funny thing was, no matter what Mama said, Uncle Lauf didn't hold it against her, only saying, *"man is born unto trouble … ."* He was forgiving.

Perhaps it would take awhile before I forgave Abel, but he didn't intend to lead me on. Although he read the entire paper every day, he was a dreamer, aloof from the world. Things simply hadn't turned out as he thought, unlike Lanford, who led me on and knew he lied to me. That I couldn't forgive.

I turned on my side, the sofa soft and the room warm. Staring at the drawings of rosemary in the portfolio, I vowed I would never grovel for money like my vivid memory of Mama in Truckee, toiling for pennies to take care of four children. Maybe I'd have to care for Abel one day, but I'd help myself too. And my daughter. That was my intent when I decided to return to work. Definitely not loneliness.

18

June-July 1911
Harrigan's Hill, Truckee

ARMS FOLDED, TINY pushed her hip out to the side. Raleigh examined his scar. Mama fumed because they needed twenty-two cents for a bag of potatoes. Alta, wanting better than potatoes, offered to get a sack of flour for seventeen cents, saying they could make biscuits and get honey from Crazy Lady Harrigan.

Mama scowled and said, "We're not starving yet, but your father better send us more money, or I need to get more work."

"Maybe Captain Ben can get us a rabbit," said Raleigh.

"He's like us, Raleigh," said Mama. "He sells rabbits to get money."

Alta said, "I think … ," and stopped, pretending to swallow instead.

Mama stared, daring anyone to say more. It did no good to remind her they could move back with Papa. She'd stormed around the house for days after Uncle Lauf's visit.

Sympathetic though she was, Mary was as dumbfounded as her brother and sisters when Mama came up with a plan. She'd talked to the new doctor about nursing women who lived nearby. Finishing off her biscuit, Mary exchanged an uneasy look with Alta.

Tiny said, "Mama, please don't go."

"We'll find more pennies," said Raleigh. "I'm good at that."

"I talked to Aunt Ola. She said you can have supper at her house when I'm called away, and Mrs. O'Brien said she'd look in on you in the mornings before school. Mrs. Harrigan can help sometimes. She's wiser than you four think."

Making an attempt at conscientiousness by wiping up the crumbs from the table, Alta said, "Anyway it'll be summer soon, so we won't have to be on time for school or anything, right Mama?"

What about Mr. Faye and the butcher?" asked Mary. "And the cow? Who'll milk the cow?"

"They understand. They know the fix I'm in," she said, lip trembling though she tried to hide it by rubbing her mouth. "Can't you take turns milking the cow?"

It came to Mary the one losing her mind might be Mama. Her mother stared off behind their heads at the watercolor landscape of dark pines and a green and gold meadow. She had found it in the saloon storage closet, probably left as payment for a room, and brought it home to decorate their bare wood wall.

Did she wonder, thought Mary, what chain of events she was setting off, coping on her own in this mountain town beside a rushing, icy river, the golden meadows and tall dark pines on the far side?

WHEN MAMA RECEIVED an offer, Mary, by far the most unhappy, begged Mama to take her along, let her care for the baby, do the dusting and ironing. She crumpled, head down in her arms on the kitchen table, as fury built up in Mama's face. Grabbing the wood kitchen spoon, Mama whacked Mary on the back of her legs as hard as she had whipped them after the accident at the river.

"What's the matter with you?" Mama wailed. "You're almost grown up and you're acting like a baby. Why can't you be like the others?"

Then Mama stopped. She was right, Mary thought, and as spontaneously as the tears began, they dried up. She wasn't like the others. Too plain, too serious.

Mama looked around, everyone frozen, watching.

She said, "What am I going to do with you, Mary?"

Raleigh ran outside, and Tiny, making herself as small as her name, slid into the front room. Pointing toward the outhouse, Alta disappeared. Mama wiped her hands down the sides of her dress, and the wrath melted from her face.

When Mama put out her hands to Mary, she shook her head and, holding back fresh sobs, said, "I'm going into the bedroom."

Shoulders shaking, Mama walked out and up the hill to the garden and got down on her knees to pull weeds.

At Mama's dressing table, Mary brushed her long, blond hair. Contemplating her ordinary, pale face and big nose in the mirror, tears welled up in her eyes. Not only was she not daring like the others, Mama didn't love her as much because she wasn't pretty.

She rubbed the red welts on her calves and hiccuped. In the front room Tiny yelled at Alta to get away from her things. Twirling a hair ribbon, one of Tiny's latest fancies, Alta flounced into the bedroom.

Hard smirk on her face, Alta said, "Why don't you grow up? What's wrong with you?"

She shoved her sister against the dressing table and jeered, "Green eyes! Green eyes!"

Mary hated that taunt. They weren't even mean words, except in the particularly vicious way Alta snarled. Shoving Mary again, Alta turned to jump on the bed. Heart pounding and vision blurring, Mary picked up the brush, whirled around, and without a word, struck Alta on the side of the head as hard as she could. Alta howled and covered her head. Mary hit again and lifted the brush to hit a third time.

Alta cried out, "Stop! Stop! I won't say it again!"

Mary escaped up the hill and burst into Mrs. Harrigan's front parlor. She didn't press her to talk, but patted Mary's shoulder and let her cry. As they came out the door, Mrs. Harrigan pointed down the hill at Mr. Faye, leaning over Mama, gesticulating, shaking his head.

"You can't go off nursing, I don't care if the doctor or Grace agreed. She didn't realize. Who knows what might happen? Even if people are around, they're too young."

Mama fanned her face with a dusty palm.

Touching her shoulder, Mr. Faye said, "Dolly, stop and think this over. It's not good."

Next day, Mama pulled the wagon from the barn and piled everyone in with a picnic to escape their troubles for a day at Donner Lake. Molly walked down the hill. Mama held the reins threaded between her fingers, as if she did this all the time. Mary rubbed her forehead, thinking about the rage that had befallen them. Uncle Lauf would say, *"trouble as the sparks fly upward ... ,"* while Mama would hope the family furor died away.

AT SUPPER ON Thursday, Mary barely heard Mama because of the racket at the table, with everyone jabbering about the last day school assembly.

"Now listen. Mr. Titus told me a lot of people are very sick. The new doctor says it's the typhoid."

Mama wiped her hands and pointed her finger.

"So don't drink water from the bucket at school. You must be careful not to catch any germs."

The next morning, Sally Faye scurried up to pass on that the principal was sick. Mary liked the principal and was the only one who felt any pity. Alta had refused to go anywhere near him since she had to apologize for smoking the cigarette.

At the assembly, wearing the gown Ola made, Mary squeezed her hands together behind her back and didn't miss one word reciting "The Last Leaf" by Oliver Wendell Holmes, in which a young person is amused by an old man tottering down the street. Smoothly, clearly, she delivered her favorite part,

I know it is a sin
For me to sit and grin
At him here;
But the old three-cornered hat,
And the breeches, and all that,
Are so queer!

And if I should live to be
The last leaf upon the tree
In the spring,
Let them smile, as I do now,
At the old forsaken bough
Where I cling.

Young and old, the audience didn't shuffle or whisper, so she knew she'd won the first prize for poetry recitation. When Mama, Aunt Ola, and the other adults nodded and clapped, Mary curtsied in the new dress and smiled. As her teacher claimed, the title was a sure winner for a girl who loved to memorize verse with fine words and lilting rhyme.

Raleigh and Tiny were already chattering about the first prize when Mary reached the house. So hot, Mary was panting.

Mama said, "Your dress looked fine and Aunt Ola was delighted."

Mary gulped cold tea.

"All my children, the gallant performers of Truckee School. I'm a fortunate woman," said Mama, hugging each with a forced heartiness, disconcerting to Mary, still anxious about Mama's temper.

Raleigh offered to pull out the old canvas tarp and some blankets to sleep outside, just as they had done many summer nights at the boardinghouse. At twilight, after arranging everything under the trees and plopping down in their nightclothes, four bodies inhaled the evening air, while frogs croaked down by the river and the cow shuffled, looking for one more patch of grass.

Alta said, "I heard the principal's sick with a fever so bad he has the deliriums."

Mary lay wrapped in a blanket and pointed at a shooting star, the last thing she remembered until Alta told her what happened five weeks later.

ALTA LEANED OVER and tapped Mary's shoulder.

"Minna said you're not in a fever anymore," whispered Alta.

Her sister appeared far away, and Mary blinked to see clearly.

Seated on the edge of the bed, Alta said, "Raleigh and I understood what

149

C. J. NOONAN

deliriums meant the next morning when you woke me up. You were rolling around, calling out, 'Stop! Don't do that!'

"I punched you on the shoulder, but then I saw your red face, and I shoved Tiny, who turned over and looked worse than you, her eyes not moving at all.

"So I pulled Raleigh up, and he ran to the house yelling to come quick. So loud, Mama ran out before he got to the door, but when she saw you and Tiny, she stopped and her face went white.

"I thought she was fainting until she took a deep breath and said, 'All right now. Well, all right.' We put you and Tiny in Mama's room. Then Raleigh ran for Minna, and I got Aunt Ola to send Papa a telegram."

Mary slowly pulled the cover over her face, hearing Alta's voice distant like wind brushing through the pines.

Her eyes opened when Alta said, "Aunt Ola came with news the principal had died and Mrs. Faye was sick, so when Minna arrived to be the nurse she urged Mama to get the doctor right away."

It seemed the next morning, Mama set off for the doctor after admonishing Alta not to forget the cold rags, which she changed once and then yelled at Raleigh to do. She left to see what was happening with Sally Faye's mother.

Hot and sweaty, Mary woke up, nobody around. She climbed over Tiny and wobbled into the front room, the doors flung wide open, letting a morning breeze blow between the front room and the kitchen. Pulling the rocking chair into the doorway, she rocked and fell asleep, the air drying off the sweat.

Then Mary remembered Minna standing in front of the rocking chair, her arms folded, blocking the breeze that had cooled Mary off. Minna dragged her out of the chair and back to bed.

Alta shook Mary's shoulder. "Minna said Tiny was sleeping calmly. You had dark red cheeks and lay there as if your torso hurt to move.

"So Minna rushed outside, but Mama and the new, young doctor were hiking up the hill."

Mary listened to Alta's voice, still far away, while the picture of whispering people came back.

Placing a stethoscope on her chest, the skinny doctor said, "Ah, her lungs, they're filling up."

Minna closed her eyes for a moment, and Mama grabbed her arm when Minna said it meant pneumonia.

"Oh, Lord, why is something happening to her?' Mama sobbed. "What're we going to do?"

The doctor rooted around and pulled some folded paper envelopes from his bag, saying something about the powders four times a day. Then Mama gripped the doctor's elbow, asking him to remember what happened with papers of medicine the year before.

Mary lifted her hand and brushed her forehead.

She turned when Alta said, "Raleigh and I were hiding out in the kitchen, but when we heard "powders," we snuck in to see the hubbub. Do you remember the doctor just stood there looking from Minna to Mama? Later Minna laughed, saying she thought he couldn't believe they would do anything other than say, 'Yes, doctor.' "

Mary pulled up the face of the doctor, skin red and upper lip sweaty. He breathed through his teeth, like he was fearful about admitting anything.

Alta finished, "He finally told Mama they're aspirin powders to relieve the fever. Minna said she held her breath because you looked so sick, but the doctor thought you'd make it."

She shook Mary again and said, "Minna went home, but Aunt Ola came and talked to Mama, in a dither for thinking to leave us to earn a few dollars."

Falling back on the bed, Alta propped up her head with her arm. Quiet, not one peep from the chickadee hopping along the bush outside the bedroom window. Mary lifted her hand and placed it on her stomach, too drowsy to say a word.

"Mama was so upset. She should have been comforted by all the help."

Alta picked at the fuzz on the blanket.

"You know, I went over to Sally Faye's to see how her mother was doing. Raleigh left the door open. He just ran out for a few minutes to go see Molly and the Jersey. Maybe we thought it didn't matter. Remember last year with the scarlet fever? It didn't matter how quiet we were or how quickly we got the doctor. The bad thing still happened."

Alta coughed like dust had settled in her throat, and Mary opened her eyes.

"I wish I'd known what could happen with the deliriums," Alta whispered.

Late in the afternoon Mary awoke, eyes drawn to the shadows filling the corners of the small room. The story of the past few weeks whirled like the bits of dust vanishing from the light into the shadow. She wondered about Alta's apology, another moment when she was her sweet self. Maybe she didn't want her sisters to disappear like dust into the shadow.

HER PNEUMONIA CHILLS and fever ended in mid-July. Mary was too weak to get out of bed, much less sit in a rocker. Tiny, stronger than her little body appeared, sat up, started talking, and climbed out of bed.

"Don't expect to go outside," Mama told her, but soon Tiny spent most of her time outdoors anyway.

Mama had stopped working for both Mr. Faye and the butcher, saying to Aunt Ola and Minna she couldn't ask her friends to do the nursing while she cleaned and cooked for others. As if Mary was her only child, Mama brushed back her daughter's hair and rubbed her arms. The only one in the house, Mary looked on as Mama was saved from collapse once more.

As before, Mama rushed around, washing, weeding, wearing a studied smile, as she prepared to ask for more credit at the grocer's. When a neighbor came over, she made tea and talked about town happenings—the typhoid scare, the latest saloon brawl, news from Sacramento about the likely suffrage election—as if she hadn't a care in the world.

At dusk, when the air cooled down, the bustle in town turned raucous, and children were shooed away, Raleigh and Alta sidled into the bedroom to play cards. No one wanted to sit in the front room where Mama brooded and searched to calm herself with passages in her Bible and poetry books.

So on the afternoon when Mr. Faye knocked and called "Dolly," Mary only slowly opened her eyes to hear "typhoid has been bad this year." Mama agreed and complained about holes of filthy water in the road where germs grew. The voices were low, but Mary heard "stop, stop talking, Dolly," and a long silence, no cough, no deep breath, no rustle.

"Alta came to see how my wife was doing," he said finally. "I'd been so anxious about her, I'd forgotten your daughters were ill. You've been gone almost a month, so I came to see how they were."

"We're all right," whispered Mama.

The door grated and wood was poked inside to heat water in the heavy kettle on the stovetop.

Mr. Faye said, "It's warm. I need to take off my coat."

"You can hang it on … ," said Mama.

After steps in the little kitchen, Mr. Faye whispered, *"Sh-h-h.* I've been so worried. About you. What's happening to me?"

Silence until he said, "I have some money to fix things here, if it will help."

Pecking at bugs on the bush outside the window, the chickadee chirped *fee-bee-bay,* but Mr. Faye sighed and then murmured, "My God, it's hard to imagine how you stay with your children way up here. No husband. No cousin or brother or … is that why I keep thinking about you? Please don't look away."

"My sister Ola is here," whispered Mama, "and I'm not the only one in this trouble. I know I need steady help, not the sometime kind. Even Mrs. Harrigan, who doesn't believe in faithfulness, knows that."

The strainer plinked against the cup, water poured over the tea leaves, and she said, "I don't know why we appeal to each other. In a different place we wouldn't even notice the other. And I'm not free, and neither are you."

The chair scraped as Mama sat down, and the table squeaked as Mr. Faye, polite like he'd never been near a woman, asked Mama to let him hold her hands. He recognized the watercolor landscape, and Mama reminded him his wife had said she could keep it. He wondered if the artist had painted an imagined meadow in a faraway world, and Mama smiled.

"I like to make you smile," he said.

Silence, until he pushed back the chair, saying he'd try to come by again and to please send a child to let him know if she needed help.

"No. No. I'm all right," said Mama.

Eyes closing, Mary's thoughts drifted to Mrs. Harrigan's talk about how men and women act in this out-of-the-way town. But, why not get help? They were in real trouble in this house.

The next afternoon, Mama gave Raleigh another message to carry to the trainmaster.

"Don't forget now, Raleigh," she said with a twitch of her mouth, a sure sign she hadn't much hope of Papa's answer.

SLEEPING OR STARING at the ceiling of her room, Mary stayed in bed all the last, hot July days after Tiny was allowed out. If Mama was unsettled, Mary felt lucky. Never had she had a bed or room to herself.

She watched bees fly in through the crack in the window, lost, she supposed, on their way back to Crazy Lady Harrigan's beehive. More than once a field mouse, crumb fattening its cheek, scurried in from the front room and out again, searching for the door to the yard. On blistering hot days when hillside noises ceased, Mary heard every whisper, as when Tiny and Hazel crept into the front room, panting and snuffling.

"O-o-o-h, Tiny, d'you think anyone knows it was us?" said Hazel.

"How could they? Anyway, maybe it wasn't. We put lots of dirt on it … maybe an old tramp had a campfire out there too," said Tiny.

Mary called, "Tiny?"

A long silence followed before Tiny's face appeared in the doorway and then Hazel's at her shoulder.

"Did you hear?" whispered Tiny.

"What'd you do?" asked Mary.

"Played campfire in the woods and cooked bread," answered Tiny.

A smoky smell was seeping into the house.

"There's a fire, and you think you started it. Right, Hazel?" said Mary.

As the little girl tipped her head, Tiny used her elbow, knocking Hazel in the side.

"Oh, I won't tell," said Mary.

From then on Tiny reported the news faithfully. The blaze burned hot and swiftly. Ash floated down from the sky. Smoke drifted over the hill, the odor filling the air. Fortunately, the main part of the fire was on the far side and was stopped after two days. Otherwise, Mama said they would have had to evacuate, and where would they have lived then?

When the smaller, scary fire began, Tiny ran into the bedroom screeching, "Get up! Get up!"

Sparks had wafted on the wind from the ridge down to Crazy Lady Harrigan's ancient chicken coop. Mary struggled out of bed to lean against the kitchen door while Raleigh and Alta yelled, running downhill for the volunteer fire brigade. Mama and Mrs. O'Brien lugged buckets to water the ground and bushes around the old coop so nothing else would burn. In the meantime, Molly trotted down the hill away from the smoke, eyes rolling. The Jersey, mooing loudly, started to run until Tiny ran alongside, waved her arms, and whacked the cow's rump to shoo her toward the barn. What stopped both the horse and the cow were the firemen, shouting and rolling a wheeled water tank uphill.

Behind the water tank, huffed Mr. Faye and a reporter. Mary pointed out Mrs. Harrigan while Mr. Faye ran toward the blazing coop and stomped on smoldering grass.

Mama came back to the kitchen with Mr. Faye, her son, and the reporter, as covered with ash as Raleigh. Each drank cold tea until the smoky dryness in their mouths was satisfied.

Rubbing his dust-covered face, Raleigh said, "Lucky those firemen had the hose. It drowned the hot bits with a great blast of water. Only chickens were left running and squawking."

In the next *Truckee Star News,* Mrs. Harrigan was all the news. She accepted declarations of help, although she said, "I'll believe them when I see the money."

The chickens scattered, pecking and clucking near Mama's garden. Some were eaten by foxes, and Tiny insisted a bobcat snatched a hen one evening, but the rest built nests under Mrs. Harrigan's porch. Tiny and Hazel searched for eggs every day.

Mama claimed Mr. Faye finally appealed to the Salvation Army. Two men dressed in uniforms stopped to ask Mary, sitting at the door, if they were heading to Mrs. Harrigan's house. She nodded and pointed.

"They told Mrs. Harrigan she was very, very lucky her house didn't burn, and some boys'll build a new coop," said Tiny. "Raleigh wants to help."

You never know, thought Mary, as Mama, humming "Oh Susanna," seemed happier for the time being, after Mr. Faye visited those July afternoons. One day he confided that the fire captain had suspicions about who started the fire, the perpetual fear in a town built of wood. Tiny was upset, and to ease her jitters she fetched for Mary and collected eggs for Mrs. Harrigan until school started.

19

August 1911
Harrigan's Hill, Truckee

MARY READ AUNT Margaret's letter out loud. Mama chopped turnips furiously, antagonized by the words "Tom stopped over. He said you were in bad straits again after Tiny and Mary had the typhoid."

"I doubt Papa admitted the least of his own part in this predicament. He must want Margaret to be his ally," she spit out.

Mary knew her brother and sisters saw Papa once in awhile, and Alta told her Papa had sneaked in one day to sit with her for a few minutes when she was still delirious and Mama was up at Mrs. Harrigan's. Mary had spent time lately pulling up her anger at Papa, especially after he sent five dollars at the beginning of August. She wasn't afraid of that mixed-up man anymore, just unforgiving in spite of Uncle Lauf's warning.

In the last part of the letter, Margaret wrote,

Tom says you're cutting off your nose to spite your face because he has to pay the hotel bill, and so has less to send over.

Mama clicked *tsk* with her tongue, but Mary wondered. The end of the letter said,

So I told a lady I know you might take her children for a few weeks while she's having her baby. I don't know if she'll come.

Mary claimed Papa had stirred the pot, so that Margaret sent Mrs. Hoy to see Mama about boarding her children the day the Jersey went dry. One after another, events began, and by the autumn wind in October, consequences blew every which way, like leaves scattered on the ground, swirled up, and discarded again.

WHEN NO MORE milk squirted into the bucket, Mama threw up her hands, railing about "the last straw." She grabbed the Chinese box and emptied the pennies onto the table to the worry of her children, who retreated to the bedroom to play cards.

Mama slapped the table with her palm and hissed, "Damn. No milk and I'm short five cents."

Tiny whispered, "Mama's never, ever said that word."

Raleigh, Mary, and Alta nodded, knowing loggers and railroad men swore all the time, part of the everyday scene in town, but not Mama. Silence followed in the house, though crickets sawed their legs in song. Molly, out by the vegetables, fluffed her lips and lapped water from the bucket.

Mama called out, "Raleigh, Tiny. Come here, please."

Mary collected the cards while Raleigh and his sisters proceeded to the front room.

"You'll have to take a bucket to the new lady who sells butter to Mr. Titus," said Mama. Ask if you can come once a week for skimmed milk left from making butter."

"Mama, I don't want to," said Tiny.

"You have to," answered Mama, adding, "She seems like a nice woman."

The next morning, lips pinched tight, Mama portioned out bread and skimmed milk for breakfast, scarcely more than Alta and Mary had endured with mean Mrs. Archer in Sacramento. Then Raleigh and Tiny put a rope around the poor Jersey's neck, but the saddest thing was Mama leading the Jersey to the butcher. Raleigh, Tiny, and Alta plodded along behind, eyes to the ground.

Mary drifted inside, sprawled out on the bed, and dozed off. Next thing, she heard Mama and wandered into the kitchen to hear about the poor cow. Instead, she found out Aunt Margaret had sent fortune their way.

Mama said, "Just as I came out of the butcher shop, a woman stopped me. She had two small boys in tow and a baby on the way. She had circles under her eyes, like she was having trouble sleeping. Her name was Mrs. Hoy."

Mama brushed hair out of her face and put her purse, fat with money from the butcher, on the shelf.

"They were from Reno. That caught my attention. Her husband is in the hospital, and no family lives there to care for the boys when she had her baby. Then she mentioned Margaret."

Mama's face relaxed. Like Uncle Lauf, always ready to help someone, Mama realized things might be going her way, even if there were two more children.

"Mrs. Hoy asked if I could take the boys right now," Mama said. "I tell you, she looked like she was going to have the baby any minute.

"So I agreed, as those boys looked like they could take care of themselves. They turned back to get their belongings at the train station. Then I hurried to get here, but Raleigh, Tiny, and Alta are waiting at the bottom of the hill to help the boys and their mother."

Mary was breathing heavily from the walk down to the flat rock. When the five children reached the pine tree, they were panting from lugging a large carpetbag and heavy satchel. Dropping onto the rock, they gulped air, and from the corner of their eyes, they looked at each other.

Breaking the silence, Raleigh declared, "Boy, this will be fun."

The two boys sat quietly, and finally Tiny said, "I wonder what's going to happen."

A scowl on her face, Alta said, "I know. We'll have to take care of them, and it's already crowded in that decrepit place."

Tiny turned to the boys and said, "She says that word a lot lately. She's showing off."

Alta didn't bother to make another retort nor say she was sorry for being rude and walked away, kicking rocks and hitting the brush with a stick like she always did when in a pique.

The two boys didn't appear upset. The taller was William Hoy, nine years old, stocky, and round-faced with dark brown hair. Little Eddie was a bundle of baby fat and soft, pink skin, but black hair. He was five.

Mary said, "Where's your mother?"

"She kissed them at the bottom of the hill," said Tiny. "I think she was too tired to climb."

William said, "She promised to come in six weeks."

"She has a beautiful watch on a chain around her neck," said Tiny. "She looked at it and then walked off."

"Maybe she wanted to catch the next train to Reno," said Mary.

The boys nodded, and Raleigh helped haul the bags up to the house.

When they reached the kitchen and found Mama peeling apples for dinner, William pulled some money from his pocket and said, "Ma said 'give this to Mrs. Edwards to tide her over.' "

Mama counted thirty dollars and said, "Your mother must want you to be well cared for. I guess she loves you very much."

The boys said nothing, but still neither appeared ready to cry. Mama crammed the money into the purse on the shelf.

"Your mother will be back before you know it," she said.

"Yes, ma'am," said William. "My ma went away before, but she came back for us."

"She did? Where did she go?" asked Mama.

"To find us a place in Reno," said William. "She was only gone for a day and came right back to us in Tonopah."

"She's going to Reno again to stay with Mr. Littlefield," said Eddie.

"Who's Mr. Littlefield?"

"The man we were staying with until Ma goes to the hospital."

Mama raised her eyebrows.

The boys lifted the bag and satchel up the ladder, across the kitchen-shed roof, and into the attic. The next day Mama wrote to Aunt Margaret to find out the real story of Mrs. Hoy and her family.

WISHING FOR A breeze, Mary fanned her face with a folded paper fan when Alta walked into the room, ill-temper flashing in her eyes.

She said, "It's so boring. Can't you sit by the pine tree, so we can watch what's going on in town?"

Though frail, Mary agreed, and Alta's demeanor changed. Gently, Alta held Mary's arm, and they slowly made it to the pine tree. Eddie trailed behind, throwing rocks at tree trunks. They sat on the flat rock and looked out past the town, following the river as it cut through the mountains toward Reno.

Alta started, "Sally went to see her Reno cousin. I bet she gets new dresses for school. Yesterday, Crazy Lady Harrigan was wearing her dress inside out, and we yelled at her to change her clothes, but she just laughed. Raleigh and Tiny showed William how they get money at the train station."

After a pause, Alta said, "It was terrible walking the Jersey down the hill. Mama patted its back all the way."

She pointed to the train station.

"And listen to this. Know what I did when I left you and the boys here at the rock?" she asked. "I followed the river path toward the train station where their ma was talking to a man—and it wasn't a white man. Something's up and I don't mean Mama and Mr. Faye. Why would those boys stay with us in Truckee?"

Alta gazed out over the gold grass in the valley.

"Did you know Mama got a letter back from Aunt Margaret? She was surprised at the lady's name," said Alta. "Mrs. Hoy called herself Mrs. Littlefield. Told Aunt Margaret she was married to Mr. Littlefield, who is a half-breed. Half Washo. I'm pretty sure that's the man I saw at the train. He looked Indian."

"Those boys don't look Washo," said Mary, "but, for sure, we don't look Cherokee either."

Eddie interrupted, "Hey, we like Mr. Littlefield."

"Aunt Margaret felt sorry for you and knew Mama needed money," said Alta.

"Mama said you boys have nowhere to go. Somebody will come for you."

"What did she say about Mrs. Hoy? Mama whips us for lying," said Mary.

Alta thought a bit, "Mama said, *'Judge not, lest ye be judged.'*"

"Mama always says *judge not* when she doesn't know what to do. And she always feels sorry for anyone worse off," said Mary.

"We're pretty bad off too," said Alta.

Hands on the rock to steady herself, Mary leaned forward, eyes on a string of ladies on Front Street, yellow ribbons around their waists, passing out leaflets.

"Those ladies have been around a lot, singing like those women we saw in Sacramento. Mrs. Faye's organizing again, now she's recuperated from the typhoid," laughed Alta, pointing out the ladies she recognized—Mrs. Titus, Mrs. Tucker, her teacher, even Mrs. Bridges.

"Are the leaflets about the special election?" asked Mary, holding Alta's arm, walking slowly back to the house, Eddie dawdling behind.

Alta whispered, "Yes. Mama's only thinking about elections and money and Mr. Faye. Maybe I'll find out what's going on with William and Eddie."

FROM THEIR SPOT on the hill, both excited and fearful after the forest fire, the children had seen the first Woman Suffrage Campaign bonfire rally, anticipating the special election to be held October 10, 1911.

With the typhoid and the boys staying, she hadn't attended any meetings or rallies, but Mama had collected pamphlets. Lying about, Mary had read many of them, her favorite a drawing of a poor washerwoman scrubbing clothes. It argued women should be allowed to vote if they were providing the income for their families.

When Mrs. Faye invited Mama, along with all the suffragettes in town, to a meeting at her house, Alta persuaded Sally Faye to invite her over. She returned, out of breath, to the delight of all, carrying a cake box. On the bed where Mary had propped herself against the wall, three boys and three girls stuffed themselves on the leftover desserts.

A delicate cake in hand, Alta related how Aunt Ola, who Mama brought with her, admired Mrs. Faye's rich house, which, in Alta's opinion, almost made Ola forget why she'd been invited. Perhaps she hadn't looked around the time she measured Mrs. Faye for the wedding, chattering until Mama grabbed her by the arm and placed her on a small sofa so the meeting could start.

It was boring, according to Alta, until Mrs. Tucker, Whitney Hotel owner, stood up. Foot forward and hands clasped in front, Alta said in Mrs. Tucker's low voice, "If we can't vote yet, that doesn't mean we can't go to the town council and tell those men what's right and what women expect."

Then Mrs. Faye reminded everyone to ask the town council members to vote for the Woman Suffrage Amendment, but Mrs. Tucker also wanted money for two more big bonfires and rallies before the special election.

Alta said, "Sally and Zack and I were behind the sofa eating cakes, when Aunt Ola told Mama it was too much for her.

"Mama told her to stand up for herself, and if they'd had some rights, their parents wouldn't have been able to order them around after they were twenty-one. Maybe the man would have given Ola money for Amanda."

Mary stopped eating her last bite and said, "I wonder. Maybe Mama thinks Papa will give her more money."

"Papa doesn't have any money," said Raleigh.

Alta laughed and said Mrs. Tucker warned everyone to stick together tonight at the meeting.

She turned to the boys and said, "Have you heard any of this election stuff in Reno?"

William said, "No, we just go with Ma and Mr. Littlefield. No time to hear anything."

"I want to see our dad," said Eddie.

THE NEXT DAY, Mary was propped on the bed, reading her favorite parts of *The Marvelous Wizard of Oz*. Through the front window, she watched Aunt Ola and Amanda climb the path to the house. Waiting for Mama to return from Mrs. Harrigan's, Aunt Ola, eyes lit up, related last night's council meeting events, not that Mary understood it all.

"Here's the best part," Aunt Ola laughed. "The meeting was nearly over when we arrived at the Railroad Men's Hall. They were passing around whiskey glasses for a nip before they left."

Having searched for Papa in a saloon, Mary easily imagined fat bearded men filling the space with chairs and loud voices, taking quick swigs, and smoking smelly cigars in a haze so heavy the far side of the room was hidden.

Next best was when Mama spoke. Their tiny mother, the opposite of Mrs. Tucker, got up her courage and stepped out to say the town council must agree to support the special election and talk to Nevada County state legislators. Votes by women would help good things happen in the town, like better water systems so no one gets typhoid.

"I didn't know Dolly knew so much about these matters," said Aunt Ola. "But she's smart, and I should know when she believes something, she just says it."

Mary listened to Ola talk about men leaning into a huddle in the back corner, pointing with their cigars at Mama and Mrs. Tucker.

Mrs. Tucker had stood and started in about coughing up money to fix the roads. If money wasn't raised to fix them, would Hollywood people come again to make another movie like last year? And who would get moving picture people to spend money? Women, of course, if the council helped with money for flyers and a bonfire so the election was won.

This was exciting. Moving pictures.

"A good idea, wasn't it? That got everyone's attention," said Ola.

She smoothed out her skirt and gave a cookie to Amanda who had wandered in from the yard, dust all over her cream-colored pinafore and little pink face.

"There's more," said Aunt Ola. "We marched out and a few took out cigarettes and lit up. Imagine, right on the street."

Aunt Ola shook her head and smiled again, but with a nervous tremble to her lip.

"Then we started home, and Dolly began to lecture me, saying I'd have to get Mr. James to vote for women's rights. I've never talked like that to him. But your mother said, 'Now, Ola, you owe me.' "

Mary imagined them walking along Front Street, a dark night, hard to see the path. Dangerous.

Aunt Ola said, "Indeed, I wonder what she meant by 'you owe me.' I suppose she still hasn't altogether forgiven me about your father. I wish she'd have some mercy."

Aunt Ola was silent for a moment. Then Mama pushed the door open with her hip, vegetables in her arms. Little Eddie carried a basket of eggs from Mrs. Harrigan. Aunt Ola told her Mr. James had agreed to vote for the Woman Suffrage Amendment.

"I didn't even have to persuade him," said Ola.

Mama's face relaxed, and the corners of her mouth turned up. The smile must have eased Ola's heart, thought Mary. Ola walked out the door humming "Polly Wolly Doodle" while swinging Amanda's little hand.

RALEIGH AND HER sisters were in the barn getting the boy boarders to help move piles of wood, so Molly had more room to wander. Mary told them what Aunt Ola said, though she kept the part about mercy to herself.

She added, "Aunt Ola remembered everything."

"I told you at the wedding Aunt Ola learned how to think," said Alta. "She just doesn't have as much book learning as Mama."

Tiny was glad Mama had stood up. It meant she wasn't so sad anymore.

Raleigh wished he had been there to see the men in the back, saying he would have punched them. William agreed, and Little Eddie held up his fists, although each sister, none of whom were against fighting back, shook her head.

Tiny said, "Raleigh, you don't hit people in a meeting. You can say what you want as long as you take your turn."

Mary reminded him, "Otherwise, there'd be fighting and shooting."

"Ma and Mr. Littlefield were afraid someone was going to shoot," said Eddie, just as his brother punched him on the arm. "Hey, stop that. Didn't Tiny just say not to hit?"

Alta said, "Who would shoot?"

The boys looked at their fists and frowned.

Mary said, "When's the next bonfire? It'll be huge. We can pass out pamphlets. Wouldn't that be fun?"

⟫◆⟪

"THOSE BOYS WERE afraid," said Lane. "What then?"

"Then leaves turned yellow and the wind blew hard," said Mary.

20

November 1963
Sacramento

In June 1963, fifteen of us retirees filled the head table in the hot, hot state dining room at the Capitol. An antique room with a well-polished California oak door and window frames, white tablecloths, and dishes imprinted with the Seal of California, the luncheon setting felt like an event for famous legislators. My pedigree? The one who had worked longest for the government, thirty-one years, all told, at the state printing office, not including fourteen years working for Mr. Wiseman's bookbindery. I was so grateful to Mr. Wiseman for taking me on at sixteen, when I looked scrawny and was tired of being poor. Only half-listening to Governor Brown's congratulations, I thought instead about my retirement trip to Hawaii with my longtime printing office pal, Edith. I felt so glad she came up with the plan.

Standing up to receive a forty year union membership pin, a smile fixed on my sixty-five-year-old face, I congratulated myself for signing on as soon as I'd been able. I handed over my initial twenty-five cent monthly dues in 1919. It came to me, as it often did, how I owed Mama. She recovered her fortitude and stood up for woman suffrage back in 1911. That's how I learned what rights were. In my time, I'd volunteered for the committees to negotiate pay raises and lunch breaks and to finally secure a state pension fund.

I knew I'd get some Social Security, but for years and years I felt practically like Mama, counting out pennies, trying to make sure I'd have enough to live on. When I told her I was retiring, she nodded and said "good girl," as if she'd never had a doubt I'd manage to find a good job, raise a daughter, and retire comfortably. I had more than enough for the boat trip to Hawaii.

The luncheon over, animated about the exotic Hawaii trip coming up, Edith and I left the Capitol for the roaring heat on the street. Abruptly I stopped, remembering the next Monday I wouldn't enter the noisy printing office and train another new employee to align the paper carefully, so it would enter the machine neatly.

STARING AT THE orchid lei in the magazine on Alta's side table, I blinked and the traumatic 1963 memory appeared before my eyes. Raleigh put his head down on his arms. Abel stirred in his captain's chair, but said nothing. Sitting in a trance as the kitchen warmed up, I was sure I'd beheld Mama at dawn, as warmth abandoned her and she slipped away.

Those first few months of retirement, I'd been busy planting more peonies and new roses, canning plums, and making blackberry jam—the homebody things I never had time for when I worked. Then cold, dark November came, and I dropped off early.

Abruptly my eyes flipped open to glimpse the sun's rosy aura among the bare plum trees. A waver in the soft pink above the plum shadows caught my half-opened eyes. Uneasy, I got up and tiptoed into the kitchen. Spread on the china buffet were my pictures of Hawaii from my first visit to paradise.

Abel, an early riser, was already sitting in his captain's chair. Coffee percolated and the furnace flipped on to heat the house. Frost was glistening on the few quince leaves outside the window. I wrapped myself in my heavy bathrobe and sat at the kitchen table, showing Abel the last of my sunny, tropical green photos. Footsteps clumped up the back porch steps and the doorknob jiggled. I knew it must be Raleigh coming by for a cup of coffee, but it was very early for him.

I looked up and knew this wasn't a chatting kind of visit. The last time I'd seen Raleigh's face stricken like that was when his wife died.

"Ah, Mary," he said, "Mama died. Alta called me. I knew she wasn't feeling good. Alta said the visiting nurse came last week and checked her blood pressure and asked her some questions. The nurse said she was all right, just old."

The china cabinets seemed far away, and the room whirled. I closed my eyes until the faintness subsided, and the light and people in my kitchen reappeared.

"I covered Mama with her blanket and came here. She looked all shrunken and stiff already. Alta went back into her room and slammed the door. What'll we do?"

Who knew how long we sat, grief pressing on our shoulders, but finally I took Raleigh's hand, telling him to go back and sit with Mama and Alta—I'd call Tiny and then go around to the funeral home on Fruitridge Road. Someone from there would go get Mama.

Raleigh rubbed his eyes, then forced himself to stand and turn to Abel.

"Can you drive me in the truck? I don't think I can walk back over."

Abel, stiff in his chair, eyes sad, but unable to respond with words other than "all right by me," stood and patted Raleigh on the back. Abel leaned over to give me a hug, saying he'd be back soon, and that's how he and Raleigh managed.

Tiny said she'd help me pay for the funeral. Good thing we agreed to have Mama cremated and buried in the local cemetery because, for sure, Mama never thought she'd die and never told us what to do. She'd never been ill that I remembered, except the Christmas in 1910 when we were so poor. She was still going until about three weeks ago when she seemed to sit a lot and not eat much, but what of it? She was ninety-three years old, and the last to go— Margaret gone, Lauf gone, even Ola gone, who we hadn't seen since she'd moved to Reno ten years ago.

After I made arrangements with the funeral home, I called Betsy, who was as surprised as the rest of us.

"Oh, Mother," she said, "I called a couple of weeks ago. Alta said Grandma was fine. I thought she'd go on forever."

Then tears welled up in my eyes and spilled down my cheeks, as Betsy talked about Mama's house and the fun she had there with her cousins. Mama did try to make life good for her grandchildren, once she had pulled out of her hard, fretful years in the mountains. I thought of the time she told us *life's but a walking shadow.* Still she kept marching, searching for the sunlight.

When Betsy hung up, I stood for a minute in the kitchen looking out the windows onto the side yard at our fig tree, branches nearly bare in November. In my mind, Mama pulled a lovely ripe fruit right off the branch in the middle of summer, peeling the skin back, eating the mushy insides. What were they for her? Something sweet and rich in life?

Then my mind drifted to the evening six weeks ago when I drove her to the New Bethlehem meetinghouse. We tried out the pink and white Desoto I'd purchased from an old co-worker. Of course, she didn't even notice I had a new car. Dressed in her black wool coat with the fur collar she must have had for thirty years, she stepped out ready for her free "holy roller" evening.

"I expect figs tonight, the text being, *'Can the fig tree, my brethren, bear olive berries?'* James 3:12, speaking about wisdom," she said, face wrinkled up in laughter.

She almost skipped, as she hurried along, not slow and slumped over like might be expected of such an old woman. I laughed to myself as she'd finally, in her way, taken Uncle Lauf up on his proposal to turn to the Lord, which long ago had infuriated her.

TINY ARRIVED ABOUT ten o'clock on the day of the funeral, Friday, November 22. She looked as sad as Raleigh, the two of them being Mama's babies most of the time we lived in Truckee.

At the cemetery, we were a regular cavalcade with Tiny in the Mercedes following Abel, and me in the pink and white Desoto steering along the curving drives to the outdoor wall of caches where the urn was to be placed. Raleigh had Alta with him. All of Raleigh's children and their families were meeting us there.

We never would have known what had happened except Abel was fanatic about listening to the radio. I couldn't believe it. Just as I pulled over, the program was interrupted to broadcast JFK had been shot. Raleigh came running. One of his grandsons had a transistor radio and had also heard the news.

Everyone was sad enough about Mama, but they were dumbstruck by the broadcast. Tears leaked out of everyone's eyes, even Tiny's, who hadn't voted for Kennedy, to Mama's chagrin. We were crying for both, a little woman who had made a bigger impression on each of us than JFK and for the handsome president known all over the world.

The funeral director stood in front of the wall, holding onto the plainest urn I could select because Mama preferred things simple but sturdy. It would hold her ashes forever. He didn't know what to do, as flustered as we were by such shattering news, so Raleigh whispered to him we had a service in mind. Everyone found chairs, wiping eyes and talking about Kennedy more than Mama, listening to his famous words that filled in time between updates on the events. Raleigh, Tiny, and I sat numb, as if we were back to Wednesday morning when Mama left the world, and we would never again hear her words.

I started off saying Mama had voted for Kennedy, of course, as she'd voted for all Democrats starting with Woodrow Wilson, the first presidential candidate she could vote for. By the time Alta and I were old enough to vote, she'd said too bad Harding won, as he was a pretty face, but not smart enough. That made everyone laugh through the crying.

Then I said we were lucky because, after all, Mama had lived a long, long time. JFK was about half her age. It reminded me again of my thoughts when I retired in June about the suffrage election she'd worked for leading to better times for women, as she often reminded us. You'd never believe times were better by the simple way she lived, and for the most part men were still running things, but I didn't bring that up. Those memories made my eyes fill again. My voice cracked, so I had to stop speaking.

The undertaker put the urn in its small enclosed space, and Tiny pulled out her elocution book and read Mama's favorite verse of the Longfellow poem "Sandalphon," which she had practiced with Tiny during her actress phase.

And he gathers the prayers as he stands,
And they change into flowers in his hands,
Into garlands of purple and red,
And beneath the great arch of the portal,
Through the streets of the City Immortal
Is wafted the fragrance they shed.

Fragrant flowers—a good choice. Tall wide-branched pines, firs, and oak trees spread out all over the cemetery. Even on this cold day, the sky was bright blue and the bushes green. In the space where we gathered, a huge jacaranda stood, bare now, but I knew by spring it would burst into purple-blue and red bougainvillea, and roses would bloom as Mama liked.

Then Raleigh stood and read the "Twenty-third Psalm" often repeated when Mama needed to restore her equilibrium. By then everyone's eyes were red and watery, tissues over each nose and mouth. Raleigh read,

Yea, though I walk through the valley
of the shadow of death,
I will fear no evil ....

The words were all that was left from those frightening days in fall 1911, when Mama comforted us. It was true, as I'd said before, she walked on in that gap between the mountains, perhaps worried, but surely fearless.

Raleigh cleared his throat to say Mama was famous because she raised nine children altogether and pulled herself and all of them up from poverty to make something of themselves. We needed hopeful words, as the radio news about JFK became more sinister—witnesses gave various versions of the shooting, reports came from the hospital, and roadblocks were established to find the sniper.

Frankie, Raleigh's second oldest and Mama's favorite, said he had a great memory from way back in 1934 when he and his brother and sisters came to live with their grandmother. He remembered how smart she was when she decided she was going to replace the outhouse with a septic system. She'd hoarded money, and to the kids' amazement began to boss the entire operation, telling men she'd found in one of the migrant camps exactly what to do. The men even built the small toilet room off the kitchen. Jimmy and Frankie went with her to the second-hand store, and she bargained for the toilet, which they hauled back in a wheelbarrow.

The kids had fun helping to dig the hole for the tank. They'd been sent to the field across the street with potato sacks to fill with little rocks to lay out for the leaching field. They couldn't believe what an engineer their grandmother was, almost like the president of her small world. Frankie thought even JFK would have been impressed. The workers certainly were, especially since who knew if any of them had ever used a toilet. Mama let each worker take a pee to see if it worked before they started filling up the open holes and pipe ditches all over the back yard. Frankie smiled and everyone sighed, grief-filled laughter mixed with tears. The funeral director was smiling too until he remembered to resume a serious look.

Jimmy told another story about Mama, then Rosalyn, and finally Margaret, whom Alta had saved and who had gone to college. Each related their memory, though I couldn't keep them in my head. I gathered my purse and papers like I knew what I was doing. I remembered to thank the funeral director. Everyone drove home to watch television for the next three days.

As we left the cemetery, Alta sat in Raleigh's car, arms wrapped over her chest and shoulders slumped forward, grieving as much as any of us since she lived with Mama and, indeed, was supposed to watch over her. Late that afternoon, after Tiny left to drive back to the Bay Area, I drove over to see if Alta needed anything. I needed a break from the repetitious news after JFK died. I felt too sad to keep listening. Alta was wandering in the back yard, pulling on the branches of Mama's huge fig tree and letting her cigarette drip ash on the grass. At least she wasn't covered up in bed and didn't smell of liquor.

She groaned, "I won't be able to live here."

In Mama's bedroom, I opened the drawer where she'd kept her papers, searching for the deed or a will. Thank God, I found the papers Mama had had drawn up three years before, giving the house to Alta. The office manager must have been surprised to see a tiny old woman walk in and ask to be advised how to transfer property.

Alta had gone into the kitchen and made some tea. She was leaning back in a chair, spinning Mr. Faye's Washo basket and staring at the woven designs, repeating the words from the Longfellow poem Tiny had read at the cemetery.

I waved the papers at her. I told her Raleigh would take her to a realtor on Monday to prepare to sell the place, and that she'd better begin to go through the things in the house and think about where she was going to live.

Shaking out some pills from a prescription jar, she popped them in her mouth and gulped the tea.

Grabbing at my hand, she said, "How'll I know what to do?"

"I just told you what to do. Like Mama always said, do for yourself," I answered.

Then, as Raleigh had done when he told me about Mama, she folded her head down on her arms.

At that moment, I wasn't kind. After all, Mama'd taken Alta in after she was released from the hospital after the war. Alta had lived in this house ever since, singing once in a while at a downtown bar, living on some kind of state check for the indigent. Raleigh's children loved Alta because she told funny stories, sang, and played the piano. Of course she didn't have to be in charge of anything, and when she'd go off on a bender, Mama'd get Raleigh to take her to the hospital for a week or so.

I said I'd be back the next day to begin cleaning up the house, thinking I could watch the news at Mama's house as well as at mine. It would probably be news about the man who killed Kennedy, and how he was caught by accident. Abel and I had a quiet supper and watched the images of Kennedy, one minute waving and the next slumped over with his car careening through the Dallas streets to the hospital. Then we watched the news about the ceremony on the plane, making Lyndon Johnson president.

Saturday I drove over to find everything gray and silent—the house, the air, even the grass. A muted tune came to my ear, so I hurried up the steps and pushed the door open, peering into the dark—not one light on. Alta cowered on the piano bench, one elbow on the piano ledge, hand holding her head, a blanket wrapped around her shoulders, leaning forward to play the notes to "Sweet Adeline." She lifted a cigarette from the ashtray, took a drag, and turned to me.

"Pretty tune, isn't it?" she said. "Mama liked it."

Smoke filled the air. She took another puff and stood up, too quickly, I supposed, as she staggered and grabbed the top of the piano to catch herself.

"Is it morning already?" she asked. "I was waiting."

Covered in the pale blanket, ashy face shrouded by a puff of graying, flyaway hair, she took another step and another, floating toward me. I was unnerved, my eyes on a wavering ghostly figure, except she didn't fade away, as often in her life she seemed to want. She lurched to the table and picked up her bottle of pills.

"Can't you at least get me something to drink?—and not water," she waved the bottle in front of my face.

She slithered down onto the floor, but that sarcastic whisper said she'd get through, though not on her own. She'd disappear if we didn't do something, for Mama's sake if not for hers.

I searched out the liquor bottle behind her bed and called Raleigh to come help me get her into the car. She fell limp from the pills and the liquor. Finally, I realized Alta missed Mama more than any of us. She hardly knew how to live without her nearby. That being so, we drove off through the streets of Sacramento to the hospital during that catastrophe-filled weekend.

BETSY AND I were on the phone for a long time Sunday while I told her about the funeral and Alta's collapse. I asked about her husband, Gus, who thought Kennedy was the greatest, both being from Massachusetts and Irish Catholic. Gus was distraught, but couldn't stop watching. And John and Polly? They'd seen plenty of civil rights violence on TV, but this new havoc, even for teenagers, was more than they understood.

Just then, *pop! pop!* and I heard Gus yell, "Oh, my God! Bet! Bet! Come look!" and Abel called out, "Mary! Come here!"

I dropped the phone and looked around at the TV. Waving a shiny pistol, that Ruby man was grabbed from behind, and Oswald slid down, though his wrist was still cuffed to the man in the Stetson. We stared at the TV. Cameras jostled, newsmen shouted, and police grabbed people in case someone else had a gun.

Later that day, Abel and I and millions of people, famous and anonymous, viewed the funeral caisson, not much smaller than our old buckboard, pulled by a team of horses all the way down the long wide street in Washington, D.C.

Not to forget, the flash of metal in Ruby's hand made me shudder over the guns we'd seen and heard in those last wild months in Truckee. At that time, to us four naive children, it seemed the world was veering off the edge.

Who of us realized in 1911 that people of little consequence had been killed—as easily as a person holding all the power one can imagine? To tell the truth, I was glad Mama didn't live to see the tragedy.

21

September 1911
Harrigan's Hill, Truckee

ABSORBED IN THEIR game of Commit, Tiny, Alta, and Mary were slow to look up when Mama walked into the front room.

"Have you seen those boys?" she asked. "Three weeks and not one word from Reno."

"In the barn," said Alta.

"Eddie's too young, but William may as well learn something. I'm signing him up for school."

The girls turned back to the cards, though Mary wondered about school too. Mama smoothed down her skirt, settled her shoulders, and went out to the barn. Little Eddie wandered in a few minutes later. Putting down her cards, Tiny looked out the front window.

"Ha, she's making them walk in front of her so they don't sneak off to the river."

Eddie said, "William'll be scared. You'll see. He's been to school in Reno, then Tonopah, then Reno again."

When the boys returned and William showed off the slate he'd bought at Mrs. Goode's, he said, "Dead sure, that school's a big place. Only three rooms at the school in Tonopah, little kids, middle-sized kids, big kids. Last year was my first time with the middle-sized kids."

Mary was surprised at the boy who rarely spoke more than a few words and never had an opinion. Little Eddie mouthed, "I told you."

Tiny said, "Don't be scared. My brother'll help you find your room."

Tipping his head, Raleigh commented, "Y'know how Mama's friends want to fix the roads? She went to see the doctor, but watched us all the way down Front Street, even though I told her we jump over the bad places."

At noon dinner, Mama said, "You're way ahead of the class, Mary, and I can't afford a relapse. Just as well because I need someone to take care of Eddie, so I can go back to work."

The others were disgusted since they didn't even like school and said so loudly. That afternoon, hiding in the bedroom, Mary, who was the only one who wanted to go to school, cried into the pillow because she couldn't return until January.

ON FRIDAY AFTERNOON of the first week of school, Mary and Little Eddie strayed down to the sawdust pile below the barn. After night rain, the sawdust was clumpy, vapor rising as the pile dried out. Eddie crawled around with a jam jar from some past game, filling it up and turning it out to make castle towers. He related a long story all the while, taking different roles, at first the prince, then a dragon that talked. Eddie threw sawdust around, as the prince and dragon battled for the castle. Mary laughed, sidetracked from reading *The Shepherd of the Hills,* which Papa brought when she was sick—a book for grown-ups, but she liked it anyway.

They heard footsteps. Moving slowly with a stiff leg and a walking stick, an auburn-haired man about Papa's height came into view.

Eddie yelled, "Hey, that looks like my daddy!"

Eddie jumped up and ran on his short chubby legs to the man who stooped, shaking his head and hugging the boy.

"Where's William?"

"At school, Dad," said Eddie, pointing down the hill.

"Where's Mrs. Edwards?" the man asked, looking up at Mary.

"Cleaning the butcher's house," answered Mary. "She'll be home soon, I think."

She hesitated, then asked, "How did you know to come here?"

"Your Aunt Margaret told me where to find my boys."

She shrugged and said, "You can wait at the house, I guess."

Little Eddie took his father's hand, and all three trudged up the hill. A stiff-legged man, a little blabbing boy, and a skinny raggedy girl looked quite a sight to Crazy Lady Harrigan, who stood in her yard with her mouth wide open in a silent cackle, thought Mary.

Mama showed up a long hour later.

"WHO'D 'A' THOUGHT she'd run away like that? I thought she was carryin' my child. Tonopah is a small town. I still don't know how she met him."

Mr. Hoy shifted in his chair and frowned. Mama was wringing her hands and sent Little Eddie off to Mrs. Harrigan. He scampered out, looking confused at the words and relieved to get away.

"Not that many Indians or half-breeds in Tonopah. I thought I knew 'em all. Including that one. They worked at the mines like me. My God, she ran away with one of 'em. Nobody even liked 'em in Tonopah, except the owner who needed miners, and they worked for nothin' hardly—when they showed up."

His face contorted into a shriveled grin. Mama looked over at Mary, and she dragged herself into the bedroom, lay down, and still listened.

"One day braces shifted and rocks came down, and I slipped tryin' to get out of the way and slid down the mine shaft. It was hard liftin' me back out. My leg was really twisted. The doc in town tried to set it, but they sent me up to the Reno hospital on the train."

The chair creaked. He groaned and stretched his leg.

"God, I didn't even know she'd come to Reno with the boys and that man, not 'til I went back to Tonopah. First I thought they'd gone to live with the Washo. He's half-Washo, y'know. Can you believe she'd go live with 'em? And take my boys? So I went back to Reno again and found her at the hospital. She'd already agreed to give away that half-Indian baby, y'know."

The chair thumped against the floor.

"I'll take her back for the boys."

A hand smacked the table.

"I found that man at the park and shot 'im, y' know, but I only winged the bastard in the arm. D'you know what the deputy said? 'Why'n't you make a good job of it?'"

Mr. Hoy laughed, a snorting, bitter guffaw. Mama was silent. Mary was rattled and pulled the bed cover over her face.

"I got it out of her that she'd gotten your name from the lady living next to 'em in Reno. At least my boys weren't up in the mountains at some God-forsaken Washo camp. That's how I came here to collect 'em. We'll go for their ma and then back to Tonopah."

Raleigh and William came home, and after scuffling and pounding in the attic, the two brothers appeared with the carpetbag and satchel. Mr. Hoy clapped William on the back and took Eddie's hand. They became smaller and smaller, as they walked down the hill into town toward the train station.

Little Eddie turned once and waved. As Mary waved back it came to her she'd be alone now all day. She'd miss the funny little boy.

Moping around the house for a few days, Raleigh finally confided in his sisters.

"William told me to come see them in Tonopah. I'll get enough money someday soon with my chipmunk."

Alta hooted, "You can't even keep two cents in your pocket!"

"Yes, I can," Raleigh shouted back.

"Leave him alone, Alta," said Mary, rubbing her throat.

With Eddie gone, Mary wondered how to get her mother to relent about staying home from school. She wouldn't go until she stopped coughing. She knew that much.

ON BALMY DAYS, Mary warmed herself outside, following tiny figures of townspeople performing the same ordinary tasks day after quiet early autumn day. Eddie and William filled her head for a while. They had seemed like any ordinary boys who might have been walking with Raleigh along Front Street. She'd never heard of a family struggle quite like theirs.

Finally, when the town arguments began, she left off thinking about the boys, forever gone no matter what her brother said. She'd droop and drift back to the house to nap until one of her siblings, most often Tiny, came home after school and entertained her with the town news.

Tiny said Aunt Ola was convinced the town council would support the special election campaign with money. Mr. Titus told Raleigh people were prodding councilmen for road improvements to attract the moviemakers.

Over at Sally Faye's house, Alta picked up Woman Suffrage Amendment leaflets the three children passed out all over town. Mary read and folded while Alta gossiped. It was Sally who told Alta that Mr. Faye wanted to be the next town mayor.

Then, as happens with many men who wish to be out in front, Mr. Faye introduced a completely different issue at the September town council meeting. At least that's how Mama put it. She flipped her hand, dismissing men, but from the tilt of her head, showing she admired Mr. Faye, who stood up for his beliefs.

Ever since Mrs. Faye had nearly died from the typhoid, Mr. Faye had exhorted townspeople like the Masons, the Volunteer Fire Brigade, and customers in his saloon. He wanted to pass local laws to get rid of outhouses. The town had electricity; now, it needed better sewage systems.

When Mary walked up to the outhouse, Mama held a flyer and measured how far away the building was from the vegetable garden. She enthused about the septic tank installed on Mr. McGlashan's property, the one on the poster. It laid out the details of the large masonry tank and pipes. It showed that the tank needs a leaching field. If a property had a septic tank, residents could install an indoor toilet. Most importantly, the containment of sewage would prevent bad germs from getting into the wells and springs that provided water to the town. Mama stopped and looked up and down the hill.

"I don't know," she said, "We're poor up here, and Minna makes me think about the Washo that live in the hills. No one cares about us or them. How are we going to afford septic tanks?"

Mama frowned, then smiled as she admitted that Mr. Faye was good at building up excitement. Humming "Sweet Adeline," she retreated to the kitchen to make soup.

Molly was busy grazing. Mary held out her hand for a lick and scratched Molly's neck. The poor horse would be puzzled if people started digging up the yard and putting in pipes. Then Tiny and Raleigh trotted up the path; Alta plodded not far behind.

Mary showed the flyer and said, "For sure, we went to a toilet like that in Mrs. Archer's room by the kitchen. One good thing about that nasty lady's house."

"We had toilets at the orphanage too," said Tiny. "Maybe because it used to be a rich lady's home."

"A very, very rich lady," said Raleigh.

Alta said, "Excuse me! If you'd all listen to me like I've said a thousand times, if we'd only talk Mama into taking Papa back, we'd move down this old hill into a decent house, and we could get a septic tank and a toilet. No one's going to dig a hole for a big tank up here by these places."

Those words jolted Mary, reminding her that Mama wasn't always wise. What if she'd been wrong herself, for hanging onto hard feelings about Papa? Right before them, Mama was distracted from her money woes, caught up by the special election, septic tanks, and a dalliance with Mr. Faye. If only to find a better place to live in this town, was it time to persuade Mama to take up with Papa again?

Mary walked into the kitchen for supper with a new outlook—all because of a toilet.

NEXT AFTERNOON, AUNT Ola, with wide smile on her face, entered on the arm of Mr. James, who had kept his word and attended the town council meeting. Flopping on the front room bed to listen, Mary considered asking Aunt Ola to persuade Mama about Papa, even if things hadn't worked out last Christmas.

A queer mix of comedy and melodrama, according to Mr. James. The Woman Suffrage Campaign received ten dollars for posters and lumber for a bonfire rally before the election. At the rally, the ladies in the audience cheered and waved flags. A patient fellow, the mayor let the noise go on a few minutes more than necessary in Mr. James's opinion.

Next, Mr. Titus proposed funds to repair roads, playing up the money-making aspect, like drawing movie makers to the mountains to film snow scenes. Council members nodded, as if they had dollars in hand already.

Mr. Faye took the floor and roused the crowd about the virtues of septic tanks. Suddenly, Mr. Vaughn, the *Truckee Star News* publisher, leaped up and boomed out that he rejected any tax proposals, whether for better roads or sewage.

Mr. Faye shouted back. He didn't believe Mr. Vaughn since his fine car had been stuck in a muddy ditch for days because the roads were so poor. Mr. Vaughn retorted, saying Mr. Faye was simply looking for a cause to help his spring mayor's campaign.

"Indeed," said Mr. James, "it was as if a pistol had fired and everyone froze."

Mr. James coughed to cover a smile, then continued the story of the ladies who booed Mr. Vaughn and the men who shook fists and swore. The mayor pounded the gavel, hollering to sit or get out. Then he said everything would be tabled until the next session, and he adjourned the meeting.

Patting Aunt Ola's arm, Mr. James said, "I've never seen a man look so relieved. I think he'll be overjoyed when the next election takes place."

Mama waved as Ola walked down the hill with a bounce in her step. Mary lifted her eyebrows, wondering when Ola might help them.

Swaying and humming "Oh Dear," Mama said, "The important thing is we've more funds for the suffrage campaign."

By THE END of September, lonesome with Eddie gone, Mary climbed the hill in the afternoons to sit with Crazy Lady Harrigan, who entertained Mary with forgotten mountain characters—Indian and Chinese, gold miners, and railroad men.

Then Mama would arrive, passing on the town's gossip and belligerent newspaper articles that resulted from the town council meeting. A *Truckee Star News* editorial accused Mr. Faye of more deal making.

In a town like Truckee where no mode of swift travel other than the railway is available, a deal with the Southern Pacific Railroad Company for a discount rate on liquor freight charges is a major cause for concern. Any sort of businessman may contract a good rate with a company for smooth delivery of the product that is the main source of his income. The fact that Nolan Faye, proprietor of the Last Chance Saloon, is also a longtime town councilman and an all-but-declared candidate for mayor of Truckee leaves the Truckee Star News *to wonder. Albeit the election is not until next spring, does Mr. Faye use his status to promote himself at the expense of his competitors? Will liquor at his saloon be cheaper and thus affordable to all sorts of vagabonds and lay-abouts much to the chagrin of the temperance alliance ... ?*

Alta reported Sally Faye's mother was vexed by the vitriol in the editorial. A week later the paper published a front-page news article that claimed

Nolan Faye, proprietor of the Last Chance Saloon, divulged this morning that he seeks a partner to finance the purchase of valuable equipment for a new business. Faye, also a current town council member, stated the equipment was designed to seal up outhouses. He had learned about such equipment in the Reno newspapers. In Faye's words, "The business will do the town good by ensuring that sewage doesn't leak into springs and wells." According to Faye, who has also indicated interest in being the next town mayor, he needs at least one partner so the proposed company will prosper. ...

Sally told Alta it rankled her father, as if he was trying to put one over on the townspeople. Sally's mother called Mr. Vaughn odious.

Late one afternoon, watching events on Front Street, Mary heard popping noises and yelling from the post office where Mama and Alta had entered a few minutes before. Men dashed to the newspaper and telegraph offices. People poured out of shops, shouting and grabbing each other. Mary jumped up and finally spied Mama pulling Alta by the arm outside the post office door.

When they reached the house, Mama waited for calm in her voice, saying she couldn't believe what had occurred, although Mr. Faye was already riled up. She'd heard him swear about the newspaper articles, and Mr. Vaughn hadn't been inside the saloon in a week.

"Mr. Faye was leaning on the counter waiting for the post office clerk," said Mama. "When Alta and I reached the post office door, Aunt Margaret's letter in my hand, Mr. Vaughn swaggered into the lobby. He and his two friends bellowed, as if next to the train's screeching brakes."

Mama thought it was too much when Mr. Vaughn pushed himself up against Mr. Faye and cracked 'good afternoon, Mr. Faye, you rogue,' which sent Mr. Faye flying off the handle, yelling he'd never speak to someone who distorted the truth.

"Anyone would agree their voices rose higher and louder," Mama said. "All of a sudden, pistols were pulled from each waistcoat. Everyone saw them. Next thing, Mr. Vaughn fell to the floor, a bullet in his chest. I don't think Mr. Faye even realized what he'd done. Luckily, the bullet from Mr. Vaughn's gun grazed Mr. Faye's shoulder and ended up in the post office wall, not in one of the patrons."

"Trouble and more trouble," sighed Mama, stirring a cup of tea until the liquid spilled into the saucer.

Retreating to the attic with Mary, Tiny, and Raleigh, Alta said, "This is what happened. Everyone started hollering and someone ran out for the doctor. One of the friends ran for Mr. O'Brien while the other one seized Mr. Faye. I thought he would run, but he sat down and held his shoulder. Mama and I stayed right by him, of course.

"Next thing I knew, Mrs. Faye came racing in, hair all flying about like the time she was upset about the car. She whispered to Mr. Faye and wouldn't let anyone come near him until Mr. O'Brien arrived. She made the constable take him into the back room and told the constable to keep everyone out, except Mr. Vaughn's friends.

"The doctor arrived and said Mr. Vaughn was dead, and someone ran to the funeral home to get the undertaker. As for everyone else in the post office, they were whispering and pointing, I guess about whose fault it was. The doctor went into the room to look at Mr. Faye.

"That's when Mama said this was no place for us to remain gawking at a poor dead soul. She dragged me out of the post office, even though we're witnesses. It was hard to tell what happened when the shouting and shooting started, but Mama did give the deputy her name. I said I'd be a witness, but you know how Mama is, pressing her lips together and saying 'You're not an adult, and there're plenty of adults here. Probably too many.' "

In the soft light of the kerosene lamp, no one said anything, but Mary was mystified by the uproar that had exploded before them.

Barely a week later, Mama was notified that she would not be a witness. Only the two friends of Mr. Vaughn, the doctor, and the post office clerk took the stand at the brief trial. Mama said the incident was notorious. Even though the trial date was set right away and a jury selected, everyone concluded it was self-defense. Alta counted that Mr. Faye spent hardly more than two weeks in the Truckee jail and never did go to the Nevada County jail.

Mary could tell the incident agitated Mama, but was disappointed Mama didn't have to swear on a Bible and testify. Alta announced she wasn't surprised that Mama, who had never been known to disavow guns, didn't want to be associated with the trial of a man killed in anger.

THE DAY AFTER the shooting, Mama picked up Aunt Margaret's letter, forgotten in the excitement.

Dear Dolly,

Mr. Littlefield and Mrs. Hoy ran away!
Mr. Hoy arrived in Reno and went to the hospital. He came here beside himself to ask about his wife. She had given the baby away to an Indian woman and disappeared with Mr. Littlefield.

Mr. Littlefield had told me he was going away, so I thought he had given up on Mrs. Hoy after being shot. I didn't say anything, but I didn't really approve of them being together and I knew people would be mean to them. Maybe they've gone off to his people. They did seem to love each other and he was very kind to William and Eddie as I said before.

Mr. Hoy was sad and angry at the same time. For days he searched, but finally he took the boys down to Tonopah to go back to their house and school.

I hope things are better now with you. I saw Tom when he came through again a week ago. He looked good. By that I mean he didn't look like he'd been drinking.

Sincerely from your loving sister,
Margaret

"Well, I never," said Mama. "First those boys come and then their father shoots an Indian and then we have someone killed in town. Now those two have run away. What did I get in the middle of?"

She folded the letter and sat still, for so long that her children became uneasy.

" '*What's done cannot be undone,*' " Mama said at last. "That's what Lady Macbeth said, you know, when she regretted all the murders."

"Who's Lady Macbeth?" asked Tiny. "How d'you know what she said?"

"Because I learned about Shakespeare and the play called *Macbeth* when I became a teacher, before you were born," Mama answered.

She paused.

"Before I met your father."

"You didn't murder anyone," said Mary. "Why'd you say that about done and undone?"

"Sometimes I regret I made your father leave. Too many bad things have happened since we've been alone," Mama answered.

"Papa could come back," said Raleigh.

"It wouldn't work," said Mama, folding her hands into her lap, staring out the window at the sliver of moon hooked to dark pines in an inky sky.

Mary wished the voice in her head, urging her, saying, "Here's your chance," would speak for her and say, "Mama, I've changed my mind, let's go back with Papa." She knew Lady Macbeth's words didn't foretell a happy end. Mary preferred Mama to sing, not quote alarming lines from a play about murder.

22

October 1911
Harrigan's Hill, Truckee

Tiny came straight home after three weeks to tell Mama she liked school. Without a word or smile, Mama peeled the skin from Mrs. O'Brien's apples.

Locking her feet around the chair legs, leaning her elbows on the table, Tiny said, "We're learning about the Indians. The Iroquois play lacrosse with a long stick and net to catch a ball. You can see totem poles up in Washington. The Hopi in the desert have kachina dolls, dressed as good or bad spirits. I really like Indian things."

Mary said, "I liked it too. Pretty soon you'll get to the Indians here in California."

"What d'you think! We learned about the Paiute and the Washo who live here just today," said Tiny. "Isn't Minna Washo, Mama?"

Mama nodded.

For a minute, Mary and Tiny watched Mama slice the apples. Tiny said, "A little rock sits on the big rock up there by Mr. McGlashan's house. The teacher said Washo and Paiute still go up there to talk to the spirits. Even though they're Methodists too, like us."

Mama laid out the slices on the crust in the pie pan.

When Mama added the top crust, Tiny said, "I'm going over to see Hazel and Minna to ask about the rock spirit."

Tiny searched for her sweater, and Mary scooped up the apple scraps for Molly. Mama warned, "Don't stay too long and bother Minna."

As Mary left the kitchen, Mama sank onto the chair. She folded her head and arms down onto the table, oblivious to the powdery flour puffing up and settling back onto the strands of dark hair detached from her bun.

As Tiny half-ran and half-skipped down the path toward the pine tree, Mary called out, "Wait!"

She caught up and sighed, "It's boring not going to school. I wish Mama'd let me go back, but she says I'm too tired and sick all the time."

"Isn't it funny? I like school this year?" Tiny laughed.

They stared across the valley, Mary saying she wished Mama would cheer up.

Smile disappearing, Tiny said, "For sure, one day she's up and the next she's down again."

Tree branches swayed in the wind. They frowned in puzzlement.

Palm against her forehead like a scout, Tiny peered at the opposite hill to Mr. McGlashan's mansion. "I can't see those rocks. But look, why'n't you come with me to Hazel's? We can walk slow."

At Minna's house, Hazel and Delilah were throwing a stick that a squat yellow-brown mutt leaped and caught every time.

Mary petted the little dog. Tiny said, "Hey, Hazel, d'you ever go talk to the Washo spirits up at Mr. McGlashan's rocks?"

Hazel held the stick in the air and said, "I haven't learned about the Indians. I'm not in your class yet. Ask my ma."

Inside, Minna stirred a pot of Spanish beans. The entire room filled with a warm, spicy smell.

She said, "Nice to see you girls. Mary, you look much better than the last time I saw you—all skinny and pasty."

"Sometimes I go out now, but no school until January. It's no fun at home by myself," said Mary, looking around. "Y'know, I think I need to sit down though. I get awfully tired," and she pulled over a straight back chair.

Tiny explained about the Indians, the rocks, and talking to the spirits, but finally Minna said, "Stop. Here's what I know. The old Washo believed a monster bird lived in Lake Tahoe and the spirits in the cave near the lake protected them. You can tell your teacher, Tahoe's a Washo word.

"Up here Mr. McGlashan built the fence to protect the rocks from people who scratched their initials on the boulder. The old Washo believe the wind speaks to them when the little stone rocks. Who knows? Maybe it does.

"There're some old, old Indian pictures scratched into the rock face high up the hill past the little creek. Did your teacher tell you about the pictures?"

Tiny shook her head.

"Washo who live way up there think those pictures belong to their ancestors' spirits," Minna said. "Washo like my old cousin, Captain Ben. He's from my mother's side, and he lives up that hill with his wife."

"How d'we find the pictures?" asked Tiny.

Minna said, "Cross the Truckee and walk up until you see the little creek flowing into the river. After you cross the creek—you'll see a place where you can cross—look far up. You'll see some flat rocks sticking out like a wall. You must look close to see the pictures."

She thought for a minute and warned, "Not a single one of you should go up there to make mischief."

Minna handed out sugar cookies and said, "I suppose I should go see your mother tomorrow. My cousin's wife's nephew is the Mr. Littlefield she asked me about. He came to see them in August."

And as they walked back home, Mary thought Mama might pull herself up if she knew about Mr. Littlefield.

Reaching the bridge across the river, Tiny said, "I bet Raleigh'll come look for the Indian pictures."

Mary was exhausted. She climbed Harrigan's Hill slowly, thinking about hiking up the hill on the other side of the creek. When Minna didn't show up to see Mama, Mr. Littlefield slipped from Mary's mind, though the Indian stories filled her head.

SATURDAY AFTERNOON'S DARK gray clouds filled the sky. Wind whipped the pine branches from side to side.

Standing by the door, Tiny said, "If those big branches are bending, I bet the little stone is rocking."

"Let's go up to Mr. McGlashan's and listen," said Mary. "It's not so far."

"Should we get Alta and Raleigh?" asked Tiny.

"Let's find them quick," said Mary. "Alta'll be furious if we don't take her."

Tiny ran around behind the house, calling loudly, climbing the ladder, and looking into the attic. Raleigh stumbled out, and Alta appeared from the barn.

Without warning, Mrs. O'Brien ran down the hill.

"Dolly! Dolly! Come quick. Mrs. Harrigan's crazy again. She's running around with a knife, shouting 'They're coming for me!' "

Wiping her hands on a towel, Mama ran out the kitchen door, and all four children stopped where they were.

Gasping for breath, Mrs. O'Brien said, "Mrs. Harrigan was at my house when my husband told me about the prisoners who escaped from Folsom. But don't worry. They've been seen over at Soda Springs. He left to go help the prison guards who are looking for them. She started running around with her big kitchen knife and screaming. You've got to help me calm her down. She likes you, and she listens to you."

Mama looked around and called, "Alta, you come with me. You're the strongest. You can help hold Mrs. Harrigan until she calms down."

Alta protested, "No, Mama. I don't want to. She's crazy."

Mama looked at her, and Alta turned to walk up the path.

Then Mama said, "All of you get inside the house and stay there."

Mama marched up the hill with Alta in front of her and Mrs. O'Brien babbling behind. The three retreated to the kitchen and found some cake, stale but edible, in the cupboard.

As they nibbled, Raleigh said, "I wonder how they escaped from the prison? Did they dig a tunnel?"

"How d'we know?" Mary answered.

"I don't want to stay here. Those prisoners might come," said Tiny. "Let's sneak up to the rocks."

When Crazy Lady Harrigan went crazy, it took a lot of tea, laudanum, and quiet words to calm her down. Mama would be gone all afternoon. Jumping up, they dashed down the hill. Out of breath, Mary climbed slowly until she reached the gate where Raleigh and Tiny waited. Opening the latch, they leaned close to the boulder with a faint depression at the top. The wind was blowing cold and strong. They pulled their collars up.

The smaller stone rocked slightly in the depression while the wind whipped around it. They kept silent, listening to a grating sound. Raleigh pointed to minute grains of rock, grinding under the shifting stone.

"What is the wind saying?" whispered Tiny.

"Maybe you have to talk Washo to know," said Mary softly.

"I just hear wind blowing," said Raleigh, "and the grinding sound."

Tiny murmured, "Will you please whisper, Raleigh. This is a holy place. Y'know, like Sunday School. You have to be quiet."

A disconcerted look on his face, Raleigh sat down on another rock to wait. They heard footsteps. Mary recognized the coat and hat of Mr. McGlashan, not surprising since they were on his property.

"Look who's here. You two don't look so cold and hungry today," declared Mr. McGlashan. "I saw you out my sitting room window."

"You remember us?" asked Raleigh.

"I do. You certainly needed something to eat that day. I hope you have some better coats by now because it's cold again. It'll snow soon."

Amazed such an important man remembered them, Mary ventured, "We were trying to hear the wind spirit, Mr. McGlashan. My sister learned about it at school."

Tiny interrupted, "But we don't speak Washo, so we don't know what it's saying."

Mr. McGlashan watched the rock moving slightly back and forth, listening to the wind.

"Perhaps you have to feel what the wind spirit is saying," he said. "Sometimes

I feel it is telling me to do something."

They stood still and mute for another moment.

"Do you feel something because you can talk Washo?" asked Tiny.

"No, no, the feeling simply comes to me," answered Mr. McGlashan.

All three remained stiff and serious.

Finally, Mr. McGlashan said, "Perhaps you must come many times before you can understand the wind spirit. The Washo would say you have to be ready to hear."

Silent, they listened again. The sun colored the clouds. It slid down behind the mountains, telling Mary it was time to go.

Mr. McGlashan said, "Upon my word, don't look so disappointed. Someday you'll hear the wind and understand. Come back anytime. I'm glad you're interested in the old things around these mountains."

At the bottom of McGlashan's Hill, Tiny said, "I think we need to ask Minna. She'd know what it's saying."

MARY DIDN'T CARE if Alta was mad, but Mama was standing next to her, fists on hips and lips pressed together, so trouble surely lay ahead.

They gathered before Mama.

"Oh, Lord forgive me, where did you go?" Mama asked, eyes filling with tears, bottom lip trembling.

"Now, Mama," said Mary, copying Alta's way to calm her mother down. "We took a peek at the rocks up by Mr. McGlashan's house in case the wind spirit was talking. We didn't do anything bad."

"I was so afraid," Mama cried, gathering them in her arms. "Those prisoners got in. They ate what they could and took what they couldn't eat. We got back and saw the mess. I was certain they took you."

"It was us eating cake," said Tiny.

"No, no, they took everything. I know they were here," said Mama. "They must be going over to Nevada. They came along the hill and saw the house was empty. Now I'm afraid to get the constable."

Alta perked up when she heard about the escape route.

"Like as not," she said, "they're following the train tracks through the pass over to Nevada. Folsom Prison isn't far from Sacramento, so they've escaped a long ways. Isn't that something?"

Mama dried her eyes with her sleeve.

"Let's get some knives and go to the constable," said Alta. "We can stab them if they try to get us."

She jabbed with her hand, then said, "Too bad we don't have a gun. Maybe we should get a pistol from Mrs. O'Brien."

Forefinger pointing at Alta, Mama said, "No, no guns. What're you saying? We're not as bad as they are."

Alta frowned. She went inside and returned with the big Chinese chopping knife. Tiny and Raleigh put rocks in their pockets, and Mary found a two by four she could hold. Excited from the near miss with the prisoners, Raleigh and the girls crept down the hill, watching every movement in the bushes, as they assumed they must do from the stories they had read about the frontier.

"Thank you for notifying us, Mrs. Edwards," said the deputy, "but the constable and those guards from Folsom Prison have already gone to search for the escapees in the woods along the railroad tracks over to Reno."

Alta smirked, satisfied she had figured out the escape route.

"And I can't accompany you. I'm the only deputy. Be careful, ma'am, though the prisoners were last seen in the woods at the far end of town, away from Harrigan's Hill."

By bedtime, excitement was well mixed with worry. All four dragged blankets to lie down with Mama in her room, keeping their weapons by makeshift beds.

At Tuesday supper, Mama announced, "Two of the prisoners were caught this side of the pass by Donner Lake. Queer how they doubled back."

First thing out of Raleigh's mouth was to ask how were they captured.

Much to everyone's disappointment, Mama shrugged and said, "I didn't stay to ask Mr. Faye the dreadful details."

Resignation in her voice, she added, "You don't have to come straight home from school tomorrow, but under no circumstances can you play in the woods or out in the meadows."

Wind sighed under the attic eaves that evening. Mary and Alta gathered their clothes and blankets to move downstairs for the winter.

On her knees, folding the blankets into a bundle, Alta said, "Thank goodness we're not going to be cooped up. I hate it when Mama's unhappy like the scarlet fever time."

Picking pieces of straw off the quilt, Alta said, "Maybe she should smoke some opium like Uncle Lauf did when he was sad. Mrs. Bridges, the lady on Back Street, told me you can get it behind the old Chinese herb shop. She's done it, and she said laudanum has opium in it. That's why people feel better when they take it. Maybe Mama would feel better and not worry about Papa or Mr. Faye."

Alta laughed her devilish laugh. Though speechless and surprised at the proposal, Mary wondered how Alta knew what Mama was thinking.

"I saw Mr. Faye stare at Mama in the post office before the gunfight. I saw how he smiled when she said hello," nodded Alta. "I see how she's up one day and down the next."

Mary pulled clothes off the hooks. She didn't believe Mama would ever fall so low she'd resort to opium. Her sister dragged a bundle to the attic door. Mary rubbed her eyes to get rid of a shadowy picture of Alta wrapped in blankets, scrawny, washed out, and barely breathing.

AT THE WEEK'S end, on receiving a letter from the influential Sacramento suffrage committee, Mrs. Faye proposed another campaign meeting. Watching Mama pull herself together after Mary handed over the note was like seeing clouds blow away and sunlight radiate over the meadow. All because the special election was coming up. Mama hoped it would be successful, not dismal like the post office murder or the prisoners or the unhappy Mrs. Hoy and her children.

To the four children's surprise, Mama came back from the suffrage campaign meeting with a box of leftover little cakes, and she was full of gossip. After the meeting, Mrs. Faye kept talking to Mama about everything they'd already done—women marching at the Fourth of July parade and the grand bonfire on Admission Day. Mrs. Faye was thrilled with the pamphlets. Mama smiled proudly since her children had passed out most of them. Mrs. Tucker offered to have one more rally right before the election and to use the field next to her hotel for the bonfire. To everyone's surprise, Mrs. Vaughn offered to print more flyers and put an article in the *Truckee Star News*.

"The wife of the lumber-company supervisor said her husband had agreed to build a stupendous blaze," said Mama. "I already volunteered you to sell popcorn in newspaper cones because I don't have any money to give to the election."

THE COOL OCTOBER evening of the bonfire, Mama refused to let Mary go. She looked pink-faced and kept coughing. In secret, Mary had no intention of staying inside and missing anything. She bundled herself into her coat, wool scarf around neck and ears, and arranged herself with a blanket folded over her legs and under her bottom on the flat rock by the pine tree.

Her family followed the crowd to the Whitney Hotel. Raleigh joined boys who piled up wood into a huge stack at the side of the hotel. Mama's women friends and acquaintances whispered together, waiting. Mr. Faye was making his way among his neighbors, and plenty of children milled around. Alta and Tiny busily passed out newspaper cones filled with popcorn.

The lumber supervisor bent over the woodpile. Next thing, flames flicked up and smoke curled into the air. As the sun set, the fire became brighter. Marching music drifted up the hill. Indistinctly, Mary heard Mrs. Tucker speaking and townspeople clapping. The moon was rising above the horizon. Too dark by the bushes around her, she ran into the house to get the lantern.

Mary wasn't inside more than five minutes, when she reached the pine tree and looked out toward Front Street to see the fire whoosh up. Bells rang. People ran toward the rally.

The fire wagon dashed to the Whitney Hotel. Flames billowed out the second-floor hotel windows; smoke rose from the roof; fire shot up as the shingles became brittle charred wood crashing inward. Though the bonfire at the side of the building was popping sparks, it blazed separately from the burning hotel.

Mary sat, frowning and squinting, when unsteady footsteps scuffled in the leaves behind her. Crazy Lady Harrigan stopped and leaned against the tree to catch her balance.

Voice soft and breathy, Mrs. Harrigan said, "Don't worry. They'll be all right. It's not the first time there's been an inferno at that hotel."

Mary looked at her, dressed in a haphazard array of three sweaters and overalls.

"I heard the noise and saw the flames and decided to come down closer. It's surprising what you can see from here, isn't it?" said the old lady.

Her face was serene and her head wasn't shaking. She seemed lucid to Mary.

Mrs. Harrigan said, "When I was nineteen, there was a huge candidates' meeting on Front Street, and in the meantime, the saloon keeper and his wife had an argument. He threatened to leave town, and she screamed, 'I hope so, but nothing will be left when you come back.' She set the saloon on fire. Every single building on Front Street, including the big hotel, burned down by the next morning. That's the story anyway."

Mrs. Harrigan cackled and sat down to gaze at the two enormous blazes. Mary recognized Raleigh, small though he was, lifting a big lumber scrap and throwing it toward the bonfire.

Just then, in the muddle of excited boys shoving and tripping over each other, someone bumped Raleigh. He sprawled out on the ground close to the flames and sparks. Glass from hotel windows burst. Burning embers shot out like sparklers down toward Raleigh. He lay still.

Mary jumped up and screamed, "Raleigh!"

Out of nowhere, tiny but unmistakable, Mama materialized and threw her coat over Raleigh. Mr. Faye dragged him away from the flames. A minute later, Raleigh stood up and threw his arms around Mama, burying his head in her stomach like he'd done with Mary in sorrow after the baby died. Mary covered her face and took a deep breath.

Mrs. Harrigan said, "See, he'll be all right. I knew it."

Silence. "Don't worry, dearie. If he hurt himself, Dolly can fix it."

Another breath. She stood to walk up the hill.

Then over her shoulder she said, "Maybe I'd worry for your mother, though. She's courting her own fix."

How does Mrs. Harrigan know what's going on, thought Mary.

The moon rose full and high, lighting up the town. People still ran back and forth, dodging each other, gawking, and backing off. Heat sending flames higher and higher, the fires became one huge blaze. The big railroad company fire engine was shooting water at the hotel.

Soon, Mama, Alta, Raleigh, and Tiny appeared, the three jumping around, yelling, and interrupting each other.

Raleigh shouted, "It was a huge fire. Hot, too. We had to stand back in the street to stay cool. They had water buckets around, then I don't know what happened."

Alta said, "A man in the hotel was leaning out the window to see the rally, and the curtains caught on fire when he lit his pipe. He must have been drunk. Everyone was outside watching the bonfire and listening to Mrs. Tucker, so no one was ready for a fire at the hotel."

Tiny added, "People took buckets into the hotel to throw on the fire. Then I heard the hotel people running to find someone to go for the fire brigade and … and … ."

"They found Mrs. Tucker," interrupted Alta, "and she tried to get everyone organized."

Tiny continued dramatically, "It was too-o-o late!"

"I know," said Alta. "Mrs. Tucker yelled at the hotel barman to get the fire extinguishers. What did he think they were for? But, you're right. It was too late by then."

Mary said, "What made you throw the lumber, Raleigh? You scared me. Mrs. Harrigan too."

Heads turned to Raleigh, who shrugged and said, "I don't know. Georgie Vaughn dared me."

He lifted his arm and displayed his swollen wrist.

Tears formed in his eyes. He said, "Mama, my wrist hurts a lot now."

"Oh, Lord," said Mama, "why didn't you show me right away?"

He shrugged again, claiming spider webs could be wrapped around to make it stop aching like Alta'd done for his gashed leg. Mama pulled him into the house, saying she'd talk to Mrs. Vaughn about Georgie, now she knew her better. Catching the lamp so it wouldn't tip over and start another fire in the dry fall leaves, Mary followed behind her sisters.

When Mama found a rag to use as a bandage, she said, "Let's be thankful everyone got out of the hotel, and no one was burned."

She picked at tiny holes in her little boy's jacket where sparks had singed the wool.

"After all that work our campaign's about finished! Everyone will talk about the suffrage rally for a long time. *All's well that ends well*. That's from Shakespeare."

Raleigh said, "Mama, Mrs. Tucker doesn't think 'all's well'."

"She means no person got hurt," said Alta. "From the hotel."

"I got hurt," said Raleigh. "I wonder if my wrist will always be stiff."

Then Tiny asked, "Where's Papa going to stay? Maybe he'll have to come here. What d'you think?"

Mary blurted out, "Yes, maybe we should go back with Papa. It's hard up here."

Her face flushed. Alta began to pick up things from the kitchen table and slap them down again.

The smile fading, Mama only said, "We'll see. Get ready for bed. It's late."

In bed, Alta whispered, "Last time he was here, I asked Papa to come say he's sorry, but he wouldn't. He was drinking again anyway."

Mary stifled a sigh, her brain mulling over what Mrs. Harrigan had said. She kept waking up, snuffling and sipping water for her throat. Mama glided through the room, bringing cold rags to wrap around Raleigh's swollen wrist in another effort to do the nursing at home.

AN ICY WIND blew leaves off the tree branches. They twirled to the ground on October 10, 1911, the special election day. Even so, the town was in a celebratory mood, not so much for the elections as in relief Front Street hadn't burned to charred rubble.

That evening Mama laughed and said, "This election is an afterthought. The excitement was the bonfire. Most men who voted are related to ladies on the Woman Suffrage Campaign. Like as not, we can guess the votes from Truckee right now."

Two days later, Mrs. Faye invited the campaign committee over once more, certain the votes were recorded by the state and a result would be telegraphed that afternoon. Alta led the way through the crowd in the front parlor to the dining room where delicate painted porcelain trays on the table displayed decorated cakes. Tiny popped one in her mouth before politely piling three on her dessert plate. Mary, Raleigh, and Alta did the same. While they ate and looked over the fancy knickknacks in the curio chest, voices from the front parlor filled the air.

Mrs. Tucker wanted to attend the next town council meeting and demand a better equipped fire brigade.

"We need more deputies to help Mr. O'Brien. I worry about those prisoners who came through town," said Mama.

Mrs. Vaughn surprised everyone when she chimed in, "I vote for septic tanks and road repairs. This town should have more concern for illnesses like in San Francisco after the big earthquake."

Pictures of haggard people streaming through Truckee by train filled Mary's head. Scarlet fever, typhoid, fire, blizzards, and men shooting guns added to her scary imaginings.

Mrs. O'Brien said, "How about telephone wires up to Harrigan's Hill?"

Raleigh whispered telephones were a first-rate idea.

Sighing, Mrs. Faye said, "We can't vote for a single thing until the state legislature releases the outcome."

Like magic, the front bell rang loudly. Zack led Georgie into the dining room. Mrs. Vaughn put her arm around her son, shrugging and scowling, but handing over the telegram with the final election results. The amendment passed by only three thousand votes in the entire state of California. Everyone clapped and ate more cake, congratulating themselves until the sun began to set.

At the dessert table, Georgie greeted Alta, who took him to task for daring her brother at the bonfire.

"Aw, I'm sorry," he said as required, but Raleigh shrugged in embarrassment. Alta lagged to cheer up Georgie, obvious to Mary he was smitten. Mr. Faye arrived as the family reached the bottom step of the house.

"Dolly," he said, holding her hand. "I've been talking to Mr. O'Brien about deputies like you asked. We'll bring it up to the council as a safety measure. How can moving picture people be talked into using the town, if it's not safe? Words like those."

His arm in a sling, he rubbed his shoulder.

"The cold makes it ache where the bullet left torn flesh. You should hurry on. Take care now, Dolly."

Mr. Faye disappeared into the warm hallway. The wind pushed the Edwards family along until they reached their own poor hill. Though celebratory talk made Mama happier, Mary couldn't ignore her own wariness. She saw the light in Mr. Faye's eyes, just as Alta had.

MAMA STIRRED THE soup. Holding her palms over the stovetop, rubbing them to warm up, Mama cocked her head and peered into the front room.

"I wonder where Raleigh and Tiny have disappeared."

"In the bedroom playing cards, bunched up in the blankets," said Mary.

"Yes, Mama," said Alta, "It's cold in this old house. The fireplace doesn't help unless we sit right in front of it. I think you should go back … "

Mama interrupted, "Stop talking about your father. I'll find a way to get more heat in this house."

Alta rolled her eyes but closed her mouth. Mama turned to Mary.

"Yesterday I ran into Minna. She filled me in on her old cousin's wife's nephew, Mr. Littlefield, but she didn't know where Mrs. Hoy and Mr. Littlefield were."

Mama stared out the small kitchen window at the pine branches bending wildly in the wind.

"I wonder if Mr. and Mrs. Hoy thought they loved each other, but later they didn't get along anymore. Then Mr. Littlefield showed up, and he and Mrs. Hoy were made for each other. Maybe she asked for a divorce, but Mr. Hoy wouldn't do it. So when he broke his leg, she left. *The course of true love never did run smooth.*' That's more advice from Shakespeare," said Mama. "It's sad, girls. You might as well know it now."

Mama smiled, biting her lip, "Maybe they'll be all right. Minna's relatives are good people. I know they are."

⟫•⟪

"DIDN'T TURN OUT all right for Mrs. Hoy, did it?" said Lane.

Mary shook her head.

23

May 1975
Sacramento and Los Angeles

I REMEMBERED THE woman with a good marriage, with the husband who never left her side. And of the women I knew, of course, my daughter was the one I loved the most.

IN THE EARLY morning the phone rang. It rang again. I threw off the covers, hurried into the hall, and reached for it.

"Mary?"

"Yes, Gus. I know what you're going to say."

"It just happened, Mary. I thought I'd better call you first. Talk to … talk to … ."

The receiver clanked. I heard breathing as it was picked up again.

"Grandma, I was at the hospital yesterday afternoon, and she seemed no different, joking with the doctor like she does. Then Dad called last night and said to come back. He was in a daze, but Polly and I held her hands and whispered to her all night. It seemed like she heard us. Then she went."

"Yes, John. I'll be there this afternoon."

"I'll call you back to know when I should be at the airport. OK, grandma?"

"Yes, dear. I'm calling now. Bye-bye."

Dizzy, I crawled back under the covers. I had to think hard to remember what my grandson had said, even though deep in my heart I'd felt Betsy wasn't going to be pulled back this time. Stretched on my bed, I couldn't catch my breath, sobs heaving up from my heart. Out the window the plum trees' purple leaves fluttered. I couldn't believe they moved. Why was the guinea hen screeching—not mute?

I forced myself up, packed a suitcase, took a shower, called the airlines, made some coffee, told Abel when he got up, washed the dishes, and called Raleigh to take me to the airport. I was keeping busy—Mama's way to not think. The most precious thing I loved was gone.

My dog Brownie galloped ahead of me into my garden. They say tending a garden helps, but sorrow was bending me over toward the earth under my feet. Flicking an aphid off the rose bush, the scent in the cool air brought to mind Betsy's favorite, miniature pink roses. She loved the planters on the bench at the edge of the deck at her house. The house where she and her family lived for many good days.

Of course, that's a mother's memory, but what else is left when someone you love is gone? Rubbing my fingers along the oily stem of a rosemary bush, I caught a glimpse of a tiny wild rabbit skittering away. Brownie pursued the rabbit into the far field. It took my breath away, as a vision of my daughter standing in front of the pet store cage exclaimed in her happy five-year-old voice, "Oh, Mom, it's so soft."

Betsy was petting it through the wire.

"Not like those wild rabbits that eat Grandma's vegetables. She's always out there shooing them off."

Betsy tilted her head, her dark red hair cut in a pageboy. She leaned closer to the cage, watching the floppy-eared black and white bunny. She smiled at me, eyes shining.

"Look at its little nose sniffing. Did you know rabbits like raisins?" she said, pointing to the piles of raisin-size poops.

She didn't understand why I laughed. When I did explain, she stored away the fact for the future, smiling all the while.

That's what kept Betsy alive for me. I smoothed dust from my peonies, the Chinese flower for long life. I planted the dark pink frilly blossoms before I left for Salt Lake City, where Betsy had married her army navigator husband. Soon he had been sent to Italy to fly bombers over the railroads and ammunition depots used by the Germans.

Brownie yapped and raced back to leap into my arms. Holding tight to her squirmy body and stepping back from the peonies, I almost crushed my pansies. Their blue and yellow faces brought a memory of Shakespeare's line, *"And there's pansies, that is for thoughts."* Betsy always planted pansies, which bloomed sturdily under the ash tree—even with kids running across her front yard all summer.

My eyes filled with tears thinking about that time I was so mad at Betsy, all because of innocent pansies spilled on the kitchen floor. We all do unreasonable things, I thought, breathing the sweet-smelling air. My world might have been peaceful if only she hadn't fallen so sick and died so young.

Abel was reading the newspaper. He put it down and we talked for a few minutes. He tried to be kind, but was never much for small talk. Abel had been lucky. His children had always been healthy, thank goodness. What would he be able to say? Only Raleigh knew what it was like to lose someone you loved more than anything. Raleigh walked by the kitchen windows to pick me up. I gathered my things, kissed my husband, and went to the airport.

By the time I found the gate for my plane, I still had an hour before boarding. Memories of Betsy swirled in my head. She amazed the women in my family because, as we knew well, length of a marriage didn't always mean love and happiness. She was the one with a good marriage.

At first I'd worried she'd married a man she knew nothing about, like many couples in that terrible war. She was petrified until the telegram came that confirmed Gus was a prisoner of war. He'd been captured an entire year before Europe was liberated. I worried about what he would be like when he came back. Then they moved to Los Angeles, far away, so I wouldn't be able to help. The arthritis flared after the birth of each child, with nothing to do for it but take aspirin.

Out the window a plane descended from the blue-gray sky onto the Sacramento Airport tarmac. The airplane sent my mind to thoughts of all those machines flying far above the Earth while I've been alive. Mama showed us the newspaper picture of the Wright Brothers' airplane when I was too young to understand what an amazing feat it was.

I didn't travel by airplane until I flew with my grandchildren to Los Angeles. That happened that same night Gus took us out to the backyard to watch the star-like Sputnik cross the sky.

My mind drifted to the long ago day in the back seat of the Ford where two-year-old Polly, baby John, and I huddled. Betsy was saying, "Go faster, Gus. See if we can get under it." The plane roared over the car as it flew onto the runway at the old airport in Los Angeles. They laughed and Polly opened her eyes wide to see the underbelly of the huge metal machine.

Soon we were sitting on the wide beach far from the shoreline. Dark blue water rose and fell, visibly touching blue-gray sky at the horizon. Betsy sat on the beach chair with her thin legs stretched out. Polly scampered around in her underpants, and baby John rolled on the blanket, reaching for sand and putting it in his mouth. Leaning over, Betsy tried to brush it out of his hand, but couldn't quite reach, her arm frozen at the elbow. I brushed the sand off the baby. Gus took photos of Polly and the baby. He lifted Polly to his shoulders and ran with her, shrieking, down to the water.

"You're so stiff, dear," I said.

"Oh, Mom," she said. "Emma next door takes care of John all the time when I don't feel well. We get by fine."

She smiled her beautiful smile when Gus and Polly ran back over the sand toward us. I found the towel and rubbed my granddaughter down, so she wouldn't catch cold. The breeze came up, the water showed white caps against the sky, and the sun in the west made the crown of each wave shine like a chip of abalone pearl. Gus helped Betsy stand. We grabbed the beach things and trudged back to the car with sandy feet, drippy underpants, flying hair, and all.

Consoling myself on the plane, handkerchief to my eyes, I thought about the new drug that was introduced—I don't mean the polio vaccine, although that was a Godsend in itself. Betsy's doctor prescribed prednisone, and for a long time, it was a miracle. She gained weight. Her puffy knees and knuckles looked normal. I remember when she showed John how to hold a bat, watch the baseball, and swing hard, saying at least he'd never be the last chosen for the teams playing in the street.

They almost always came to Sacramento over the Fourth of July. They'd leave the kids and go off for a few days by themselves. I'd drive down to Los Angeles two or three times a year in the blue '55 Buick convertible I'd bought secondhand. I'd listen to the radio and watch the fields change on Highway 99.

That day before Easter vacation in 1956, I was thinking about the beautiful dress I'd made for Polly, green and white plaid with small pink embroidered flowers. Suddenly, I slammed on the brakes and gazed at red taillights stretched as far ahead as I could see. Traffic halted because a tractor-trailer truck had crashed as I reached the pass called the Grapevine over the mountains into Los Angeles. By the time the lanes on my side of the highway were allowed through, I worried whether I'd make it to the kid's school where Betsy was to receive an award for her service to the PTA.

Slipping into the back of the auditorium, I was amazed at the huge crowd. There was hardly room to breathe. On the stage with Gus holding her arm, Betsy walked forward to the podium. She was handed the plaque and shook hands with the principal of the school and the president of the regional PTA. Wearing shoes with heels and a suit that didn't look like it was hanging on a skinny frame, she turned and smiled her grand smile. The crowd stood, clapping and clapping. I was truly proud when she walked down the staircase, people shaking her hand and congratulating Gus. It was only a school PTA award, but it felt like an extraordinary celebration.

Tears were streaming again and my handkerchief was soaked. I didn't even notice the plane landing. Collecting my purse and jacket, I recalled Mama's comment about Betsy's award. She was glad for her granddaughter and, to her mind, it was one of the things that came about from getting the vote all those years ago. Women weren't allowed to open their mouths at the schools when she was a teacher. It made me smile for a minute before I'd have to face the funeral.

There wasn't much to do until the following evening at the viewing. Betsy's best friend from college talked about how much she loved the week that Betsy and Gus would spend at their home in Sonoma every summer. She laughed about the time Gus was picking wild blackberries and brushed some poison oak. He spent days daubing himself with calamine lotion while they played gin rummy and drank wine from the local vineyards.

Maybe that good time story brought to mind the memory of the year things began to fall apart. Suddenly, the tiny wonder pills had overwhelmed her body. There had been warnings that people's bones and internal organs were affected by that miracle drug. Ha. It wasn't a miracle. It made her better, and then it killed her.

Betsy lived for a rough ten years, her bones breaking and her skin so thin it split apart simply touching it. Gus, try as he would to make things appear normal, became less and less able to cope. John, graduating from college, was caught between Vietnam War peace demonstrations and a very low draft lottery number. The arguments distressed us all. Though he hated the army, Gus tried to protect Betsy. She could only remember her fears during World War II.

I've lived so long I don't want to think about the wars I knew already—four big ones for God's sake, if you count the Spanish-American War that began the year I was born. I knew what it was like to be frightened the one you loved wasn't going to come back.

One night when John returned from a demonstration with a black eye, Gus bawled out his son, when really Gus was frantic because Betsy was frightened. In the end, rather than be drafted, John volunteered. Luckily, he found himself in Vietnam as a reporter for the army newspaper, long before he knew about the famous few who made their way in and out of Vietnam in the same manner. John didn't return a wreck, and received his discharge well before all hell broke loose at the end of that war.

Not long before her final sickness, Betsy planned an entire wedding for her daughter with a hundred people at the house. Sitting in her chair, her fingers twisted by that miserable disease and wearing a long dress to cover her legs, Betsy bantered with Gus, who looked handsome in his tuxedo. They drank and laughed—relieved it was a good party.

By Saturday morning, I was worn out. At the services for the throng that followed us to the burial site, I felt myself descend into a deep grief. I finally understood how Mama must have felt those months after baby Florence died.

If only … indeed, it's what Mama had finally said when we kids saw and heard that other tragedy long ago. It was always if only, if only. If only the doctors had another medicine, then a good marriage would have had a good ending.

Sunday lunch after the last out-of-town guest had left, Gus and I sat down for sandwiches. He looked as sad as I felt. That's when it came to me—not a single member of his family helped him with anything. He'd had to help those two old ladies back east, his mother and his sister, who loved him above all, but who never left home, nor ever had any idea how fragile Betsy's health had been.

"Friday I went down the hill to the market," Gus said, "I was surprised. I turned to see if any traffic was coming, and there was Betsy, dressed in the blue Mexican skirt she loved, sitting next to me in the car, smiling as we drove along. At the stoplight, she turned her head and rolled down the window.

"Guess who was in the car next to us? Humphrey Bogart and Lauren Bacall in their big Rolls Royce. Betsy and I had seen them a long time ago right at that corner when we first moved to Los Angeles. Remember? We told that story all the time.

"Humphrey put his arm on the Rolls Royce window ledge and turned to look at us.

"Betsy lifted her hand, waved at him, and said, 'Nice seeing you again.'

"Both Humphrey and Lauren waved and drove off. Betsy gave me her beautiful smile once more and was gone too."

He used the napkin to wipe his eyes.

"We had great times together," he said.

24

Mid-October 1911
Harrigan's Hill, Truckee

AFTER THE ELECTION, the wind stopped and the sky cleared to azure. Tiny and Mary yelled for Alta and huddled with Raleigh in the attic, conspiring on a hike to the Indian pictures.

Raleigh said, "Should we bring weapons?"

"It's a holy place, Raleigh," said Tiny. "Y'don't bring rocks to church, do you?"

"What if the other prisoner is hiding up there?" he asked.

"He's not hiding near those rocks," she protested. "Captain Ben lives up there."

A few moments passed before Mary proposed meeting at the train station.

Finger on her chin, Tiny asked, "D'you remember how to get up there?"

"I know how. I've been there before," announced Alta.

Surprise and wariness combined on their faces. Mary, Tiny, and Raleigh waited until she added, "I didn't have anything to do and followed Captain Ben last summer, but not all the way to the top. I got tired, and it's lonely up that high—even when a woodpecker is *pick-pick-picking,* or wind rushes through the pine trees."

THE MOON ROSE late that night—no owl, no crickets, no ruffle of leaves. The house remained dark, except for wood glowing in the fireplace. Mary dreamed a woodpecker *tap-tap-tapped* until she awoke to knocks on the front door. Raleigh and three girls rushed into the bedroom and dived under the bedcovers.

"What is it, Mama?" whispered Tiny.

Raleigh clutched his mother's nightgown and mouthed, "Prisoners."

Alta begged her to get the Chinese chopping knife. Mama put a finger to her lips and disappeared into the front room.

"Please don't send us away," pleaded a woman's voice when the door shushed open. The voice murmured, "We didn't know where else to go. Mr. Littlefield's aunt was frightened when he visited in the summer. We came on the late train from Reno after we heard people had been looking for us."

Mrs. Hoy walked in to stand by the fireplace, her hands stretched forward to feel the heat. Wearing a heavy man's jacket over her shoulders, she still shivered when she turned to Mr. Littlefield. Eyes almost closed and face gray, she wasn't pretty like the first time she came to Mama, as Tiny pointed out later.

Mr. Littlefield helped Mama put a log into the fireplace and fan the charred pieces until the fresh wood burst into flames.

He said, "We hid in the woods, waiting until it was late and no one was around before going to my aunt."

"Then I thought of you," said Mrs. Hoy. "Your sister Margaret came to the hospital when the baby was born and said you know the story. I thought you might know how to get help. We need horses to ride the back trails over the mountains to Sacramento."

Mama said, "I can let you use our Molly. She's sturdy and has already pulled a wagon over the mountains. You'd be all right on her, Mrs. Hoy, but my sister is wrong. I don't know the whole story."

Mr. Littlefield, a square-faced man, as tall as Papa, wearing the flat-top, wide-brim hat favored by the Washo, said, "We're not bad people, Mrs. Edwards. Things … "

"Oh, Mrs. Edwards," said Mrs. Hoy, "I gave the baby away to a young woman who would love a mixed-blood child. My husband said he would raise her, but I know what would have happened when he saw the baby. He shouted at me when he found out I'd given the child away. That's when he hollered he was taking my boys to Tonopah. He yelled I'd better get back there when the doctors let me go, or I'd be sorry. What did that mean?"

Mr. Littlefield took her arm.

"My husband shouted like he was losing his mind," said Mrs. Hoy. "So I wrote to my brother in Wyoming and asked if he could take the boys. I told my brother I was afraid of my husband and I was going to San Francisco, but I'd go to my brother's for the boys."

"Oh, my Lord," said Mama, circling the room.

She rubbed her hands over her face.

"Who am I to judge?" she said, walking around again. "Get the horse tomorrow after you find another. Let me show you where she is. Molly's very gentle. Tonight stay up to your aunt's house."

Mama grabbed her coat off the hook.

"You can't stay here, not even in the barn. You'll have to ask your aunt how to get another horse."

Mr. Littlefield shook his shoulders, as if to pull his body together. He followed Mama from the house, thanking her as they left and promising Captain Ben would bring Molly back. Mrs. Hoy held her hands for another minute before the fire. Then she yanked off her scarf and dragged her fingers through her hair. A groan escaped her mouth. She rubbed her hands down the front of her dress, straightened the scarf, pulled the jacket close, and left the room.

Raleigh and his sisters crowded at the window, watching dark forms descend the hill, a tiny lantern swinging next to the tall one. The half-moon was rising, the hillside no longer shaded in gloom, but the two bodies walked quickly. They had a long way to go, down the hill, along the river, up the far hill, much higher than any of them except Alta had ever attempted.

THE NEXT MORNING, the kitchen door squeaked, and Mama's voice called out.

"It's Sunday, but go to the trainmaster, Raleigh. Perhaps your father passed through and left some money," she said.

"Let's all go. Maybe Papa's at the livery stable," said Alta. "Maybe he'll come back to Mama and say sorry now he has to sleep in the smelly tack room."

Mary was surprised Alta knew where Papa lived since the Whitney Hotel burned down. Tiny and Raleigh brushed hay off their coats and climbed over the side of the wagon where they'd been sitting, expecting Mr. Littlefield to come for Molly.

"Wait. I need my wool scarf. I'll go too," said Mary.

Hand on her hip, waggling her shoulders and pointing her finger, Alta said, "You'd better keep your mouth shut. No matter what, we want Papa to make up to Mama."

"I know. I've agreed, haven't I?" retorted Mary.

"I don't know. Mama'll see you're up to something. Your face is a dead give away," said Alta.

Mary lowered herself out the bedroom window to the ground and separated her coat from the bushes. Alta and she kept behind the trees in case Mama was watching birds, rabbits, or children. Outside the Trainmaster's Office, Raleigh and Tiny met them, no envelope in hand.

Breathing heavily, Mary sat down on the bench, rubbing her hands and pulling her collar up around her neck. The other three grumbled, in a hurry to beseech Papa to do something. Finally, Mary stopped gasping for air, and they walked down to Papa's new home.

The Truckee Livery Stable was a plain wood building not far from the collapsed Whitney Hotel. Mary peeked under the overhang shading the front doorway, wide enough for small wagons. Faint light filtered into the barn-like room through filthy windows in the front wall. Old hay and horse sweat filled Mary's nose. Tiny, Raleigh, and Alta paraded in.

"Hey, Bill," Alta called out.

Horses shuffled in wood stalls, one lifting his head to watch them. Someone was talking to the livery boy. The children stopped.

"If you don't mind, I don't want to take the train," said the man speaking to the livery boy. "I prefer a horse able to take me over the summit and down to the valley."

The man took a step—Mr. Littlefield stood in a shaft of dim light—shoulders pinched, hands clasped at his back.

"Look, the owner of this livery don't sell nothin' to no Washo," said Bill. "The train people'll sell a ticket to anyone with the money. I don't know where they'll let you sit, but they'll take y'r money."

"Find out how much. You don't know me, but I have money. My uncle, Captain Ben, will vouch for me. Everybody knows him. I'm good with horses. I don't like trains," said Mr. Littlefield.

Looking down and dusting off his pants, Bill said, "Oh well, y'r right, I know Cap'n Ben. I guess I c'n ask the owner, but he's pretty against Washo, or any Indian f'r a fact."

Bill was hiding a bald lie, Mary thought. He wouldn't ask the owner. What did he have against Washo? Or Chinamen and Negroes and other sorts of people who weren't like him? Only Uncle Lauf didn't care who was who. If the person accepted the Lord, it was all right by him. Tiny grabbed Mary's arm and pulled her away from her thoughts. Bill called to them.

"You want y'r pa?" he asked.

"I'll be back with money," said Mr. Littlefield, heading for the door, scratching the horse's forehead on the way. He strode past the children without a glance.

Alta said, "D'you know when he's coming?"

"Couple a days or so seems t'me," answered Bill, walking over and squinting to see where Mr. Littlefield had gone. "Trainmaster paid up front f'r the room."

They hustled to Bridge Street to find Mr. Littlefield, then sat on the rocks between the river and the railroad tracks.

"He must have been in some hurry to get away and up the hill so quickly," said Mary.

"Bill. He's mean," said Tiny. "What'd Mr. Littlefield do to him? He said he had money for the horse."

"Maybe Papa can get them a seat on the train in a good spot," said Raleigh.

"They don't want anyone to see them," said Alta. "Remember how Mr. Hoy tried to kill Mr. Littlefield? That's why they want horses to go on the back trails to Sacramento."

Raleigh and Tiny sucked in breath.

Mary said, "Maybe Mr. Littlefield can give Mama money to buy the other horse. Without telling that nasty stable boy. Bill'd end up the fool."

"That won't happen," said Alta. "I know how it is. A man has to take the money. I don't even think Mrs. Bridges from Back Street could walk in and buy a horse."

Tiny and Raleigh ran ahead to distract Mama with the news Papa wouldn't be in town for a few days. Mary dragged herself to the wall under the window and slumped against it. Alta held her hands together and lifted. Mary pulled herself level with the window frame. She fell into the bedroom, shuffled to the bed in the front room, and didn't move until supper. Mama sat down by her daughter, and Tiny told the livery story.

"Please don't make yourself sick again," she said, feeling Mary's forehead, smoothing her hair. "I don't know what I'd do."

Gazing out the window at the first evening stars, Mama rubbed her forehead and began the melancholy song about unhappy love.

> *The cuckoo, she's a pretty bird.*
> *She sings as she flies,*
> *She brings us glad tidings,*
> *And she tells us no lies.*

"I'll go see Minna tomorrow. We'll figure some way to buy another horse for those two. We're a piece of this story now, and I suppose we must do our part to finish it." Mama's hands shook as they caressed Mary's hair.

Falling asleep, Mary promised herself not to run around for a while after they went up the hill to see the scratches on the rocks. That seemed a good compromise. Much later she admitted it was willful. The Indian pictures weren't going to disappear. They could go up the hill anytime.

ON MONDAY, MARY sat on a bench up against the station wall and watched the Sacramento-bound train screech and halt. An older woman descended, catching a child who tried to leap down, then a tall man, limping slightly, beat-up hat pulled down low, and last Mrs. Faye, holding her skirt and giving her hand to the porter. Mary wondered why Mrs. Faye, dressed to the nines, went to Reno. Then the conductor passed down packages from the shops.

Shoving her hand into her pocket, Mary found a cookie. She stomped her feet and walked all the way around the station to warm herself, eating the cookie and keeping an eye out for her brother and sisters. By the time Raleigh, Tiny, and Alta came running down the street, the passengers had disappeared.

A mottled, long-nosed dog sniffed in the weeds along the track, scaring a field mouse that leaped the rails into the brush. Though a sunny day, cold settled silently over the valley. Mary shrugged her hands inside her coat sleeves and waited at the steps.

Raleigh yelled, "We were arguing with Hazel."

Struggling for air, he put his head down, hands on his knees.

Chest heaving, Tiny said, "Hazel said Minna told her to go straight home."

"I wonder if Mama went over to Minna's," said Raleigh.

They watched the dog until Alta said, "Let's go. Or we won't be back, and Mama'll look for us."

Mary slipped in behind Alta, following her across the bridge over the river. They jogged along the dirt trail until they arrived at the creek, stopping to watch the rivulet vanish into the Truckee.

"Come on," said Alta.

Picking her way along the narrow path next to the creek, Alta watched for the easiest place to cross. She found stones serving as a bridge. Mary swallowed, panicky about slipping into the icy creek, but the water was low, and the rocks remained dry on top.

They did as Minna had told them and looked up. Wide-branched pine trees blurred the view of gray granite containing glints of mica and dots of obsidian and quartz.

They climbed quietly in single file, keeping their heads down to watch the narrow, steep track. Though shadowy from the tall overhang of trees, the sky was still blue and sunny where it showed between the branches. Mary glanced upward from time to time to see if they were getting close to the granite wall. Off and on she picked out the burble of water from the creek hidden by brush and brambles.

Mary walked slower and slower until Raleigh stepped on her heel. She tapped Alta on the shoulder to stop. Hands at her waist, she waited for her heart to stop pounding. No breeze rustled through the trees. Mary glanced up again. No hawks disappeared and returned in a slow survey high overhead. She leaned against a tree trunk. No crows chastised the children for intruding in the woods, not even a woodpecker's *bap-bap-bap-bap* filled the air. Looking down, she frowned. No scuffle from a rabbit, scrabbling deeper in the undergrowth to hide.

Alta pointed to the rock outcropping. Slivers of mica in the granite glinted between the tree branches. Footsteps swished through pine needles. A figure with a well-worn felt hat loomed in front of the rocks.

"The prisoner!" mouthed Raleigh.

Alta clapped her hand over his lips as words carried in the silence.

A woman's voice cried, "My Lord, how did you find us?"

Tiny whispered, "Mrs. Hoy."

A man's voice mumbled, " … saw you at the train in Reno … asked around,"

A loud male voice said, "What d'you want? I don't have any money. We're staying up here with my aunt until I get enough to go to San Francisco."

Tiny opened her mouth, but Alta put her finger to her lips.

They heard, "Come back with me … " and " … Indian bastard."

The woman's voice pleaded, "No, don't, no."

Mary looked up and between dark branches to see a silvery metal gun barrel reflecting light from the sun. She grabbed her sister's arm and pointed.

Alta mouthed, "Let's go! Fast!"

At that second, a loud crack reverberated, and then another. Alta waved her hands to say go, go, but the others stood petrified by a harsh groan, tumbling rocks, long-drawn silence, and then relentless, vociferous sobbing.

They ran. Tiny led the slide down the path as fast as possible without crashing into each other. They didn't slip on the hard, clean track. With their lips pinched closed, they sprinted through the creek, ignoring the stone bridge and letting water leak into their shoes. Cutting down along the river, they crossed the bridge and fell onto the bench at the train station. Mary's lungs heaved; her throat throbbed. She laid her head back against the wall. Alta put her head down between her legs. Raleigh covered his face, and Tiny cried tears as big as raindrops.

She sobbed, "What'll we tell Mama?"

Everyone fell silent until the station bell signaled the next train's arrival in five minutes.

Alta said, "Let's wait and see what happens. Anyway, we didn't see a person exactly. We saw a gun and heard something."

Raleigh sat forward and shook his head, as if to get the terrified look off his face.

Then he grabbed Mary's arm, pointed, and said, "What d'you think?"

"Put your hand down!" hissed Alta.

"Mr. Hoy," whispered Raleigh.

With his hat sheltering a face like cold ash, the tall man limped up onto the far end of the platform. At the window he asked for a ticket to Reno and Tonopah. His hands shook as he placed coins on the counter.

Raleigh waved his hands, urging his sisters to leave. Taking a step, he tripped on a loose nail that was raised on the platform. He fell, catching himself with his sore wrist, and let out a scream.

The man's face whipped toward the children. Lifting his hat, he stared, head pushed forward to show skin soot-colored around glistening red eyeballs. He jerked his hat back down and took a stiff-legged lurch toward the bench.

"Here're the tickets. The train's coming," called the station clerk.

The man turned to grab the stubs. The train whistle echoed along the track and its brakes screeched. Lifting Raleigh, the sisters pulled him down the train station steps at their end. Darting away from the station, hiding in the shade of the steep-roofed houses, they raced along Church Street. They stopped to catch their breath and peered around the side of the Methodist Church, wondering if the train carried its passenger, or if a stiff-legged man watched from the station platform.

"Should we go to Mr. O'Brien?" gasped Mary.

Her brother and sisters shook their heads. They took off along Front Street for Harrigan's Hill. At the Last Chance Saloon, Mr. Faye stepped out, and the four children screamed and halted.

"What's the matter with you?" said Mr. Faye. "You look terrible."

Mary gulped, "A man tried to get us. At the train station."

"That horrible Mr. Hoy," said Alta. "We saw him, well, we heard him and saw the gun."

"What? Where's your mother?" said Mr. Faye, eyes moving from the train station to the mountain where Raleigh pointed.

"At Minna's maybe," said Mary.

Tiny shivered and cried. Mr. Faye held her by the shoulders, saying to go home and not let anyone in. He would get Dolly and the constable. The four of them ran for the bridge and the hill.

INSTEAD OF ENTERING the house, the four staggered to the wagon in the barn, wheezing from fatigue. Mary's legs were weak, so Raleigh and Alta shoved her over the side. They huddled under blankets.

Tiny spoke up. "We'll have to tell Mama."

"You already said that. Mr. Faye will get her," said Mary.

Tiny fiddled with her jacket buttons, hiccupping while she held back sobs.

"Poor Mr. Littlefield," said Tiny. "He was a Washo, like Hazel. I'm glad Hazel wasn't there."

Raleigh joined in, his voice trembling, "That pistol sounded so loud."

He turned to Alta.

"Was the noise that loud at the post office?"

Alta nodded, watching a spider crawl on the side of the wagon.

"But everyone was shouting and hollering. Not like at the rocks. Remember how quiet it was? Like the forest knew something was going to happen."

Alta squashed the spider with her forefinger. Tiny burst into tears again.

"Why'd you do that, Alta?" said Tiny.

"What?" Alta asked, looking out the barn door as if she saw something in the twilight.

Raleigh brushed his arm across his eyes to dry his tears. He choked as he tried to hold back more.

Finally, he said, "Who d'you think was groaning? It was most awful."

Shaky all over, Mary answered, "I think it was Mr. Littlefield. At least, it sounded like a man."

There they stayed—Tiny sniffling, Raleigh coughing and choking, Alta bent over, flicking away another spider, Mary squished in the corner with hands under her armpits, biting her lips.

"I guess the rocks rolled around when Mrs. Hoy fell over," said Mary.

Alta pulled herself up and said, "What d'you think happens when a bullet goes into your head?"

Tiny drew in a harsh breath.

"We were lucky Mr. Hoy bawled like he did … so he didn't hear us," she whispered.

Pointing at Raleigh, Alta said, "You and Tiny better stop crying. Like Mama said 'what's done is done.' She's not going to be mad about sneaking off. She'll be in a state because we heard it and saw the big revolver, not a little pistol, Raleigh. She won't let us go anywhere. Think about that!"

Mary said, "I don't want to go anywhere. I wish Mrs. Hoy had never come to Mama. It's not right what she did."

"William and Eddie never said anything bad about their mother, not about their father, and not about the Indian man either. So how d'you know who's wrong?" said Raleigh.

"Anyway, everyone's always mean to the Indians," said Tiny. "Why should Mr. Littlefield get killed? He wasn't mean."

Startled at Raleigh's and Tiny's words, Mary closed her mouth.

After a minute, she said, "It isn't right to leave your husband."

Realizing she'd condemned Mama, she added, "Or your wife, either way."

"It's not right to kill people either," declared Alta. "Mary, I don't think you listened to what Mama said day before yesterday. No one's all right or all wrong, which is how you think a lot of the time."

Taken aback, Mary looked away to the twilight sky. The sun nearly gone, shadows wavered among the trees and the horizon's filmy, golden translucence. Without another word, they scrambled out of the wagon.

Empty and dark.

"When's Mama coming?" whispered Raleigh.

A step scraped at the front doorway. After a moment's silence, another step grated on the wood.

Raleigh murmured, "Who now?"

The four children scrambled into the bedroom and threw themselves on the floor behind the bed.

They froze when a voice called out, "Mrs. Edwards, you here?"

Mr. Hoy jiggled the door open, shuffled toward the bedroom, looked at the cold fireplace. Pulling out a handkerchief, hands shaking, the man wiped his face.

"Mrs. Edwards?" he called.

Before anyone grabbed her, Alta walked out and said, "She's not here."

Watching the man's pocket, she said, "Only me."

"I've been looking for my wife," he said, wiping his eyes, "and wondered if she came here. She ran away y'know."

Mary was certain he lied. Alta waited, but he didn't say more.

She said, "We haven't seen anyone since William and Eddie left."

That was a lie, too, and Mary wondered if he would leave.

"I don't know when my mother will come home," Alta said.

Mary peeked from behind the bed at Alta, her arms crossed and feet spread apart. Mr. Hoy sat on the chair, his leg stretched in front of him.

"I was going back to Reno, but thought I'd come up to see Mrs. Edwards."

He stood as if to leave, then swung around.

"That woman lied. She lied about the baby. About that half-breed. Then she took my boys," Mr. Hoy yelled, waving the handkerchief and stomping across the floor.

Alta stepped back to the chair. Mary slid from behind the bed and found the hairbrush. Raleigh and Tiny grabbed blankets.

He stopped suddenly and said, "I was sure I saw you at the train station. Didn't I?"

"No," Alta lied. "Maybe some other kids."

He paced the room, pulling off his hat, shoving it back onto his head, calling out his wife's name. Then he put his finger to his lips.

"You hear that?" he said, touching the fireplace bricks. "Softly, softly. She's called to me."

He caught hold of the chairs and shoved them around. He stopped again at the fireplace.

"*Hsst.* She's calling."

Alta gripped her chair.

"My boys talk about you four all the time," he hollered. "What'm I going to do?"

Raising his arms, he lunged at Alta.

Alta screamed and Tiny ran out. Tiny threw a blanket at Mr. Hoy's head. Mary hit him with the brush. Raleigh tackled him around his stiff leg, and he fell. They sat on him and held his arms, like they had done to Alta. He thrashed and then lay silent, staring at Alta, who had run into the kitchen and seized the chopping knife. She poised the sharp side above his chest. Her hand shook, but she didn't strike him.

Tiny cried again. Raleigh lifted his terrified face. Stunned at her strength, Mary held the brush, waving it in front of Mr. Hoy's face, ready to hit. Alta stood with the knife wobbling in her hand. She told Tiny to stop crying—it wasn't going to make it any better, although her cheeks were full of dripping tears too.

No one heard the door latch click, huddled as they were over Mr. Hoy, still mumbling to his wife. Mama came in with her arms flying, as she pulled off her muffler and hat. Mr. Faye followed and Mr. Hoy turned, vowing he didn't mean to frighten the children. Mama's face faded white as a bed sheet.

Mary told her about the pictures on the rocks and revolver and train station. Alta kept the knife pointed at Mr. Hoy's chest. Tiny didn't open her quivering lips.

Finally, Raleigh blurted out, "Mama, what about the gun?"

Sooty black circles around his eyelids, Mr. Hoy's red eyeballs almost popped out as he apologized again vehemently. He said to feel his pockets and Mr. Faye checked. All the while, Mary whacked the brush against the chair back, and Alta still waved the chopping knife. They found no revolver.

Mr. Faye watched while Mr. Hoy pulled himself up. Anxiety in his eyes, Mr. Faye said he'd have to tell the constable they found no gun and no one had seen Mr. Hoy shoot on the mountain. The three girls stood guard, knife, hairbrush, and blankets in hand. Raleigh rushed out to meet the constable, and Mr. Faye walked with the family down to the bridge.

"What can I do? Mr. Hoy scared the children, and he's talking to his wife. But has he harmed anyone?" Mr. O'Brien said.

Mama pulled the constable to the side of the bridge. Waving her arms and pointing to the mountain, she sent a flush up Mr. O'Brien's neck and his hands brushed furiously through his bushy hair.

Mr. Faye stayed with Mr. Hoy, babbling about his wife. He didn't look around to see if he could escape. Of course, he couldn't run far with his stiff leg, thought Mary.

Mr. O'Brien said, "Mrs. Edwards saw your wife, dead up on the hill over there."

"She couldn't be dead. I've heard her," said Mr. Hoy. "She's up at one of those Washo camps. You've got to go up and get her. I'm going back to my boys. You send her back to me in Tonopah."

"Mrs. Edwards saw your dead wife, but no one saw the murderer. You'd better get back to your boys and stop talking about your wife. The Tonopah sheriff will put you away for being crazy," said Mr. O'Brien. "Very suspicious."

Mama glared at the constable. The entire family marched to the train station, guarding Mr. Hoy. The man left on the Reno train, under the conductor's supervision. Mama remonstrated, "All the luck just left with Mr. Hoy. Not crazy, he's crafty like a fox."

25

Mid-October 1911
Harrigan's Hill, Truckee

"WHY DIDN'T YOU listen? Why were you out there after the bad things that've happened. Good gracious God's sake," said Mama, rocking faster with each word.

Tiny covered her face. Raleigh slid down next to the chair.

"I know about Mrs. Hoy," said Mama, "because Minna and I walked up to Captain Ben's."

"Oh, Mama," said Mary.

"Oh yes," she said. "I'd talked to Mr. Faye about that wretched boy at the livery stable, and he agreed to buy the horse if Mr. Littlefield had trouble again, but he thought cash in hand would do the trick."

She smoothed her cheek.

"Mr. Littlefield did have money from Captain Ben, and they left to get the horses and reach Donner Lake by nightfall. That's when their luck ran out."

Mama took deep breaths, clicking *tsk* against the roof of her mouth.

"Minna and I were sitting outside Captain Ben's house when we heard the blasts. We knew it was a gun and hurried down. Captain Ben went back for his sons to carry the bodies up to the house. We argued about getting Mr. O'Brien, but Captain Ben said no. Of course, I didn't know you children had been anywhere near those rocks."

Mama stood to wrap a cold wet rag around Raleigh's wrist, swelling and bruised.

"I bet Mr. Hoy threw the gun in the river," said Alta. "What d'you think?"

Mama said, "I think everyone was wrong. I was wrong to let Mrs. Hoy leave the boys with us, and she was wrong to leave them. Mr. Littlefield was wrong to take Mrs. Hoy away. Mr. Hoy was surely wrong to use a gun. You children were wrong to go up there where you hadn't been invited."

Squeezing the rag, she added, "Maybe Mr. Hoy was mean to her but good to the boys. Perhaps her parents made her marry Mr. Hoy even if she didn't love him."

Mary's head and heart hurt. Alta gazed out the window at the far mountains. Tears slid from Tiny's eyes down her cheeks. Mama wrapped a blanket around Raleigh's shoulders, and the girls dragged in more wood for the stove and fireplace.

They ate in silence until, of a sudden, Mama said, "If only the stable boy hadn't been so black-hearted, Mrs. Hoy and Mr. Littlefield would have been long gone."

Carrying the quilts into the bedroom, they collapsed in a jumble. Mama comforted them, saying nothing bad would happen that night, and tomorrow she would see the constable to make him promise to send a deputy to Tonopah. She murmured,

> *Yea, though I walk through the valley*
> *Of the shadow of death,*
> *I fear no evil …,*

while Mary and her brother and sisters lay quietly. The rockers grated over the dust. Mama turned the pages of her books and whispered other lines, searching, Mary believed, for advice.

MARY AWOKE WITH another sore throat. Mama said for Mary to accompany her to the saloon, and Alta, Tiny, and Raleigh should get ready for school.

"Can't I please go with them?" Mary begged. "I'll stay out of the cold."

"No," said Mama. "You did a foolish thing yesterday that turned out more terrible than you could have imagined. Now look at you. You can rest on one of the beds, and you won't get into trouble."

Pointing at each of the other three, Mama said, "Absolutely no sitting around here while I'm gone. You hear me, Alta? At school you'll have school things to think about. Look for me on Front Street afterward."

At the door, Mary trembled and the others hunched up under their coats, facing the autumn air. The wind blew again, scooting yellow and brown leaves along the ground.

"I told you so," said Alta. "It'll be forever before we can go off anywhere."

The three started down the hill. Alta stomped off ahead with her hair flying in the hard wind. Tiny, her tears flowing, and Raleigh, his back stiff, descended at a snail's pace. Mary knew Alta, filled with bravado, would pretend nothing was wrong, but the two youngest … perhaps afraid Mr. Hoy was on his way back, perhaps fearful they would cry in class, maybe alarmed by the weight in their hearts.

They made it to school, but Tiny always swore to Mary she didn't remember one minute of the entire day or any other day in the next few weeks.

WARM BY THE hearth, Mary muffled a cough and waited. Grim-faced, Mama folded the mess of blankets, took an apple to Molly, and piled wood by the fireplace. Finally, they arranged their coats and scarves against the cold weather and walked silently down to the Last Chance Saloon.

Mary offered to dust the furniture. Mama changed the sheets in the upstairs rooms, emptied the chamber pots, and cleaned the bathtub at the end of the hall. Needing to rest, Mary lay down on the best bed and closed her eyes. Pictures swirled in her head from the day they met the boys to the previous afternoon. Heart thumping, she squeezed her eyes tight until Mama came in to shake out the curtains.

"Mama, Mrs. Faye got off the same train with Mr. Hoy. What if he decides to come for her? An old lady got off too," she said.

Gloom covered her mother's face, though she said nothing and left to clean one more room. A clock struck noon, and Mary got up to search for her.

" … too much," said Mama. Muffled sobs carried to the hallway. "It's too horrible what's happened. I can hardly think."

"We don't know. Maybe I can find a way to help," whispered Mr. Faye.

He paused. "You're shaking. Let me hold you."

"We shouldn't do this. What if your wife sees?"

"No, no," said Mr. Faye. "That won't happen."

Then shoes shuffled, voices murmured, and the barely opened door clicked shut.

Mary turned back and lay down on the bed, the quilt touching her chin, and stared at the ceiling. How often had she overheard conversations in this small town, and now, she had no doubt about Mama and Mr. Faye. She blinked, and a vision of Mrs. Harrigan appeared before her, whispering, "Surely it was bound to happen."

Her mother returned soon enough. They ate stew in the saloon kitchen, but Mary avoided looking at Mama. After they laid down clean sheets in the room nearest the landing, Mr. Faye hollered up that the constable wanted to see Mama. Puzzled how her mother would act, Mary followed her down into Mr. Faye's tiny office.

Pulling on her coat, Mama said, "I expect to be gone most of the afternoon, Mr. Faye."

He patted her shoulder and said it was all right, asking her to pass on his sympathy to Captain Ben, Minna, and all the family, acting as if nothing had happened.

Mr. O'Brien greeted Mama from where he sat at his round table.

"Minna Finn and Captain Ben will be here soon. I'm glad you arrived first because I've been thinking."

Face stern, Mama remained immobile in the chair across the table. Mary waited on a wood carton seat.

Clearing his throat, Mr. O'Brien said, "You knew this lady … ."

"Matthew O'Brien! What d'you want?" cried Mama.

The constable blinked.

Clearing his throat again, he said, "Now most of the time, the Washo bury their people and never tell me anything. This time it's complicated because of the white woman. We have to find out who did it, I guess. So is it Mrs. Hoy for sure or not?"

Mary covered her mouth, and Mama slumped in the chair.

"I told you it was Mrs. Hoy," she said. "You need Mr. Hoy. You let him get away yesterday. I don't care what he claimed."

The constable replied, "Now, now, he's only one suspect. Maybe some other Washo man tried to rob them. Maybe the half-breed was married and his wife killed them. Maybe he killed the woman and then himself … "

Mr. O'Brien smoothed his mustache with a finger, a flush appearing from his neck to his cheeks.

"I'm sorry I said … In front of your daughter … " he stammered.

Mama shook her head and said, "Matt, you'd better send your deputy to Tonopah. Who knows where Mr. Hoy'll go. I'm afraid for my children, and what about Minna's cousin's family up there all alone on the hill? If you had more deputies in this town, I'd have someone to watch out for us, wouldn't I?"

The constable said, "Yes, yes," and mumbled about who'd bring the body of the white lady down.

Wearing a suit and flat-top wide-brim hat like Mr. Littlefield's, arm looped through Minna's, Captain Ben entered the office. He nodded to Mary and Mama.

"Constable, my mother's cousin is a kind man," Minna said. "He's known for his powers to give true advice."

Mr. O'Brien stroked his chin. Captain Ben began. "In August my wife's nephew came to me because he no longer had power. Being half white, he'd been with the white people too long. He'd been shot in the arm by Mrs. Hoy's husband."

He waited a moment and then said, "He came to me to cure him. We had a night ceremony, but afterwards I had a warning in my dreams."

The captain intoned, "The one-eyed, one-legged giant appeared. He grabbed my wife's nephew and threw him high into the land of the dead. I followed his soul to rocks where warriors defend the sacred spring. My wife's nephew ran past them, but I had to fight until I beat them back. So my nephew's soul outran me. He reached the spring, and he would never come back. My power wasn't enough."

He stopped again, and Minna patted him on the arm.

In a normal voice, Captain Ben went on, "It was a fearful dream, so when he came back two nights ago, I told my wife's nephew to go stay with his other aunt, my wife's second sister, who lives near Donner Lake, until he had enough money to reach San Francisco. I gave him money for a horse. I could see he loved the lady who was with him, but she was white."

Waving his hand, Captain Ben said, "There was nothing wrong with the lady. She was kind and sad also. I don't blame her. They were going down to get the horses when it happened."

Interrupting, Mr. O'Brien said, "What exactly did you see?"

The captain repeated what Mama had told Mary the night before, but he added, "We reached the rock wall where you can sit to think or pray by the sacred pictures. They had fallen in a heap with bullets in their heads. These two women saw it too."

Shaking his head, he pointed to Mama and Minna.

"It's hard to believe someone could be filled with enough anger to kill them by those sacred pictures."

"Did your nephew have a wife who might have done it?" the constable asked. "How do you know your nephew didn't kill the woman and then himself?"

"He wasn't married. He didn't want to die. He didn't have a gun. He wanted to go off with the white lady somewhere to be safe," said Captain Ben.

"Well, that settles that," said Mr. O'Brien, slapping his hands to his knees. "We'll get the bodies and bury them. I don't know about the husband."

"That's not the whole story," said Minna.

"We don't want ghosts," said Captain Ben. "My sons took the bodies up to our graveyard. We burned them and their belongings last night and buried the ashes this morning. I wish it had rained to erase their footprints, but I brushed them away as best I could. My wife and I prayed they would accept death."

The old man stirred in his chair and held up his hand.

"Please leave it alone. Don't go looking for the lady's husband. My wife is afraid her nephew's ghost will come back to avenge the lady's death. We have done everything we can think of to help my wife's nephew and the lady journey to the land of the dead."

"I explained the law, but he prefers the old Washo ways," said Minna.

Mr. O'Brien remonstrated, "We must get the husband's statement. Also Mr. and Mrs. Hoy had children. I'm sending my deputy tomorrow."

Mention of the boys made Mary whisper, "What about the baby?"

The captain answered, "It's a girl baby. She's safe with my wife's nephew's cousin. The daughter of the aunt who lives by Donner Lake. She'd lost her baby and was happy to take the child."

Mary sighed and looked over at Mama, who waved her handkerchief in front of her face.

Minna said, "That's all now. Captain Ben must go back before it gets dark."

When the old man left, Mama said, "Matt, I'm not afraid of a ghost. I'm afraid Mr. Hoy'll come after us."

"Now, now, nothing will happen to you. The Tonopah constable will watch him," he answered in a voice that was supposed to be soothing, but wasn't.

"Matt, I'm going to Mr. Faye because Mrs. Faye was on the same train with that man when he came to Truckee yesterday. Mary saw them," said Mama.

The constable said, "Why didn't you tell me?"

"Would you have arrested him?" retorted Mama.

"I'll go see Mr. Faye," said Mr. O'Brien. "He gets excited, you know."

"I'm still going," said Mama. "I want the town council to hire more deputies. They won't listen to women even though we can vote."

Thrumming his fingers on the desk, Mr. O'Brien stared at Mama.

"Are you really going to do something about Mr. Hoy? Or are those two murders going to be put aside?" she asked.

He waved his hand in dismissal. Outside, Mama set off for the saloon. Mary didn't want to see or talk to Mr. Faye. She wasn't like Alta who would smirk.

STANDING IN THE saloon's small office, Mr. and Mrs. Faye were examining a new-fangled, coal-burning Round Oak heating stove.

Mr. Faye turned and said, "Hello Dolly."

His eyes slid back and forth and blinked as if flipping through a list of reasons Mama might have returned.

"Mr. Faye, I have a proposal to discuss," said Mama, speaking formally, meaning business. "The constable may come to see you about this also, but I must impress on you how important it is that the town council hire more deputies."

Mrs. Faye sat down, and Mr. Faye brought a chair for Mama. Uneasy about what she knew, Mary turned away to marvel at the fancy stove.

"As it is, a number of people in town have met Mrs. Hoy and her children or have seen the lady's husband. You know he's most likely the murderer," said Mama. "That man acted a good role yesterday, and Mr. O'Brien simply wanted to get rid of him."

Mrs. Faye nodded, but Mr. Faye said there was nothing to hold him on, not even for entering the house when everyone saw how he was acting.

"Be that as it may, Mrs. Faye, you came in on the train yesterday from Reno with Mr. Hoy. My daughter, here, was sitting on the bench and saw you. Remember the tall, slim man with a slight limp?" said Mama.

Mrs. Faye covered her mouth and said, "Yes, yes, I did, but men get on and off the train here all the time. I didn't think anything of it."

Mama put her arm around Mary, who flushed.

"I'm telling you because I'm afraid for my children, and for my sister Ola and my other sister in Reno, and for you, Mrs. Faye, and for the station clerk. What if, after thinking about it, that man comes back again? Or sends someone else to hurt us?" said Mama.

"We have some say in the business of the town council. We need more deputies. I don't want vigilantes prying into everyone's business, but the town is getting rougher. There we are up on the hill with no electricity, much less telephones to call for help. I know septic tanks are important, but this is for our safety too," she said, voice fierce.

Mr. Faye placed his hands on the table. Mama leaned forward in her chair and gazed at Mr. Faye, his neck becoming ruddy while Mrs. Faye turned to look at him.

"Dolly, as you know, I've already asked for deputies at the last town council meeting. That does cost money."

Mama frowned.

"Find some," said Mrs. Faye, cheeks reddening and tears filling her eyes like the time she was frustrated about the Model T. "Mr. O'Brien can hardly handle the load he has now. Maybe some new deputies will make a difference."

Mrs. Faye felt well heated by the new stove, and she pulled her shawl away from her shoulders and flapped the edges in front of her.

She said, "My dear, surely you can devise a plan to raise money to hire two more deputies. After all, you're a businessman."

She smiled and waited.

Mama said, "My children are very unhappy about the murders, being good friends with the little boys. It's a terrible story. Hiring more deputies would be one good outcome."

Mama stood, pulling her coat close. Mary tucked her mittens inside her sleeves, preparing to meet the cold air when the saloon door opened.

Flapping her shawl, Mrs. Faye said, "Dolly, we haven't sold the old wood stove. Wouldn't it be good to have it in your house? We can find some men to bring it up. We all need to help each other, don't we?"

Stunned, Mama whispered thanks and enfolded Mrs. Faye in a hug. Mr. Faye crossed his arms and fixed his eyes on one woman and then the other.

THEY MUST HAVE watched from the lumber barn.

Raleigh yelled, "Mama, 'member Joe who had scarlet fever when we had it? He went back to Reno with his cousin when they got better. I didn't think I'd ever see him again. Like William and Eddie. But he was at school today!"

Tiny pulled out a lollipop from behind her back and laughed, too boisterous to be light-hearted, but better than the sadness last night, thought Mary.

"Where'd you get those?" asked Mama.

"Alta bought them, " said Tiny, "and cornflakes too."

Mama said, "I must say, I'd forgotten about cornflakes. That seems like a long time ago, doesn't it?"

The gaiety faded and Mama wandered off to get supper. Mary walked up to the outhouse, wondering why Alta spent money on her brother and sister—a kind, unexpected gesture.

Mary pulled on the outhouse door, which was hooked shut. She waited, and the door opened a slit. Alta peeked out, and smoke escaped.

"What d'you want?"

"What d'you think?"

Grabbing Mary's arm, Alta whispered, "Come on. Come on."

Sitting on the edge of the privy, cigarette between her fingers, ash hanging, ready to drop into the hole, Alta said, "You better not tell, you goody-goody."

"Will you stop calling me that name? Maybe I'm different from you, but I don't tell, do I?"

After a moment, she said, "You're only fourteen, Alta. Where'd you get the money?"

"Oh you know, errands for the ladies on Back Street. Go buy soap or coffee when they run out. They give me money and cigarettes if I ask. That's how I bought the lollipops for Raleigh and Tiny."

Alta sighed.

"They've been so sad. I felt sorry for them."

She paused. She inhaled.

"I have cornflakes. Want some?"

Alta pulled out the green and red box. Mary reached in for a handful and ate them one by one. Alta exhaled.

"I thought I'd smoke up the hill in the woods, but I think that's how the fire started while you were sick. Anyway Crazy Lady Harrigan might see me and tell Mama. She's not as loony as you think."

"I know," said Mary.

Alta took a long pull and dropped the cigarette down the privy. They watched smoke rise. Then, unable to hold off, Mary related what she'd heard in the bedroom at the saloon.

"What did I tell you?" said Alta, lips twisting uneasily. "I've been waiting for this to happen."

Picking up the cornflakes and stepping out, swinging the outhouse door back and forth to make a breeze and get rid of smoke, she said, "I'll wait out here. I've got something to tell you too."

In the lumber barn they slid way down into the wagon to stay out of the cold wind that blasted through. A minute later, Raleigh and Tiny appeared with a blanket, wrapping up in it against the cold.

Alta said, "Papa was at the livery stable today. Raleigh, Tiny, and I had been walking around on Front Street waiting for Mama, and he came off the train. We've been to see him before at the stable. I think even Mama'd been at the hotel once or twice to see him. She's been getting money from someone, not only from stingy Mr. Faye. Otherwise we'd be starving."

"Papa looked first-rate," said Raleigh.

Mary said, "You may think Mr. Faye's cheap, Alta, but he's going to find a way to get the town to pay for more deputies, isn't he?"

Conspiratorial in the outhouse, Mary and Alta stared each other down in the wagon until Tiny said, "We've been so scared. Papa told us about the time some boy accused Papa's brother of stealing a horse. He cut him with a knife, leaving him to bleed pretty bad. This was after the war when everyone was poor where they lived and fought with each other all the time. Their father said never to tell the mother, and they didn't."

Bundled up under the blanket, Mary watched Tiny, such a tomboy, and yet crying all the time these past two days.

"It's so hard to not say anything at school," Tiny said. "Raleigh's lucky because he can play with Joe now. He's a nice boy and friendly. Minna made Hazel go home again as soon as school was over, so I'm afraid I won't have anyone."

Squished up, they gazed out the barn door, inspecting the dependable orange glow left by the sun and the bright stars beginning to twinkle one by one, no moon in the early night sky to obscure their brilliance.

Mary said, "I wonder what Papa would say about the baby? Remember how sad he was about Florence? I found out Mrs. Hoy's baby is with Mr. Littlefield's cousin."

"What d'you know," said Alta.

Mary passed on Captain Ben's version of the events. She imagined what it would be like when the bodies were laid out, burned hot, and charred. Did flames swirl into the sky, sparks rising to the heavens?

As she finished, Molly wandered into the barn and settled herself in the corner away from the door and the wind. Mary and Raleigh climbed out of the wagon to brush her down. Mama called, and the children dashed through the cold and into the house.

"THIS TIME I mean it. Go to Aunt Ola's tomorrow after school. I know you're sad. It'll be a long time before it fades away, like with Florence," said Mama. "Maybe your aunt will help."

"Papa came to town today," said Alta. "We visited, and then we came up because we thought we missed you."

"Well, did he give you an envelope?" asked Mama.

Raleigh shook his head. Mama smoothed her hands along her apron and turned to stir potatoes boiling on the stove.

Finally, Mama whispered, "Remember the line from Ecclesiastes, '*a time to keep silence.*' It's hard, but you must do your best. Think how William and Little Eddie would feel if they ever found out you told what happened to their mother. That wouldn't be kind."

<hr/>

"DID WILLIAM AND Eddie ever find out?" asked Lane.

"I don't think so," said Mary.

"Did anyone ever find Mr. Hoy?"

"More happened before we knew about him," said Mary.

26

Late October 1911
Harrigan's Hill, Truckee

AFTER SCHOOL, RALEIGH and Tiny leaned against the saloon bar until Mary came down, and they climbed McGlashan's Hill to Aunt Ola's home.

"Sit, sit, sit," said Aunt Ola.

She gazed at them and sighed, "You look so cold and sad. Take some cookies and tea. You'll warm up and ... and feel better."

They settled in armchairs and ate cookies until Ola said, "My goodness, where's Alta? Dolly told me you would all come for the afternoon."

"Alta'll be along. She's doing a job for Mrs. Bridges on Back Street," said Raleigh. "That's how she gets money. Me and Tiny find things at the train, and you know, Mary doesn't go anywhere much until the doctor says she's better."

"You're here, Mary," said Aunt Ola.

"Mama's been taking me with her because she's afraid for us to be alone at the house after the bad thing the other day. You know she wants more deputies."

"Mr. James'll support more deputies," said Aunt Ola. "Now, I can too."

Just then Alta waltzed into the parlor, but Aunt Ola didn't say a word and passed the plate of cookies.

Raleigh said, "It was a very bad thing that happened. Mama said and Papa said after a long time, it won't be so scary."

"Yes, that's so," said Ola. "How is Dolly feeling today?"

Mary said, "She cried this morning, even though Mrs. O'Brien brought good news. The constable sent a deputy to Tonopah."

Aunt Ola turned to Alta and said, "Did you get some money for helping Mrs. Bridges?"

Alta's face began to burn. Tiny grinned and Raleigh swung his feet back and forth under the chair in an effort not to laugh.

Alta tilted her head and said, "Yes, ma'am, I did, and I didn't buy anything either. It's all for Mama."

She spread her pretty lips in a virtuous smile. Mary knew perfectly well Alta hadn't decided to be generous. On the other hand, she had bought lollipops for Tiny and Raleigh.

Her hands smoothing the arms of the chair, Aunt Ola said, "I've been wondering about Dolly."

Mary blanched, perhaps her aunt knew Mama's secret, but instead Ola said, "I know she thinks I'm foolish, and it's true, I'm not as smart or educated as she is, but Mr. James is generous, and I have my own money from sewing. I wish I knew how to get Dolly to agree to let me help."

"Aunt Ola, can you help us get Mama to go back with Papa?" blurted out Raleigh. "It'd be better that way, even Mary thinks so."

Biting her lip, Aunt Ola placed the plates and teacups on a tray.

"That's a hard request, Raleigh. Dolly doesn't like to be told those kinds of things. I'll have to think on it."

The trees bent in the wind when Raleigh and his three sisters set off down the hill, Aunt Ola giving them each two bits when they walked out the door. To feel better, she said. Coins in their palms, they stopped at the grocer's on Front Street.

New tiny silk pouches of tea leaves perched on the counter, and Mary said, "Let's get some for Mama."

Raleigh proposed a pound of sugar to sweeten up their muffins and fruit. Lastly, they each bought a nickel's worth of candy. With money left over and an irreproachable sense of goodness, they started up Harrigan's Hill, heads down against the wind.

Holding her coat collar, peppermint stick at her lips, Tiny asked, "Where'd you really go, Alta? Off with Georgie?"

"Shut your mouth, Tiny. What d'you know? I did go do an errand for Mrs. Bridges. George came to help me, that's all. You're another tattle-tale," said Alta, fury on her face.

Tiny and Raleigh guffawed at Alta's wrath, but ran off ahead calling "Georgie-Georgie." They knew it was the better part of valor to disappear.

Alta's rage turned when Mary said, "Why Georgie?"

"You better not say anything to Mama," Alta shouted. "He's sweet on me, so why shouldn't I get him to do things for me?"

"All right," said Mary. "What do I care?"

Silently they walked, Mary rested at the flat rock while Alta continued up, whacking leaves as they flew into the air. In her heart Mary cared that Alta hadn't told her about this boy. She wondered if it was because, although she still played games like Run, Sheep, Run, Alta had grown up while Mary was sick. Mama said she'd become a woman.

Mary wished they were more sisterly, like Mama and Ola, who laughed and comforted each other now they had gotten over the bad part about Papa. In the hard wind, tree branches cracked into each other and swung apart, like she and Alta, never swaying together.

TWO DAYS LATER, Mr. O'Brien sent for Minna, Captain Ben, and Mama. Mary sat on a stool, peering at papers neatly laid out, typed with the polished writing machine on the deputy's desk.

Mr. O'Brien's deputy said, "I typed up what I found out. Mr. Hoy spoke about his wife's disappearance from the hospital and how he took his boys back to Tonopah. As for Mrs. Hoy's relatives, Mr. Hoy said she didn't have any. A Washo man told him about Mr. Littlefield's relatives. He admitted coming to Truckee, but only to ask around he said.

"He disavowed her to me. He'll wait the proper time and then apply for divorce. If she's dead, he wants the papers that say so."

Everyone sat quietly.

Then jabbing her forefinger at the deputy, Mama said, "That man lied. He knows Mrs. Hoy has relatives, and you know he was acting a crazy man part when he was caught by my children."

The deputy protested, "I was supposed to get a statement. I'm not the lawyer or the judge."

Mama said, "You don't want to know where Mr. Hoy had been that day. You don't care if Mr. Littlefield and Mrs. Hoy were murdered. You don't even know or care why she ran away."

She made a *tsk* of disgust and turned aside, her hand over her eyes.

"Now, now, Dolly, we're waiting until the justice of the peace has a date for a hearing. We'll explain the case to him, but if no one comes to claim Mrs. Hoy, I don't know what to do. Captain Ben doesn't want to press charges," said Mr. O'Brien.

Captain Ben nodded and said, "I'm satisfied. The law won't bring my wife's nephew back, and she doesn't have the strength to keep watch for ghosts."

Patting Mama on the knee, Minna whispered, "All right. All right."

The constable added, "Mr. Hoy's never going to set foot in this town again. He knows we're suspicious of him. You don't have to worry about your family."

"Yes, yes. Everything's fine. My children are unhappy, and whether you say so or not, they're afraid Mr. Hoy will get them. Those two boys will never see their mother again. The only child who's all right is the little baby who has a new mother and who'll never have to know about all this," said Mama. "Is that the end you want?"

MARCHING UP THE hill, Mama talked to herself about how she was going to confront the justice of the peace. Pitiful how the laws were set up for men. She threw up her hands as she walked, and Mary worried she was acting like Crazy Lady Harrigan.

Gulping breath, Mary jogged along to catch up. Mama kept walking faster and faster. When she flung open the front door of the house, she found Alta, Tiny, and Raleigh sitting on the bed, eating their penny candies, waiting. She stared, then her face softened, as though her brain had stopped arguing and noticed where she was.

"See, Mama," said Tiny. "We all came home together, so no one would be alone."

"Well, that's fine," Mama said, pulling off her coat and scarf, rubbing her hands in front of the fire.

When Mama had boiled water for tea and set food on plates in front of each child, Mama said, "Mary'll go stay with Aunt Ola on some days from now on. I won't have to worry about her, and you all can go up to Aunt Ola's after school. Why weren't you at Aunt Ola's today?"

Alta said, "Now, Mama, we were at Aunt Ola's, but the sun set. See how dark it is."

Mama's eyes flitted from one child to the other and to the window and the fire.

She sighed, "Yes, I see, and here's what I think. After Mrs. Hoy left her husband, I think she was confused, and no matter what she did it made things worse. Mr. Hoy was so angry he took revenge, which is an evil, cruel thing to do. It's sad the men in charge in Truckee and Tonopah don't care because it's a woman and an Indian who were killed."

Masses of clouds covered the sky that night. Sorting the blankets in the shadowy room, Tiny said, "Maybe Mrs. Hoy had nothing to do, and Mr. Hoy was away all the time in the mine. William and Eddie, they were probably out playing all the time. Maybe it was hot and boring out there. Maybe she was lonely, and Mr. Littlefield and she started to talk and it just happened. Isn't that sort of how Mr. James got together with Aunt Ola, you know, the lonely part?"

Mama said, "I hadn't thought of it that way. Maybe so. Maybe so."

Raleigh murmured, "Let's not talk about it. I want it to go away."

THE SKY WAS still covered with dark rain clouds on Monday morning. Mary trudged up McGlashan's Hill, her arms crossed to hold her coat close against the icy wind pulling at her hair. She was relieved to entertain Amanda inside Aunt Ola's warm house rather than stay with her mother. Raleigh and Tiny, but not Alta, came by after school, and the three of them hiked up their hill.

At the outhouse, the door was hooked again.

Mary shouted, "Open up!"

"Who's with you?" Alta whispered.

"Nobody," she said. "Open the door!"

Alta pulled Mary in. Wind blew in the cracks in the roof. Cigarette smoke filled the space and escaped into the air outside.

"It's cold, cold, cold in here. I've been smoking in the back hallway at Mrs. Bridges' house where it's warm until she told me I was too young," said Alta, rolling her eyes. "Want to try?"

"No!" said Mary, waving her hand in front of her face to make the smoke disappear.

"Oh, quit that good-girl look," said Alta, cigarette drooping between her fingers over the privy hole. Mary waited, arms crossed, leaning against the splintery wall.

"The cigarette helps me think," confided Alta after a time. "Mr. Hoy was out visiting Back Street in Tonopah all the time, gambling and drinking and you-know-what, and Mrs. Hoy was made to stay at home to take care of those boys. So she found someone else. Too bad he was a half-breed because that made Mr. Hoy even madder when he found out. Stick with your own kind, I guess."

Now Mary had seen Alta cry and knew she wasn't as unfeeling as this version sounded. Alta dropped the cigarette down the hole and left the outhouse, swinging the door to draw out the smoke, not that it did much good, before she let it slam.

ON THE DATE of the hearing, the justice of the peace entered from the back of the constable's meeting chamber just as Aunt Ola and Mary arrived. Mama, Minna, and the old cousin sat at the front. Mr. and Mrs. Faye walked in and sat down right behind them.

Surveying the array of people gathered before him, the justice of the peace raised his eyebrows, brought down the gavel, and asked the constable to begin. Fortunately, Mr. O'Brien was brief because the audience had had enough of the story. He ended with Captain Ben's evidence.

The minute the justice heard the old man didn't want to pursue an investigation into the murder of his wife's nephew, he held up his hand and said, "Just send that man in Tonopah a death certificate. He'll have to deal with his children and her family, if they ever show up. That's all we will do."

He tapped his hand on the table, and then, irritation in his voice, he stated, "I hope you have all the forms ready so I can sign them and we don't have to spend more time on these deaths. It's been quiet for a good while, and lately you've had too many shootings in this town. Bad for business."

The justice of the peace shook his papers and said, "Let's get on with the other matters before us."

Mama leaned over to Mr. O'Brien, and he whispered to the justice.

Top lip curled in a sneer, the justice turned and said, "Yes, madam?"

"Your honor, while I recognize Captain Ben's reluctance to go further with this incident, I have something to say that may change your mind with respect to Mr. and Mrs. Hoy, but I would rather speak privately."

The justice of the peace turned back to Mr. O'Brien who shrugged.

"Please approach, Mrs. Edwards," said the justice, agitated, pulling his sleeves.

Mama leaned on the desk. The audience heard murmurs. Mama's hands spread out, and the justice's eyes turned fierce. He pointed at the constable and back at Mama. He whispered and stabbed the table with his finger.

Mary was apprehensive that Mama had told the constable and the justice about the letters from Aunt Margaret, the talk in the livery stable, the night visit, or the hike up to the Indian pictures. As she sat down again, Mama shook her head at what Mary thought was the justice's lack of sympathy.

Looking at Mama's vexed face, the justice snapped, "Madam, if you'd had your husband around, you wouldn't have needed money and taken in those children, and you'd never have been involved."

Mama's jaw clenched like the man had stabbed her, and she flung back, "Your honor, I would've taken in those children even if I had been with my husband. We had a boardinghouse. I would've given them everything I gave my boarders. I try to be a kind woman. A town survives on more than business. I think that's all you care about. You think if these murders haven't gotten in the way of business, then don't bother. Well, civilized people need more than money. I never would've left those children alone."

"Speaking of civilized, madam, it appears your children wander all over town like regular ragamuffins," said the justice, eyes squinting as if aiming a gun. "They may not be cursing street urchins, but they ought to be at home where they belong. Not out where they shouldn't be, like little hooligans people say started the fire this past summer. They wouldn't see and hear things they shouldn't know about."

Furious that the justice was turning on her, Mama didn't stand down. Instead, she aimed sharp words.

"Your honor, why should children have to stay at home all the time? The buildings may be old in this town, but the river, meadows, and woods are beautiful. Children stay healthy when they can run and play. Unless the reason is you government men and your business friends don't want to pay for a deputy so they can be safe?"

The justice of the peace looked down at his papers and grabbed his gavel. He rubbed his other hand over the top of his head, fingers shaking. Mr. O'Brien and Mr. Faye exchanged looks.

Once more Mama spoke, "Your honor, more deputies would help the issue of safety. No matter whose family they belong to, rich or poor, children wouldn't have to worry about things they shouldn't see or hear."

The justice pounded the gavel and shouted, "That's enough. This session is adjourned. Mr. O'Brien, Mr. Faye, I'll see you in the other room."

Mama stood outside with Captain Ben and Minna, her hands shaking, but her eyes glittering, certain she'd had the better of the justice. In a tight circle, they shivered as the wind blew hard, the air cold enough for snow.

"I have no idea why the justice said those things to me," said Mama. "I wasn't rude to him up at the table. I've never met that man."

"I think Mr. O'Brien and Mr. Faye had already talked to him about county money for a deputy," said Mrs. Faye, finding a spot in the group. "Maybe this justice doesn't like people asking him for help, and he took it out on you. My husband did say he was stingy and conservative."

Minna reminded them all no one should feel safe since they still didn't know about Mr. Hoy.

Old Captain Ben nodded and confided, "Mrs. Edwards, I think I know what you told the justice. I saw all those little footprints, as I looked around on the path down the hill. But what's the purpose in telling? I've done what I can to keep my nephew's ghost and the white lady's ghost from visiting this world. That's the best I can do to keep Mr. Hoy from searching for more revenge."

Coats flapping open, Mary and her mother struggled home against the wind, grabbing coat lapels and holding hats to keep from freezing. Once inside, they threw wood into the kitchen stove and the fireplace to bring warmth to the rooms.

Sitting in front of the fire, hands and feet close to the flames, Mary recounted the events floating in her head. What if Mrs. Hoy had wanted things she couldn't have? What if Mr. Hoy was mean because she kept asking? She fell in love with someone else who in the end couldn't get her what she wanted either. The lies and killing came from wishing for what you couldn't have and placing your hopes in the wrong person. Or maybe Alta was right. Maybe Mr. Hoy would've been glad to get rid of her if she'd just picked a white man.

Offering that version to Mama, Mary already knew her mother would say it didn't make it right to kill someone.

Mama added, "Your story is very grown-up, Mary, but *'what's done is done.'* I wish it were long passed."

IN THE AFTERNOON, a man from the Last Chance walked up the hill to borrow Molly and the wagon.

"For the Franklin stove, Dolly," said the man. "Mr. Faye's going to help me bring it."

Saying, "well, well, well," Mama walked around the room, and the man helped her move the bed to another corner. Wrapped in her coat with a blanket around her shoulders, Mary coaxed Molly away from the sparse clumps of grass on the hill. They hitched her to the wagon, and Mary was sent down with the man to get some hay at the livery stable. It looked like snow any day, and Molly would have trouble finding something to eat.

Tiny and Raleigh met them on the way back, so they felt like a caravan again traveling home with the treasure. Soon after, Mr. Faye huffed up the hill. Mama had doused the fireplace flames and scraped out the ashes. Mr. Faye and the handy man sat the stove properly on the hearth and angled the pipe up the flue. The fellow climbed onto the roof and covered the space at the chimney top around the stove pipe. Then he waved and hiked on down the hill.

Pulling on his overcoat, Mr. Faye said, "Dolly, was the justice angry at Mr. O'Brien for not asking the right questions?"

Mama nodded.

"Now I understand when my wife said the constable can no longer handle the difficulties in town. So, here's what I know. Even though the justice was rude, he's going to see if the county can help us pay for at least one more deputy. That's what he agreed to after the meeting.

"He was against the suffrage amendment, you know, and doesn't like it when a woman is involved in a legal matter."

Mr. Faye laughed and asked Mama to walk with him to the pine tree as he had some other news for her.

Striding up the path, Alta stopped and waited as Mr. Faye stood with his hand on the trunk. Mama stood with her back to the tree. The wind died down and their words, even whispers, carried down the mountain. Alta smothered laughter, thinking they were unaware of anything except each other.

Mr. Faye leaned over Mama, saying, "I can't let you go."

She smiled, as he smoothed her hair again and again.

Wrinkling her forehead, she said, "I'm caught too, but I work for you. I have four children. I have a husband."

"I have children too. We can go to another town," said Mr. Faye, pulling Mama against him.

"I don't want to be known around town. Or hurt Grace. She's done good things," Mama protested.

He held her hands against his cheeks and said, "She's busy, all the time, off doing who knows what."

He murmured, "How did this happen?"

"I don't know what to do. I'm afraid we'll be found out," she whispered, leaning back against the trunk.

Mr. Faye put his arm around Mama's shoulder, guided her to the stone bench, and whispered into her ear almost like kisses. Alta finally walked down the slope and back up loudly singing "Sweet Adeline." By the time she showed up near the bench, Mr. Faye and Mama were shaking hands. He doffed his businessman's hat and walked down the path.

THE ROCKER SCRAPED along the floor and burning wood snapped in the stove, but all four heard Mama.

"I'm certain of it. Mr. Faye took my side because I do a lot of work for him, and he felt he owed me something. If only a new deputy would get Mr. Hoy."

Alta smiled, and before being told a word, Mary guessed Alta had heard something besides news of a deputy and Mr. Hoy.

"For certain, Mr. Hoy was clever and lucky," Mama said and waved her hand in front of her face to whisk away her thoughts.

MARY'S SORE THROAT returned, and she stayed inside engrossed in Rudyard Kipling to keep her mind away from October's unhappiness. Tiny talked again about her desire to be an actress and collect jewelry. She dropped her interest in Indian things. Joe and Raleigh often fished, but he refused to play games with guns. Alta withdrew from the family little by little, coming home as close to suppertime as possible, though she had to walk in the dark on moonless nights.

27

End October to Mid-November 1911
Harrigan's Hill, Truckee

ANOTHER ROUND OF coughs and spikes in fever seized Mary. Confined to the house, she was told to flee to Mrs. O'Brien if bad people came. Those unhappy thoughts faded when her book-loving friend, Etta, handed over Mary Shelley's *Frankenstein*.

"You might like it because it's about a monster and goes with Halloween," offered Etta. "Are you going to Sally Faye's party?"

It was the first she had heard about a Halloween party, but she determined to get better before the raucous holiday in their town. Holding her head over a steaming pot of water, Mary breathed vapors of Mentholatum that her mother had obtained from Minna.

In the middle of supper chatter, when Mary asked if her brother and sisters were invited to the party, Mama interrupted, "I think it was the uproar this month and the judge's comments about shootings. Something to ease a ruckus, which will also help Mr. Faye's chances to be elected mayor. I told you he's a clever man."

"Now Mama, Sally told me her mother talked him into the party. She's the clever one," said Alta.

Once settled on the front room bed, they whispered about rowdy Halloweens and decided nothing was as alarming as the past month. It wasn't even scary last year, Raleigh remembered, when those mean kids found a drunkard reeling down Front Street and threw rotten fruit, setting off a brawl. Raleigh and his sisters laughed until Tiny began to cry, thinking about poor William and Eddie with no mother and no fun on Halloween.

Then for Mary's ear alone, Alta asked if she thought Mama would run away with Mr. Faye.

"I think she's all mixed-up," murmured Mary.

"I hope not. Papa makes me angry, but Mama has to go back with him. I don't want to happen to us what happened to Mrs. Hoy and Mr. Littlefield," sighed Alta, who didn't sound certain.

"Papa wouldn't do that," said Mary, not sure she knew what happened between men and women.

Snow rolled in the weekend before Halloween. Out of sorts, Mary and Alta bickered over each hand of cards. Raleigh complained about going to the pump. Sad-eyed, Tiny huddled under the blankets. When the storm stopped early Sunday morning, everyone but Mary scraped their way downhill to church. Snow piled on the tree branches, but not so deep on the pathway.

Reading *Frankenstein,* Mary heard a knock and ducked under the quilt, holding her breath and keeping her eyes tightly closed. The latch lifted, and she scrambled out of bed and bolted to the kitchen, only stopping when a voice called "Dolly." A tall, haggard figure, disheveled with his soggy hat, raggedy beard, dirty pants, and wet coat dripping on the floor. Walking stiffly from the cold, Uncle Lauf could have been Frankenstein.

Holding onto the table, he removed his smelly coat, put on Papa's old sweater, and sat listlessly. Mary scooped snow into a large pot and heated it on the stove. Lauf looked better after he washed in the hot water. Never one to admit he was starving, the garrulous man wasn't talking either. Mary found some crackers and applesauce.

Finally, Uncle Lauf said, "I've prayed to the Lord to direct me. I knew He wouldn't let me suffer. Bless you, Mary, for being the Lord's helpmate."

She offered more crackers, thinking she, all by herself, was making sure Uncle Lauf didn't suffer. But if he thought she was helping the Lord, so be it.

Uncle Lauf had recovered some by the time Raleigh, Tiny, and Alta came home. In spite of blowing snow, Mama had sent them ahead while she went with Mr. Titus to his grocery.

"I almost didn't make it through the wild mountains this time," Uncle Lauf began. "I returned to Seattle in September and received a train ticket as far as San Francisco. Then I walked. But the Lord has provided me with sturdy legs, so I don't mind. I conducted glorious meetings in Sacramento, and I was directed to go to Reno … ," he stopped for a moment to gaze at them, " … where I found the Lord, if you recall. There'll be a grand assembly with ministers and witnesses from all around Nevada and California. Thus, I began my journey up here."

"Why didn't you work in Sacramento to make money for a train ticket?" asked Raleigh.

All eyes on Uncle Lauf, Raleigh's expectation seemed like an obvious solution.

"Or maybe you could've found Papa. I bet he would've given you a ride," offered Tiny.

"I hardly know your father," said Uncle Lauf. "I don't think I'd recognize him."

"Or sent a telegram to Aunt Ola," suggested Alta. "She would've helped."

"The Lord always provides," said Uncle Lauf. "Jesus walked everywhere. He didn't ask for help. He only took what was offered. I'm his disciple, and I try to win over those who have lost their way by following his example."

He waited for approving nods, but they only said, "Oh."

"Anyway, near Colfax, I met two men, and we joined together for companionship on the road. By the time we reached Soda Springs, the wind's bitter sting was unrelenting and heavy snow piled high. We pushed on through drifts until finally we looked for shelter in a world so blinding we squinted as if the desert sun glared down on us.

"Only by moving did we keep the blood flowing in a white world with fantastic icicles drooping from overhanging rocks. Only the heavens were dark and menacing, except when completely white from snow flying into our faces."

He stopped. Though listening politely, Mary had seen plenty of snow, lovely flakes that fell until freezing cold settled into the bones. Uncle Lauf's talk seemed full of fancy words for a snowstorm's aching misery.

"The wind lifted for a second, a railroad snow shed flitting in and out of my vision, and certainly the Lord was looking out for us when the swinging light from a watchman's kerosene lamp approached.

"I convinced the fellow we weren't tramps with plans for mayhem. God must have touched his heart because he directed us to a train workers' bunkhouse. Beds with dry straw and buckets of coal to build a warm fire in the stove brought us back to life. I lay quietly, giving thanks to God for our fortune, and soon fell asleep."

Radiance filled his eyes, so Alta and Mary later agreed he must have been practicing for one of his meetings.

"We awoke to a glorious sun, the snow-covered trees laden with sparkling diamonds. We started early, sure God's grace was with us, but the sky clouded up at Donner Summit, and we fought the howling wind and snow until the storm relented. I left my new friends at the saloon and made my way to this refuge, thankful I had endured."

All four breathed relief.

"*Whoo!* I'm exhausted, Uncle Lauf," said Raleigh.

"Too much like the poor Donner Party," said Tiny. "No more death for me.

We've had enough."

Mary didn't say anything, but in her secret opinion the story wasn't as thrilling as the history of Roxane.

Alta said, "Let's hear about Japan."

"Save that for tomorrow," answered Uncle Lauf. "I admit to exhaustion."

Alta led him into the bedroom, and immediately they heard snoring. Returning home, shaking her head at her brother's latest escapade, Mama laughed and sorted through her purchases.

"He's older than me. He should know better," she said. "I'm happy he finds comfort helping others, but he goes too far. He probably talked those men's heads off about the Lord all the way through the snow and wind."

When dinner was served anyone could see Uncle Lauf hadn't eaten well for a long time. Nothing was left for the next day.

GOBBLING THE SAME oatmeal the children ate every morning, treating it like a gift from Heaven, Uncle Lauf was full of energy again. He offered to chop wood and take the horse and wagon into town to get supplies for Mama.

"Dolly, I'm certain poor Molly needs exercise, and the house needs repairs," said Uncle Lauf. "I've been blessed with the knack for such handiwork."

Mama was short of money for those kinds of repairs and needed all her money for food. Eyes afire, he assured her if she didn't mind putting him up, the Lord would allow him to wait until the middle of November to go to Reno. He'd get money working at the box factory.

"I have faith," he said.

Mama patted his hand. Uncle Lauf went off to the box factory, and they waited until evening to hear the story of Japan.

"Remember my vision?" asked Uncle Lauf, eyeing his audience.

For sure, thought Mary. Each child had a clear memory of Uncle Lauf's desire to take them to Japan to save people who were ignorant of the Word.

"Remember I left from Seattle?" he said, rolling up his sleeves. "It took twenty-one days to reach a land where I couldn't speak the language. Brother Martin, my missionary friend, thought I was insane, being completely bereft of funds when I reached Yokohama. I must have a direct line to Heaven because I prayed, and next thing, I found a job teaching English, and I still had plenty of time to devote to the souls who needed me."

"What's on your arm?" interrupted Tiny, pointing to the mysterious design on his skin.

"This? A tattoo in the Japanese style, a prayer for strength. A man in my English class had tattoos all over his body. He asked if he could pay by giving me a tattoo," Uncle Lauf said.

"Like pictures in my book," said Mary. "How strange."

"An entirely different world, everything smaller—the buildings, the fields," he said. "It's the people I remember, not the land. I think the tattoo helped me save the man. He came and lived at the mission. Sometimes I tell about the tattoo to show the way to bring people to the Lord."

"Why'd you come back?" she asked.

"I became ill like you, Mary. Not the typhoid, but another fever that turned to pneumonia. Rest on the ship cured me, and strength from the tattoo prayer inked onto my arm."

Uncle Lauf stopped them on their way to Mama's bedroom. Ola had written him the distressing tale, and it was lucky he'd received the letter when he disembarked, before it was loaded on the ship to Japan.

"Ola's quite anxious about your mother, you know," he said. "How she's so up and down, but you can help her. That's what the Lord asks of you."

"Get her to let Papa come back," said Alta. "That's what would help."

"Well now," said Uncle Lauf. "Well now."

He put his hands together and whispered to himself, not asking them to get down on their knees. The kitchen door squeaked, footsteps stamped on the doorsill, and Mama crossed into the front room, back from looking in on Mrs. Harrigan.

Settling into their quilts, Mary murmured, "What would've happened to us in Japan when Uncle Lauf got sick?"

"I still hope I get there someday," Tiny mumbled. "But I never expected Uncle Lauf to get a tattoo."

Raleigh said, "He's some preacher."

"I bet you can get a tattoo in Sacramento," said Alta. "Let's just pray he gets Mama to let Papa come back."

Mama and Lauf spoke quietly on this quiet night. The snowfall muffled any outside noise. Guided by the Lord, with help from Ola and Margaret, Lauf felt certain to save Mama. She sighed.

"You're a good woman, Dolly," Lauf said. "You did right to protect your children. You don't have to rebuke yourself. Even if you told some lies, the Lord will forgive you because you did it for love of your children."

"I didn't lie," said Mama in a fierce whisper. "I didn't tell anything extra, but I didn't lie. The husband lied. Furthermore, I told them to get Mr. Hoy, but they ignored me because I'm a woman. They wouldn't do anything because he killed a half-breed and a run-away woman. Now you tell me, Lauf, who was following the laws in this country? Or the ways of the Lord? Who?"

The chair hitched forward.

Uncle Lauf said, "The Lord provides for everyone, even the Japanese and the Indians. They only need to take Jesus into their hearts."

Mama snorted, "I read the Bible all the time, Lauf, and I've never found the place where the Lord said to love or help only those who love him, like some people believe. The world is full of shades of gray, Lauf, not all light or all dark, as you seem to think."

Lifting her head, Mary peeked into the front room. Sitting in the straight back chair, with her elbows on her knees, Mama covered her face and swayed back and forth. Then Mary glimpsed her uncle's long legs in the rocker. She lay back, and through the doorway, she watched the shadows.

Mary remembered Alta accusing her of being too sure of right and wrong. Gliding forward and swaying back, the rocking chair's outline played on the wall. Mary rubbed her face and blinked, her thoughts sliding along with the gray shadow until Mama took up the talk.

"Certainly I've looked for a way to explain those murders, Lauf. People do evil things and get away with it. The sad part is I feel like I need to be forgiven because I didn't help more."

"If you ask … , " answered Lauf promptly.

"I've looked for the words," interrupted Mama. "The Lord doesn't have time to stand around and help me feel better. We need to go on."

A swoosh in the hush, ashes fell to the bottom of the Franklin stove.

Then Lauf said, "You're a strong woman, Dolly, but you need someone to help. Please, forgive your husband, and have him come back. If you recall, Jesus did indeed say to turn the other cheek."

"Yes, yes, I know," answered Mama. "Is this what Ola really wanted you to tell me? Now I've heard from everyone, all of my children, and you're the latest. The new Methodist minister, who loves the rich people and ignores the rest of us ordinary souls, sermonized about forgiving your neighbor. Only Cyrus and Frank haven't sent me letters. And my friend Minna, who'd never interfere. It's hard, Lauf, when I feel Tom should ask my forgiveness. It's hard to be wise and generous."

ON HALLOWEEN THE sky cleared. Uncle Lauf headed off to the box factory to fill in for someone who had quit. That afternoon, hot and tired, he assured the children the Lord had helped him endure. He had provided stunning white meadows and mountains rising to Heaven to enjoy while Lauf worked loading wood boxes by the train depot. That evening Uncle Lauf allowed he was staying home to read his Bible. He didn't want anything to do with witches, demons, and ghosts.

Mary wrapped up and walked with Mama to the Faye's house. Alta, Tiny, and Raleigh set off to meet Georgie, Alta's hanger-on, and to wander around town soliciting treats. Soon they rushed into the Faye's front room, laughing and out of breath. Sure enough, the usual boys had thrown eggs and fruit at Raleigh and Georgie.

Mary took a bite of gingerbread and gazed around the dining room in which every lamp was lit, not one corner gray and gloomy. Guests wandered about, smiling and contented. Out the wide window, hills gleamed icy blue-white under the three-quarter moon on a night usually mysterious, forbidding.

Aunt Ola asked Mary if the fever and cough had disappeared. Mary told her about Uncle Lauf's Japanese tattoo. Ola smothered a laugh and then closed her mouth, staring at Mama and Mr. Faye in the far doorway, looking out the window at the moon. Oh no, thought Mary. Mr. Faye turned, and his mouth said, "please," as Mama shook her head, put her hands up, and covered her eyes.

Rubbing his stiff shoulder, Mr. Faye walked off. Patting his waistcoat pocket, he stopped and gazed at the table filled with food, the fringe on the hanging candelabra, the curios in the oak cabinet, and his daughter who came up and threw her arms around his waist. He nodded to Mrs. Vaughn and to Mr. and Mrs. Tucker. But Mr. Faye didn't seem to see anything. He bumped the dining table, stumbled into a chair, and apologized to a fellow after knocking the cigar from his hand. He turned around and around, finally picking his way to Mrs. Faye, and pulled himself straight, smiled, chatted.

"Oh, Mary, what did I see?" said Ola, a pink blush rising from her neck to her cheeks.

In the meantime, Mama gathered everyone and meandered to the front door, stopping and starting, pulling at her coat. At the door, Mr. Faye took her elbow and said good-bye. The four children followed Mama down the steps, down McGlashan's Hill, across the bridge illuminated in the moonlight, and up Harrigan's Hill to their little place.

While they laid themselves out in the bed, Tiny sighed, "I wonder where Papa is. He would've liked this Halloween."

Patting her stomach, Alta mused, "Maybe I should ask him again to say he's sorry."

The next afternoon, she found Mary out in the barn brushing Molly.

She smoothed the horse's mane and said, "I saw Mama get rid of Mr. Faye, you know. Now the trainmaster thinks two weeks before Papa returns. I guess I'll wait around the livery stable that day."

Walking away, Alta said, "Papa's afraid of you. I'll tell him you want to go back, though."

What d'you know, Mary said to herself. In her head a light illuminated Papa's face—Papa afraid of her, while she stood in the glare, her hands on her hips. She concentrated on Molly's warm back, brushing to dispel the picture.

BY MID-NOVEMBER, UNCLE Lauf made enough money to buy nails and repair the attic roof. He bought food for the family and bales of hay for Molly. Aunt Ola sent over money, enough to take the train with a stop in Reno as far as Denver. Sorry to see him leave, everyone waved to the tall fellow disappearing once more down the hill.

"The tattooed preacher," Mama said, "Indeed, we've received far more help from him than from the Lord. Though Lauf will never admit it."

28

October 1985, The Following Monday
Colfax

ON MONDAY MORNING, Tiny discovered Alta's blue silk dress and exclaimed she never would have guessed Alta still had lovely clothes. Coming up after Raleigh's funeral, Tiny found Alta roaming around in Mama's old brown dress and a moth-eaten sweater. That's when Tiny decided to pay for an assistant to come in daily to get Alta up and going.

We folded up the blue silk dress and her well-preserved wool coat with the fur collar, fifty years old for goodness sake, and filled plastic trash bags with things too raggedy for the Salvation Army. Tiny wondered if we should offer the dress and the coat to the assistant who, after all, found her on the bedroom floor.

Tiny and I sank onto the bed, thinking of our beautiful sister, whom Mama loved more than anything, and who drifted through life unable to cope. Alta exerted herself only enough to play the piano, sing, and make money for her bad habits. She did find the merchant mariner, but as far as I knew, they fought and drank until he disappeared to the Pacific well before World War II.

"She'd never talk about Bill Hutchinson," murmured Tiny. "Said to mind my own business."

I knew all this, and I stared instead at the silk screens of dainty Japanese geishas that Hutchinson brought the one time after the war when he came to see Alta at Mama's house.

Raleigh found the Colfax retirement community, and his grandsons must have tacked up the pictures when she settled into the small cabin. Except to wander into Colfax for cigarettes and liquor, Alta withdrew from the world.

My great-grandson, Lane, came in to get the bags of rubbish.

"I thought Aunt Alta lived in San Francisco," he said. "How'd everyone end up near Sacramento? Truckee sounded exciting."

"You'll hear about leaving the mountains," I said.

"It was exciting until the day we left," said Tiny. "And now there's only the two of us to remember."

We pulled ourselves up, and heavy-hearted, we sorted through the last knickknacks. For a memento, Tiny only wanted a Murano glass bowl she gave Alta after a trip to Italy. I took the tiny woven Washo basket with the beautiful designs, Mama's only remembrance from Mr. Faye. I carefully wrapped the silkscreen geishas for Lane's mother and John.

Waiting for the fellows who would take Alta's paltry furniture, Lane dug into the back of the closet, and we discovered the snapshot postcards of bombed buildings in Tokyo, a skinny little village girl with a baby on her back, and a beautiful untouched garden. Hutchinson sent them when he was in Japan, the messages noncommittal—"miss you," "the girl's mother is gone," "lovely garden in this bombed out city." He kept in touch, though Alta kept him secret.

We opened the studio photo of Raleigh, handsome at twenty years old, with an easy twinkle in his eyes. Rubbing off dust, I wondered if it was taken about the time of his marriage.

"Raleigh had a good funeral last year, didn't he?" said Tiny. "I'm glad John brought me up to Sacramento that day to see all his children and grandchildren. I hadn't seen them together since Mama's funeral."

The last time I saw him, Raleigh held his fishing rod and leaned against the grape arbor, chatting with Abel before he went out on the river. He was smiling as he walked down the driveway to his grandson's car. He wore the same kind of shirt and overalls he wore as a kid, and he had the same eager step to catch up with us girls when we roamed around Truckee. Eyes swollen and red, Raleigh's grandson Davy came by that evening, and he didn't have to say a word. I buried my head on the table, crying, barely able to listen to the story.

Davy and Raleigh and a granddaughter rowed one boat. The other grandkids were rowing along next to them, each watching their line and chattering at the same time. Raleigh had been laughing and throwing back a fish too small to keep when he keeled over into the middle of the boat. He hadn't complained about his arm or his chest hurting; he simply looked surprised and cried out. Davy tried CPR as the granddaughter rowed back to shore, but Raleigh had stopped breathing when he fell over. Abel said the one good thing was he died while fishing, the thing Raleigh liked to do best.

"The funeral was nice," I said. "I'm glad Raleigh didn't know he was sick and just went all of a sudden."

Smiling at our little brother's photo, it should have been obvious Alta wasn't right—she wouldn't come down to Sacramento for Raleigh's service.

"Thank God, I made those arrangements for Alta with the people here," said Tiny. "The assistant must have been frightened to death when she discovered Alta on the floor crying, blood oozing out the side of her head. Who knows how long she'd gone on drinking and taking pills before she tried to shoot herself? How did she even have a gun?"

"I wonder where she hid it?" asked Lane, in his matter-of-fact way.

I had no answer. The retirement people said her hand shook, so the bullet only grazed her head. Lane barely knew his great-aunt, and he didn't understand how often she'd looked like she wished nothing more than to disappear.

Tiny walked around the little kitchen, searching for a box of cookies, putting on some tea water.

"You know, I never thought Alta wanted to quit the world. It seemed like the pills consoled her."

She found a plate and fanned out the cookies.

Then she said, "I wonder about baby Florence, pretty and charming and smart like Alta, even when she was only six months old. But she was sweet, and Alta was trouble even as a baby, wasn't she? Maybe Mama grieved so because she'd thought Florence was one more chance."

Tiny passed the plate to Lane.

"What are you saying? Mama tried her best for all of us. Papa had something to do with us too, didn't he?" I said.

The struggle between our parents … Mama always was confused about Papa and made wrong decisions, like she said about Mrs. Hoy. Leave him, stay with him, leave him, find another man, go back to him. The best thing Mama ever did was agree to leave Truckee, and that turned out better than for poor Mrs. Hoy.

Lane passed over the photograph of Mama when she was fifty. So healthy, almost plump, smooth skin, wearing her black coat with the fur collar, she was still appealing in the only expensive clothing she ever owned. To have money, that was another excellent reason we moved to Sacramento.

Good-looking and smart, no wonder Mama caught Papa when she was young; and no wonder Mr. Faye was attracted, even though she couldn't bring herself to go off with him. All long passed, I thought as I dusted my hands off.

Tiny peeked into the box and lifted up the Chinese chest with the painted flowers and miniature drawers, the object forever associated with Papa.

"I wouldn't have guessed Mama gave this to Alta," said Tiny, rubbing it with a cloth to bring out the black lacquer shine.

Mama saved enough money in that little box to feed and clothe us kids, even when she became skin and bones. I turned the woven bowl with the intricate designs, musing that perhaps Mr. Faye was good for her—perhaps the attention helped. But as she said, while putting another coin in a drawer, she'd better find a way by herself.

"Could be Mama gave it to Alta as a memento when she moved to San Francisco," I said. "Maybe to depend on herself instead of counting on Mama to get her out of every fix."

Maybe that's why Alta and Hutchinson fell apart. Like Mrs. Hoy, maybe Alta wanted things, and that man wouldn't agree to them or didn't have the money. Though it didn't explain Alta's and my belief we should stick to our own kind. I did, and look what happened.

"There's one more picture in here," Lane said and lifted out the watercolor landscape. "You told me about this picture from the house on Harrigan's Hill."

The landscape of soft blue sky, spring green meadow, and pale blue river with the stripe of sunshine, fir, and Ponderosa in the back. Any one of us, staring at that watercolor, might pretend to walk into paradise, searching for a happy day. Watching for love. Wishing for peace of mind. All those desires that eluded us.

"I think it was in Alta's bedroom in Mama's house," I said.

Setting the watercolor up against the teapot, I said, "Did I tell you about the last time I came to see Alta?"

Tiny shook her head, so I told Lane to take the plastic bags out to the front of the cabin, so Polly could collect them. I prepared to reveal the last secret.

Alta's front room appeared in my mind. Looking out the open window at the black oak, branches full and round, I listened to a little gray wren hop from limb to limb, *churr*, cock its tail, and *churr* again. It was Alta's private entertainment.

Once Alta had neatly made the bed and displayed the Murano and Washo bowls on the windowsill, she'd sat in the armchair, cigarette between her fingers. Honestly, she'd seemed pleased to have company. She brought up the day ages ago when I'd left Betsy with Mama, and Alta took her for a walk way out into the country to Noguchi's farm with the beehives.

It was hot and Alta and Betsy drank from an outdoor faucet until a bee buzzed up and landed on the lip of the spigot. The bee stayed there no matter how much they tried to shoo it away. Betsy finally brushed it off and took a gulp before it landed on her nose. She yelped, but Alta swept it away before she was stung. Betsy just said that was a close call. She must have been six or seven. Alta laughed and said it showed how clever and brave Betsy was.

Then she teared up, but of course, I was dabbing my eyes and could only nod. Scrabbling around in her drawer, she pulled out bottle after bottle of pills and finally swallowed one without even taking water, and she became more and more calm.

Beginning to slur, Alta rambled on about her brother's children, as if he wasn't my brother too. By now she was limp in the chair and asked if I could get her some water. I don't know why she wanted it then and not with the pills, but she drank most of it in one long swallow and put the cold glass against her cheek. Then she dropped the bomb.

"So how's Raleigh's youngest, that cute Margaret?" Alta said, voice garbled and low. "Darling little kid, but haven't seen her in a long time. Naughty for a while as a teenager. Others come by once in awhile."

I shrugged, not having seen Raleigh's children in a long time either.

"I love babies," she said.

A bit confused about where Alta thought she was, I asked her what she meant. She'd never had children.

She said, "I know. Of course not. I got rid of the one I would've had. How was I going to take care of it? You were the lucky one."

I was so surprised, I couldn't speak. All those years I felt like she'd lorded it over me. How she was the one that did whatever she wanted. How I was too timid. Too good. And here I'd had a job I liked and a beautiful child, and she was envious of me.

I reached for the teapot, knocking over the watercolor, and Tiny grabbed it before any tea spilled on the lovely landscape.

She said, "Mama and I knew she'd gotten rid of it. That's why she ran off to San Francisco right after World War I. She knew Hutchinson then."

"My God," I said, "I was the only one who didn't know? Why didn't you tell me?"

Lane stomped back into the kitchen, and Tiny shrugged.

"What difference did it make?" she said. "Alta wouldn't listen. Didn't we all have our own lives to worry about?"

My lips pinched shut.

"Mama was afraid Alta was going to get the Spanish influenza and die there in San Francisco alone," said Tiny. "Of course, she didn't. She kept going."

The day I visited, I watched Alta drift off to sleep. Then the assistant came into the room and shook her head when she saw the pills all over the table. It wasn't more than a week or so later, they called and told me about the gun and then called again that she'd died, but not from the graze by the bullet. I was always unsure Alta ever came to grips with why she did what she did. Whatever Tiny thought, Alta finally took enough pills to make herself disappear.

Still waiting for the men to pick up the furniture and for Polly to come and take us back to Sacramento, Lane ate all the sugar cookies, and we drank the tea.

"You know, 'The end is not yet,'" said Tiny.

I nodded. I knew. We gave the Chinese box to Polly and the watercolor to John since Betsy wasn't alive.

29

December 1911
Harrigan's Hill, Truckee

WITH NO WARNING, telegram, or whisper from Alta, Papa showed up one afternoon before Thanksgiving when Mama was making dresses with material leftover from Aunt Ola. Intent on guiding the fabric and pumping the sewing machine's foot pedal—a hand-off after Ola bought an electric model—Mama was slow to look up. Papa lowered himself into the rocking chair, covering his cough with a red handkerchief.

Clearing his throat, he said, "I've come by, Dolly, because I've been to Tonopah."

To keep her hands from flying into the air, Mama grabbed the piece she had finished sewing. Scissors clattered on the floor, and Mary jerked her head up.

"You know Raleigh, Tiny, and Alta told me everything. They said you were beside yourself, Dolly, and Mr. Faye at the saloon told me about the justice of the peace and about Minna and her cousin. When a brakeman was sick in Reno, I thought why not. I took the brakeman's place and worked the line going up and down Nevada, stopping at Tonopah to see what I could see."

Mama's eyes opened wide, and Papa put up his hand.

"Dolly, let me finish. When the train stopped in Tonopah to load silver ore, I went into town to find the sheriff. I thought he might tell me something. I didn't want to sneak around. I'd never seen those boys and didn't want to be accused of robbery or worse."

Papa coughed and rubbed his chest.

"The sheriff did tell me something. Mrs. Hoy's brother turned up, worried because he hadn't received a letter for a long time. Mr. Hoy acted surprised to see him. The boy William told his uncle she'd run away with the Indian, had a baby, and died. The sheriff doesn't think William knew the whole story. Still, the brother, very upset according to the sheriff, cursed Mr. Hoy about the things his sister had written, which may have been true, but I don't know.

"Indeed, even before the brother showed up, Mr. Hoy had broken down. He'd looked terrible for weeks, said the sheriff, and then he went a little crazy, drinking and having nightmares. The mine owners wouldn't let him work, scaring the other men when he claimed to hear voices coming from cracks in the rocks."

Mary blurted out, "What about Eddie and William, Papa?"

"They wandered around town, the neighbor women giving food and such," said Papa. "The brother showed Mrs. Hoy's letter and took the boys to Wyoming where he lives with a wife and a boy and girl. Quite a trip to find out about his sister, but the boys're safe for now. Mr. Hoy for a while was in the little hospital they have for miners. Now he's at his house all alone. I went into the saloon he frequents."

He stopped and put up his hand again.

"Only one whiskey, Dolly. The doctor has been on me.

"A bottle on the table and a drink in hand, you couldn't miss Mr. Hoy, his leg sticking out. Face gray and hollow, with black circles under his eyes like the children told me. He squinted, then his eyes opened wide, and they're red where they should be white. The sheriff said he's living far, far down in his own kind of Hell. He'll never, ever climb out."

Papa twitched his lip and stared at the yellowed walls of the room. Mama picked at basting stitches, pulled out a loose thread, and blinked like she was turning over photographs of the past three months.

Mama turned to Mary and asked her to run up to Mrs. Harrigan and get some eggs, so they'd have enough for Papa to stay for supper. Surprised at the request, Mary climbed the hill and told Mrs. Harrigan Papa's tale that finished off the terrible things that had happened.

PAPA SAT FORWARD.

"Dolly, I need a place to stay. My room at the Whitney is gone, and the livery stable is dusty and drafty. When Alta, Tiny, and Raleigh visited me, they said it's hard up here, though I'm glad Mary's better now."

Mama interrupted, "We're all right, Tom."

Papa said, "No, I've missed my children. I know I'm a trouble, but I'm trying to do right. May I please come back?"

Mama peered at Papa, light vanishing from the room as the sun slid behind the mountains. She lit the lantern. He no longer looked muscular like men who did physical work and his face had a grey tinge.

She said, "Why'd you go to the doctor?"

"A bad cold since September. The cough doesn't stop. That's when the doc said to stop smoking and drinking."

Smoothing the material on the sewing table, Mama said, "I'm tired all the time too."

She picked at flecks of dust on the fabric.

"I wonder what I'm going to do," she whispered.

She peered down at the stitching and breathed, "Tom, I can't keep going on without someone to help."

Brushing back strings of hair, her eyes roamed from the watercolor to the dark bedroom doorway and back to Papa. Then Mama sighed and words slipped from between her lips.

"So we'll let bygones be bygones, all right?"

Papa pulled her up close, placed his forefinger on her cheek, and smoothed her skin.

Bodies touching, arms massaging her back, he whispered, "Dolly, ah, Dolly."

Mama leaned against Papa and pressed her arms against his back. Her face softened and her cheeks turned rosy—from the warmth of the stove or from Papa's warm arms, Mary didn't know. Holding the folded newspaper basket of eggs, Mary reached the kitchen doorway and watched them.

Tiny, Raleigh, and Alta slipped in behind her. The lamp glowed. Mama's voice was soft. Papa sat, smiling at them as if all evenings were this bright.

AT SUPPER, WISHING her sister would control herself, Mary kicked under the table when Alta said, "Can we move back into a house in town? I hate this old place."

"Maybe. It was comfortable, wasn't it?" said Papa. "You should've seen the house where I grew up in Tennessee. It had so many bedrooms, we'd play Hide and Seek. Two separate outhouses and sixteen seats at the dining table. A fireplace in every bedroom and a covered porch so grand you could play outside even in the rain."

Papa rocked, shuffled his feet, and watched Mama, head down, catching the threads to hem a sleeve. He drew in a breath and coughed from deep in his chest, covering his mouth with the red handkerchief.

When the spasm stopped, he sighed, "I have a few days, so I'll go around and ask. There's nothing in Truckee, though, as grand as that house."

He didn't stalk out the door and stomp down the hill, but sat, legs crossed, pressing his chest with one hand, his face translucent as ice. Mama took his arm and pulled him to his feet, whispering he should lie down. They disappeared into the bedroom and the door closed, an occurrence so rare Mary had forgotten there was a door.

SHIVERING IN THE attic shadows, the sisters put on coats and scarves over their nightclothes, rolled themselves in the blankets, and began to whisper.

"Remember how Mama always felt sorry for William and Eddie? Sad they were almost goners, except the uncle finally showed up. I wonder if she fixed on giving up her grudge against Papa because he found out the end for that wretched man," said Mary.

Alta rolled about and said she was glad Mr. Hoy was living in misery.

"I wish she hadn't taken her time to change her mind about Papa. Aunt Ola's right. She's willful, sticking with Mr. Faye so long."

"Papa's a drunk and lets his eye wander too," said Mary. "But I think maybe those days are over."

She blew out the flame in the kerosene lamp.

"That coughing is much more dreadful than mine."

Then Alta asked, "Isn't it strange Papa was talking about Tennessee? I thought he left home because he was the bad boy."

Closing her eyes, Mary murmured, "They're both willful."

PAPA DIDN'T GO to the saloon. He plodded steadily through town, but found no affordable lodging for another boardinghouse. Then late one afternoon, Tiny flung open the door, hand in hand with Aunt Ola. Dressed in a cream-colored wool suit, blond hair covered with a white wool scarf, Ola lightened up the twilit room.

"I came to see how the party dresses look, but really, Dolly, I have some news too."

"Go find your sister," Mama said to Tiny. Tiny disappeared into the bedroom to sit with Mary by the door and eavesdrop.

Aunt Ola said, "I'm glad for you Tom's back."

A sigh while the rockers grated over dust.

"What're we going to do?" Mama said, plaintively. "I can't stop thinking if I'd had money, Florence wouldn't have died, and Mary wouldn't have been so sick, and I wouldn't have gotten mixed up with the Hoys."

Shadows filled the corners of the room, closing in on Mama and Ola. She found the lamp and the room lit up again.

"Dolly, you must move on," Ola said. "You were happy, Tiny said. But, good Lord, you're not up at all. You can't keep sinking down like this.

"Besides Dolly, now you know what happens. I saw Mr. Faye at the Halloween party. I saw how he looked and … and how you looked."

Mama covered her face.

"I gave it up, Ola."

Leaning over her sister, Ola said, "I can tell it's not quite over."

Mama rubbed her hands on her skirt.

"And another thing," said Ola. "No matter what, the children did hear that murder."

Ola settled onto the straight chair and smoothed a crease in her beautiful wool outfit.

Mama said, "Also Tom's not well."

Eyes shining as if the lamp was lighted in them, Ola said, "But listen, Dolly, things will get better. Here's my news. Mr. James and I are moving to Sacramento. His business is growing. We've money to buy a good house. Why don't you move to Sacramento again and stay with us for a few weeks? Tom works the train routes from there anyway. Plenty of time to look for a proper place you can afford without worrying about the children. And you'll be away from Truckee. What d'you think?"

"Yes, good news," answered Mama, folding her arms across her chest as if to hold herself together.

Mary and Tiny peeked in, the flame flickered, Aunt Ola patted her sister's shoulders and kissed her cheek. Mama lifted her hand to wave good-bye and shut her eyes.

ON MONDAY BEFORE Thanksgiving, Papa groaned that his blood boiled and froze. Then he coughed up clots of blood. Mama sent for the doctor, and Mary watched for his head to appear by the pine tree.

Old Dr. Charles said, "Hello, Mary. Fevers and coughs stopped? Keeping warm and rested? It's funny. You children are rarely sick, but when you do catch something, it's very affecting, isn't it?"

Then he turned. One look and the doctor said Papa had developed consumption—and it wasn't an early infection anymore.

"Rest, isolation, nutrition, no liquor, no smoking," recited the doctor.

Mama sighed, resignation showed in the slump of her shoulders. She asked how to keep him isolated, what to feed him.

"He needs thick soups and oatmeal," stated the doctor, not gentle like the time he tended to Florence. He talked like he'd answered the same questions a hundred times.

He stood for a few moments, jiggling the handle to his black bag and shifting on his feet.

"There's a new sanatorium in Roseville for people with lung infections," he said. I'll send his name to the admissions office, but he'll have to wait for an opening. And don't ask about the money. They have funds for railroad men. I'll request financial help."

Mama looked warily at the doctor, saying she'd heard about those places people never left, but Dr. Charles assured her it wouldn't be longer than a year. Papa wasn't that affected yet.

Dr. Charles edged out the door. Light spread across Mama's face, and her eyes, filled with a sudden energy, displayed relief that Papa wasn't dying yet.

At Thanksgiving, the three sisters sauntered down the hill off to Aunt Ola's, the air warm enough to leave coats unbuttoned. Each swished the skirt of her second new gown in one year and fluffed the ruffles. Raleigh, with only new shoes to keep unscuffed, ran along in his happy-go-lucky way, paying no attention to his sisters even when they yelled at him to watch out for the ice. At the bridge they leaned over to watch the ribbon of running water in the middle of the river and disputed the amount of ice thickening along the edges.

After satisfying themselves with a bounteous dinner, as good as last Christmas, Mama took the step.

"I'd like to take you up, Ola, Mr. James, on your offer to stay with you in Sacramento. I must wait until a space becomes available for Tom at the sanatorium in Roseville, but I thank you ahead for your kindness."

Aunt Ola beamed.

Alta said it's how Mama came to her senses, though Mary claimed it's how Alta got her way.

Just before Christmas, Mama dispatched Raleigh and his sisters to town with Molly and the wagon to pick up hay. To their surprise, Mr. Faye showed up as they dragged the bales to the wagon.

"Mr. James said you were moving to Sacramento. My wife has relatives there. What d'you think? Maybe we'll see you," said Mr. Faye.

"Some excuse," muttered Alta, as Mr. Faye ordered Bill the livery boy to come help.

"How about if I lead my old horse up the hill?" offered Mr. Faye.

"I guess so," said Raleigh, "but Mama agreed to give Molly to Joe's family."

Mr. Faye climbed onto the buckboard and held the reins up Harrigan's Hill. Tiny sat with Mr. Faye, chattering about Papa, who had made the wagon and a sled when they brought Molly to Church Street. Raleigh and she had pulled out the old sled and took Molly out to the far meadow with Joe, Hazel, and Delilah. For the last time, Tiny sighed, before she never saw them again.

She rattled on about Raleigh turning over the chipmunk traps to Joe. The deal was Joe gave Raleigh the leather trapper's bag in exchange. He'd wished for a bag like that for ever so long. They wouldn't use chipmunk traps in Sacramento anyway. Mr. Faye smiled, but Mary doubted if the Truckee saloonkeeper even knew the kids Tiny blabbed about.

Molly pulled herself up beside the barn, and Raleigh jumped from the wagon, hollering for Mama. Waiting to find out where to place the bales, Mr. Faye folded his coat neatly. Alta, tapping her foot, and Mary, fingers interlaced over her stomach, could have told him, but it was obvious Mr. Faye wanted to see Mama.

Smiling when she appeared, he laughed, "Hello, Dolly. I thought it was one last time to see Molly, but your son said you're giving the horse to Joe. I suppose I can see her anytime."

Mama looked from Mr. Faye to Raleigh to Molly.

"I saw the children in town, and I thought I should help," he said, folding his shirtsleeves. "That stable boy is no good, and I know Mr. Edwards is sick."

Mama nodded and pointed out where to place the hay bales, not too far from Molly's food box.

Catching Mama's hand, Mr. Faye said, "You know, we visit my wife's cousins in Sacramento, so perhaps we can visit your family once in awhile."

Mama said yes, that would be nice and shook his hand. She watched while Mr. Faye sweated with the children, lugging bales into the barn.

That done, "Come along with me a ways," he said, and Mama nodded, eyes glossy and lip trembling.

Raleigh and Tiny took care of Molly and the wagon. Mary went to warm up under the blankets in the front room.

Alta said Mama took Mr. Faye's arm, and he stroked hers for the longest while before he pulled a small woven basket from his pocket and pressed it into her hands. She turned it this way and that, examining the Washo-style designs. She smoothed the lapels on his businessman's jacket and started back to the house. Mr. Faye watched Mama, strode off a few steps, and turned to look again. He navigated his way until Alta couldn't see him anymore.

FLOPPING ONTO THE bed, Mary found Papa with his face flushed, rocking restlessly, and rubbing his palms along the arms of the rocker. Papa's afternoon nurse, Minna, sat on her chair, exuding patience from her relaxed shoulders and quiet breathing. They traded stories about the old days. Minna mused over nursing school in Sacramento. Still they needed her up here, and she couldn't stay away from the old Washo ways, gathering piñons from trees on the Reno side of the Sierra and beating tall meadow grass to drive rabbits into nets. Even if she was only half Washo.

Raleigh and Tiny wandered in and spread out on the bed.

Tiny said, "Alta and her boyfriend have gone up the hill. You know, Georgie Vaughn."

"Who?" demanded Papa.

"Alta's friend from school, Georgie Vaughn," answered Raleigh. "He used to be mean, but not anymore."

So he finally showed up, the one Alta wouldn't talk about, following her around, Mary thought, bemused.

"Georgie Vaughn," repeated Papa, drawing out the vowels, adding a touch of Tennessee twang. "I wonder if we're related."

Papa rocked for a moment.

"Your Cherokee great-grandmother was a Vaughn. Maybe his family's from Tennessee."

Mary, Raleigh, and Tiny raised themselves up, all attention. Minna leaned forward and placed her hands on her knees. Papa settled back in his chair.

"She married a white man named Vaughn," he began. "I never knew him though. He died when my mother was young. That's how we'd be related to that boy, if we are."

"Well, I'll be," said Minna. "You never know."

Papa pressed his hand to his chest and said, "For sure, Minna, you never can tell. She lived with her eldest son's family, my mother's brother."

He took a few gulps of air.

"Now, my father's family treated my grandmother fine," said Papa. "I mean my father knew my mother was part Indian, but he didn't care. My father wasn't even upset when they came to tell the Negroes they were freed.

"He just wanted to be left alone. When soldiers were fighting near our house at the battle by Stones River, he just fed them and sent them on. From both sides. It was cold, too, and winter, so we didn't have much food. No one cared about the Indians during that time, and afterwards for a long time, everyone was just trying not to starve."

Papa sat there rocking, contemplating the ceiling, and rubbing his chest.

MAMA COLLAPSED ONTO the chair in the front room, combing her fingers through her hair. Amused in spite of the fever, Papa called out about the connection between great-grandma Vaughn and the boy Georgie. Tiny wondered if Mama remembered the grandmother, and Mama said yes, but Tiny shouldn't expect the Cherokee to welcome her to their tribe.

Papa said, "It's why I can't understand about Mrs. Hoy and Mr. Littlefield, Dolly. Our family got along all right. They would've been all right, too, if they'd made it to San Francisco."

"But, not in the mountains," said Minna.

"They didn't get away quick enough, and that Mr. Hoy was a hard, hard man. Indeed, a hard man," finished Papa.

Then Mama sniffed and heard feet running down the hill and puffing breath and feet stomping back up.

"Now what?" she called as she reached the kitchen door to see Alta throw water at the side of the outhouse. Smoke floated into the air at the back of the building. Georgie came racing down with a bucket and started pumping water.

Mama yelled, "Oh, my Lord. A fire again? Get those old buckets, Raleigh. Hurry!"

Tiny grabbed one, ran to the pump, ran up the hill, dumped water on the outhouse wall, and sat down to catch her breath. By the time Mary reached the outhouse, more dried-out grass was burning. She threw dirt, sneezed, and covered her mouth with snowy dust.

Snorting and stamping her hooves, Molly trotted out of the barn. Mary tried to catch her mane and coax her out of the way, but the horse, watching and snuffling, stopped in the middle of all the kids running around with buckets. Raleigh dumped water on the blanket Alta had flung out of the way and smothered the glowing splinters on the back wall of the outhouse.

Mama grabbed Alta, the edge of her coat blackened, her face covered with streaks of burnt charcoal, her eyes bleary and cheeks red. She turned to Georgie—skinny, dark eyes set back under heavy brows, with ash all over his clothes and face—lifting a pail to run down for more water.

"What in the name of Heaven and Earth were you doing?"

Georgie's eyes flicked to the outhouse corner, a flask shining on the ground, a can of cigarette butts spilled onto the dirt. Minna held onto Papa, wrapped in a quilt, his hat smashed on his head. They gazed from the outhouse to the burned grass.

Violet eyes open wide, Alta said, "Now, Mama, we went up the hill, but Mrs. Harrigan yelled at us, so we came back and sat down against the outhouse wall and put the blanket over us to keep warm while we talked. Georgie had the whiskey and cigarettes, so I thought why not."

"Stop lying," said Papa. "Don't you think we know when you're trying to get out of something?"

"Mr. Edwards, I did bring the whiskey, but, but … "
Georgie paused.

"You stop too, young man," said Papa. "Don't cover for her. What happened?"

Smoking and sipping from the flask, they covered up so Mrs. Harrigan couldn't see them. The cigarette burned a hole in the blanket, and Georgie flipped the cigarette away. While they stomped on the sparks, neither saw the cigarette begin to burn the brown grass next to the dry wood of the outhouse. The flask tipped and liquor leaked out because, next thing, they turned around and the grass and wood were really burning hot and fast. So that's when he ran for water.

"I'm sorry, Mr. Edwards, I am," said Georgie. "But I can help. We can get wood from your barn and replace the back of the outhouse. Just can I ask, please don't tell my mother."

Papa laughed and choked, laughed some more. Raleigh, Tiny, and Mary tittered. Molly licked Mary's hand and showed her teeth. Mama held her hand over her mouth. Even Minna cracked a smile, though Alta and Georgie stood without a hint of a grin.

Shuffling down the hill, Mrs. O'Brien, with Mrs. Harrigan on her arm, surveyed the mess. Mrs. Harrigan pointed her finger at Alta, whose face turned pale.

"Whatever that girl said, there's more," said Mrs. Harrigan. "She and the boy were enjoying themselves up there on the hill. Now, I don't care about that. What do you think happens when they get to be that age? But she was leading him on without one thought of what other people might see or think. You'd better watch out for her."

"Mama, we were just kissing," said Alta.

"That's all, Mr. Edwards, I swear," said Georgie.

"I started yelling at them, or it would've been worse," Mrs. Harrigan said. "I may be crazy, but I know what I saw, and I know what I'm talking about. That young woman better be careful, and you too, young man, before you're sorry. Very sorry. I know what happens. And how sorry you'll be."

"She didn't lead me on," the boy said. "I brought the whiskey. Just to try it out. We weren't doing anything very bad. Honest. And I'll fix the wall tomorrow after school. Just don't tell my mother."

Mrs. Harrigan trembled, shaking her head, grabbing onto Mrs. O'Brien's arm. Alta slid behind Molly, out of the way of Mama's eyes and Papa's arm.

"I know what's true," shouted Mrs. Harrigan, "And I know I'll be gone soon, so I'd better say it now."

The old lady struggled back up the hill.

Hitching the quilt higher on his shoulders, Papa said, "I've heard enough. I won't talk to your mother, Georgie. You're too old for that, but we'll have a new outhouse built by our strong and healthy long-lost cousin. Right, Minna? Upon my word, this is grand."

Papa coughed again, wiping tears from his eyes and covering his mouth with his handkerchief. Georgie switched his eyes from Alta to Papa.

"Are you listening to me, George Vaughn?" said Papa. "Don't talk my daughter into anything or worse let her lead you on. I know about boys your age."

As for Alta, Papa said she was too old to punish as before, but she'd better come home right after school and follow Mrs. Harrigan's advice too.

Mary was surprised he even remembered those whippings since he was so drunk most of the time. And why was he taking charge all of a sudden? Becoming part of the family again? Making sure Mama wouldn't forget him? Was he afraid the consumption would soon do him in?

Alta stood with her arms at her sides and her eyes nearly closed, as if she had made herself walk off into the far meadow through the woods and up the mountains until she was gone forever. The look on Alta's face so distant, Mary feared it was the moment Alta began to leave, as she threatened all the time.

"And clean up this mess. George. Alta. Mary, get the horse out of the way."

Papa stopped to catch his breath—gulping air, shivering. Minna took his arm, ready to lead him back to the house. At that moment, brilliant yellow-orange flared in the blue sky above the western ridges. Papa lifted his head and guffawed, coughed, and guffawed again. The bursts of laughter resounded in the vast bright yellow air. The laughter was catching, and everyone found the outhouse fire hilarious. To Mary, it was a relief to laugh long and hard. She held Molly around the neck, the horse turning and gazing from one to another.

JUST AFTER CHRISTMAS, Tiny roamed the front room, her hand brushing against the window, the door, along the walls, until she said, "Shall we sneak away to the Indian pictures, Mary? I bet the path isn't full of snow, and it'll be easy to cross the creek. It's probably frozen."

Without a hitch, they hiked up the mountainside. The space in front of the outcropping was merely a ledge that widened the path going up the side of the mountain as far as the ridge on top for all they knew.

Broken off and tumbled onto the ledge, small boulders had been arranged so a visitor could sit and contemplate the signs carved into the rocks, but Mary and Tiny climbed onto them. At first the scratches looked like cracks always found in large granite faces. Then up close, Mary discovered four connecting oval shapes, reminding her of a caterpillar. Once she knew how to search, her eyes followed scratches shaped like a snail. Tiny called her over and traced a spoon.

Gloved hands under their armpits, they jumped off the boulders.

"I wonder if someone just liked to make pictures, or if Captain Ben knows the story," said Mary, stamping her shoes.

"I think you have to know what it means, like at the rocking stone," said Tiny. "Maybe the wind was telling us to go see these pictures."

Mary picked up an arrowhead-shaped piece of granite, turning it so the mica and obsidian glistened.

"I bet the Washo people sit here and think of stories to go with the pictures. I wonder if great-grandma Vaughn would like the carvings?"

"I wish Mr. Hoy hadn't done something evil up here," said Tiny. "She probably wouldn't want to come, and now I want to go."

"No, no. Just a minute," said Mary, stomping her cold feet again.

"I think bad things happen everywhere, even nice, quiet places like this one. But sometimes things happen you'd never bet on, like Mama's taking Papa back. That's better, I guess. And, isn't it good Mrs. Harrigan told Alta to be careful?"

Rubbing her mittened hands together, Tiny said, "I don't know. How d'you think of these ideas? Alta's always going to go off, no matter what Mama says or Papa does."

Mary turned the granite piece so it sparkled. Tiny turned her eyes from one curious picture to the next.

"I just can't figure out the puzzle," she said. "Let's find chips of granite for Alta and Raleigh."

Why not, thought Mary, and they inspected the ground for three more shiny souvenirs. Pulling their collars over their ears, they scuffled along the path, snow carefully pushed to the edges of the forest undergrowth. Unafraid, Mary had time to see fallen pinecones and tiny rabbit prints and bright red snow plants, a blur the last time they'd made their secret journey.

THAT VERY AFTERNOON, Mama had received the admission letter to the sanatorium in Roseville. The letter set off the entire family, rushing to give away the few pieces of furniture and possessions too awkward to take to Sacramento.

The next morning Tiny, Raleigh, Mary, and Joe led Molly down the hill, across Front Street, and out to the field at the back of their old boardinghouse on Church Street. It filled Mary's heart to think how often she'd forgotten all about their horse, but even so, Molly took care of herself, eating the grass on the hill, drinking from the bucket by the pump, nuzzling when Mary showed up, as if she was Molly's best friend in the world.

The horse seemed content putting her head down and pulling up grass where the snow had melted. Joe combed her mane with his fingers, and Molly turned to nuzzle his hand. His family had a shed where Molly could stay when it snowed, although that day the sun was shining and, as Uncle Lauf said, icy snow sparkled like diamonds.

WIND RATTLED THE pine branches on the morning they were to leave, and snow clouds built up on the ridges. Mary barely felt the change in weather, she was so giddy with the excitement of this train ride—different from all other times when her stomach turned and her head ached at the thought of a new place. Now she was almost grown, and ready to put those worries away.

Mary and her brother and sisters hurried down Harrigan's Hill carrying their carpetbags and sacks of food and gifts neighbors and town friends had given them during the week of good-byes. Everyone plopped down quickly because the early morning train with seats for six free passengers—still allowed to Papa even though he hadn't worked for almost two months—was rolling out of the station.

Mary pulled out her tattered copy of *The Marvelous Wizard of Oz,* and Tiny said, "I hope there're no bad witches where we find a house."

"I hope we find a good witch with money," said Alta. "Because I think we should go to the nickelodeon. See what it's like."

Young bankers that they were, Raleigh and Tiny rooted around in their boxes and pulled out twenty cents. Just enough to get in.

A good omen for the new life ahead, thought Mary, as she passed out the granite souvenirs. Her brother and sisters leaned against the windows, and the train clattered along the track through snow sheds and tunnels and down the mountains toward the foothills. Careening along, they shouted about the cliffs of sheered-off rock and sunlight glinting off the mica and tiny specks of obsidian, just like the shine off their souvenirs held up to the window.

Soon her brother and sisters drowsed in the rocking car, but Mary, determined to stay awake, recited verses.

The train entered a mountain tunnel, so lengthy the car was pitch-black. If she squinted, she could see the tiny dot of blazing light at the far end, coming closer and closer.

> *How far that little candle throws his beams!*
> *So shines a good deed in a naughty world ... ,*

she whispered, so literal and so prescient, as the train burst out the other end, hurtling toward Sacramento.

30

May 2003

Sacramento

Days crawled by like the inchworm on a hollyhock stem. I whispered poems to myself while eating alone at the retirement house. With fuzzy vision, I had been happy to hear everyone's tales, and Yuki's were the best. Maybe because she was one of the Noguchi daughters and went with them to Tule Lake. Small world.

Then Yuki died. Toward the end, my supper companion drove me crazy, unfolding my napkin, moving the water glass closer, saying, "Eat this now, Mary," as if I couldn't do anything. I may not see well, but I know where everything is, or should be, if she hadn't moved it. I felt bad the evening Yuki said she couldn't hold down her food and her heart kept beating too fast. I felt around on the table until I reached her hand and held it for a while.

That's one thing about me. My heart is as regular as clockwork and my blood pressure is perfect. All I take is one aspirin at night.

I got myself to that busybody director and demanded my aspirin back after my assistant tattled. She said I had to have a prescription and the nurse would give me one aspirin each night. I said hogwash and made Polly hide a bottle in the treasure box Betsy gave me when I was forty. My granddaughter agreed the director was a rigid woman, but Polly said the helper was only trying to do her best for me. Maybe.

Anyway, Yuki stopped wheeling her walker into the dining room the very next evening. Two days I waited, but no one said a thing. Finally I searched out the director. She hemmed and hawed and at last said Yuki's family had taken her home. Believe me, I knew what she meant, and Polly wrote a sympathy note to Yuki's family.

Truth is, I loved Yuki and missed her so. She'd listen to my stories and lean over and talk right into my ear to tell hers so I'd understand. Day after day, no one was seated at my table. Then it dawned on me, no one else wanted to sit with me because I couldn't see, and I touched food with my fingers to feel what it was before I used my fork.

What a bunch of fools. Like Jaques from *As You Like It* said, they're from the sixth stage,

> *the lean and slipper'd pantaloon,*
> *With spectacles on nose and pouch on side.*

The oldest and healthier than most, the residents act like they're so above me. I may be in the last scene of all,

> *Sans teeth, sans eyes, sans taste,*

but not *sans everything*. I still know what I'm doing.

And I'm 105. When we set off in the train from the Sierra to Sacramento, and a mountain girl became a city woman, how could I have known I'd live during three centuries?

ABOUT TWELVE YEARS ago, after Abel died, I realized I couldn't manage the house. One evening I sat at the fireplace petting my tabby kitten, and a loud ping burst a tiny round hole through the glass window. My grandson said it looked like a pellet rifle shot.

A few nights later, a truck rolled up the driveway and two boys not much over twenty jumped out. I took down Abel's old rifle and held it up at the front door. One knocked and the other said they needed to use a phone, they were out of gas. What a stupid thing to say. I knew they were checking to see if someone was home.

I told them to turn right around and go to the next big street. They'd find plenty of gas stations, and if they tried to get in, I'd shoot them because I was holding a gun right in front of me. I was petrified, of course, and the gun was so old who knew if it would work, or if I actually would have shot it, but I must have sounded younger than I was because they left. Eighty years after we left Truckee I held a gun in my hands. What we do in this life.

Soon after, my beautiful gardens were sold off. The house wasn't much, but the grounds were worthy of a tiny park, and I came here, not far from Polly.

Twelve years now, and all dead, even Tiny. At her last phone call, Tiny said she didn't want to go on. Until then she'd seemed content enough in her ritzy condominium for wealthy old people. She kept in touch with her golfing buddies, inviting them to lunch in the fancy dining room.

She spent time working on her stock portfolio after rich Ralph died, but considering how poor we were as kids, she didn't hoard her money. She gave a lot away to charities and foundations. Mostly that's what she talked about, but on the last call she didn't say a word about stocks. I guess she gave up, even though she'd had live-in help for about two years. Honestly, my granddaughter drove me to her apartment many times, and the assistants did everything for her.

THE DAY BEFORE my birthday party, I sat by myself—thinking about Tiny, reciting poems, waiting for the helper to bring my food—when I was sure my old friend Olivia sat down with me. I was surprised. Though actually, I couldn't see her very well. Everyone's a gray shadow.

I asked Olivia how she was, and I rambled on about Tiny in those swell rooms looking out to the hills on one side and the San Francisco bay on the other. Olivia laughed when I said it was funny how I remembered things one way and Tiny had a completely different memory. My voice broke when I told Olivia she'd died.

Olivia confessed how sorry she'd been when Lanford Truitt turned out to be a bad case. I'd never forgotten him, no matter it was a long time past, but I only patted her hand. We were chatting happily, when I felt a hand rubbing my elbow and turned to see Lanford, smiling like I remembered. I caught my breath and felt for his hand and said how nice it was to see him once more.

Then Polly leaned over and spoke to me. She said Olivia had left, and now my grandson, John, was sitting next to me. I sensed the silence at the tables around me and knew they thought I was demented, so I vowed to be careful, though I was so lonely. The helper brought my plate, and my grandchildren talked while I ate, although I wasn't hungry and couldn't taste the food. After a few bites, I ate my ice cream, the only thing I really like, sweet vanilla.

Polly and John took me back to my room, and I asked John to be careful with the wheelchair, my bones so fragile the tiniest move feels like something has cracked. In my room, he helped me sit in the armchair, the one piece of furniture that didn't make my skinny bottom ache. Polly picked out a dress that still fits for the birthday party tomorrow. I've lost so much weight most of my clothes feel like bags on me, but what's the use of buying a new dress?

Polly said I seemed sad. What was wrong? I was going to be 105 tomorrow. Amazing.

I was all right, though I couldn't even turn on the radio and listen to the news without dozing off. I'd entertain myself with memories, but the only ones I remembered happened ages ago. Then I'd get so sad when I thought about Betsy, living only to fifty-four.

It's astonishing how Tiny and I lived long, long beyond our imagined time. Even Betsy's husband, Gus, died a couple of years ago. Tiny and I kept going, as Mama used to say, walking on through the world we had learned about during our growing up days in Truckee. Now it's only me, glad for grandchildren to lean on.

I pressed a hand over my mouth and felt around until Polly handed me a Kleenex. My granddaughter, the English professor, told me it was all right, William Faulkner said something like the past isn't dead and buried, it isn't even past. I laughed and the ache in my heart gave way. She said to think about the good things that have happened in these three centuries.

Then, of course, I remembered my Model T, and John said, "Remember the blue convertible Buick? That was a great car. We had fun when we sat in the back seat watching Fourth of July fireworks shooting up into the sky out by the lake, didn't we?"

Always warm on those evenings, I loved eating watermelon on the grass while we waited until it was dark, time for the fireworks display.

By the time John and Polly arrived for my 105th birthday celebration, I was exhausted. All morning I'd been the center of attention, aides fixing my hair, putting make-up on me, helping me get dressed. The Retirement House bigwigs came and a newspaper photographer and reporter. So tiny now, some of the audience probably couldn't see me. The director handed over the microphone and my voice boomed out.

"Today I'm famous. The oldest grandma at the retirement house. Not only am I famous, but I've met famous people. At thirteen, Charles McGlashan, who wrote a famous book about the Donner Party tragedy in the Sierra Nevada, told me how to listen to the wind. He was a smart man. I shook hands with Eleanor Roosevelt in New York City not long after the war. She was wonderful. In England I ran into Pearl Bailey at a shop in Cornwall. I said, 'Pearl Bailey, fancy meeting you here,' and I shook her hand. And when I was ninety-one, I saw George Burns at one of his last performances. When I was introduced I told him I always watched Gracie and him on TV. He said she was a great gal, but she's gone, and he gave me a kiss right on the mouth. He was a funny man."

The audience clapped and laughed. They probably couldn't believe a 105-year-old lady could remember all that, much less be funny. The entertainment fellow sang "Sweet Adeline" and other old-timey songs, and I ate some cake and had about a dozen pictures taken. I'm not sure why anyone wanted a picture of my old face, but I smiled and hoped my hair wasn't frowsy. By the end, when John and

Polly took me back to my room, I was so weary Polly helped me get ready for bed.

Though I could barely move, my eyes didn't close. I wondered if I should have given the audience a piece of advice. If you know it's time to say good-bye, have courage. Tell your family it's all right.

WHEN RALEIGH ARRIVED a couple of days later, I'd stopped getting up. I'd been daydreaming about spring days when we took turns riding Molly in a Truckee meadow, and, warm and sweaty, I went back to Front Street for penny candy.

Bundled up under the covers, every bone aching, I heard, "Hey, how're you doing?" said in the happy-go-lucky voice I loved.

I opened my eyes and couldn't believe he'd appeared. I was so happy to see him. Not too tall. Strong shoulders and reddish hair.

I said, "How're you? How's Mama?"

And I told him Tiny had died.

That's when he said, "Grandma, it's me, your great-grandson Lane, not your brother."

What could I do? I turned away to hide my sob. Everything was shadows. He looked like my brother at twenty-five, and I remembered the happy sound of his voice. That's what had lived on.

Then Jaques whispered, *"sans eyes,"* in my head. The catch in my throat turned to laughter. Lane laughed too, sitting down next to the bed, so he could talk in my ear.

He said, "You've some great genes, Grandma."

And I said, "Who would've guessed after the scarlet fever and the typhoid I'd live to 105."

Lane fiddled with something. Funny how some noises are clear, and for others I might as well be completely deaf. He had a new iPod, one of those machines that came too late for me. I couldn't see to use a computer either. He wanted to record one more story, but I was too tired.

Lane said to do the poem about the last leaf, so I lay there, my arms on top of the blanket, and repeated the poem for which I'd won the recitation prize. It sounded good. Then I gave him my last treasure, the tiny woven Washo basket, and I said, "don't forget all those stories I told you."

My great-grandson gave me a kiss, and I managed to wave good-bye.

MY WINDOWS ONTO the deck face the west, so every afternoon the light lasts later into the evening. Through the gauze curtain, a golden glow suffuses that side of the room, while the other corners are dark. Lying in my bed, I think back on the soft gray mourning dove that built a nest and laid an egg in my azalea pot. She was a gentle mother, sitting on the egg, calling *ocoo-ooh* to her mate. I'm sure a cat waited until the one day when the dove's mate didn't appear, and the dove flew off to find food. Then the cat knocked the egg out of the pot in an attempt to eat it. The dove returned and cooed, sad and sweet at the same time. She flew from the pot to the ground and back, her wings whistling, as her search grew more frantic. Her mate never returned, and after a few days, she disappeared also.

Now, like the dove, I'm crying, lonely for the people long gone. My bones crack, dried up like the last leaf on the limb, twisting in the slightest breeze, holding on by a frail strand. Spring has come. I feel weightless, breathing lightly, catching the glow shining in the narrow break in the curtain, and the world left far behind. My legs begin to move because it's time to go. I see the way.

ACKNOWLEDGMENTS

I thank friends and supporters for their comments as I wrote, especially Kim and Dawn Chase; my writing group, the 950 Club; my sister, Paula Noonan, and sister-in-law, Margaret Goodman; the Summer-Fall 2006 workshop and its writers who read and gave excellent criticism for some of the original chapters; and above all Helon Raines, who read and reread the manuscript offering helpful suggestion after suggestion.

I thank the Truckee-Donner Historical Society for help with this manuscript, by consulting pictures and old records after my phone calls and emails.

In addition, I thank the Sacramento library and other Sacramento historical organizations that answered my questions with grace and diligence.

Finally, I wish to remember the real Mary Edwards Ashton Ames (1898-2003), who told about her time in Truckee, and from whose stories I have written this fictional account about a series of events during an impressionable time—events that led to choices that made an ordinary life unique.